M.J. Mollenhour

# AMAZON AVENGER

To my friend, Carl,
Here's something to read while you're recovering. Get well soon,

Mike

Learn more at:
www.MJMollenhour.com

TALAVERA
media

To purchase copies of *Amazon Avenger*, visit major online book retailers and search "mollenhour" or visit the author's web site at

www.mjmollenhour.com

This novel is fiction. Characters and their names are the product of the author's imagination and are used fictitiously. Any resemblance to real people, living or dead, is coincidental. Places and incidents are either fictitious, or are cited fictitiously. The story cites some real events, facts and places to support the plot, but the story is fiction and any resemblance to actual events is coincidental.



Published by Talavera Media, P.O. Box 9299 Knoxville, TN37940

Talavera Media and the Talavera Media double-sabre logo are registered trademarks of Talavera LLC.

Printed in the United States of America
*Hardbound Edition*

ISBN 13: 978-0-9799672-4-5    ISBN 10: 0-9799672-4-4
Library of Congress Cataloging-in-Publication Data Control Number: 2011923483
Layout by Cory Mollenhour, cory@mollenhour.com
Cover design by Cory Mollenhour, cory@mollenhour.com
Author photograph by Kelly Rogers Photography

Fonts: BellMT; Trajan Pro

*Printed in the United States of America on acid free paper*

1.0

# Part I: The Amazon Avenger

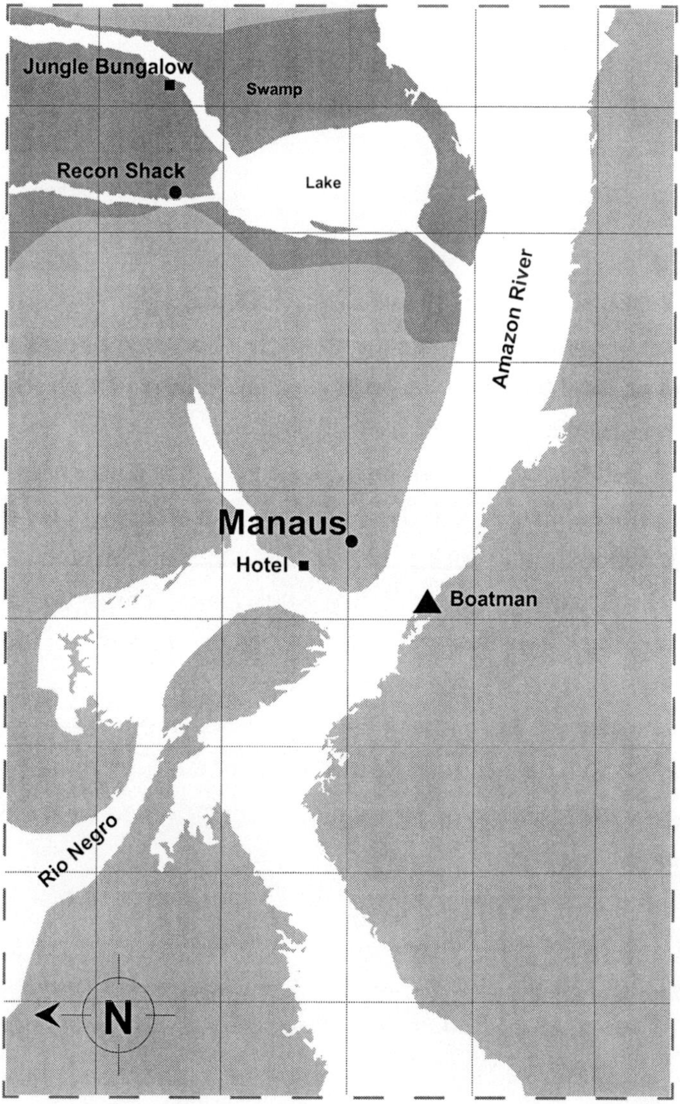

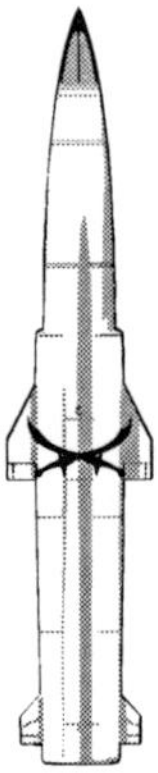

# 1

*Daybreak*
*Amazon River backwaters*
*South of Manaus, Brazil*

Screams. Screams drove Jack McDonald on. Screams tightened his grip on the throttle. Screams played over and over from the video surveillance he'd just watched.

Her screams.

Jack had watched the monitor's surreal, black and white, night vision camera images in horror as Consuela screamed, thrashing against the men who tore at her dress. Her skin, bronzed by years under the Brazilian sun, glistened, slick from fighting for her life. Her long, dark hair flung wildly about as she kicked and clawed her two attackers.

She screamed his name at the covert microphone, begging him in English to help her, urging him to come, to hurry and to kill these two men who were pinning her down even as Jack dashed to the canoe.

Racing through the Amazon River backwaters as fast as the motorized canoe would buzz, his tortured mind reverberated her screams for rescue. Time slowed, unyielding to his curses and rage. Time mocked him, forcing him to listen to the echoing screams. Time and space refused to warp to his will, leaving him droning slowly, slowly through the swollen swamp toward

Consuela. Nothing could cut his short canoe run through the jungle waters by even a precious minute.

As if time's stubbornness and Consuela's repeating screams were not torture enough, other screams rose in dissonant chorus—screams from a different time, a different jungle, and from a different woman. From a different—death.

In this familiar vision from the past, a woman pressed her hands to her gaunt face and gaped down at him in shock and grief. *Or, did her eyes accuse?* He knelt on both knees in front of her, cradling her husband's bloodied head in his lap, groping for the severed artery, desperate to stanch the bleeding. Jack stuffed his own Combat Gauze into the wound but blood flowed, unabated. Jack screamed, "Doc! Quikclot!"

The woman's husband, conscious of fading away, mouthed, "Thank you," to the young American officer holding his head. Then, having absolved his would-be rescuer, the dying man peacefully shifted his gaze upward to his wife, unafraid of The Grim Reaper, concerned now only with trying to console his love. She looked back into his face, saw her husband's life ebb away, and she screamed again and again.

That memory had returned from years ago in the seemingly suspended time and still of the jungle night. The rage-grief duet screams from the two women struck ethereal disharmony in the mind of the man choking the motor's tiller—and then *that other* scream returned to join them.

Unlike the other two in the maddening trio, he had never heard this punctuated scream. He could only imagine his wife's scream, her violent death, her loneliness at life's abrupt end, without him there to treat her wounds or to console her. He had been away—again—at her death; but, on many nights, he had relived her last moments, her terror just before the crash—and he heard her screams in his nightmares.

High-pitched, outboard motor whines cut through the haunting cacophony. The angry engine churned and moved the canoe forward from the channel into the lake. His ghosts pleaded with him to hurry! Their voices urged him on toward the yet-living woman, but the wound-out motor argued with them, scolding the lone American in the slender wooden boat to slow down, threatening him with a breakdown. Threatening him with *failure.*

But, not tonight. Not again. He would not lose the woman just ahead in the jungle, pinned on the floor of the bungalow. Not like he failed the woman whose husband he lost in that bamboo hut in the Philippines.

Not like he had lost his wife.

This time, he would *not* arrive just tiny time-slices too late. He crouchred, set his jaw, and squinted hard ahead, jungle to the left, open lake water to the right. The sun's rays probed through the forest at the edge of the lake, determined to make morning break through the canopy. He twisted the throttle with all his might, as if to squeeze more drops of gasoline through the fuel line.

Jack wanted to scream, too—scream with fury at the evil men who, right now, might be claiming his agent's life. He bit his lip and stared ahead, straining to spot the creek's mouth from among the rising mist-curtains of tangled brown and green.

There! He almost missed it.

He shoved the outboard's throttle handle hard right. The canoe canted and slowed in the sharp turn, but the canoe creaked from the strain and obeyed, piercing the narrow creek mouth.

Now, straight ahead. Only a few hundred yards more. Only the whining motor's time-space limitations stayed him from the throats of the men who would slay her—who would slay Consuela.

Not this time. Not like the Philippines.

The bow cut through murky waters, darker here than on the lake, with jungle pressing in. The tall, broad-shouldered man seated at the tiller overbalanced the canoe just a bit. When he ducked from the snare of a low-hanging vine, the canoe lurched crazily, slamming against a rubber tree root, almost capsizing. The collision pitched him headfirst into the gunwale. He struggled to his knees, fought the vines away and seized the throttle again. The canoe leveled, regaining lost speed as he aimed it up the creek channel like a dagger. He wiped the blood trickling into his narrowed eyes and glared at the bungalow emerging from the gloom ahead. He checked the magazine and chamber of the short carbine slung on his back.

He prayed to God that Consuela still lived and that God would grant him the furious grace to fall upon them in time to save her life.

Not this time. Not like that other jungle dawn in the Philippines.

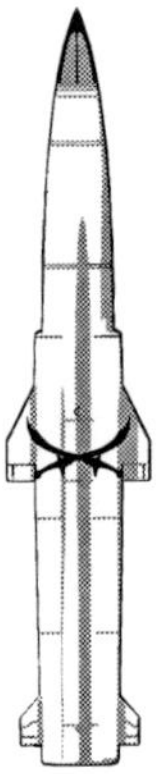

# 2

*December 2002, daybreak*
*Cartowan Village*
*Basilan Island, Philippines*

"Attack first light Lieutenant Jack! What you think? Slip away again if we not hit Abu Sayyaf now—hit hard. What you think?" Batenga urged the tall American Army officer, now almost as brown as he.

Jack thought his counterpart in the Filipino Marine Light Reaction Company was as bloodthirsty a little soldier as he'd ever seen, that's what he thought. "Fierce and Fearless at Five-Five"—"4F" Jack had nicknamed him. Jack would fight with 4F anywhere.

4F squatted low, wound like a tiger ready to spring, waiting for his American adviser's agreement. The American rolled over and peered into Batenga's fiery eyes. He looked past, at Batenga's men, or at least toward those he could see. Between the camouflage and weeks of mud, all of the men blended with the rich jungle earth in this murky mixture of night shadow and new day.

"What you think? What you think, L-T Jack?" Lieutenant Batenga whispered, grinning wickedly from ear to ear, barely able to contain his primal urge for combat, for rescue—for revenge.

"I'll tell you what I think, 4F," Jack started to say, but checked his speech.

Lying prone, 40 yards from the enemy just wasn't the time for Jack to tell Batenga that he thought Batenga's hot, dank little corner of the Global War on Terror, here in the extreme southern Philippine Islands, to be the strangest place on earth—the Far East version of that line in Europe roughly marking the furthest advance of the old Ottoman Empire. South of here, you entered Moslem Indonesia's islands at your own risk. Sometimes, staring out over the Celebes Sea, Jack saw this line, like a boundary between alien beings, shifting like a long, strung out swirling mass of venomous sea snakes, but clearly marking the two different worlds—as different as land is from water.

"I say 'Go.' I say 'Attack,'" Jack whispered to Batenga, instead.

Batenga gave Jack thumbs-up and grinned wider, if that were possible. Already, Batenga popped the caps from the ends of the M-72 LAW anti-tank rocket and extended the launcher tube until it snapped into place and locked. He glanced behind to make sure no hapless soldier was about to be roasted in the back-blast. Up on one knee to clear the brush, Batenga fired the portable rocket that boomed out the unmistakable attack signal. The Light Reaction Company men rose from the earth on line as one, their rifle fire and curses rolling before them like a wave of sudden death.

It was over in two minutes for these Abu Sayyaf terrorists.

The village mayor's intel had been solid. The Light Reaction Company caught the Abu Sayyaf holding the kidnapped Americans right where the mayor said—in the abandoned village between the road intersection and the creek.

Bad choice. Desperate, Jack guessed. Cornered. Tired. Hungry. Weren't they all? Time to end it.

The Company moved in at midnight and spent a stealthy night crawling into position for the first-light raid in the morning. One squad set up on line in ambush along the north road, another blocked the east road—no escape either way for the enemy. The other two squads deployed on line across the creek, crossing this "danger area" by rushing in unison just as Jack had trained them, exposed for only a flash, disappearing into the brush on the far side, then crawling forward as one. Then, the two squads stayed on line as they stalked in the dark as close to the abandoned—but now Abu Sayyaf-occupied village—as possible.

Good plan. Combat choreography. The blocking squads ambushed the leftover Abu Sayyaf trying to run away. Good men. Good mission: free the hostages grabbed at the seaside resort over a year ago—and kill any Abu Sayyaf they caught terrorizing Basilan Island. Oh, yes, all within the Rules of Engagement, of course. Oh, yes, the ROE. But, out here, with Batenga's men, far away from camera lenses, forgotten by the American public, and with the military lawyers covering commanders' asses in Afghanistan and Iraq, they adapted the ROE to their nasty little war against the Abu Sayyaf beheaders—the "Abee-headers" Jack and his men called them, to make sure they didn't forget the kind of enemy they hunted.

Without speaking, each of the men had decided that he would take no prisoners today. Each somehow understood the Light Reaction Company's unanimous agreement—and the concurrence of their sun and grime-darkened American Army advisor. Maybe keep one of the wounded for questioning. Maybe. For a while.

And the Filipino Marine Corps Light Reaction Company had succeeded—finally.

What a mix of emotions! His men soldiering expertly, raiding just as they'd been taught. And victory.

But also loss.

Relief, but grief.

And guilt. Numbing guilt.

Success, but First Lieutenant Jack McDonald, U.S Army, 1st Special Forces Group, assigned to organize, train and advise this Light Reaction Company, would second-guess this raid now and forever.

Later, back at their base camp, weapons cleaned, gear hung and ready for the next mission, still in his filthy uniform, Jack sat at his laptop and stared at the screen. What else was there to say? Finally, he keyed into the report the terse final phrasing: "Husband died; saved wife."

It was the violent death of long-held hope that finally broke her. Their yearlong captivity frayed their sanity, but always the kidnapped couple hoped and prayed. Hope endures so much. They had endured and encouraged the others, but they had seen others in their group singled out by their kidnappers, some raped, others beheaded. Still, the young missionary pilot and his wife had always clung to the hope of seeing their children again.

Then, this new morning of captivity crackled with gunfire and the promise of imminent rescue by the soldiers. This time, the two could tell, their Abu Sayyaf captors had been caught lax, their three perimeter guards dozing. This time, the machine gun fire clearing the dirt street and the charging men swarming toward them assured victory mere seconds away. Rescue. They'd dared to hold to hope, to faith, and now the Filipino Marines had arrived.

But hope whiplash-reversed again in the dawn crossfire: assassination by one of the Muslim kidnappers, bitterly exacting one more death before facing his own? Or, was it a stray round, an accident, a "friendly fire" tragedy, perhaps fired by the very American officer accompanying the band of men bent on rescuing them?

Either way, her husband, hands still tied to the post, drooped and fell on the floor, his blood pooling.

It was this realization of their enduring hope, raised to immediate reality, then shattered in front of her, that released her screams from within her as Death clutched for her husband's bound, exhausted body. Even as the jubilant young officer sprang up the steps into the hut to greet them in excited English, she screamed for her husband, finally, finally despairing.

Her screams stopped the soldier's own jubilant cheers.

He stood, shocked for a moment, then dropped to his knees and began first aid, shouting for the medic, groping into the mess for the artery to close it off, urging the man to live, to live. He stuffed a blood-clotting bandage into the bullet hole, but rolled the wounded man over gently and saw the gaping exit wound—and knew.

Had it been his round? He'd killed their guards, hot to get his red-dot sight on their black hearts, pressing the M-4 trigger quickly to kill them before they could present the hostage couple as shields. Two to the chest—shift the dot—two more to the chest in two quick trigger presses—shift the dot and press twice more—taking out all three guards in less than two seconds. Finished off the one still moving with a head shot. Good shooting, he thought, but it all happened so fast.

Had he been too eager?

Did she blame him?

He looked up at her and knew her grief.

Oh, God, had it been his bullet?

Afterward, Jack shifted and steadied himself with his M-4 carbine against the palm tree, his mind and eyes blurring even as 4F gently led the rescued American woman away to the waiting Blackhawk. Jack turned again and stared at the young missionary pilot's lifeless body. Jack shielded his eyes from the rest of the men as if to guard against the chopper's rotor prop-wash kicking up dust and chaff, and he wept.

For the young man. For their four, fatherless children. For their mother.

And, Lieutenant Jack McDonald, a young man himself, though hardened by Rangers at Fort Benning and combat in Afghanistan, Columbia, and now in the Philippines, wept for salvation from all the seemingly endless evil in the world.

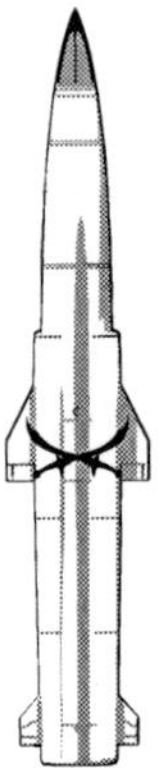

# 3

*Two months before present day,*
*middle of night*
*Iran, Gulf of Oman Coast*
*Across the Bay from Behesti Port*

The president wept tears of insane joy and danced. Saya-dar pretended not to notice. Instead, Saya-dar turned, straightened his black and white-checkered Arab *keffiyeh* so that the disguise wrapped his face and hid all but his nearly black, Persian eyes. He solemnly shook the hands of the two portly Russians standing with him in the harbor office three stories above the docks. The Russians stood with hands resting together on their bellies, fingers intertwined, and smiled thinly up at him. They, too, tactfully avoided discourse with the president, choosing instead to make a show of studying the missiles being loaded aboard the *Mi Fortuna*. Saya-dar's eyes laughed at his president, but he spoke no word. His Arabic was imperfect and he chose to raise no questions about his Iranian identity. Besides, he loathed the language and would not deign to refine his accent.

Crews manipulated cranes and lifted the last missile aboard the ship, placing it carefully in the specifically-adapted shipping containers. Then, the crane operators placed the tops on the modified containers. Stevedores removed the hoists. Saya-dar peered through binoculars, inspecting the loaded missiles from the air-conditioned office above. Bright lights from the steel superstructure blazed like stars illuminating the port.

Lit up below sat weathered, faded, red and orange containers like thousands of others. The dents and rust spots added an especially nice touch, thought Saya-dar. Just as he had specified. Art. Pure art. Except, these shipping containers were façades. Once harmless, now they served Saya-dar's covert purpose.

Standing ramrod straight, looking every bit the Arab chieftain to fool the Russians, Saya-dar watched the missiles being loaded and hidden from sight, daydreaming desert death.

In this, his favorite death vision, desert warriors topped the dune, scimitars raised, sun glinting off the sharpened blades, horses snorting. Faces wrapped against the blowing sands, the warriors plunged downward onto the unsuspecting Western camp.

The fools looked up and screamed. The desert warriors screamed "*Allahu akbar*!" as they slashed across and chopped downward, then upward, around and back down as trained cavalry learn to fight, leaving no one alive.

Yes, he, too, would cause death to plummet from above onto the unsuspecting, screaming Americans. Already, despite 9/11, they'd grown complacent. Good!

Saya-dar, The Shade, The Protector of The Faithful, the Iranian terrorist mastermind and financier would change that. He'd picked up where bin Laden had left off. The Western world would look on in horror, and they would wonder from which direction Saya-dar and his men would strike next. They would wonder where he had struck from this time. They would wonder *who* had struck them, for one of Saya-dar's many secrets remained his identity, at least for now.

The president babbled on.

Let him. Certainly this was his moment to celebrate. Each in his own way, Saya-dar figured. The Saya-dar held back though. He would celebrate in his own way too, aboard his yacht, *Babylon*, only once the consuming missiles fell from the sky. Then, Saya-dar would revel in the chaos. Saya-dar already had a select Scotch whiskey waiting in reserve as the special reward he would give himself at the right time.

But not yet. This phase of the operation was complete, but the next phase was more intricate, less under Saya-dar's direct control. This nagged at the master terrorist. As distracting as the president was, he was Saya-dar's president and Saya-dar could count on both his passions and his craftiness. For the next phase, though, Saya-dar had to rely on others. Powerful others, but others with their own motives, their own hatred not harnessed to Iran's theocracy.

Saya-dar watched the tugs turn *Mi Fortuna* out to sea and smiled thinking about the rest of his navy being prepared by those others far across the oceans.

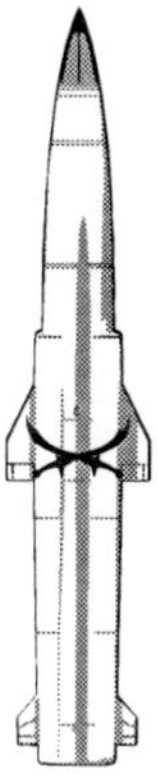

# 4

*One week before present day,*
*Monday, lunchtime*
*Café Antiquario*
*Brasilia, Brazil*

"Jack?"

"I'm Jack. And you are?" Jack rose and asked of the dapper thirty-something just arrived at his table.

"I'm Richard Pye—really, no code name for me although I asked for one—just for the fun of it," the man said, grinning and extending his hand.

British. Sounded like West Midlands maybe. *A Brummie from their Birmingham?*

"Please join me," Jack invited, speaking to Richard and smiling but checking behind Richard and to the side as Jack indicated the chair.

"Skylark," Richard Pye whispered, opening his eyes wide, adding drama.

"LeSabre," Jack responded in hushed tone.

Both men laughed as Pye slid his chair out and sat.

"Who writes these little rituals, Jack?" Pye asked.

"Someone from Detroit who just closed out his grandparents' estate," Jack offered.

"Well, I don't know about you, but I'm famished," Richard Pye addressed Jack, but looked at the serious-faced waiter approaching. "These Brazilian waiters are like the European waiters, not like your American "servers," my boy. These chaps know how to make a guest feel like a million pounds sterling. Let's see what Brasilia's finest lakeside café has to offer and enjoy a fine lunch overlooking the *Lago Sul.* Then, we can take a stroll along the shore here at their South Lake," he said to Jack, nodding toward the lake, just south of Brasilia's beehive of government office districts. "I recommend the stroganoff," Richard added, appearing to be absorbed in the menu.

Jack zeroed in.

"Let me guess. Identifying accents is a hobby of mine. Vicinity of Birmingham, in the Midlands," Jack hazarded, eyeing the slender, sandy-haired Englishman sporting the thin mustache as his grandfather might have decades before.

Richard snapped his head up from the menu, his blue eyes sparkling, perfect teeth shining in the Brazilian sun vibrating off the lake.

"Very *good*, old boy! I'm calling you 'old boy' because you Yanks get such a kick out of the expression. You seem to expect us to call you 'old boy' about every 20 seconds and I don't want you to be disappointed. I'm not a Brummie, though," Richard made sure to say, using the slang term for one from the English Midlands city of Birmingham, "but I do hail from just west of there, overlooking the River Severn and out toward Wales. Ah, what a valley, that, now! The Severn Valley! Dear God, would that I be so blessed as to rove its green hillsides and pastures again!" Pye proclaimed, sitting back, raising his limed ice-water in a mock toast, pretending to gaze faraway, but really checking the lakeside walk just to the front of the café's open-aired dining patio.

Jack liked Richard immediately.

"And you, I suspect you, Yank, are from the town of 'Around,' righto?" Pye asked, barely able to contain his glee.

"Yes, I'm from 'Around,' Jack chuckled, wishing for some reason he could say more, and just relax and talk, normally, as if with a newfound friend. "And, you can no doubt tell from my accent, I'm from our Dixie, so as much as you Brits like to call us all 'Yanks,' we southerners resemble that remark," Jack said, borrowing from Rodney Dangerfield.

The men relaxed but gave away no more and, in a somewhat constrained way, finished their beef stroganoff, left the necessary Brazilian Real notes to cover the bill (no trace-leaving charge card), including a reasonable tip—an amount not to garner attention either way—and stepped off the open-air, covered, stone-patio dining room onto the sidewalk winding down toward the lake. They turned along the lakeside walkway and strolled toward the sweeping, modern-design suspension bridge in the distance that marked the eastern end of the lake.

At first, the men said nothing, walking through well-trimmed gardens designed for relaxing, casual walks. Pye knew Jack simply could not say much, and Jack—Jack just felt distant.

This work was different from his Army service as an infantry officer. He had camaraderie among the soldiers: first as a young rifle platoon leader with three other platoon leader second lieutenants, his company executive officer and their company commander and all of those young, sharp sergeants; then, among the turbocharged men of the $1^{st}$ Ranger Battalion; then, among the elite Special Forces community and later, commanding Charlie Company at the storied $101^{st}$ Airborne Division (Air Assault). There, his first sergeant always stood with him, a strong, older, more-experienced soldier, backing him up, diplomatically correcting him just before he screwed up, stopping Jack with a little cough and then, "Suh, p'haps…" this and that.

Camaraderie. Jack missed 4F, too.

Talking with this pleasant Brit reminded Jack McDonald how "alone" he really was now.

"What do you do for the British Embassy?" Jack asked.

"I'm the aide to the military attaché," Richard replied. "I'm not some covert operative; I really am the aide to the military attaché."

*Right.* Jack fought back the impulse to roll his eyes in disbelief.

"How'd you get mixed up in—things like this, Richard?"

"No one else appropriate to do the job was around," Richard said.

"Are you appropriate?"

"Sometimes. My boss wants to keep this real quiet. I serve part-time as our consul in Manaus. I fly from Brasilia up to Manaus a couple of times a month. You know they have an international airport in Manaus, even though it's in the heart of the jungle. Well, you see, two weeks ago, I'm there to check in, sign forms, present an award, and attend the opera, when my secretary comes in with this worried look on her face. Says there's this woman in the lobby insisting she see the 'chief British spy' at the consulate. We have no bloody spy in Manaus; it's 1,000 miles into the interior—not exactly Vienna during the Cold War. Shipping. Rubber, of course, 100 years ago, but now it's the main commerce hub for all the people 'up' the Amazon. Lots of bananas come through here. Lumber. Oil comes in from Peru by barge and they refine it at Manaus and send it on. Did you know that? Tourism. Ship-building—oh, yes, that brings me back to my story.

'Anyway, the secretary ushers in this gorgeous, fortyish,

bronzed, Brazilian-Amazon woman in a flowing print dress—the kind women wear more into the interior, in the country, you might say—hardly chic—not young and urbanite like you'd see in *São Paulo*—the big city or here in Brasilia among the government office workers out husband-hunting and bar-hopping. Very distracting, I must say. I had a hard time attending to what she had to say. That changed real fast, though."

"Why?" Jack asked. He'd just meant to make appropriate small talk but this was quickly getting down to mission-connected. Good.

"She's Venezuelan by birth, she tells me. Her mum was Mexican. Both her parents died long ago. Speaks both Portuguese and Spanish and pretty good American television English. Shame she didn't learn the Queen's language right! It would have complemented her poise, her athletic grace. I digress.

'Turns out, she's the personal housekeeper for a Venezuelan ship-builder with his shipyard just downriver from Manaus. The boss's name is 'Fats.' Yecch! Fats. Rich, but eccentric. A hermit sort. We checked him out. Not a lot on him. His paperwork trail starts in Manaus. Odd, but not terribly so. He's been in the Amazon for 40 years. Records weren't kept quite so meticulously in the jungle that long ago. He just seems to have plopped down there 40 years ago with no history.

'This Mr. Fats set up a welding shop decades ago and grew it into this successful barge-building business and custom shipwright operation. You'll see what I mean. These barges that traverse the Amazon are massive! The river will handle huge barges hauling—well, I could go on, but they're very efficient transportation."

Jack gave him a "Can we stick to the point?" look.

"Of course. You're wondering how barges and voluptuous,

tanned housekeepers tie into your government's—someone's—sending you down here on this pleasant social visit to the sophisticated cousins representing the far-flung corners of the Queen's empire in South America. Well, these barges have to be built right along the river on big rollers. Crews of maybe 25 men will weld them together. When they're done, they remove the blocks and roll the barges down into the river for launch. Down the Amazon they go and out into the Atlantic. Fats sells them all over the western world. They truly are massive. Your country—your states along the Atlantic coast—buy some for garbage hauling. That brings us to *her* story.

'New York City's Port Authority ordered one. That's ordinary enough, but then, as the NYC barge neared completion, about four weeks ago, these three men show up at her employer's house. Now, here, generic Jack, old boy—is that really your name, I don't think so—we really must talk about Fats' house a bit.

'He's very reclusive. Mr. Fats lives in the same bungalow he built years ago. It's located up a tributary, off a swampy lake about seven miles downriver from Manaus and a mile off the Amazon. Back 'in the sticks' as you Yanks would say. Where the foxes say 'Good night,' to the rabbits, as the Germans would say. He values his privacy, apparently. Commutes from home, by boat usually, to the Amazon and then a few miles upriver to his office and shipyard. Does his business and that's pretty much it. He is rarely seen in Manaus. He contributes to the Opera House Foundation there but never attends. His house rests over the water on stilts, but a footbridge leads to higher, drier land and a path, which leads to a dirt road, which leads to a paved road that would take you into Manaus. His is very much the jungle bungalow. Therefore, we call it 'The Jungle Bungalow.'

'She—the housekeeper—boats to market close by often but

only once per month or so to Manaus. She orders and does his other personal business by mobile phone and online. Yes, the Manaus area has excellent wireless service," Richard added, noting Jack's look of surprise. "Flat. A tower carries a long, long way across a miles-wide river," Richard explained.

"OK, I get the picture. So, this heartbreaker housekeeper hoves into your office wanting James Bond. She's star-struck. Been to too many movies," Jack said. Might as well have some fun with this stuff.

"You might be right—maybe that's why she looked for us Brits instead of you American types. We're far more suave. Yes, there, I said it. 'Suave.' That's why you hire us to do your radio ads. The accent lends instant credibility, don't you think? Regardless of why she chose me, she brought us some very interesting news of matters that you cousins should be aware of," Richard said, knowing he had Jack's full attention now.

"I reported up the chain, briefed our MI-6 station chief in Brasilia. Thought the spooks would handle it from there and I'd be back to enjoying the Brasilia night scene. Lovely town. No, *ghastly* town but those *thousands* of government jobs draw thousands of young earnest ladies looking for work—and for Mr. Right. That would be me. I'm bound to be Richard Right for one of them, don't you think, old boy?"

Jack eyed Richard. Medium height, medium-to-slender build, in sound physical condition, wavy blond hair, brushed back. That so debonair pencil-mustache. Aristocratic features that Jack conceded the young females Richard hoped to impress would probably call "ruggedly handsome." No scar marring his face, like the one that marked Jack's left cheek. (Jack had developed a hard-to-break identifying habit of rubbing that scar when he was thinking, and he touched it now.) Sporting plainly Anglo-Saxon white skin even in the tropics. *My, but it must be lonely here for a blue-blazered blueblood. He is, at least, enthusiastic. Is he just playing some part? Is this Brit to be taken seriously or is he someone frivolous who Gordon has tossed my way as a practical joke?*

"Oh, I'm *sure*," Jack jibed. "So, tell me, is the housekeeper *The One*? Were you smitten by this isolated and lonely, somewhat older, maiden of simple country tastes?" Jack asked, playing along to see whether he had a valuable ally or a nuisance.

"No, well, yes, but I was more urgently smitten by what she reported," Richard said, returning just as abruptly to business.

"I'm ready," Jack said. He meant it. Let's get to the mission.

"I think she's more than the housekeeper there. I think she's the boss's comfort on sweaty jungle nights. She knows more than she should about his habits and business. He tells her the three men—Mr. A, Mr. B, and Mr. C we shall label them for now—visiting him from afar do not like 'western' women who are too—immodest—or forward. He tells her that she should stay out of sight for the most part. Tells her to wear some of her better—and less revealing—dresses. Tells her to avoid the men altogether, if possible.

'She asks if they are homosexual. He laughs and says, "No, their attraction to women is more like master-slave," he tells her. "They might just kidnap you and take you back to some desert harem if you entice them too much. They are Middle Eastern," he tells her. Tells her they placed a big order. They are here to pay for and pick up two vessels, fabricated by Fats. "These guys were sent to me by Carlos Guevara himself," he brags. Now, this is where it really gets interesting.

'She knew Fats did business with Carlos Guevara. Special-outfitted some of the Venezuelan president's tankers and container ships. That wasn't surprising to us. What was surprising—and a bit disconcerting don't you think?—is that men from Iran personally are voyaging to Manaus and buying these custom-outfitted barges and container ships. And, they were referred to Fats from *el Presidente* Carlos Guevara! I see no sense in that at all, do you? Neither did Consuela.

'What a musical name, don't you think, Jack? Not 'Jack,' of course: 'Consuela.' Consuela. Oh, my!

'Anyway, she's right, don't you think? These Three Kings of Orient Are have no business following any star from Iran, 6,000 give-or-take-a-few miles, to the jungle paradise on the Amazon known as Manaus. I mean, good heavens! Most *Brazilians* have never been to Manaus. And, buying customized vessels. Can they not weld together a barge in Iran? Why here, in *your* hemisphere, right under your noses? Does it not miff you a bit, old boy, that your would-be-nemesis Guevara is chums with your sworn enemies? There you have it; an odd match up of your sworn enemies, in an odd place for them to cavort," Richard finished.

"Yeah, yeah, it does miff me a bit," Jack agreed, trying to work out the implications and impatient to hear more.

"Well, here are three Iranians, bearing a personal introduction from Guevara, visiting this Fats in his jungle love-bungalow whether you Yanks—and rebels—like it or not. The lovely Consuela made it a point to watch and listen, and what she saw and heard frightened her.

'One man is older and soft—Mr. A—but two of these men are hard, hard men. They send chills down her spine. Softy is soft, groomed and expressive of his designs toward her. He seems to be the boss and the other two seem to be gorillas—bodyguards she thinks—executive protection. We'll let the goons be Mr. B and Mr. C. Should I continue?" Richard asked.

"Do go on," Jack said, taking it all in and trying to fit the pieces together.

"For the most part, she manages to stay clear as told, though she serves them food and drinks just like she serves Fats. While the softy-playboy is not beyond making his interest in her known, the other two remain always armed and—while she catches them eyeing her—they express absolutely no interest in her, always remaining on high alert, instead. All of this puts the lovely Consuela on high alert, too.

'Then, a few nights ago, she was resting in a quiet corner of the bungalow, an out-of-the-way porch spot she found that is usually breezy, when softy-playboy and her boss stepped out onto the veranda. Night was—of course—hot and no barrier blocked the sound of their voices. They spoke in English, the language they all share in common. She heard them refer to—get this—*already* having created a compartment for smuggling men into the U.S. on a tanker specially welded and outfitted by Fats. *Already.* Done deal. In the past. This had worked well and they are here to pick up another special ship.

'She might live in the jungle, my furtive friend, but she keeps up. She knew about the 20 suicide truck-bombings at the department stores all across your country in 2007, and had read about how the suicide-bombers probably entered on some cargo ship through one of your southern ports. One of your TV reporters observed the pattern of the 20 bombing sites spreading like a fan from the Gulf Coast. He speculated in the story that Consuela read that the bombers entered the U.S. to the east of all of the Texas oil ports, perhaps through your huge port at Mobile, Alabama.

'That, too, made sense to her. You see, Jack old boy, she is not only sultry; she is intelligent! Truly a treasure of the rain forest! Is she not? Don't you agree?" Richard asked, in a finishing flourish, but not in an unfriendly way, pausing to catch his breath and get Jack's reaction.

"Perhaps," Jack responded.

"Perhaps? Is that all? Perhaps what? Come on, man! Guevara! Oil. Oil tankers! Container ships! Lots of tankers and container ships coming to Mobile. Not all that far from the mouth of the Amazon, is it? If the tanker leaving the Amazon on Brazil's northeast coast headed to Mobile, avoiding the open Atlantic, it could go through the Caribbean, pass between Cuba and the Yucatan Peninsula, and into the Gulf of Mexico in short order," Richard insisted, wanting Jack's reaction.

"It would pass all along Venezuela's coast," Jack observed.

"Precisely! Plenty of opportunity for terrorists already staged in Venezuela to link up with the tanker and book passage to America in the custom-outfitted and secret luxury quarters hidden in the bowels of the otherwise mundane vessel!" Richard concluded.

"Guess where else the linkup might occur?" Jack added.

"Where?"

"Cuba," Jack stated grimly.

"Well, how would *you* do it, Jack?" Richard asked.

"I'd pick Venezuela. The world ships to Venezuela and its ports. Oil tankers leave from Venezuela all the time. Empty tankers in; full tankers out. Tankers coming and going. A tanker outfitted right could carry *jihad* types from Iran to Venezuela and then on and we'd never know it. Unless our agents in Venezuela reported it," Jack concluded.

"How are you fixed for intel sources in Venezuela? Never mind. Forget that question. I got a bit carried away. I hope your CIA's been busy there. We are," said Richard.

"Well, I wouldn't know unless they got me directly involved,"

Jack said.

"You are directly involved," Richard said.

"Yes, I guess I am. Looks like our agent is an unpaid volunteer, drop-dead gorgeous housekeeper who is a lot smarter than her boss gives her credit for," Jack said.

"How's your Portuguese?" Richard asked.

"You kidding? I'm good with Spanish, so I can try to understand Portuguese, but I don't—it's not a language I know," Jack admitted. "The similarities to Spanish and all of those Latin word roots help me read it somewhat, but all of those 'tang,' 'bang,' and 'bong,' sounds throw me."

"You don't speak Portuguese, do you?"

"No," Jack admitted.

"Not to worry. You will have your own personal interpreter."

Jack looked at Richard.

"Consuela?" Jack asked.

"You Yanks get all the women! The beautiful, exotic, jungle maiden will be your personal companion and hold your hand as you infiltrate, set up surveillance, and save the world. You will be just like our James Bond! Well, no offence, but you won't be just like 007. Hard for you Yanks to emulate that level of charm. Tut, tut."

"What's your involvement? Why are you here? Why is the Queen's own spy running this show?" Jack asked.

"Not a spy. Not a spy. Oh, no, dear boy. I told you that! Good question, but here's why. For some reason, she picked our consulate in Manaus to report these shenanigans. Little place, our office in Manaus, you know. Sleepy little post, mostly there for all of the eco-Brits taking rainforest tours to lodge their complaints about boorish tour guides or lost credit cards. Show the flag of the far-flung empire and all that. You know, they still respect us there. They have an expression. Something about making a show of looking busy and industrious for the British. They know we British get things done. Goes back to colonial times.

'Anyway, I was there—in the office—when she came in wanting the top British spy. Mrs. Moneypenny sent her to me since no one else was in the office and Moneypenny wanted to get back to checking her E-bay account. Consuela confided in me. I must say I was taken with her—her story. I reported to my boss, the military attaché here in Brasilia. Now, rumor has it that he is indeed the MI-6 station chief. He called your CIA station chief, and we all had the most station-chiefly lunch right here at the *Café Antiquario* where you and I just met. I had the beef stroganoff then too. Quite savory. Did you like it?"

Jack just stared. Richard caught the hint and resumed.

"We, too, strolled along the lake here. The two chiefs hatched the most devious plot, most of which I don't know. All I know is that your CIA guy wanted this one off the books for some reason. Hush, hush. We just wanted to pass the intelligence and the opportunity to you since it involved the 2007 suicide truck-bombings. We would get a few Brownie points and have some chips to call in as a favor. You Yanks do so much in return for a little appreciation. You must be absolutely desperate for continental acceptance, what?"

Jack made a show of glaring at Richard, but could not keep himself from laughing. Richard joined in, then resumed.

"Well, instead of pouncing on this as some kind of CIA op, your CIA guy somehow got your Army involved. You are Army, are you not?" Richard asked, cocking his head, eyes sparkling.

Jack opened his mouth to answer yes and stopped. He *felt* Army still. Suddenly, a wave of a feeling he immediately recognized as "homesick" hit Jack.

He sighed and answered, "No, Richard, I'm not Army."

Pye obviously didn't believe him.

"Well, who…? Never mind. All I know is that your CIA guy got a General Ortega and some anonymous American down here real fast, pulled me in to brief them, and—next thing I know—my boss is telling me to meet code-name 'Jack' for dinner here in Brasilia and support his op," Richard divulged. "All of this has happened just within the last few days—while the Middle Eastern jungle visitors-customers are still at the bungalow in Manaus. We thought we'd do you the favor and you would be eternally grateful and have warm feelings about us, but take care of this nasty business yourself. Seems you just can't function without us!"

Jack smiled and understood. The new CIA Director was furious when he found out Ortega had been the first to name Saya-dar as the secretive leader behind the 20 suicide-bombers who ignited America's heartland. He was particularly piqued that Special Operations Command Central had been tracking the man through a defected Cuban intelligence officer. Miffed that the Cuban had not defected to the CIA, Jack supposed. Seems this Director's purpose was to "tame" the CIA and the broader intelligence community, and here was SOCOM, running amok.

The career intel and ops types at CIA stayed mission-focused though. They suspected General Ortega was running his own intelligence agency from SOCOM—Central in Tampa's McDill Air Force Base. Given the political state of things, and the lack of support from their own Director, they decided to take advantage of "subbing things out" as they thought of it. Off their budget. Off their books. Side-stepped any illegal domestic spying stuff. If things went wrong, then it was the Army's fault. If things went right and SOCOM looked heroic, then CIA would be coy, humbly accepting praise for its shadow role. And, besides all that, it got the good work done while the CIA was stuck playing footsie with their new Director.

All of this signaled Jack that the CIA had embraced the idea wholeheartedly and was now in with Ortega "thick as fleas."

That wasn't good.

Jack knew his legal status was questionable; the fewer who knew of his existence the better. And now, here was Richard Pye, the MI-6 spy who insisted he was a mere under-diplomat, assigning him a dangerous mission. SOCOM. MI-6. CIA. Just who all knew about him? Who was calling the shots on this one?

"So, who's my CO on this one?" Jack asked.

"CO? Oh. 'Commanding Officer.' You most decidedly *sound* Army. Fact is, *Jack*, or whomever you really are, I really don't know. I think our chaps passed this off to your General Ortega and his anonymous shadow, and we are just providing local support here in Brazil. The intel about the previously outfitted Trojan-horse tanker maybe involves those 20 truck-bombers. That might connect the action down here to inside the U.S. and we Brits thought you might want some revenge. We thought you Yanks would want to run this exclusively. Besides, you'll have greater latitude to handle this than we would if the fracas moves into the U.S. Wouldn't do at all for some congressional staffer boinking some news babe to impress her by accusing the U.K. of running a spy operation in America. Wouldn't look good on the telly, would it? Re-invasion or some such rot. Not talking about the Beatles, either. So, you've got it, we're helping you, and your General Ortega figured you might as well start here with the source—in Brazil—in Manaus."

Jack nodded. This had his employers, General Paul Ortega and Gordon Noone, written all over it. For now, Gordon's simple orders were: meet the Brit and get the mission from him. So be it.

"Mission, please," Jack asked quietly.

"Infiltrate to Fats' barge-building operation and into his home, if necessary, by 0600 hours three days from now and initiate surveillance by video and audio. The primary mission is to learn the purpose for this barge just bought by these Iranians. Secondarily, you're to report anything you learn about Fats' connection to smuggling in those 20 truck-bombers. Finally, once you've learned all you can, you're to prepare to kill Fats and the Iranians, if ordered." Richard ended, quite matter-of-factly.

"Ordered by *whom*?" Jack demanded, not so quietly.

Jack wasn't beyond assassination, but his ground rules were plain: he took orders from 'No one'. Gordon 'No-one' Noone, to be precise. Jack enlisted in Ortega's and Gordon's *Team Arcturus* but that didn't mean he was out for hire generally, even to close allies like the British. He'd work with the British—and for them if ordered by Gordon—but he wasn't about to snuff a man without Gordon personally ordering it. He'd call as soon as this little lakeside stroll ended.

"By whom? Who knows?" Pye laughed and savored his own joke. "Get it? The anonymous *Who* knows?" he continued. "You can't seriously think that such a person would ever slap his name onto your mess!" Richard said.

"Yes, I get it. Someone will call another and '*Who*' will issue the order. Later, everyone will wonder who "*Who*" was. Mine would be the only name on the wanted poster. Real funny. Well, tell you what. You pass this back up the chain: 'I take such orders from No One.' Say that exactly: 'No One.' Tell them that: No One must order me to kill anyone—and they *who* must know will know what I mean," Jack said.

Richard turned to face Jack—no joking around now—and his

eyes got big, questioning.

"It'll be OK, Richard. Just tell them that. 'No One' must order me to kill," Jack emphasized deliberately, just in case Richard was recording the conversation. He'd originally thought Gordon's adopted code name to be corny; now, he appreciated Gordon's knowledge of literature, Homer's cleverness, and the name's Ulysses-inspired utility. Came in handy.

The men said nothing, both making a show of looking ahead eastward at the sweeping parabolic supports dipping, intertwining, intersecting and forming the dramatic bridge across Brasilia's South Lake—*Lago Sul. That bridge is like this twisty, crazy but exciting world, loopy but somehow with order* Jack thought. Jack pointed to a bench along the walkway.

"Richard, why don't you tell me what the Operation Order calls for next?" Jack asked. "What's the Concept of the Operation?"

"Yes, of course. You probably already know that a highway runs northwest from here, across the dry country, into and through the Amazon jungle, all the way to the south bank of the river, directly across from Manaus. Remarkable achievement. Few in the world are aware that a city of a million sits on the Amazon more than a thousand miles upriver. More so, who would dream a highway runs to it—and then north again once you've crossed by ferry. No American interstate or British M-class highway mind you, but a paved road, nonetheless. It's a long drive from here, though. For that reason, you're flying from here. Got to get you in there before these Iranian customers leave.

'The "books" will show you arrived here in Brasilia by commercial jet, cleared customs, checked into a B&B—one of ours—and we'll create a trail of charges on a card in your name.

I will enjoy your dinners, thank you. In reality, we'll fly you by private plane to Borba, south of the river and south of Manaus, where you'll link up with a tractor-trailer freight hauler—actually hauling actual freight. You'll ride through the jungle up Highway 319 to the Amazon, but you won't ferry across with the trucker. The Marine Police check traffic on the other side. He'll drop you off with one of our agents who will small-boat you across the river." Jack interrupted at this point.

"'Small boat'? Explain 'small boat' please," Jack said. To a Ranger, small boat first meant 8-man rubber rafts paddled by exhausted, starved men. He could just see himself single-handedly paddling a rubber raft across the miles-wide Amazon—or maybe they planned to give him a dugout canoe. Pye laughed.

"Characteristic on the Amazon are these colorful passenger ferries and freight-haulers the size of one of your American stern-wheelers. Also, you'll see hundreds of slender motor-canoes—the main "motorcars" of this jungle river highway. You'll have one of those waiting for you—with driver. This way, you will leave no trail—no record of ever having been to Manaus at all. Let's cover the details," Richard said.

The men returned to the parking lot. Pye opened his rented VW Gol G4 and drove to an apartment block where mostly hundreds of young government workers rented. So did the British government. Here, in the rented safe house, the two poured over every detail of the plan. Richard unfolded the map.

"Your river boatman will enter this lake just off the Amazon and drop you off at a pier where you'll find your own motorized canoe. You'll continue past Fats' channel—sort of his watery driveway—and work your way up another channel to your very tiny, abandoned shanty on stilts. I've no idea how you'll do this. It will be the middle of the night and you'll be in the jungle.

I'm told you infantry types love this sort of thing, what? We checked. Your abandoned shanty base is on land Fats owns, but, for some reason, he never, ever goes there. There is no sign that this shanty has been occupied by anyone for decades. We know because we outfitted it to supply what you need but—no comforts. It's got to still look ordinary. Consuela has verified that her boss never goes there. She doesn't know why, but he knows of it and avoids it like the plague. Otherwise, we'd had to have found you some other hide-out and that would have been really hard to do, considering the terrain. So, you'll sort of be hiding in the open." Jack started to protest and Richard interrupted.

"You'll have a dugout like these jungle Brazilians use: strictly one-man. You'll also have a trolling motor for silently moving about the area. You'll also have a faster, motorized canoe, one of those long, colorful types you see there with a weed eater-looking motor. Good for fast escape.

'The bungalow is a half mile from your shanty by water, straight through the flooded forest. That would be slow paddling through the rubber trees and vines. Instead, it's faster if you motor down your channel toward the Amazon, left into this lake, then hang a left again up Fats' private boulevard channel.

'You tie a red rag around a bridge piling here at the Amazon bank and that lets Consuela know you're in position at the shack. She'll remove it after returning from market and link up with you at your shack. Set up the microphones, cameras, and transmitters. You're *surveillance.* She'll bring you documents you want. You'll have a good digital camera and a smartphone capable of uploading them. Here."

Richard handed Jack a netbook with Windows already running.

"My op order," Jack said, seeing what he had just been handed.

"I want to see my toys," Jack said.

Jack scrolled quickly to the end and found what he was looking for: a section titled whimsically "Shack Annex." It included a list of all supplies and equipment that—supposedly—would be staged there for him. The list included batteries for electronics Jack would need to run the surveillance and uploads. The Order with its annexes exuded "Gordon," all neatly in the Patrol Order format used universally by trained-up troops taught at Ranger school. Clearly Army. Pye puttered in the kitchen brewing tea while Jack read it over.

"Something's missing," Jack said.

"What?"

"A way to reach you," Jack said.

"Righto, old chap. Official policy and all that. Too many ties between the Mother Country and the colonies already, don't you think?" Pye replied. "Like your own government and Army, the Queen is concerned about having her hands dirtied. Yes, we're all chasing foxes here on another continent, but, come on, man! You are here without official cover! Your own government won't make you officially OK; how can mine?" Pye asked—logically, Jack thought.

"Damn them all to hell," Jack swore.

Pye's eyebrows lifted.

Jack looked at Pye.

What was there to say? It's lonely out here.

"Richard, don't get me wrong. I'm grateful for your help. However, this lonely, crude, jungle recon-shack, owned by the enemy, stands symbolic. Our countries need dirty jobs done, but the too-large, complacent, soft, and unsullied percentage want someone else to occupy these outposts. These people would throw me to the crocodiles in less than a heartbeat. I'm here in a friendly country, putting secret cameras on a foreign businessman. I can hear it now:

'Worst foreign policy in America's history.'

'American relations with our South American allies are now at an all-time low.'

'Heath Overstreet would have a field day on NNN—that's Nasty News Network—smirking and making the president out to be the worst person in the world just because Jack got caught running around in Brazil on the U.S. payroll. Maybe if the job is so unimportant that neither of our countries is willing to undertake the mission, it's just not that vital. Maybe I should just thank you for lunch and go home." Jack said. "The stroganoff was very good, by the way."

"Sure. Wouldn't blame you a bit. Eat at the Queen's table and leave, if you must. Maybe once the mushroom cloud goes up over Chicago your people will be more willing to back you up, openly and officially. Maybe they will put aside some of your pay in a retirement account. Healthcare benefits for Jack. Medal for you when it's all over. You'll be a hero and get book deals. Hire back on as a highly-paid consultant. Just like a Congressman. So, are you calling it all off?" Richard asked.

"Of course not. I don't mind the jungle—the Amazon jungle, that is. Been to Jungle School in more ways than one. It's the up-the-Chesapeake jungle I don't know how to navigate. I just want this contained as tightly as possible. Hey, what about the Brazilians? What do they know about this? Anything?" Jack asked. "This is their country, after all."

Richard coughed to clear his throat. Might as well lay it all out.

"Yes, this went to their ABIN—their intelligence service—just on the question of helping infiltrate an American surveillance operative, mind you. Not on who you are or even who your target is," Richard said, raising his voice and his hand, seeing Jack about to explode. "They know your target is not Brazilian, and they know Guevara is implicated. That's good enough for ABIN. They just cannot be put in the position of telling their people right now that they have given permission to the Americans—or the British—to run around in their country doing ops. Unofficially, they want to help your country and they want Guevara to get his fat face punched in. Lula was livid that Guevara comes down here, using Brazil to conspire and cooperate with terrorists. But, they just elected that communist agitator as president and ABIN is nervous about her being worse than Lula about taking pot shots at the Americans. You blow your cover and the Brazilians have a national scandal that could set back your relations by another century. But, as long as Jack is a dull boy and you don't blow your cover, they win, too. So, be nimble and quick—jump *over* that candlestick or get us all burned. ABIN is quietly issuing instructions to a few of their people in the Manaus area who will provide you limited help—on a need-to-know basis, only. The truck driver insertion is an example. He's theirs, not ours. The boatman who will get you across the Amazon is ours but he's theirs too. They lined him up for you. If you absolutely blow the whole thing and end up in jail in Manaus, I'll know it and start the quiet calling necessary to slip you out before the news gets so high up that no one could ever spring you free.

Jack glared.

"Here," Richard said, smiling a little and passing Jack a small note. "My mobile phone number for this op. Officially, this ends my participation in your adventure and I stay here in government-ville, resuming my place in the bureaucracy. Unofficially, I'm setting up south of Manaus, close by your hide. I'll be monitoring your audio and video uploads. See, old boy, I won't be enjoying dinners on your fake credit card after all. If you get into trouble, call the Redcoats. Sort of Paul Revere in reverse. See? We have no hard feelings over your little temper tantrum back then."

"Well, why didn't you say so in the first place?" Jack asked.

"Ha! It was far more fun to watch you burn. Call if you must. Memorize the number on that slip and eat it," he joked.

Jack did both on the spot.

The men shook hands.

"Hey, does this mission have a name?" Jack asked. "Missions are supposed to have names."

"'Piranha.' Operation Piranha. Keep your body in the boat, and your feet out of the water. We just never know what is lurking down there," Richard advised.

"Yeah. I saw the movie," Jack said.

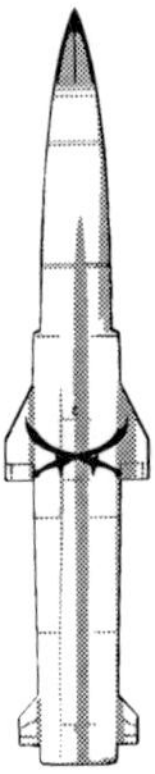

# 5

*Tuesday morning*
*Borba air strip*
*Amazonas State, Brazil*

Jack looked to his right as the pilot reduced altitude to land at tiny Borba. The Madiera River glistened on its way to add its water to the Amazon, 150 miles to the north. Borba claimed space from the jungle, but the river stopped the town's growth ambitions cold on Borba's north and the trackless rain forest closed in on the town on all other sides.

Looking out the front window, Jack McDonald prayed that the pilot knew what he was doing. The airstrip was long enough but, if the pilot overshot, they'd become one with the triple canopy jungle. Jack looked for the road he knew ran northwest away from Borba to connect up Highway BR 319 south of Careiro, 75 miles away, but the jungle completely hid it.

*There, there's the ferry landing. That truck waiting by the terminal must be my ride.* Jack looked for an ambush but the jungle masked all.

The pilot circled the airport once. *Giving me a look at the tactical situation below before he goes in,* Jack thought. *Very expert.* Jack flashed the stoic pilot a smile and a thumbs up. *Was that a smile back?* Jack wondered.

Now, the pilot shed altitude fast and leveled off just above the runway. He'd spoken no word at all during the entire flight from Brasilia and Jack had respected his sense of covert operations security. *Hell, he could be one of ours for all I know.*

No sooner than had Jack stepped onto the tarmac, the pilot became human. Grinning, with gray eyes flashing, he surprised Jack by handing him a Butterfinger candy bar. Laughing at Jack's obvious surprise, and still without a word, he straightened the bill of his cap as a good-bye, nodded to Jack, closed the Helio Stallion's door, turned and lifted off again. The short-takeoff, specialized airplane with its slender nose and swept forward look appeared eager to get out of town. The pilot dipped his wings after he left the runway and, with that, he left Jack in the hardscrabble working man's town of Borba, deep in the Amazon basin.

Jack peeled away the yellow wrapper, took a bite from the bar, and laughed, understanding the pilot's candy bar message. The pilot must have flown Ranger School support. Those chopper pilots, knowing that the Army drove the Rangers half mad by starving them, offered the ragged Rangers a flight bag full of illicit candy bars on the way to landing zones during the Florida training phase. A delicious tradition.

Jack munched the Butterfinger, shouldered his trying-to-look-civilian daypack, and strode to the only tractor-trailer rig parked nearby. A man leaned against the cab, smoking. He flicked the cigarette away as Jack approached.

"Come, my hitchhiker friend, we are to leave immediately," the man said, in a not unfriendly voice. "I am Jose," he said, laughing, introducing himself falsely and generically, and extending his hand.

"I am Jack."

"Right-brain."

"Observation deck," Jack answered.

These linkups throbbed fraught with almost palpable danger. Jack could never know for certain the mission hadn't been compromised. At every point involving another person, he could be walking into a trap. Jack hated linkups with "partisans."

However, Jack saw no sign of any threat. Jose stayed relaxed, waiting for Jack to get comfortable. Jose watched with some amusement as Jack eyed the back of the tractor rig and motioned for Jose to open it up. Jack watched Jose's every move as he complied. Jack half-expected Ulysses and his platoon of Greeks to rush him as the doors swung open, but no one waited inside in ambush: only pallets holding stacked bags of soybeans. Jack nodded and turned to shake Jose's hand.

"Let's roll," Jack said.

A soldier has to trust someone, somewhat. He just can't do it all alone—at least not and get the mission accomplished on time.

Time. Time was Jack's enemy. Time—the lack of it—forced all of this logistical support on him. Otherwise, he could have kept this whole job tighter, with fewer people knowing he was out in the woods. Every helper could be a traitor—a trap.

Jack hated the truck ride. Almost the entire route was a potential ambush site. After an hour of trying to see into the green walls of the jungle tunnel pierced by the rude road, he accepted that risk, crawled into the sleeper, and did what soldiers do when they can: Jack McDonald copped some "Z's."

The blaring radio woke Jack up to what sounded like the Bee Gees singing in Portuguese. He climbed out of the sleeper. Jose stood outside the cab waiting for him.

"Sorry, *senhor*, but turning the radio up is safer than grabbing your arm and shaking you to wake you up," the driver said. "I did not want to find myself with your knife at my throat."

Truly spoken.

"No problem," Jack said, agreeing.

"We arrive at the ferry across the Amazon in about 15 minutes," Jose said.

Jose had pulled the truck off onto a scraped but abandoned lot. Jack could see a few tin-roofed buildings ahead. No other vehicles passed by.

"Why are we stopped?" Jack asked.

"To give you time to get your things together and for me to tell you about the next leg of your trip through the jungle," Jose said. *Careiro de Varzea* lies ahead, the last town we come to before the ferry. I don't want to delay there because that's where the Federal Police station is. They might get suspicious if they see me stop for too long short of their checkpoint, especially if they see you get out and take off on foot," Jose explained.

"On foot?" Jack asked. *To where?*

"Yes, on foot. I'll stop briefly at a tire shop just before we reach the ferry landing and make a show of looking at tires. You'll get out too and just not get back in. You'll be met at the shop by your guide. I'll keep going like a good little truck driver with a delivery to make and you'll be on your way after a casual pause," Jose said, apparently proud of the plan. "OK?"

"OK. Let's do it."

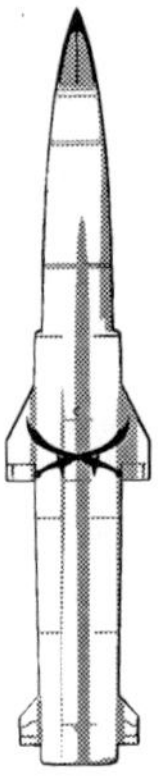

# 6

*Tuesday afternoon*
*South side of Amazon River*

Highway 319 sloped downward and then entered a cut into an even steeper bank, leveling out onto a flat plain before reaching the ferry landing. A cluster of buildings appeared alongside a short line of waiting trucks and cars up the road at the ferry. The structures were the usual string of businesses, each painted a different bright color, front open to the air and sun, corrugated tin rusting. Stacks of used tires in front of one caught Jack's attention: one of the many *Borrachoria* tire shops you find in Brazil. *They must wear out a lot of tires here.* A man sat in the shade in the ever-present, white, plastic chair, reading a newspaper. Jose slowed and halted just before the tire shop. Jack climbed out with him.

"Thanks, Jose. Good job," Jack said, making his good-bye.

"You're welcome, and good luck," Jose said, and the Brazilian, maybe British, trucker-agent smoothly became just a trucker again.

Before Jack could seriously wonder what to do next, the man sitting by the *Borrachoria* appeared, extended his hand in greeting, and introduced himself as "Boatman, the boatman." He grinned broadly, delighted with the joke. Jack accepted the code name as appropriate if unimaginative. Boatman and Jack exchanged the challenge and password for the day. So far, so good. The Brazilians might be only unofficially involved, but they were handling their end of things like champs—like clockwork. Jack stepped back a few steps and took in his new contact and his surroundings.

The Amazon rolled by about a quarter mile ahead. *Careiro de Varza* scattered about, clustered mostly around a truck stop, a couple of *Auto Mecanica Electrica* repair stations, some open-to-the-front eateries. A Bohemia beer sign hung by a single bolt and threatened to fall into the street onto the three chickens picking about below. Jack spied a few blocks of secondary businesses and residences across the street. Plainly, not many visitors hung out in this town.

At the riverbank, a cacophony of sounds and color throbbed. Red, white, and sky-blue painted passenger ferries rocked. Passengers on the ferries lounged in hammocks hung in the open air from hooks above the deck. A gentle breeze from the river cooled the day. Jack expected rain forest swelter, but the river—looking at least five miles wide at this point from what Jack could see—channeled a constant breeze, helping out and moving the mosquitoes along without time to alight. A loaded ferry chugged away from the shore and an incoming ferry approached. Also tethered to a quay floated a gunmetal gray boat bearing the name of the Federal Police, specialized waterways unit, the *Policia Maritima*, reminding Jack that he wanted no attention. He had no idea which agencies were on board supporting the operation and which would consider him a criminal.

However, everyone bustled about his business. *Either they ignore you or try to bully and bribe you*, Jack thought, noting the Latin American way of checkpoint policemen and soldiers. Jack perceived no interest in his arrival—no threat—and turned to Boatman who seemed to know what Jack was doing.

"*Senhor* Jack, we must go. We are not the only people to avoid the *Policia Maritima* at these ferry landings, and one of them will eventually take notice. Come with me, please," he said. Without looking to see if Jack followed, Boatman turned and entered a gravel path threading its way between recklessly stacked tires behind the *Borrachoria.* Twenty yards down the path, they emerged into a field sprouting more stacks of tires and came to a motorcycle.

"Our ride to your crossing, *senhor,*" Boatman explained.

Jack climbed on the back. The man rode five minutes to a rude dirt road and turned. Five more minutes—all downhill telling Jack they continued to descend to the riverbank—brought them to a clearing. Cattle grazed below tall trees. Across the clearing, Jack saw the river again, and a house on stilts. Nearing the house, he saw several boats tied up.

Boatman stopped, both men dismounted, and Boatman kicked down the stand.

"Welcome, *senhor*, it's humble but it's mine. We'll eat first and cross the river later, inserting you at night," he explained.

"I don't need to eat," Jack said, anxious to resume full control of his situation when he was so little in control of the operation.

"But, I do, *senhor,*" Boatman smiled. "Come, it is all right. Enjoy some hospitality. Some beans and rice, of course. My orders are to time your passage to drop you at 3:00 a.m., and we are early for that."

Jack followed, stepping onto the wooden plank porch completely surrounding the shack on stilts. The inside was surprisingly neat, clean, and warmly decorated. No one was in the shack, but beans and rice with slices of sausage sat in bowls on the kitchen counter, prepared and waiting.

"I sent the family out," Boatman explained simply.

Jack didn't like it. That's what he would do if he were playing Judas, but he'd also do the same if he were on the up-and-up. The man would be foolish to needlessly expose his family to danger, and Jack represented danger. The food did smell delicious. Jack realized how hungry he really was.

"I'll be back in 10 minutes," he said. His host nodded.

Jack spent the next 10 minutes walking the perimeter of his surroundings. Careless ambushers would assume he'd just stay in the kill zone and they might have set up too close. Jack's recon revealed nothing but a small riverbank farm with a shop for keeping boats and motors repaired. What a relief.

He turned his attention to the single-story structure. Tin-roofed, plank sided, on stilts but low, very close to the water's surface. At one end, a portion of the structure was open to the elements, creating a porch. At the other, a lean-to roof shaded the porch for laundry work. The planks were painted white, but faded. Some had been replaced without painting them.

Boatman cleared the table after the men ate and Jack helped. Good upbringing. Mom would have been proud of him. Boatman pointed Jack to a cot in the corner and laid down nearby. Soon he was snoring. Jack followed suit.

Jack's wristwatch alarm sounded. He rose from the cot and awakened Boatman.

"Time to go," Jack said.

Boatman motioned Jack to the porch above the river, connected to the shallow wash from the Amazon by a ladder. The ladder led them into a smaller red, white, and blue boat—a long, slender arrow of a canoe with a canopy overhead and a motor on the back. The motor looked like a weed eater, with an 8-foot shaft diagonally stuck into the water. Jack found a straw hat and a bottle of water waiting.

"It will take two hours, *senhor,* even though you can see the other side. We're going in here," he said, handing Jack a hand-drawn sketch map marked "X."

Jack compared the sketch to his own map. They'd cross and also go downriver about eight more miles where the frenzy of Manaus would be left behind.

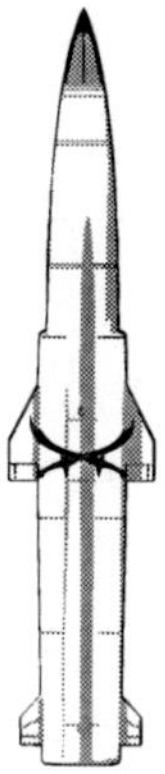

# 7

*Tuesday, midnight*
*Amazon River bank,*
*four miles south of Manaus*

Boatman tugged the engine to life and expertly maneuvered away from his house on stilts. Jack noted the children's toys on the deck, the plastic rain catch-barrels on the porch at the laundry area, and the single-paddle wooden canoes. He pulled his baseball cap down over his eyes more and settled in as Boatman swung the canoe around and headed east down a smaller channel, away from Manaus and the Amazon River.

Instead of heading across the river and directly to Manaus like the ferry would do, they planned to stay off the river, on this channel taking them away from Manaus, until coming to the end of the island that lay on their left side. Then, they would turn back to the west, cross the Amazon well downriver from Manaus, and approach the doorway to Fats' secretive world. Fats' bungalow perched on stilts above one of the hundreds of backwater lakes. Boaters accessed this particular lake by a narrow channel, hardly visible from the river. Once through this narrow channel the lake opened up. Instead of this lake being smoothly oval-shaped, its banks were irregular, broken, and permeated by scores of secondary waterways leading away into the rain forest.

A village lay on this lake, situated on one of the main side-channels and invisible from the Amazon. This little village included the market near to Fats' bungalow, the market Consuela frequented. Fats' and Consuela's hidden world ranged from market, village, marina, docks, and homes to jungle, swamp, and isolated narrow inlet, with the Amazon's vast waterway only two twisting, watery miles away.

Jack had to admire the setup. Fats' barge-building and welding operation occupied the riverbank exactly 6.3 miles from the narrow channel-doorway to his secluded, watery world. The commute to work by boat couldn't take more than 30 minutes. From his bungalow, Fats could escape by road, too. The man never had to enter the city if he wished to avoid the public. Once through the narrow passage connecting the Amazon with the lake, and cloistered on his own tributary, he might as well be in the heart of the rain forest.

Jack checked his compass: still navigating eastward with the island on their left. He checked his mobile phone and was surprised to find three bars of signal. He looked back at Boatman who seemed to be enjoying his discoveries. Boatman, throttled back and drifted quietly.

"Did you expect to be blow-gunned by head-shrinking cannibals, *senhor*?" he asked, not waiting for Jack's answer to roar with laughter.

"Manaus and pockets along the river generally are busy markets, but Manaus—well—it's 'something else' as you might say. In some way, that always surprises Americans," he said. Boatman had quickly reasoned that Jack was American, despite Jack's efforts to try to appear British or Canadian or German or something else. Jack still marveled that some ethereal quality gave Americans away. He'd heard many theories. Boatman continued.

"I know you cannot say much, *senhor.* I will assume you are diligent to keep operational security and not just rude," the man said, and smiled. "I'm sure you were told that Manaus is busy but it's hard for someone from the outside world to grasp what goes on here. Here's this beehive with oil tankers and container ships and barges and passenger ferries coming and going, a thousand miles into the jungle. In fact, step outside Manaus and you're in it. Few Manaus residents ever put foot in the jungle and they'd be as hard-pressed to find food and water there as you—well, as any American tourist might be, yet it is their backyard.

'You'll be inserting about eight miles downriver from the city's developed area. Still some huts and businesses along the bank and around, but where you're going in it's much less inhabited, I assure you.

'I'm to drop you off at your own smaller canoe, watch you check it out and operate it, and make sure you have gas. Then, I'm to wave good-bye to you. I do not know where you are going," Boatman ended.

Jack nodded thankfully and said nothing. He'd have liked a guide who could lead him through the creeks and sloughs to his objective, but he also liked the man not knowing exactly where he would be. He marveled at all the help lined up to support him but felt so alone in his enforced, compartmented silence. He'd liked to have known more about the man. This agent obviously had a life of his own outside of espionage, and he had a family to protect. As if reading his thoughts, the boatman added:

"*Senhor* Jack, I know very little about you. Obviously you're an American (*There it was again!*), but no one told me that. They told me my government wishes your success. They said your enemies are my enemies, and you are our friend. I was ordered to keep silent with you and told you would do the same. You are so diligent in the performance of your duties! Alas! I'm Brazilian! How can I keep silent? I hope I've not bothered or offended you by my chatter. I do want to say, before we part, 'Thank you' for whatever you are doing that helps my country and I pray for your success.

'Now, we'll insert you and you'll be gone. I will return to my house on stilts. But—and this is breaking my orders, *senhor*—my mobile phone number is written on this slip of paper. It's a pre-paid bought just for your little trip to our humble area and it goes into the river when you're done, so don't worry about leaving something on it that might get me in trouble. I'll leave it off but check messages four times a day—6—12—6—12. I will help you if I can," Mr. Boatman ended.

The men shared a look: gratitude, respect, lonely camaraderie, and then Jack swiveled back to his front.

Boatman throttled up again, entering the main Amazon River channel. This time, he maintained enough speed to creep upriver against the current, but stayed as silent as possible. Another hour brought them close to where Jack's GPS told him the insertion point would be at the narrow inlet.

Boatman slowed. Jack's senses heightened. There. On the right. Jack spied a channel almost masked by its angle and by the green carpet cloaking everything on its banks. Boatman slipped into the channel. Another half mile of travel, and moonlight revealed a lake and what appeared to be a few buildings across its surface. Boatman veered right and cut the engine, pulling up to a pier. There sat a replica of Boatman's slender, motorized canoe, only smaller, about 16 feet long.

"It's yours, my son," Boatman proclaimed grandly, play acting to relieve his own nervousness. "Don't drive it too fast, now."

Jack stepped out onto the rickety pier. In 10 minutes, they had verified fuel, oil, and Jack's ability to start and use the engine. As the men parted ways, they waved, Boatman pointing his bow back toward the Amazon and Jack pointing his down this narrow channel toward the lake.

Jack hated to see the man go, but his sense of excitement grew as he navigated toward the lake. Time to breathe, relax and discipline his emotions and mind to view this as no more than a technical military patrol problem to be solved. First, he had to find the shack, no small task in the primordial blackness lit only by the moon, vanishing and returning among the clouds.

These missions blessed Jack with meeting so many fine, brave people. The same missions dictated a serial string of farewells to comrades-in-arms of all nations. Unless something went terribly wrong, he would never again see Boatman or—for that matter—scores of other good men and women—fellow soldiers. Quietly puttering up the channel, he missed his deceased wife, Donna. God, how he missed her. He missed the company of other men who fought for their country. *Just what was he doing here…?*

*Stop! Don't go there. Certainly not now!*

For a time, he'd work for Gordon Noone and serve his country this way, out of uniform. Not forever. It'd not define him.

The giant rubber trees dwarfed him. Jack had faith that Gordon had not sent him to this remote corner in vain. Jack cut the engine, slowed and checked his GPS. He confirmed the GPS' position using a red-lensed flashlight and map. Time to paddle. It would be so easy to miss his own channel and take the wrong one. This channel to the right led to Fats' bungalow. Another quarter-mile and Jack would find a smaller channel. His surveillance post stood on its stilts up that one. Jack looped the cord of his compass around a support, set the compass on the floor of the canoe in front of his knees, folded the map, and dipped the paddle into the moonlit waters.

Ten minutes of quiet paddling brought him to his own turn. He turned his canoe into a channel no more than 10 feet wide.

Here, navigation became almost impossible. The GPS struggled for signal through the canopy of trees. Jack verified the direction by his compass. At first, using a man-made structure so close to the target had made him nervous but, as he thought about the terrain, he appreciated the ingenuity of the chosen observation and listening post. He now dipped the paddle more infrequently, stopping to listen every 40 yards or so.

"Two if by sea," his operations order, Command and Signal paragraph had said. Jack spied two dim lights ahead. These were to mark the shack for him in the dark. The closer Jack drifted toward his objective, the more he felt his own vulnerability.

In a foreign country. Deep into Brazil's interior. Reliant on a number of others, each of whom could betray him. Fats' bungalow only a short canoe trip away. Jack was truly on his own and at the enemy's front door.

Jack dipped the canoe's paddle again and eased the slender, covered, dagger-shaped boat forward. No sign, but he'd not expected anything overt, even if men hid waiting in ambush for him.

Here, the breeze was stifled by the jungle. The heat hung. Few mosquitoes, though: he'd expected clouds of the satanic little beasts.

Jack stopped for a "security halt." He paused, completely still, oriented himself to the ambient sounds, and "felt" the terrain and the night. He studied the jungle night. Joined the jungle night.

To his left and right shimmered backwaters as far as Jack could see, which wasn't far. Rubber trees loomed skyward. Vines hung in tangles. Ahead on stilts sat the shack, unpainted but looking in solid repair. Tin roof. Covered porch. There was a ladder to tie up by. No sound at all coming from it. Jack waited, floating, for 10 minutes. Night cloaked the jungle. The moon tried in vain to light the creek. The two signal lights shown like animal eyes in a cartoon drawing. No sound. Ten more minutes. Between creaking shack-floors, night's stillness, and the water, Jack calculated he would have heard any ambusher by now. Nothing.

Again, he dipped his paddle for a single stroke and glided to the right, slipping behind a rubber tree. Jack spent the next hour circling the shack and performing security halts.

Nothing.

Finally, and from behind the shack, Jack approached, mounted the ladder, and climbed up. Nothing happened so he began to take stock of his supplies and locate any weapon left for him.

A hammock with mosquito net hung unsurprisingly in a corner. A large, plank-built locker sat all along one wall, creating a seat. A plastic table with two chairs stood by it at one end. Jack moved toward the locker to locate its lock. He was pressing in the combination when he heard three soft whistles from the direction he'd come. Silence—then three whistles again. Silence. Then again.

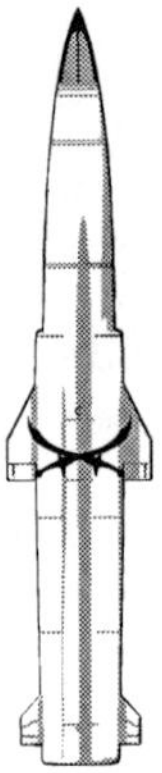

# 8

*Wednesday, surveillance day one*
*Three hours before dawn*
*The surveillance shack*

Jack receded into the shack behind the lights—where he could not be seen. Jack felt a canoe bump the shack supports and felt the slight jar of a weight shaking the shack as someone stepped from canoe to ladder. He waited. The lamps lit the doorway and ladder with a golden glow.

A brown arm came up. A hand gripped the ladder's top post, two feet above the floor level. A second small hand came up and Jack gripped it, supporting and pulling upward. A shapely, brown, bare leg next appeared, the bare foot finding purchase on the shack porch floor. A woman swung forward and upward and into view, pulling herself upward by Jack's extended hand. She stood, straightened her dress, looked at Jack, and smiled.

Before Jack stood a woman of maybe 40, medium height and fit build, clad in a flowing, loose, sleeveless, flower-print dress. Her shape rippled beneath the gauzy dress, not immodest, but cut minimalist to help keep its wearer cool in the jungle heat.

The woman's eyes searched Jack's in the flickering lamp light.

"Powerball," she spoke in heavily accented English.

"Jackpot," Jack replied with the password to the challenge, the security ritual completed.

The woman surprised Jack by falling into his arms, pressing close to his chest. He instinctively lifted his own arms and held her. She clung closely. Jack, alarmed, glanced around but saw no danger. He moved his hands over her waist and hips. No weapon. He felt only her breasts and face pressing against his chest and belly—no gun or knife there, that was for sure. Jack relaxed and gently removed her from the tight embrace, backing slightly away and bending down to search her face.

Tears rolled down her cheeks.

*This is my help? Uh, oh.*

She addressed Jack in accented but clear English, sounding a bit dramatic, a flare, Jack thought, picked up from the television dramas that must have been her teachers.

"*Señor,* I am so glad you've come! So glad! I am so frightened of these men!" she exclaimed.

Jack said nothing yet, but appraised her further: straight, dark-roast coffee-colored hair ending in a gentle upturning sweep over her browned shoulders; eyes chocolate-brown pools reflecting the lamps' glow—opened wide and afraid; breasts full and unrestrained, partly visible in the loose "V" of her dress; arms sinewy, waist narrow, hips round but not fat; legs and feet bare from mid-thigh down. Disarming in her beauty but plainly unarmed. He'd have spotted any weapon underneath that outfit.

"You are Consuela?" he said simply, in Spanish. He did not introduce himself and had no intention of revealing he was American.

"Yes, I am Consuela. I called for you. Or for *someone.* They sent you. I did not know they would send an American. I am so glad you are here. We are all in great danger," she ended.

Jack sighed. Of course she identified him as American, despite his fluent Spanish and his "bought off the Brazilian economy" duds. Somehow, all foreigners knew immediately you were an American. How did they *always* know?

"First, please relax. Are we in *immediate* danger? Were you followed?" Jack demanded.

"Oh, no-no, not that kind of danger," she assured, taking his hand again, moving into Jack. "I came to show you where his bungalow is and to do whatever you tell me," she replied.

Jack blushed, though she could not see clearly enough in the flickering lamplight to know. He squeezed her warm hand, smelt her light, flowery perfume, but gently left her embrace again to keep hands free.

"Good. You may call me Jack. Let's look to see what is in the box over there," Jack said. He directed her to the supply locker. He was anxious to get his own hands on a weapon.

She moved with him toward the locked box. Jack worked the four-digit combination and opened up his staged supplies. Consuela retrieved one of the lamps and returned to his side.

With Consuela pressing distractingly close and lighting the contents, Jack retrieved a gray, molded-plastic case.

"Well, I'll be John Brown," Jack exclaimed aloud, so astounded that he reverted to an expression his grandfather had used dating from who knows how far back. "Somebody out there in spy-land is having a good time with the toys."

Inside the case, he found a Bersa Thunder Pro in 9mm. He figured the Argentine pistol must have been easier to find in Brazil than trying to smuggle in some more commonly found weapon. Gordon must have wanted to bypass the American embassy, too. Jack appreciated the Bersa, a well-made, fine weapon, under-rated in the states but perfectly serviceable. Jack worked the action, finding it clean and lubricated. Three magazines accompanied the pistol. He tested the magazines, pressing down hard on the top round. They barely moved. Good. Fully loaded.

He put the Bersa aside, and marveled, feeling well-taken care of. It was what lay next to the Bersa that had so surprised Jack.

An odd, ugly, blackish, plastic conglomeration, looking more like a politically-incorrect Lego kit than a firearm, sat next to the Bersa. It offered some familiar hints of being a gun, but no gun could be found. Jack recognized it as the Israeli-made Roni pistol-carbine conversion he had familiarized with at the King Abdullah II Special Operations Training Center in Jordan.

Jack laid the conversion flat on the chest, and opened it like a book. He cleared the Bersa, fitted the bracket on the back of the slide, placed the Bersa into the conversion kit, and latched the cover over it. Now, in five seconds, the Bersa, encased in the Roni, became a compact carbine, complete with vertical forearm grip, adjustable shoulder stock, and Aimpoint Micro red dot sight mounted on the rail on top. Jack attached the single-point sling also in the box and turned on the Aimpoint, dialing it up to "8." He took out his Gerber multi-tool, unscrewed the battery cap, polished the battery and cap with his shirt, and screwed it back on. Since this Roni kit came already fitted with a sound suppressor, he'd test fire it in the morning, further away from the shanty.

*Gordon, thanks, man!*

Jack palmed a magazine home and worked the action again, chambering a round this time. Jack checked the loaded chamber indicator, slipped his arm through the sling, popped the forearm grip to vertical, and practiced getting the Bersa/Roni up from high-ready to on-target a few times. Very light weight; very compact; very handy weapon. The Roni quadrupled his accuracy with a pistol and controlled recoil so well that it could be fired almost as fast as a fully automatic weapon.

He looked at Consuela, happy and smiling until he saw Consuela's expression. Consuela shrank away, then recovered and returned to his side with the lamp, nervously watching his every move.

"Let's see what else they have for us," he said, trying to put the woman—his source, his agent—at ease.

She was not ready to relax.

"Who *are* you, *señor*?" she asked. Seeing his smile fade, "My life—it is in your hands," she explained.

Jack unslung the carbine, set it down, and turned to face her and study her again. *Would she bear up under this?* He peered into her face and she seized his hands again.

Every moment of Jack's training screamed at him.

*Grabbing my hands! Is she setting me up? Do I kill her or turn on my "Manage the agent, McDonald," charm?*

For the tense, frozen moment, though, Jack perceived no tangible threat.

"They will *kill* me, *señor*, if they discover I'm helping you," she explained, trembling.

Her face was only inches from Jack's in the lamp's light. Her hair fell across the corner of her eyes, opened wide. He felt her warmth adding to the damp Amazon heat surrounding them both. Her hands were warm, firm, urgent. Jack could feel her fear. Rational fear, too, as she had pointed out. She was risking her life—and maybe torture—to be helping him.

"Sit down with me, please, *senorita*," Jack said slowly in careful Spanish, directing her to one of the two chairs. He eyed the carbine, but the rest of the equipment would have to wait. Just as Consuela counted on him, he must rely on her. Yes, they were both in grave danger and both their lives hung in the balance—

held by the other.

"First, you must know that I cannot tell you who I am—or anything about me. Doing so would only place both of us in even greater danger. You know that, don't you?" Jack asked, adopting more formal Spanish since that was the way Consuela spoke.

She nodded, but a tear fell alongside her nose. Jack touched her tear, gently wiping her face with his fingertips.

"I, too, have no idea—really—who you are. I know you told the—authorities—about certain dangers that lurk here and that you have bravely agreed to help stop bad things from happening. You could not do that alone and you needed help. I am sent to help you." Jack said.

"You are American," she said.

"Where I am from is of no consequence, Consuela. It is who I am and where I am going that matters," Jack said.

"Who are you and where are you going, *señor*?"

"I am a soldier for now, going to Heaven when I die, but before that day, there are many evil men to send to hell," Jack said. "I will not harm you; I will help you and try to protect you. It is the evil ones I came to stop. You summoned me. I walk a road prepared by you, Consuela."

Jack knew she would identify with his explanation if she truly was who she said she was. She was afraid and needed protection. He came from far away to be that protection. She, too, had acted in the face of great risk to stop evil men. She didn't seek out danger but danger came to her anyway. He watched her eyes and could not help being struck by her quiet courage and natural beauty. She had made herself desperately vulnerable to help his countrymen. He loved her for that. He resolved to do more than just use her as their agent; he would protect her.

Consuela nodded her head slowly, determinedly, taking in the truth of what Jack had spoken. The woman smiled.

"Consuela, I want to prepare immediately for whatever dangers might befall us. Let's look now at the equipment we've been supplied with. Then, we can speak of these things further," Jack said.

She got up with him and returned to the locker. Jack found the usual fare of freeze-dried food, several gallons of water, water purification tablets, one of those new straw water-purification filters and other personal hygiene articles. A bag of Werther's hard candy. Nice touch. A machete. He also found the miniature surveillance camera and microphone sets he knew Consuela must place. He glanced at the woman standing next to him, her bare arm brushing lightly against his. She would have to be brave. She must be brave to have taken these risks already. Good thing. He did not want to think of her fate if caught placing the equipment.

Jack showed her how to place and activate the miniature camera-microphones. She spoke his name, and he turned to see what she wanted.

"I must leave," she said and before he could react, she kissed him and was gone. As he watched her step into her canoe and disappear into the pre-dawn dark, the awful "aloneness" surrounded Jack again. Consuela had brought back the emptiness left in Jack's heart by Donna's death.

Jack shook it off. He got about the business of setting up shop, preparing the surveillance receivers to record and re-transmit video and sound via the satellite phone he'd found in the locker. When Jack finished arranging the shack to be operational, he stepped back and approved of what he had been supplied.

Jack lay down in the hammock after giving up on the idea of moving his hammock outside among the trees. He'd rather not stay inside, such an obvious target, but he'd have to stand by in case Consuela returned. Besides, he'd need to closely monitor the receiver and re-transmitter equipment. Lacking more secure options, Jack did the obvious; he rested.

Sometime in the next few hours, Jack awakened to the beeps of the recorder in his ears. The device was set to signal Jack once the placing agent activated it. It looked like Consuela had gotten to work.

Jack flipped open the wireless digital monitor and powered it up. From the diagram Consuela had given him, he recognized the view on the screen: shot from the open-air veranda, into the entry and living room. In the wide-angle, fish-eye lens, Jack saw what had triggered the motion and sound-activated camera to transmit.

A man stood slouched over the rail, smoking. Minutes later, he flicked the butt into the water and turned, disappearing into the living room. Jack heard his steps fade and then grow louder as the next microphone picked him up.

"Oscar, this is Jack," Jack spoke into his own transmitter.

A voice Jack did not know answered: "Oscar, over. You're loud and clear. Pictures are good. I say again, pictures are good. Over."

That was it. Someone, somewhere, was watching. CIA, Jack assumed. Jack would never learn who, but he knew Gordon was watching and listening somehow.

"Jack, out."

What else was there to say?

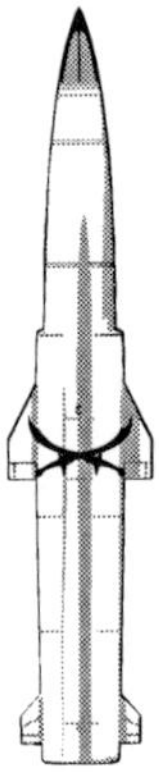

# 9

*Thursday, surveillance day two, 0300 hours*

Jack arose well before dawn the second day, heated a packet of food, and ate. He donned the jeans and camouflage-looking but civilian shirt bundled in the locker, slung the carbine over his back, climbed down the ladder, boarded the wooden one-man canoe and checked the GPS. Must be cloudy; no signal. Jack turned it off and retrieved his luminous-dial and needle compass.

Consuela had pointed him in the right direction. Fats' bungalow sat on its stilts approximately 500 yards away. Jack planned to work his way paddling directly through the swampy jungle, slipping among the vines and trees to approach from a way Fats would not expect. Now, it was time for a recon with the night vision device.

Thirty minutes of careful paddling brought him within sight of a cloth tied around a tree—the signal he'd asked Consuela to place 100 yards from the bungalow. Now, Jack slowed, selecting his next concealment among the trees, working his way closer. He arranged the camo netting to cover himself and part of the boat. He must be invisible.

Before morning twilight, Jack approached Fats' compound.

Ahead, through the trees, on stout stilts, stood an unpainted, lap-sided, palm leaf thatched roof bungalow with covered porch completely surrounding it. Simple design. Door in the middle of each of the four walls. Perfect square. About 1,500 square feet. Lots of room for a place down here. A covered walk—also on stilts—started from one of the porches and formed a pier extending about 50 feet from the porch. Tied to the pier were several boats: a wooden covered canoe like the one Jack occupied, a pontoon boat, probably for hauling heavier equipment and supplies, and one of the longer, slender, colorful canoes with the weed eater-style motor on the back. Finally, and out of place, a wave-runner bobbed at the far end of the pier. Its speed and maneuverability concerned Jack. *That's more speed than I've got.* Jack paddled quietly out and around to the wave-runner. Finding no key to steal, he palmed water from the creek into the gas tank.

He'd risked enough and left, paddling away at an angle, not directly back toward his own shack as the morning sun stretched out to reach through the canopy and dapple the Amazon's backwaters. These hellish missions led him to some wondrous places. Certainly, this was one.

As he returned, zigzagging among the trees, in no great hurry to get back, Jack formed a plan. He'd check in with Gordon by sat phone as per the Op Order. He didn't expect to hear from Consuela unless she had something to report by one of the surveillance microphones. At least until that night. She was to return from one of her market trips, if possible, and give him the exact arrangement of the devices, plus answers to his more specific questions about the number of men, their ages, size, behavior, and the rundown on any weapons.

Arriving at the shack, Jack listened as beginning twilight turned to dawn and daylight brightened. No sound. Jack tied up the boat—this time behind the shack and climbed up, warily. He brewed some coffee in the aluminum coffee pot on the propane stove from the storage trunk and moved a chair to the doorway. Jack sat, sipped strong coffee, and listened for the chirp that would signal transmission from the bungalow. He felt restless. Got up. Stepped forward and sat on the wooden plank porch, feet hanging down, staring at the water. Subconsciously, he patted the carbine slung across his chest.

Jack remembered how it began. Just like this: *Water, water everywhere....*

He had stood at the rail of the *Arcturus* on a morning like this, on their first mission, before he knew what Gordon was up to or who Gordon really was, smelling the salt sea spray and taking in the Caribbean sun and sea. Donna had sneaked up on him, bringing him a cup of coffee. She'd seen him touch his Colt .45 pistol and thought better of surprising him. Instead, she had teased: "What are you about to do, Jack? Shoot some albatross for breakfast? If you've read *Rime of the Ancyent Marinere,* do you know what that would do to us all?"

One year. One year ago, everything had changed. He'd contemplated a more or less normal life, with Donna, and she was gone.

A call. On the way home. What to do tonight? Want to go out? Lovers' banter. Jack had settled in, actually looking forward to becoming "normal," but it was not to be.

Another call. An accident. On the freeway. Gone. So mundane in some ways and so cataclysmic in so many others. She and their child-to-be—along with their new life together—over in an instant of time.

“You ready to do some work?” Gordon had asked after four weeks.

“Work?” Jack had responded, shaken from the fog of shattering grief. Unshaven. Lost. Depressed.

“Work. You remember. There’s still so much to be done, you know,” Gordon had said, sounding tired. Donna and he were close for niece and uncle and, well, the three of them had survived much together on that first mission.

But, Gordon was right. Everybody had his own tragedy to deal with. Life went on while evil never took a rest. Donna’s death ended her adventure here but did not change that fundamental truth. Losing her just made it harder to cope.

Cope? *What’s with “cope”?* Rangers don’t *cope.* Rangers conquer. Gordon was in his late 50s, and he drove on. He continued the mission. What right did Jack McDonald have to just check out?

“None,” was the answer Jack had arrived at. No right at all. He’d said yes to Gordon as always—as Gordon had known he would. Gordon offered an otherwise out-of-the-action soldier the way back into the fight. Gordon offered Jack life.

Still, Donna’s death left Jack altered. Before, he’d been a young, late-twenties, previously-single, ex-Army Ranger captain, full of it and looking for more. Donna and he had married in the heady wake of the *Arcturus* adventure, bewitched by the Caribbean Sea, enriched by the treasure they’d found, and intoxicated with having outfoxed death together. Might have been an impetuous wedding on a Coast Guard cutter, but it worked. The marriage, that is. They loved each other.

Jack smiled thinking of the look on Gordon's face when they told him they were getting married. He'd opened his mouth to spout off some wisdom, but stopped before the first word of protest left his lips. Life grabs you fast and leaves you before you're ready unless you just outlast it. He saw love in the pair's eyes, and who can reason against love anyway? Gordon lost a recruit to the *Arcturus* operations team formed by General Ortega. Or so he'd thought. *Guess what, Gordon? Jack's back!* McDonald reflected bitterly.

No. Not bitterly. That was just the ugly demon of loneliness gnawing at his heels, clawing at his legs, trying to drag him down, down, down. Jack was back, thankfully. He was thankful to have his health, to have his freedom, and to have the trust of men like Ortega and Gordon, "No One," Noone.

Jack laughed aloud. He had the trust of "No One." Those two men had invited him back to the fight against America's enemies where he belonged. *Thank you,* Jack voiced in his soul. *Thanks for the mission.*

Donna! How could Jack have resisted her? It was Gordon's fault, anyway. He recruited Jack as a bodyguard aboard the *Arcturus.* The luxurious yacht. The Caribbean Sea. Donna LaRue. The electric tension of adventure in the air. Battling pirates. Then, facing down terrorist assassins bent on revenge and sent by the mysterious Saya-dar to Gordon's lodge to kill them all. Jack had saved Donna's life and the two were bonded forever.

Continue doing missions for Gordon once they married? Jack didn't need the money—not after what they had found on the island—but Jack had to get back into the action. Donna understood him and even backed him in his decision to stay on the

*Arcturus* team. Jack worried that she'd insist on getting into the fight again herself.

Then, Donna brought home the news. Pregnant! She never asked Jack to change his mind about *Arcturus*, but she didn't have to. A life working for Gordon was always being gone, for undetermined months, to undisclosed places, for underground reasons. He could be killed and his family would simply never know. Add to that the threat of criminal prosecution by his own government. "This is no life for a married man and father," Jack had concluded and told Gordon. He was working on accepting true civilian status—when *the* call came that day.

And Donna was gone, just like that.

And Gordon was calling him to Team *Arcturus* again.

Saya-dar. The man who had caused so much death and grief. Jack wouldn't recognize him if he bumped into him—had never seen him clearly—but the man he captured at Gordon's lodge—and later interrogated—told him plenty. This Saya-dar had attacked his country, had sent 20 suicide bombers into the American heartland, and killed hundreds of his countrymen. He'd gotten away with it, too, for now. Saya-dar had almost tripped up fatally at Gordon's lodge, but had escaped Jack's lined-up tritium sights by seconds. Only a second earlier! He'd vanished and Jack burned for revenge against the man who had almost kidnapped Donna and who had planned the bombings. Jack wondered where he was and renewed his vow to kill him someday. It was as if Jack could somehow undo Donna's death if he could kill Saya-dar, even though Saya-dar had failed and Donna had died in a soul-rending automobile accident instead.

But he couldn't undo anything. That moment aboard *Arcturus* when he and Donna stood in the spray from *Arcturus's* bow and fell in love was gone forever.

Jack tossed a stick into the muddy water below and watched the ripples. He'd always thought he'd walk the "road to come what may" in the bold company of others. Comrades. Men to share hard times and then celebrate victories with afterward. Now, here he sat, in a shack, up a creek, hidden among the vines and trees, 1,000 miles up the Amazon, the immense Amazon, immensely alone.

Jack tossed another stick into the water and smiled from the childhood memory the ripples stirred. He was a young, young boy watching the rainwater run through the ditches, imagining where it would go, imagining the roadside mini-torrent as a mighty river tearing at its banks, and daydreaming that the leaf curled at both ends floating along was Jack's raft carrying him to—destination unknown, but certainly to adventure along the journey. Adventure *was* the destination! He'd spent many hours in his youth, quietly in the woods, learning to find his way, learning to hunt, learning to embrace the wilderness as his friend, stoking the fires of that imagination and now, here he was. Living it.

But, living it alone. As if this solitude weren't enough to drive a man insane, out of this mission's mists came to him a brown, warm beauty *needing* his comfort. Donna was dead, and Jack wanted those kinds of feelings to be buried with her.

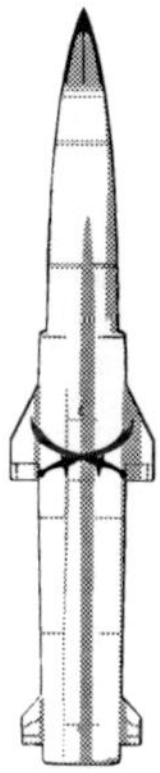

# 10

*Thursday afternoon,*
*surveillance day two*

Thursday dragged. The jungle pressed in hot and not even monkey-antics high in the canopy cheered Jack. He'd never felt so alone, so vulnerable, as out here, his life dependent on the good will of a woman no one could vouch for. Jack knew men who could lie in an ambush position, or in a surveillance hide, or on stakeout for days, never losing focus, never letting their minds wander. He envied them. He respected their skill. He was not one of them.

The sat phone chirped.

"Jack," Jack answered, and gave the day's challenge.

"Oscar," confirmed the caller.

"Whassup?" Jack asked, over-casually just to irritate The Voice.

"First, a question. I've got to authenticate you. I've been given a question for you to answer."

"OK. Shoot."

"What was Bobby's favorite beer?" The Voice asked.

"You asshole. What do…Never mind."

It was a good security question, really. It just pissed off Jack to have The Voice remind him of his friend, killed in action during the *Arcturus* mission. No doubt, The Voice had gotten the question from Gordon. *I really need this right now!*

"Can you answer it or not?" The Voice demanded.

"Amber Bock."

"Right. Consuela is on her way to your shack," The Voice said, quickly changing the topic.

"How do you know?" Jack asked.

"She said so. Right into one of the microphones. You could see her tonsils. You need to tell her not to do that. If they see her talking into a vase, she's toast," The Voice chided.

"I *did* tell her. I'll tell her again. Anything else while we're on the phone?"

This guy really irritated Jack. He hated someone telling him he "needed" to do such and such, or that the "had to do" this or that. Why? The guy was just one more desk commando, enamored of his own authority, feeling superior because he was smart enough to be in an air-conditioned office in D.C. while field rats like Jack sweated and bled in far-flung corners of hell.

*Why am I letting this guy get to me like this? Everybody's got a role to play in Kipling's Great Game and he is doing his job, too.*

"Nothing. Out," The Voice replied and broke the connection.

"Sorry," Jack spoke into the dead phone.

Jack sat on the narrow porch that surrounded the shack, dangling his feet, looking at the phone. He laughed at himself.

*You got a problem, Ranger? You need some counseling? I'll give you some counseling! Drop and give me 50. And one for The Big Ranger in the Sky, too! Now, you got a problem,*

*Ranger? I didn't think so. That's why they made me the counselor for you mule-shit maggot Ranger wannabees! I'm a counseling genius! They should call me Sergeant Freud! Every muleshit, ragbag, sorry- excuse-for-a-Ranger wannabee I counsel gets cured!*

Jack laughed aloud, remembering his Ranger School Tac Sergeant's method of solving Ranger "personal problems." Anyway, it worked. Problem gone.

"Push on! Continue the mission!" Jack ordered his ghosts, muttering the commands the crusty old Tac Sergeant was legendary for bellowing out.

Ten minutes later, scanning the trees and shadows, he spied Consuela approaching. This time, he extended his hand and helped the lady up.

"Hi, Consuela." *God help me, it is good to see her.*

Consuela got right to business.

"*Senhor*, you must come," she said breathlessly, chest heaving, not even saying "Hi."

Jack heard immediately that Consuela reverted to addressing him in Portuguese under stress, instead of in Spanish, though she knew he spoke Spanish but not the language of Brazil. Her skin glistened from exertion in the day's heat. She must have paddled her canoe out and across the swamp between the bungalow and Jack's surveillance shack instead of motoring up and down the channels. *It's calm the agent time.*

"Sit down and tell me why," Jack said, leading her to one of the two plastic lawn chairs that furnished his quarters. Jack sat back, showing her he was relaxed, open, and patient. Consuela sat forward, tense, gripping the chair arms, catching her breath, her bosom rising and falling, and finally settling to a more normal pace.

"The men and my—employer—met and discussed what you would call a set of papers. Plans. Uh, drawings. On big sheets of paper. Like an architect or engineer might do to build one of Fats' barges. I cannot think of exactly the right word," she gestured and gushed, embarrassed.

"Tell me more about those," Jack said.

"Drawings, but not by hand. Drawings by machines. With measurements, numbers, all printed in blue. Blue! That's it! You call them 'blueprints'," she said.

"Very good. That is the kind of detail I need. Any title or label on the blueprints? Anything that told you what these were plans for? I mean, this is what your boss does, Consuela. He builds barges and outfits other steel ships. It's not at all unusual that he would be looking at blueprints," Jack said, slowly, trying to move Consuela toward the more important details.

"I did not see a title, but I did not get to see all the sheets, all drawings, all blueprints," she corrected. "*Señor*, the men were *very* excited about these. Fats builds steel barges, you know—and he changes other ships." she added.

"Other ships?"

"He has many men working for him. They build barges, mostly. He sells them to other men all over the world. He is very rich from this," she added, somewhat confidentially, Jack thought.

"I'm sure. What ships does he *change*? How does he change them?" Jack said, a bit short.

"I don't really know. I do know this. In his home, he has changed ships for the president of my country, and entertained him in our home." she said.

"President of your country? You mean President Lula or this new president has been here to see Fats?" Jack asked. That didn't make sense.

"No, no, not the president of Brazil. The president of *my* original country: Venezuela," she corrected.

"Carlos Guevara? Carlos Guevara has been to the bungalow?"

Neurons fired madly, searching out and creating new connections, incited by a new urgency, fueled by danger.

"Yes. I am Venezuelan you know. *Señor* Jack, I am not stupid. I read. I listen. I learn. I 'keep up' as you say. I taught myself English from your TV and from my boss, who speaks it," she said. "We speak mostly English when we are alone. He has lived in America, Jack! Born there. I thought you knew."

*American? I bet that's a story!*

"More about these ships and about Guevara, please, Consuela."

"Fats makes barges, but he also works on steel ships, tankers, and container ships mostly, for many customers, but also for Guevara. Guevara himself flies here to Manaus bringing plans, then returns to inspect them when his tankers are finished. We have an international airport, you know. They—party. They drink. Fats curses your country. Guevara curses your country. He pays Fats, stays at the bungalow for a while sometimes (She shifted when she said this.) and leaves. He visited us—Fats—before those 20 bombs went off all over your country, in those stores, killing all of those poor people."

*Modifying tankers. Fats is modifying tankers for Carlos Guevara.* Jack would have to get word passed to CIA—The Voice no doubt—and check this out. Seemed to him that Guevara sold oil and didn't need it tanked in. Did oil exporters ship in their own vessels? Venezuela had refineries, but not enough to keep the country motoring around. Perhaps Guevara needed tankers to import gasoline from his capitalist nemesis to the north. Container ships he could see, but tankers? *Two years ago. Did Fats modify a tanker to smuggle in the truck bombers?* Well, the research doggies could work on this one. Either way, he believed Consuela and respected her instincts on this.

Jack continued looking at Consuela, but the television footage of the carnage flashing across his thoughts took him elsewhere—back to the truck bombings of 2007. His eyes narrowed. Without realizing it, his chin set, his face hardened. He saw Consuela's eyes widen, and saw her shrink back. *I'm scaring her.*

Jack turned away from Consuela, and walked to a window, looking out onto the still water, listening to the jungle afternoon.

The carnage. They never caught the man who planned the 20 bombings, and they never figured out who smuggled the bombers into the country.

He would do anything to find and kill these men.

"*Señor*, you must come and see these blueprints," Consuela interrupted, settling down now, but insisting—again.

Jack turned to face Consuela and moved close to her, bending down and examining her face. He searched down deep into her eyes.

Beautiful, deep, chocolate pools stared back, full and direct, into his own scrutinizing eyes. Her black hair fell across her brow. She brushed it back and behind her ear. Her gaze did not avert. She cocked her head, and gave him a puzzled look.

Consuela. Exotic. Sexy. Bearing vital information. Now, urging him into her boss's lair. Tantalizing him with the promise of information he could not resist? Setting him up? Enticing him? Baiting the hook for his capture, torture and death?

For some men, it was a prickly chill up the back of the neck. Others crouched, whipping their heads around left and right, checking their six, feet planted in a good, solid combat stance, knees slightly bent. Some answered the urge to jump just to the right or left, and swivel 180 degrees. Some told him they experienced this more Ninja-like deepening sense of smell, taste, sight, and thought, all without ever actually seeing or hearing any threat—just sensing it.

For Jack, it was far less profound and more dramatic. Absurdly, the image of the robot in '60s reruns of "Lost in Space" appeared, frantically waving his arms up and down, and shouting, "Warning! Warning! Extreme danger!"

And now, as he stared into the face of this soft-spoken, hot, bronzed jungle enchantress, Jack saw the robot.

Here was this alluring woman, working her way into his weaknesses, drawing him in by her intimacy and their shared vulnerability. She came now, urgent, offering him intelligence she knew he could not turn down.

Jack searched her eyes, only inches away. She stared back, face relaxed, open, then quizzical at his intensity. She did not back away. Instead, she took his hands and said, "*Señor* Jack, what is wrong?"

One man looked into Putin's eyes and saw a man he could do business with. Another saw the letters, "KGB," flashing warning signs. Jack wished he were a better, more instinctive judge of character. He knew he had a weakness for women.

Really, he had no choice. He was here to explore Fats' connections to terrorist threats, past and present—threats passed on by this agent—Consuela. Without her, they would not have known. He really, truly had no choice but to trust her—but he'd do this bit of spy work on his own terms.

Jack stood back and gave her space.

"Tonight at 2:30 a.m., I will arrive at your east porch. Meet me and show me these plans," he ordered.

"*Señor*, what if the men are still up—still awake?" she asked, logically.

"Tie a strip of cloth on the rail by the ladder when the coast is clear—if and when it is safe for me to come in. Can you do that?" he asked. "Do not speak into any of the microphones again," Jack added.

"Yes, I can do that. I will do that, I will be careful," she agreed.

"Anything else?" Jack asked, observing her hesitation.

"Yes, *señor*. These men—they are very excited. Something is about to happen—big. Also—," she said, hesitating, clouded and looking down.

"What? Tell me, what?"

"They grow more—bold," she said quietly, looking down still. A tear formed and ran down her cheek. She wiped it away with her hand.

Jack's heart went out to her. He took Consuela gently into his arms and held her. Her face rested on his chest as she cried.

Every tactical instinct screamed "No, you blithering fool, no!" He was supposed to have a plan to kill her if need be, and here he was. *Uh, oh.* The Ranger TAC Sergeant reappeared suddenly, his weathered face contorted in mock rage, inches from Jack's own face, wool beret perfectly straight across his furrowed brow, jowls working, screaming: "You stupid piece of mule-shit! Maggot!"

Fair enough. *I am properly chastised.*

He couldn't help it. Jack wanted to protect Consuela.

He pressed her closer, bodies hot in the swirl of emotions

stewed by jungle danger. He held her, felt her breathe in and out, pressed his fingers into her back. Pressed his face into her hair. Then, finally, slowly, gently, so gently, Jack relaxed his embrace and moved from her.

"You are very brave, Consuela. You and I may never know how many lives we are saving. For certain, the people you are saving will never know. Do you believe in God?" Jack asked.

She looked up, surprise in her face.

"Of course," she said.

"Then, pray to Him and draw strength from your faith. I will come tonight. It may be that these blueprints are all we need, and you can end this soon. Now go, before they think you've been gone too long."

*And before I ask you to stay.*

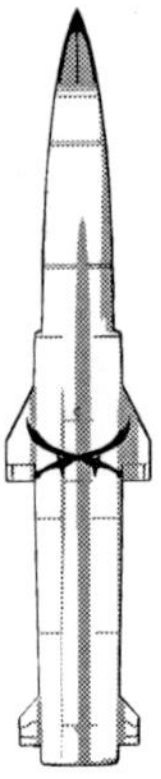

# 11

*Thursday evening,*
*surveillance day two*
*Jack's reconnaissance shack*

"Oscar, this is Jack, over."

"This is Oscar, over."

"I'm going in tonight for a close recon. Just want you to know," Jack said.

"Why? That's not your mission. Don't do it. You're surveillance! Listen to the microphones—and to me!" The Voice ordered.

Jack just looked at the sat phone and sighed. You know, you report to somebody just so that someone else can know what you are doing and where you are, and this guy you're reporting to presumes to be your boss. Jack saw "Dilbert" written all over this comic-strip conversation. He opted for a frontal assault to end this silliness.

"I conduct surveillance as I see fit. Don't forget; I'm actually *here!* Just shut up and listen. Take notes, intel-boy. The source tells me she has what are probably shipbuilding blueprints that the Iranians are very excited about, and the customer is—drum roll please—Carlos Guevara," Jack explained.

"So, your point is?" The Voice demanded, obviously stung by Jack's sarcasm and missing what Jack had just said.

*Obtuse*! "Just write it down. I'll take pictures and upload, if possible. Out."

*Good grief!* He'd need to call Gordon and get someone with some sense on the support end. Who was this dweeb and who hired him?

Jack set about collecting what he anticipated needing. He checked his digital camera. Battery on full charge. Settings right for close and dark, no flash. Waterproof bag. Good. He removed the Bersa pistol from the Roni conversion kit, and cleared the weapon by removing the magazine and operating the slide. He caught the ejected round and pocketed it. Jack field-stripped the pistol and felt the slide rails for just the right amount of lubricant. He reassembled the weapon—omitting the magazine, replaced it in the Roni kit—and maneuvered the carbine, getting used to the length and weight of the sound suppressor. If all went well, he'd not need the gun. But then, that was the way of guns. When you needed one, you *really* needed one and nothing else would substitute. The brilliant Surefire flashlight fastened to its rail underneath the barrel worked. All set to go.

The knife was another matter. Gordon had spent no money there. Oh, yes, sharp enough, but how cheap! Well, it wasn't going to be traded for big bucks at a gun show. It'd stick and slash. Jack noted it was one of those WWII British commando knock-offs and smiled. He bet the Limeys supplied that. Some of that wry British humor, no doubt. The knife would do for one mission anyway, and he'd fuss to Richard later just for the fun of it.

The sat phone had to come along. Got to have commo. He

might need to upload the pictures immediately.

Jack reached into the bottom of the bin and pulled out the trolling motor. He might need both hands free tonight. And, some rope—because Rangers need rope. They just do.

At 11:00 p.m., Jack moved out for the 800-yard approach. He'd told Consuela 2:30 a.m. but he'd be out there watching well before then. So often a soldier's life lay in the hands of anonymous others. You had no choice. You were the field weapon—the eyes and ears—but were by no means the only person involved. Any one of the others might betray you or inadvertently give you over to the enemy. He believed Consuela to be trustworthy, but could not tell, and could not afford to trust her more than necessary. It was not necessary that he simply show up at the appointed hour hoping the girl was legit. He'd recon the objective well before time to launch the mission.

Again, Jack slipped through the sodden forest, avoiding the channels. He controlled the trolling motor with his left hand. The able Bersa, locked into the CAA Tactical, Roni conversion kit, hung from a single-point sling to his front, with Jack's right hand on the pistol grip, finger indexed outside the trigger guard.

Jack took his time. He slowly circled a wide area around the bungalow, reconnoitering first for any ambush parties. His circles tightened. Soon, he could make out bungalow lights, flicked off one by one. One room stayed lit. From it, raucous laughter rolled, magnified in the night. Jack recognized Farsi but did not speak or understand the language except for a few key phrases and words—terse, gritty commands soldiers might know. He heard Consuela's voice in English, pleading, and eased the canoe in, on high alert, every sense tuned, body tense—poised.

However, when he came to within 25 feet of the window from which the light shone out, the light went out. He heard doors shut.

*What?*

He saw Consuela emerge from the door and run to the porch rail. For 30 minutes, Jack watched her from the jungle shadows. She cried. He wanted to go to her but tactics took over. She was at least physically safe for now. Then, she returned into the house, on bare feet, making no sound.

Jack eased 10 feet closer over the next 20 minutes.

No sound. No laughter. He opened his mouth slightly to improve his hearing and smell, tasting the jungle night.

In 10 more minutes, Consuela emerged, walked straight to the rail, pulled something from her dress pocket, and fussed with the rail. Then, she sat in one of the wicker chairs, pulled her feet up under her and cried some more. It was now well beyond midnight.

From his waterproof bag, Jack removed a device like one of those laser rangefinders hunters and shooters use. He pressed its on/off button, checked through its eyepiece for the green light indicating "operational" and scanned the bungalow.

This night vision device checked not only for infrared and thermal, but it also included a radar detector. They might have their own night vision devices set up, or even ground surveillance radar. If so, he could detect the radar and infrared, but not the use of night vision devices that merely amplified ambient light. He figured any night vision device used out here would have to also use infrared, there was so little ambient light. Also, he could detect heat.

Jack hoped he detected no such counter-surveillance devices.

He'd have to go into the water, in that case. He did not relish treading water in the Amazon's swamps any longer than necessary.

Detecting no IR coming from the bungalow told Jack a lot. He switched on the device's IR emitter—his IR "flashlight" and began circling the bungalow again, spying no sign of movement. At 10 minutes before 1:00 a.m., he eased the canoe toward a tangle of vines just off the porch on one side of Consuela, tied up, and went over the side into the water for what he hoped was a very short swim.

You can get used to almost anything. Exposing your body to all manner of nastiness is outside the norm for ordinary human behavior in the modern age, and soldiers are no different—except for what comprises ordinary experience. Part of training is "acclimating" yourself to the environment. In other words, crawl through some slime, ignore the snakes and alligators, and get used to being crawled on and bitten. Suck it up and just do it. You'd be surprised what you're capable of quickly learning to tolerate.

Jack hadn't acclimated to the Amazon, but he'd done the Philippine jungles and mangrove swamps. Just don't think about the movie, "Anaconda" or about those piranha! Besides, he'd seen the documentary—the one where the guy went looking for piranha and had a hard time finding them. Then, once they finally located some in the vast swamp of the *Pantanal*, the guy dove overboard and swam around with them. Incredible! Jack had always figured that if you dangled your foot anywhere in the Amazon, a thousand piranha would instantly shred it bare. He laughed inwardly. If that fear were realistic, then he should be able to walk to the bungalow on the backs of the piranha. Anyway, put all thoughts of nasties out of your mind and continue the mission.

He felt no bottom, but he did not expect to. He'd already sounded the surrounding waters and found them generally to be about 12 feet deep. The black caiman crocodiles should slither out of his way. At least, he'd read that they ate only fish—and dead things. *Why would they limit themselves to hunting for fish?* he wondered. He hoped they knew their dietary limitations. He eased his way to the veranda, careful to create no waves. In the distance, something slapped the water. At the porch, he stopped and listened for another five minutes. Then, Jack swam again, this time, under the stilts.

The bungalow creaked as if alive. However, he heard no footfalls, coughs, whispers, or dropped gear from above. Either all of the bad guys were dozing or they were very, very good. He did not think they would be that good. *Never rely on underestimates of the enemy.* Someone snorted and his bed creaked as he turned, and then, all fell silent again.

Jack emerged underneath Consuela, climbed the ladder rungs, and heard her gasp as his face broke over the floor of the veranda, taking the tied cloth with him on the way. Jack smiled at her in the dark.

She started to speak, but Jack held his finger to his lips in the universal sign for "Shhh!" She nodded, smiled, and motioned him inside.

This was it. Either he'd been betrayed or she was legit. Nothing exploded when he stepped inside, so he followed Consuela through the dark room.

Consuela held his left hand lightly. His right gripped the Bersa, held at the high-ready. Jack so badly wanted both hands free but indulged her need. Still, its rankled him that a perfect tactic was for her to seize one of his hands and take him at least that much out of the action.

No one attacked. Jack relaxed a bit. NO! That's when they always attack.

Still no attack. No sound. No footfalls launching at him. Only this warm woman leading him from the kitchen into the den.

Jack had memorized the floor plan Consuela had sketched for him. He knew that the den also served as Fats' office. On the large, wooden, work table lay the blueprints, some rolled up, some spread out, weighted down by what appeared to be shrunken heads. They *were* shrunken heads!

Quickly, Jack removed the camera from its waterproof bag and readied it. Gloves on. Snap a picture of the table top before moving—things. Done, now to get down to business.

Jack touched the blueprints. About 20 pages thick. So be it—get to work.

The pictures required a felt-eternity, most of which was ever-so-slow page turning. Finally, Jack turned and nodded to Consuela. Jack brushed her hair just away from the side of her face, placed his mouth directly next to her ear, and whispered from his lungs and the depth of his mouth to avoid hisses: "Done; let's go."

At the ladder, Jack held Consuela's face, drew his mouth next to her ear and whispered again, "Come to me tomorrow afternoon during your run to market. I'll know by then if you must stay longer or if you can get out."

Consuela nodded.

Jack kissed Consuela lightly and their lips lingered. Neither the robot, nor the TAC Sergeant even bothered to sound off, just frowning and shrugging and looking really mad.

He relaxed, backed away, and looked at her. Then he turned and ever so slowly and noiselessly went over the side.

Consuela's kiss burned his lips on the way back as he paddled, feeling his way among the trees, probably not as alert as he should have been. He maintained enough presence of mind to circle his own shack to check it, and spent an hour reconning before re-occupying his "patrol base" which he wanted so badly to move but couldn't. The jungle night mocked Jack's utter "aloneness."

Returning to this same place, this rather obvious patrol base scared Jack. He'd accepted the necessity, but—like so many of the things he found he had to do—it violated all of his training. Carefully recon the planned patrol base. If you have time. Occupy a false base just before night and then slip away later, to establish the real one. Use it for reporting, weapons cleaning, distributing ammo, personal care and food and—if time—getting some sleep. Go on high alert at first light—before dawn—and move out just after dawn. Don't go back.

Don't go back.

All good, sound, tactics. All taught for good reasons. Experience. Here he was over several sequential days, occupying a base picked by someone else. That meant someone knew his base before he occupied it. He was returning to the same base night after night. Not only that, he had someone—a civilian partisan in Jack's thinking—visiting him, probably taking the same route in and out every night.

This better not go on long! Jack hoped the blueprints would prove to be the intel Gordon had been looking for. He set right to work to find out.

Jack set his Iridium satellite phone to upload data and keyed in the number for his controllers. With the connection confirmed, he uploaded all of the photographed document images. When the upload was confirmed, Jack retrieved the tarp from the bin, took out the flashlight also there, and pulled out a pen and notebook. With these in hand, he crawled underneath the tarp, switched on the flashlight, and viewed the pictures on his camera, ready to write.

The blueprints immediately revealed clues. "Title: *Invisivel Barco.*" Odd. Looked like Portuguese for "invisible boat." Was old Fats developing some kind of new "Philadelphia Experiment" technology down here?

What the blueprints did not say stood out, too. No print-shop name. No engineer stamp like would be required in the states—probably here in Brazil, too. No logo boasting these were the work of so and so engineering firm. Why not? Didn't want some outsider to know about them, that's why not.

On the front page, the designer had drawn the outside dimensions and shape, without details. The barge was huge: 100 meters long by 60 meters wide. Jack knew very little about barges, but this struck him as pretty darn big. He supposed big coal and garbage barges reach that size. Someone else could check that out.

Page two proved more perplexing. Many notes in margins about special waterproofing products and seals. Top deck—a solid sheet of welded steel panels, but not flat. Like a mountain ridge top sort of, tapering from the barge's center slightly to the bow, stern, and gunwales. Thus, the top deck formed a raised lid it looked like to Jack.

The next page gave the supporting truss detail and it was considerable. Jack supposed the top deck slope and supporting trusses underneath did—what? Trusses supplied strength to support loads, he knew that much. He couldn't form a theory explaining their function on this barge. Well, even now, the bright boys in the back room were pouring over the same plans. They'd figure it out. Yeah.

Page 4 proved the strangest yet. This barge plan incorporated a set of what looked like stubby wings, before and aft, on the sides, below what Jack thought would be the water line. These "fins" or "flippers" looked almost like what you'd find on a submarine. Stabilizers maybe? Maybe an improvement in ocean-going barges that Jack just didn't know about.

The remaining pages showed—of all things—inside compartment details. He'd figured barges were like bathtubs. You fill them up. Coal. Gravel. Grain. Something. You didn't need inside compartments. Yet, here they were.

Finally, the last pages proved the most enigmatic. Tanks and a "compressor room". Tanks for what? Oil? Surely not. There were tankers aplenty built just to haul oil. Maybe old Fats was designing a new kind of oil tanker, hoping to sell it. These tanks, though, included ports or jets to the outside of the barge, very low, all around. Besides, he didn't see any mechanism for pumping liquid cargo in and out. Well, maybe. At the bow, between massive towing hooks, emerged some sort of umbilical-looking connections. The plans detailed those too, labeling them in Portuguese words derived from Latin for "electrical," "air," and "control." Odd. Then, again, he was no barge builder.

Enough. He'd think about it. Time for a couple of hours of sleep. Jack listened. Nothing but jungle ambient noises. Swish of crocodile tail. Lapping water against trees. Night birds and bats. Even in the distance, an occasional ship horn or engine. Jack drifted to sleep and dreamt of a living, rusty-steel, monster barge, rising from the deep, ridden like a horse by none other than a grotesquely huge Fats.

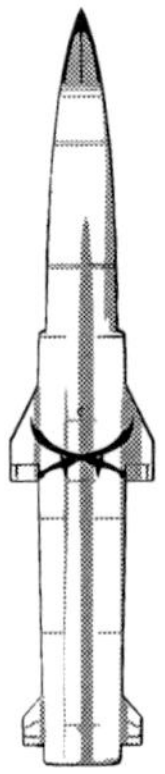

# 12

*1968, 3:15 a.m.*
*South of Las Vegas, Nevada*

"Our sins will find us out," Fats mocked Monty. "What are you worried about? It's our 'sins' that's made us a *fortune*. Besides, only the coyotes and vultures are going to find *this* out," Fats added.

Fats emphasized his little life's lesson by planting a rage-powered kick into the casino head-bookkeeper's side. Then, Fats shifted to the other foot; a toe-kick just above the kidney revived Chauncey enough to protest. The formerly dapper, but now blood-caked Chauncey, moaned pathetically and forced a swollen eye open to look at his tormentor.

Face huge and raw-boned. Mouth twisted open in a sneer that seemed impossibly big. Teeth all the same length, yellow, the two front ones splayed outward leaving a wedge-shaped crevice between them. Sandy-colored hair coarse, wild, bushy, not at all like a lion's noble mane, but more like what Chauncey imagined Mr. Hyde would have looked like, stuck out in all directions.

Ugly.

Fats' jowls shook. Curly tufts of hair continued into sideburns way, way down onto his blubbery cheeks. Then, those muttonchops stood out in all directions, enhancing Fats' fierce, even monstrous appearance to the already terrified Chauncey.

Fats' mouth worked. He was yelling something, Chauncey was sure, but he couldn't hear any sounds right now. The pounding he'd received stunned him.

Now, Fats bent over, his face inches from Chauncey's, Fats' eyes huge, bulging, eyebrows like hedges untrimmed and uncut. Teeth crooked, lips bulbous and flopping wildly.

Sounds returned, and the stunned Chauncey began recovering from Fats' last beating and kicking. Fats roared in his face and this time Chauncey made out his taunts.

Chauncey's failure to respond like Fats wanted him to enraged Fats even more. Of course, any response Chauncey offered enraged Fats, too. Everything enraged Fats. Young, strong, rage. Evil.

Fats glared at the recovering accountant and screamed at him to get up. This was absurd, if Fats really wanted him to get up; Chauncey was broken, internal organs hemorrhaging, brain already damaged from the blood seeping out from Fats head-kicks. Chauncey would never get up.

Of course, getting him up was not really Fats' objective here. Killing Chauncey was Fats' objective, and Fats was well on his way to accomplishing that. But, before finishing off the poor Chauncey, rage compelled Fats to get down in Chauncey's face and scream at him, epithets punctuated by kicks now that Fats' knuckles hurt from slugging Chauncey's skull. So, Fats finally straightened from his squatting position. As Fats glared down at Chauncey's swooning, bleeding body, battered beyond recognition, Fats' rage settled to ice. Fats calmed, just like he always did when killing an already-pacified victim. He'd had his fun, and now it was time to finish Chauncey off and get on with it.

Rage. If any descriptor immediately clung to Fats, it had to be *rage*. From early on. Fats' distraught parents had fled Taos before the sheriff could question Fats-the-teenager. They had no idea what they could do other than run. Fats had led them out to the sandy gulley where he'd left the boy's crushed body, face down, where the water collected in the soft, cool sand in the gulley's bend, by the steep bank, by the red sandy rocks. His mom had been horrified; his dad furious. Fats had just laughed and pointed to Billy Wainwright lying there, head crushed in, arms and legs askew in weird positions. Fats thought it funnier the more he looked at Billy, all limp and lifeless and misshapen. His parents had wanted to know where he'd been, and why he'd come home bloody? Well, he showed 'em, and they went berserk.

Packed up, made an excuse about work somewhere else, and cleared out before the sheriff could make any headway.

That was Fats' first killing.

He liked it. He liked it a lot. He'd have to do more of that.

And Fats did. But, he grew more clever, even as he grew more deadly. Killing just for the primeval thrill didn't get him anything. In the future, he linked it to money. Fats killed for money, or at least connected to some heist he'd done. Killing just for the fun of it just wasn't worth the risk of getting caught. He might as well be stealing someone's cash at the same time.

Fats was also big on not leaving witnesses. He always had to weigh that against the extra attention leaving a witness beaten to death seemed to garner. "When in doubt, strew the body parts about," Fats always said.

Fats had eight years' experience strewing body parts and grief about. But, not at random, and not just to express his rage.

For money. Always now for money.

So, there lay poor Chauncey, head messed up pretty good, most of his ribs cracked. When he tried to move, the pain exploded around his chest and cleared his head a little. Fats, staring down, now saw Chauncey as business, just business. Chauncey could have told the story of the casino rip-off, could have pointed to Fats and Monty, for Chauncey had spotted the bookkeeping transactions that didn't look right.

That diligent little Chauncey! Good for him! Detected embezzlement, did he? Yep, but he didn't know what to do with his forbidden knowledge. He confronted Monty, his assistant, and Monty brought the matter forthwith to Fats. Fats knew how to handle such matters.

Chauncey didn't beg; he'd done that already. He'd begged hard. He'd cried. He'd squealed. Finally, he'd accepted his fate. Once he let go of his life, that freed him to get past the terror and hate Fats. It was plain to Chauncey they'd kill him. The blood mixed with sand in his mouth choked him, but he threw at Fats all he had left, rasping out his final threat.

"Bosses—bosses kill you! Kill you! Kill—you. Bosses. Bosses—kill—you." Chauncey faded and passed out.

"Bosses kill *me*?" Fats sneered again. "You're pathetic! With this haul, I'll—uh—*We'll* be the bosses. Right Dracula?" Fats said, now turning to his partner in robbery and murder, Monty MacAfee, using his clever "code name."

Dracula just stared at the lavender-suited, kicked-in corpse, broken, bruised, and bled out into the dry desert streambed south of Las Vegas.

"Yeah. I mean, right, Wolfman," Monty mumbled. Blood-sucking "Dracula" or not, Monty felt sick, but he was so afraid of Fats-the-Wolfman, he somehow held his stomach.

So, there lay Chauncey, teeth broken, blood forming bubbles on his split lips, trying to start begging again, Fats figured. Chauncey opened his mouth to curse Fats and Fats chose that moment. Fats shifted his weight and reared his right leg back. The rage now turned to concentration. Concentration on aiming that kick. Fats collected all of his beef behind that leg and swung a powered kick straight into Chauncey's face, breaking more bones. But the blood did it. Chauncey choked on the blood now pouring out. Chauncey died at Fats' feet, choking and bled out onto the sand.

Fats stared a moment more at the expired Chauncey, savoring the kill. Then, Fats turned toward Monty and just looked at him with impassive, impossible-to-read eyes, those eyes peering from that massive face, that wild-looking, coarse face. Monty shrank involuntarily. Fats saw that and felt good about it. Monty was a witness too, but he and Monty were partners for now, and Fats had plans for Monty's skill at the books. Fats turned again to look at Chauncey. He bent down to feel for a pulse. None. Just needed to make sure. Just like that Billy Wainwright. In fact, Fats thought as he stared at his latest victim, Chauncey looked like Billy a little. It had been so long. Face messed up. Hard to tell. *Looks like ole Billy, though.*

Fats had come across the younger boy, Billy Wainright, down there in that gulley. Billy was building a tree house he told Fats. No one else around. A tree house! That enraged Fats. Looking back, Fats wasn't quite sure why Billy's building a tree house had set him off so. A tree house. How cute! Years later, Fats decided it was Billy's peace that doomed him. Billy was so content there in that cool sandy ditch, his private little woods-world, clomping around collecting limbs to use to build his "tree house" there in that drying little ditch of a creek. Billy was having so much fun there by himself in his imaginary world.

It made Fats sick. Then, it made Fats mad. That turned to Fats' rage. That doomed the hapless Billy, who died surprised, disbelieving, unable to comprehend any reason for the older, bigger boy's descent into the gulley, destruction of the tree house frame, and bullying. The bullying turned to a beating, and Billy was already unconscious when Fats picked up the red sandstone rock just lying there suggesting itself to Fats as the murder weapon. Fats crushed poor Billy's skull with it and put the rock right back where he found it.

Fats jumped up, panting. He scoped around and saw his own tracks all over the moist sand. It took him 20 minutes, but a bundle of light twigs held together made a broom, and he obliterated his tracks. He turned Billy's corpse over and laid Billy's face on the rock, to make it look like Billy might have fallen there. He swept Billy's red plaid-shirted body with a light coat of sand just to make him harder to find, clambered up the gully bank and walked home, whistling, feeling very good about his power. Feeling strong!

A foolish killing, he later decided, determined not to do that again. He'd kill for money or for other good reason, but he'd not take that risk again just for the heck of it.

He had enjoyed it though.

Now, the older Fats eyed his partner again. Monty stood there, shaking, staring at the corpse of Chauncey, his former boss at the casino. Monty's face contorted in terror and his eyes darted back and forth, like the cops would emerge from behind Nevada's rocks and cactus any second.

"What we gonna do, Fats? What we gonna do? Where we gonna go now?" Monty whined, pleading with Fats for answers.

Deep Purple's new version of Jimi Hendrix's hit, *Hey Joe*, shook the truck, but even the hard rock, eight-track blasting didn't drown out Monty's wailing. *Music to murder by*, Fats thought, watching Monty like prey.

Monty would have to be controlled. Later, Fats considered, he'd probably have to kill the shaky bookkeeper. Fats shrugged. No problem there. Just pick the right time. For now, they had to get out of town. Just like Taos.

When Fats had seen his mom and dad gawking at him, their faces all horrified looking, he had lost all respect for them. That's why he left them when he turned 16 and never saw them again. By 16, he was his own man, and by 24, Fats was flush with cash. Looking at Monty gave him that same feeling. He loathed the bookkeeper.

This job was special though. The haul from the casino staked Fats. Oh, yeah, and Monty, too. Monty was good with those books, man.

"Come on, let's get out of here," Fats growled, grabbing the soon-to-be, ex-casino assistant bookkeeper's arm and roughhousing his partner toward their battered, stolen Ford truck. "Get in, get in!" Fats yelled at the still-stumbling Monty and then—seeing that his partner was losing it—opted for a different tack.

"Look," Fats cooed in his graveled voice, calming his tone intentionally. "Look!"

It seemed to work. The smaller man slowly pulled his eyes from the lifeless, lavender, vaguely Chauncey-shaped lump, and raised his stare into Fats' fierce eyes and huge face.

"You done *gooood*, boy! You a rich man! *Rich*! You got it *made*! Education! A good-looking Latin-lover wife and now the dough to keep her happy! You on Easy Street, man! This is the hard part—I know it's hard—hard on me too—and it's over! Over!"

Fats thought his motivational speech to his failing partner to be quite good. And so, so deliciously true!

Not quite. It wasn't quite over. Deep Purple proved prophetic.

"No joke, Fats, that's who the guy was. You best quit flashin' cash man; that kind of stuff gets noticed. They ain't gonna overlook this," California whispered, looking around as the diner door squeaked.

"He was a weasel *pencil-pusher*!" Fats protested, in denial over what his ex-cellmate had just told him.

"Don't matter, you killed *their* pencil-pusher! Besides, just whose money was that I just *know* you must have taken? They'll check their books and figure your game out. Ain't everybody here who will keep his mouth shut when they come looking fer ye. Fer that kind of money and the hurt those Chicago boys can bring down on you, even your old buddies…," the coy California said, trailing off, rubbing his thumb and two first fingers together.

That was it. No choice, really. Fats thought about it not too long, paid his old buddy California off with the obvious hush money, and took Monty-Dracula along. And his wife.

Oh, yeah, the wife! Monty's Mexican chic-a-rooskie. Couldn't very well leave her here to squeal. If the mob really did own the "End of the Rainbow" casino like California had said, they'd lean on this squirrelly assistant bookkeeper hard. No, he'd break before they leaned hard. And Fats knew who Monty would blame once he broke and squealed. Too weak, and the wife to try to save too.

*I'll have to take them both along.* Well, that had fringe benefits.

Already brewing plans about how he'd next use the sharp-minded and sharp-penciled bookkeeper, Fats ground his way over the desert into Mexico. Seemed like the thing to do. Mexico. The power of suggestion: *Hey, Joe! Where you goin' wit dat gun in yo hand?* blared over and over on the truck's stereo.

"*Maybe I'll try Mexico way,*" Hey Joe suggested to Fats. Fats thought he'd run far enough.

Nope. A cousin—third or fourth, he couldn't remember—tipped him off about the Mexican Mafia.

"Get out of here fast," Cuz had said. "They've subcontracted the job out of Chicago to the boys here in Mexico. You know what that means. They will have no mercy on you. Those knives!" Cuz said, shuddering.

Fats scoured the map for the remotest hole he could find where a man could spend some newfound cash in style and still be far, far away. Geography wasn't his strong suit, but Chicago and now Mexico motivated Fats to learn. There! What place is that? Manaus! 1,000 miles up the Amazon, still got some class and some money left over from the rubber plantation days. A man could get there by small plane without the Brazilian government even knowing it. Manaus. Hell, *nobody* would look for him there.

He first scared Dracula about them Mexican boys, and then held out the "only" option.

"Set up shop in a new city. Manaus. Look here. They'll never find us there. They'll never even look for us there. Manaus. 1,000 miles up the Amazon River, boy! Big city in the middle of nowhere. Boomtown! You can work with that, you so good with the numbers. Monty, they got an opera house there! Opera, man! So-so-*phisticated.* Just outside the city, you in the jungle. Ain't but two ways in: got to either fly in or get in going upriver. We'll fall off the face of the earth, but in *style*!"

They tried Venezuela first, though. Not quite so far away. Not so remote. Caracas was wild, but not in a jungle sort of way. Didn't work, though. Same thing. After two years of living it up and loving Caracas, word leaked back to the Mex about the three rich Americans dropping dollars and broad hints about their exploits.

So, on to Manaus, after all.

And, sure enough, the boys from Chicago didn't look for them in Manaus. The Mexicans hunted them in Caracas, drank and whored awhile, gave up, and went home. Both Fats and Monty learned from their own very public carousing in Caracas, and they stayed discreet in and about Manaus. They got in quietly. They settled in quietly. They made money—legitimately. Got established. They stayed to themselves, mostly. Enjoyed the city life when they wanted, but not like in Caracas!

It worked for two years.

It was that wife who eventually threatened to bring down the whole sweet deal.

She'd more and more plainly refused Fats' gropes and finally, he guessed, told her husband the truth. Unfortunately, part of that truth was she was whining to stay with Monty despite Fats' charms—and whining for Monty to take her home to the states. Must have been the baby she'd had in Venezuela. Now, she insisted on getting out and going back to the states. Fats did not care if they left, but he gave them about two weeks before Chicago would find them, torture them, and learn about his little jungle hideaway. If you've run as far as Manaus, how much farther can you run?

"Raise our little Venezuelan-born baby girl in the states. We're leaving you," she screamed at Fats. "And I mean all *three* of us. You keep your tropical paradise! It's just like you: lots of green but stinks like slime!"

Oh, that was a big mistake.

Her taunt could have done it, alone, but that really wasn't it. He'd had her and wanted more, but now that the kid had come, she'd grown cold. More—responsible or something. Fats could throw her off with no problem. But, that mouth! All she had to do was run that fat mouth and let slip to the wrong person that he was living in Manaus, and.... She'd do it, too, vindictive bitch!

So, in the quiet, completely black jungle night, in the stifling still of his own bungalow, he reached his decision. The rum helped.

Fats paddled his wooden canoe down the creek, into the larger creek channel and out in the direction of the Amazon. The creek poured out onto a lake just before joining the river's deep, powerful flow. Fats paddled, clinging to the shore, and cut up the next channel, dipping the paddle in strong, regular strokes.

There it was. Monty's and his Connie's shanty on stilts hid from the churning, hungry Amazon across the lake. Their lantern still cast a beam of light out, down the narrow waterway, through the vines and trees, toward the approaching Fats.

Fats glided up and tied up beneath their porch, hearing the angry, arguing voices as he tightened his clove hitch. He listened.

Arguing about him? No, about him *and* the kid. The girl, the little whelp, now about two years old. The woman cursed her husband. Monty's own voice—urgent but more muffled.

Blame. She blamed Monty for being in this hellhole. She blamed him for being insipid and impotent to deal with the amorous Fats. Blamed him for his failure to deal first with her whoring, and then her repentance. She blamed him for being too chicken to take from Fats his rightful full share of the casino haul. Too cowardly to insist on his share of their new business profits. She blamed him for being too limp to do anything about it when Fats took her. She blamed him for their child.

"I *hate* you. I *hate* you!" She'd screamed at Monty. Fats barely held back belly-laughing down in his canoe below.

But, by now, Fats had made his mind up for sure.

In the River Styx-like gloom and utter blackness of his own hidden bungalow, it had all descended upon him so clearly. He could take care of his accounting problem, his leftover baggage from the Vegas job, his duty to split profits with his partner, and his lust for the fickle Connie all at the same time—and pocket the rest of the take.

The lure of taking Monty's share featured highly in his logic.

Simple. Cold. Businesslike, really. That's all.

Fats stepped from the canoe and mounted the ladder. When he stepped onto the deck, all of a sudden, they stopped screaming. Must have been they felt the canoe drift and bump into one of the pilings below. When there are no city noises from other people, you notice things like that.

Fats reared back and kicked the ramshackle plank door in. Monty shrank, very un-Dracula like, wide-eyed, seeing his own death. But Connie—oh, that so-beautiful Connie! Always so full of Mexican fire—fire that still burned in Fats. Connie was going for their Mossberg pump shotgun. In the corner. Too far.

Fats didn't slow down. Took all that in even as the splintered door pieces clattered across the shanty floor. Fats gripped his thick tree limb, cut earlier just for this purpose. Raised. Swung just as she grabbed the shotgun's barrel. Too late.

Fats felled his lover with one blow powered by the force of both lust and rage. She moaned only once and dropped like a stone.

Fats twisted to Monty and leapt at the transfixed man—his old partner—in two bounds, completing the second bound with a swift downward arc of the club. Both hands. Body weight and momentum behind the blow. Solid. Straight, like a well-hit high line drive, only down, down.

Death crashed down on Dracula's head, his skull cracked open, his brain destroyed. No stake in the heart necessary.

Now, his blood pounding, his senses alive, Fats sprang back at the dazed Connie. He tore her dress from her, shredding the cotton from her shoulders in strong, downward, jerking, ripping spasms. She began a protest—

"The baby!" she moaned—but Fats' open-handed smack starting way out from the side stunned her and dislocated her jaw.

She tried to mouth "Baby!" again but couldn't and protested no more, even as he forced himself into her. When done, he sprang from her, and, before she could try to struggle to her feet or plead again for mercy for the child, Fats took up his death-club once again.

Silenced, forever.

Three can keep a secret, if two are dead.

In the back room, the child cried.

Fats howled. These "sins" would soon disappear forever, he thought. The caiman crocodiles and piranha ate carrion.

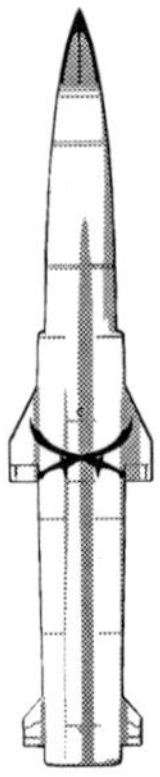

# 13

*Back to present day,*
*Friday's early hours*
*The recon shack*

Jack lay in his hammock, listening for what the night would tell him. He squinted, shook off a restless sleep, and checked his watch: 4:25 a.m. Still oh-dark-thirty. Time for normal people to be in deep sleep, repairing for the next dawn, around the corner.

Time for Jack to send in his 0430 situation report.

Jack pulled the poncho over his head to contain the flashlight and keyed in the code for all is well on the Amazon front. He hit the button to burst-send his SITREP to the satellite angel watching over him above. Within seconds, the friendly confirmation code appeared on the Iridium phone's display. Somebody out there's not dozing.

Jack returned to monitor the night noises. By now, he'd learned the sound of the river-world's breathing and sighing. The forest played its ceaseless sonata, but night cloaked it with the peace of fewer monkeyshines in the trees. *Nocturne* thought Jack, Chopin playing in his head. But, hearing nothing like the tell-tale sound of water slapping the wooden sides of an approaching boat, Jack lay back hoping to return to sleep at least until the dawn sun broke through into the bungalow.

Instead, he thought of Consuela.

# 14

*Friday's early hours*
*Fats' jungle bungalow*

Consuela lay on her back, staring at the ceiling poles, sleepless after leaving Jack, feeling his kiss linger on her lips. The jungle night heat pressed in. Long ago—as a little girl—she had grown comfortable in the Amazon's sweaty heat but tonight the jungle quiet offered her no peace.

Consuela was betraying a man she—loved? Loved? She shook her head and frowned. No, not in the man-woman way she saw among couples in Manaus and on television. Not in the romantic way. But loved, indeed, in some way she couldn't understand. Revered, even, at one time. Revered as a savior might be revered, a rescuer. As a legal guardian might be revered, even as he was feared. It was true, Fats had rescued Consuela, *hadn't he?* That's how she remembered it, but she was just a little girl.

She was five when Uncle Fats came to pick her up. Consuela recalled the day so clearly. That day, Uncle Fats had come to her at the convent. She didn't remember exactly why she had been sent to the convent.

An accident. Both parents dead. When you were a baby. That is what the nuns had told her when she grew old enough to ask questions. Now that odd word.

"Adopt." The man spoke the word in English to the nun. "Doppt?" What was "doppt?" "*Adoptar*" she then heard the two say, conversing in Spanish, the language of the nuns, the language they taught her.

"I'll take care of you," the promise.

And he had.

She supposed. She had taken care of him, too.

At the market, though, she saw other women her age—and younger. Laughing. Happy. They had husbands, families, babies and friends.

Somehow, Consuela did not fit in. She would never fit in. Consuela knew that now and it made her sad. The American man who had answered her call, who had come to help her had awakened in her a longing. She touched her lips involuntarily, thinking again about Jack's kiss. What life had she missed? She shopped, and did Uncle Fats' business in town, but always returned to her secluded, watery world downriver from Manaus.

Uncle Fats had given her so much. Hadn't he? Took her in when she'd lost her parents. No one knew if she had any relatives. That's what the nuns had told her.

The nuns. They had treated Consuela kindly. Fussed over her when Uncle Fats came to get her. Didn't want to let her go. They'd whispered among themselves, thinking Consuela out of earshot. *How could this happen? How could God let this happen? Why would God let this happen?* they had asked each other—angrily, even.

Nonetheless, Consuela walked out that day, her little hand in

Uncle Fats' big hand. She turned and waved to the nuns who just stared. They looked tired, Consuela remembered. Consuela never saw them again.

Consuela grew up outside Manaus in Uncle Fats' home on pilings, out in the jungle. She knew no other. Later, as a teenage woman, she had given into—been with—the man many times. Then, he'd given her to other men. Now, she was secretly giving him over to—someone in authority she didn't even know. She agonized for a year over what to do, but it was the coming of these last foreign men that determined her course. Something fundamental had shifted

And it was right. She was right. She knew this.

They'd come in a fancy boat and taken over. Plainly, they coveted her, with their eyes, loins, and words. And Uncle Fats just laughed. He kept her before them like—like bait—baiting their eyes with her body. He made it clear he did not care.

She'd cared for him. Prepared his food, kept the bungalow, kept his books, run his errands, exposed his embezzling employees. Said nothing to anyone about his sobbing, pleading nightmares. She'd helped him grow wealthy—always there for him.

She'd kept him warm. Done the tender things he'd guided her to do. All of them. Now, he had cast her off.

This all had been so confusing to her.

Then, the men from the Middle East—the "Arabs" she thought of them as—erased her confusion. They boasted of killing Americans. Their drunken boasts took on an even more sinister and concrete tone as their two weeks with Uncle Fats passed. They planned something—like 9/11—and Uncle Fats played some key part in their evil. They planned to hurt the Americans.

And, Consuela understood.

They planned to hurt her, too.

And Fats would let them.

She couldn't accept it at first. She shook her head and rejected it. When they toasted Uncle Fats over the blueprints and made him an "honorary *mujahideen*" she could no longer deny what her guardian had become. No—really had always been.

Now that she had taken action, there was no going back. She didn't know how this would end, but Consuela knew she'd be leaving the jungle bungalow where she'd grown up. She'd be leaving Uncle Fats. Just Fats. Not her uncle. Not her uncle at all.

*I will leave.*

And that felt so *right.* She felt *clean* just thinking about making her plans. Maybe she'd find a man like the other women in the village and in Manaus. Not the prostitutes. Women with husbands. Children.

Maybe the young American who kissed her…?

Where would she go? How would she leave? She had no money of her own. She'd never before needed any money of her own!

Fats had money. So much money. He paid his workers. Why not her? Why had he not ever paid her? She'd never asked for pay. If she needed money for a new dress, he gave her the little she asked for. But never pay. Never any money to save for her own.

Consuela thought about her age and felt suddenly old. Forty. No home of her own. No child. Pregnant before, but….

She knew what she must do.

Consuela slipped from bed and pulled on a loose, earth-colored dress hanging from a peg. She knew this house perfectly from memory. She'd awakened many nights, unable to sleep. She'd wandered the bungalow with all lamps and lights off, many nights, letting the rhythm of the river sooth her heart and mind. She'd pad from room to room wanting so badly for this bungalow to be her home—but it wasn't. She'd pass from kitchen to den and walk by Fats' room. Always, she'd shudder at passing and feel guilty for hoping she would not arouse him. But, she knew this place. It was like the bungalow knew her, too.

And now the bungalow mocked her for lacking the courage to leave.

Suddenly, Consuela *hated* this bungalow and *hated* the man who kept her in it. It was not just a wooden pole structure on stilts. It's foot-thick, palm-thatch ceiling and roof weighed down on Consuela, pressed in close and heavy. The whole bungalow was an affront to the jungle—to the river—to her! The bungalow was an affront to everything wonderful all around her and inside of her. It—no, *he*—was a disease, a "cancer." They cut those out, didn't they?

Clarity crystallized in Consuela. She padded through the deep dark into the den, and threaded her way around the furniture to a corner by a bookcase. She did something she'd done only once before.

One night, long ago, she'd sat curled up in a corner of the den and had fallen asleep there. She had awakened to a soft noise, but not a jungle noise, to find Fats with a lantern, standing by that bookcase. For some reason, she'd said nothing. Instead, she'd watched, spellbound, as he reached underneath a shelf with both hands and then slid the bookcase sideways! A room! A secret room, just like in the movies! She'd grown up here and never known of its existence.

Fats had stepped into the secret room, holding the lantern before him. Consuela knew he couldn't see her. His eyes adapted to the bright light held in his hands, and he'd not been able to see her in the shadowed living room, already mostly concealed in the corner between the cabinet and the wall. She had gotten up from sleep naked in the night heat and dark, and no brightly flowered dress reflected the little light cast that far from the lantern. Her tanned skin perfectly camouflaged her for the night, with her long hair flowing past her brown shoulders, swirling about and around her face, blurring her image.

She had watched every move he made. The box. The papers. He had written for half an hour. He had groaned softly, but still not loudly enough to awaken her had she been asleep. He had carefully replaced the box, papers, pens and all, and had stepped back into the den. Fats stood at the secret room's threshold. He sighed, his shoulders slumped, and then he slid the bookcase back into place, all silently as a stalking snake, padding then to his room.

Consuela sat curled up until sure he was asleep. Then, she crawled straight to her room. She'd seen something forbidden, and it frightened her.

Weeks passed and Consuela shied away from the bookcase. Fear of being caught looking behind it? Fear of what she'd find. Fear—undefined? Fear.

But, Consuela had grown more curious. Eventually, during one of her many nighttime roamings, she had put her own hands beneath the shelf and touched the two latches there. Both wine and sex had assured he would sleep soundly until early morning, but she had moved ever so quietly regardless. There! Slight pressure on the latches and they moved! She stopped, re-latched them both, left immediately, and went to bed.

Fats rarely left the bungalow. Years ago, he'd left the barge-building operation to his manager and the bookkeeping to Consuela as much as possible. Still, she knew he'd have to leave and she had waited.

Finally, he left for the day, taking clothing suitable for an exclusive party at the opera house. She had sat before the shelves for an hour before reaching in and unlatching the bookcase. She slid the bookcase aside on its rollers. She beheld the secret room. She knew when stepping into the tiny room's mysteries that she'd never be the same, but she did not know how she'd be changed.

Before her stood her guardian's secrets. The box. She noted its position and then stepped back out of the room. She retrieved her digital camera and took several photos of the room to assure she could replace the objects exactly as they had been before her.

The box. Metal. One of those workmen's toolboxes. Handle on top. Tray. In the tray were photographs instead of tools. She had removed them gently, reverently.

The pictures—six in all—showed a young man, a young woman, and a child. In the first, the parents held a baby by a car parked by a stucco-covered house on a street with palms. In the second, they pushed the child, maybe a year old now, in a stroller down a busy street with Latin-American people hustling up and down the marketplace. In the third, jungle framed the photo of a toddler, a little girl, standing by her mother, holding her hand. Instantly, Consuela knew these were her parents. She had known she was the girl in the three photos.

The next picture showed that same young man side-by-side

with Uncle Fats, arms on each other's' shoulders, smiling. The fifth picture showed the young woman, only this time without the man or the baby or Fats. She posed seductively in revealing lingerie, and beckoned in lurid color to the photographer with her outstretched hand and finger gesturing "come hither." The sixth and final photograph, an older picture, black and white, and worn, showed all three of the adults in front of a brilliantly lit sign announcing the Las Vegas Dreams-Come-True Hotel.

The pictures told some story, of that she was sure. She just didn't know what. She did somehow know what *kind* of story these mere six photographs told. Consuela's thoughts raced; she felt a bit sick to her stomach.

Not a time for weakness! She determined to know more while Fats was away. She removed the tray, looking for more pictures that might reveal more of the story. Her story. Instead of pictures, Consuela found documents and money below the tray. She stepped back. So much money! All in American dollars, not in Brazilian *Reals*.

Again, she carefully braced her elbows and photographed the surfaces of the documents before rifling through them. Then, she set the money aside and lifted the first of the papers. These appeared to be some form of business books kept in "partnership" with Monty. She set these aside, too.

Below the business records lay a worn, brown, leather-bound, handwritten notebook. She stared at it, suspecting her own fate lay written on its pages. No, not her fate, her history. She slowly opened its cover. She must know.

A journal. Uncle Fats' readily-recognizable handwriting. He kept a journal! Why? She read and marveled.

The dated pages were filled with passionate writings about a woman named "Connie." She understood Connie to be the woman in the picture—her own mother! Consuela read for an hour as Fats poured out his feelings and detailed their experiences. Then, the tone of the impassioned pages changed, became more tense, more demanding. Became darker. Finally, in the last pages: hate—black, bottomless hate.

And then no more. The last entry date was 1973. Consuela examined the photograph of the little girl again, straining to pull details out of the cracked black-and-white gloss.

She'd been adopted at age 5. She knew that from the nuns.

Consuela sat back, thinking. The meaning of all this swirled and evaded her reasoning, but not her emotions. Some as-of-yet undefined understanding grew within her and it frightened her. Her revulsion for Uncle Fats also welled. Consuela was perplexed. She could not understand why she felt so sickened thinking about Uncle Fats. She'd gotten beyond .... Now, this new revulsion.

After reading Uncle Fats' journal, Consuela replaced all the documents and cash and pictures exactly as she had found them, checking their order and position against her digital pictures. She returned the horrible metal toolbox to its exact place, closed the secret room off again, and never returned to it. In the months to come, she shunned the bookcase that hid the room. Consuela imagined that the bookcase leered at her, mocked her. Uncle Fats complained that its shelves were neglected and gathering dust. After that, she wiped them and always made sure in the future that he had no further reason to suspect she had any aversion to the corner. But, she did.

During the times afterward, when she awakened in the dark hours of the night, she wondered at the meaning of all, but she never breached those secrets again.

Consuela stood now before that same bookcase. She stared at it.

Shelves. Only shelves. Only a façade thinly hiding the truth.

She listened. No sound came from anywhere within the bungalow. *Quickly now*!

Noiselessly, she unlatched the bookcase and glided it silently aside on its casters and tracks. Stepping in, she removed the metal box and spied papers lying on the shelf—papers not there before. She took both the box and the new papers onto the veranda and tiptoed toward the boathouse.

In the way of people preparing for some momentous event without knowing exactly why, Consuela had done something else remarkable. She'd prepared her own secret place—a rectangular, wooden box underneath the boathouse flooring, holding a plastic storage tub. She'd gathered there a few things dear to her. Dried flowers mostly. Assembling this collection gave her a sense of having her own life—of not belonging to Uncle Fats completely.

Now, climbing over the rail and back underneath the flooring, she placed Uncle Fats' box and papers in her own box and listened. Silence.

Consuela worked her way back out through the pilings and supports and peeked over the veranda floor.

A boat. The men. Uncle Fats. They returned!

Consuela stayed as still and quiet as the crocodiles. The men docked and clambered onto the deck, cursing and laughing loudly as they crossed the veranda, entered the bungalow and headed for the back.

She waited almost an hour.

Consuela stirred, climbed onto the veranda, crossed it, entered the bungalow, and began to tiptoe across the den toward her own room when she heard low voices. She took two more cat-like steps, intending to complete her evasion, but curiosity whispered into her ear. Consuela turned and crept instead toward the opposite side of the bungalow—toward the office, Uncle Fats' bedroom, and the guest beds. She squatted in a dark corner and listened.

The murmurs, now rising in volume, came from the office. She recognized Uncle Fats immediately, then recognized one of the Middle Easterners, as well. She rose and eased behind a display case only six feet from the door to the room where the men talked. She cocked her head and strained to hear.

Laughter erupted. *They are drinking*, she decided, from their volume and tone. No, wait. Only Uncle Fats was drinking. She now recognized the voice of the visitor as the older Middle Eastern man. This one always spoke in careful, measured English. Had he been drinking, he'd probably have lapsed back into his own tongue. Instead, she could tell he was choosing each word with great care. His tone was like silk, and quieter than Fats. Who were they talking about? Had they discovered the American?

"Why should I care?" Uncle Fats asked, more a challenge than a question.

"She is your—companion—is she not?" the Iranian purred.

"Companion! That's a good one. That's really a good one!" Uncle Fats sneered. "No, she is not my *companion*."

"Then, she is your—responsibility, yes?"

Uncle Fats grew sober. No reply for a moment. Then, he spoke, more clearly, more quietly.

"I took her on long ago. You could say that. Now, I find her—useful. I sure as hell don't owe her anything. No, she's not my responsibility," Fats concluded, as if to convince himself.

"Indeed, she must be very useful, then; you are demanding such a great sum. Of course, you did adopt her. You must think so highly of your daughter," the man continued, working his way around the delicate transaction, angling for a cheaper price. The drunken Fats took the bait.

"That's a good one! Daughter be damned! Let me tell you something I've told no one else before. Her old man and I was partners, see. We came here with a stash from the states and then robbed a man here and made out real good, see. That's how I got started and got all this," Fats bragged, gesturing.

"But, we fell out. Won't tell you why. Bottom line. You need to know just who you are dealing with here if you think you're just gonna steal a looker like her for nothing. I killed them both, you know. Her parents. I *killed'*em! With my bare hands. If he was gonna get to keep her, then both—well. I killed them both. See? That's how I got Consuela. Couldn't very well kill the kid, could I? Packed her off to the local convent first for a few years. Then I got this idea. Paid off the local government with her own dad's share of the money. Nuns didn't like it one bit, but I had papers. The papers said I got her, so I got her. I *adopted* her. Told Consuela her folks had died in an accident. Sorta true.

'She's mine now. I'll sell her, but, if you want her, you gotta pay big bucks because she's *mine.* My investment. And—(Here Fats paused and leered at his customer, knowing what he really wanted.)—she is one hot piece, too!"

Consuela heard and knew. She squatted in the corner, stunned.

A force jerked Consuela from her Amazon jungle stillness and hurled her amidst a Hades of swarming demons. From afar, across a gaping chasm, her mother reached down to her to rescue her, but could not stretch across the chasm to grasp her hand and pull her up. *Momma! Oh, Momma!* Behind her mother stood her father. Both looked down on her with such sad, sad eyes. Consuela looked up at them, tears running.

Then, Consuela saw their faces more closely. Battered, bones crushed, blood dried over their eyes, noses and lips. Hideous in black and blue and crusted red. From behind and beneath her, from the horde of demons, she heard Fats sneering at her parents—and at her. Calling her father vile names. Calling her mother a whore.

Behind Fats, the gallery of riotous demons howled their encouragement to him and joined him in mocking Consuela's virtue. They taunted her with all she had done with Fats. Fats held his raised, upturned hands out to them. To stop them? In her defense? No, he was demanding something from them.

Now, the demons threw gold at him. He turned, leering directly at her, gold dropping from his fingers, gold falling onto him like rain, and he leapt at her and stripped her dress from her. And he raped her. She cried out to God and to her parents. Her parents held each other, and sobbed, and faded away.

*God, oh God! Where are you? Save me from this!*

A tree frog's louder-than-usual croak, and belly-tightening, real, sickening, physical fear jolted her. Her parents' last wisps vanished.

A dream? A nightmare? A vision?

No! A warning. God *had* heard her cry out! God had *warned* her in this horrible dream! She was to be sold like a slave!

Rage rolled against Consuela's horror and shoved it back. Truth electrically super-charged the crackling rage.

Truth.

Know it, and be free.

The man, Fats, had murdered her mother and father.

And she'd been living with him ever since. Slaving for him. Doing his bidding. The bidding of the man who tore her own parents from her! And now, he was bargaining to sell her to these men, to be taken away and used by these men.

The vision of the screaming demons tried to linger but gave completely away. As they retreated, they howled at her and mocked her more, ever the louder because they saw that they had lost their hold on her, but they and their crass voices ran. Strength from somewhere returned to her. Supernatural strength. Consuela's quaking legs regained their power. Her mind's voices quieted and calmed.

Consuela listened for danger. She eased away from the doorway. She breathed deeply and forced herself slowly and deliberately to her own room. She crawled into bed to think and sleep, but she wept, instead, in bitter, deep, silent sobs. Then, in the very early hours of the morning, her shock resolved to grief, and then to anger, and then to that strength she did not know she had.

Consuela formed a plan. Everything now made so much sense. Fats taking advantage of her in shameful ways. The pictures. His old journal, at first so tender and then so vile. The timing of her adoption. The nuns' worry. And now Fats' design to cast her off to these slave-masters.

And now came the young American who honored her.

Everything now made so much sense. God's timing had arrived.

Exhausted, a resolved Consuela slept.

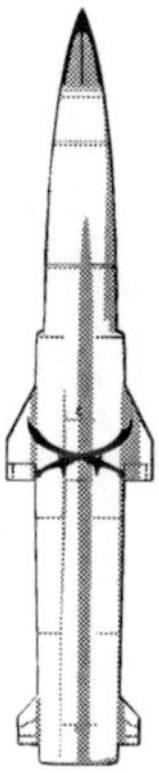

# 15

*Dawn, Friday,*
*surveillance day three*
*The reconnaissance shack*

Morning broke over the city of Manaus and the jungle surrounding it.

Jack stared at the sat phone. Then the video monitor. Back to the sat phone. He wanted word from—whomever—that the blueprints were exactly what they needed. He wanted this operation over. He wanted Consuela out.

"Jack, this is The Voice," the guy would say.

"Jack, over," Jack would say back.

"You did a great job man. Got just what we need. Get out of there. Shut 'er down," The Voice would say. "Shut 'er down and go to the house. You're done, man. Get a hot shower. Get a steak."

"What about extracting our agent?" Jack would say.

"Who? Oh, yeah. Her. The housekeeper. Extract from where? Her own home? They call that kidnapping. She's free to leave. No extraction. Not your responsibility. Get out! Those are your orders, soldier. Out! Out."

That's what The Voice would say. Jack could say "Roger,

wilco, out," and it would all be over. For him anyway.

Jack wanted Consuela out of there. Problem with that was, would that compromise the mission?

Of course it would compromise the mission. She had to remain in place or Fats and the Iranians would immediately know something was wrong. By God, if she wanted out, he'd get her out and the powers that be could crucify him later. If they could find him. Speaking of..., why didn't they call? He wanted this thing over.

Jack paced back and forth to and from the shack doorway. He flicked the Roni-wrapped Bersa up, down, back up, back down, Aimpointing trees, leaves, and monkeys. His left hand confirmed the spare magazines on his belt. He kept glancing at the radio, as if to make it speak. Nervous behaviors by an agitated operator.

The brightening green world outside pressed in. The placid waters seemed to make the slow, morning time drag.

*Patience! What's wrong with you? Get a hold of yourself!*

Jack knew exactly what was wrong. These jobs were not just missions. They always started that way, even while he was still in the Army. Written mission handed down from above. Short, terse, plain statement of what someone wanted done. Accomplish such and such at such and such grid coordinates by such and such date-time group. Then, all-business Warning Order to your guys. Lots of planning when there was time. Put together the full plan—the Operations Order. Revise as more intel came in from higher up. Sand table models. Sergeants and troops drawing equipment. Get everybody around to go over the Concept of the Operation. Rehearsals. Big enough mission, and you had lots of testosterone-charged up officers insisting on giving their input. Top sergeants stood off watching it all become a chicken foxtrot.

Some headquarters far away always wanting to know what the hell you were planning to do. The more junior NCOs watching it all shake out and then efficiently going about the business of getting the men ready. Everybody getting all pumped up to do the mission. Then, you launched, landed, and lead started to fly.

And real people started to die. Real people. All kinds of people. People you never expected to even be there got hurt.

Bobby! His old XO from the 1st of the 506th Currahee Infantry Battalion! Bobby, may God give you rest. Dead, killed in the pirate assault during the *Arcturus* mission. *If I hadn't called you up and convinced you to get on board with me on that—.* So many others. Great fun for the survivors but along the way, real people got killed—or worse. With you one moment, fighting, laughing, or just standing there next to you, and then, gone. Some mortar round lands, and when you get up and your thinking and hearing come back, they're turned into a bloody, life-drained husk.

Consuela. Consuela was the "real people" in the kill zone on this one. Consuela was the casualty just waiting to happen. Not a soldier. Not a spy. Not a professional, anyway. An "agent." *They are going to write her off!* Had it not been for her, they would not have even learned what was brewing out here at all.

What *was* brewing out here with those blueprints? What kind of barge is that? Haven't all of those geniuses figured that out yet? *Call, and let me get her out of here.*

On cue, the sat phone warbled. Jack darted into the shack and answered.

"Jack, over." Challenge and password out of the way.

"Very good. Listen—I've—."

"No, you tell me what you found on those plans. Are they what you need?" Jack demanded.

"Are they! I'll say so! It took some time and we had to call in some Navy types but we just cracked it. We know their scheme. It all fits!" The voice said, excitedly, even courteously. Maybe even with a whiff of respect.

Jack was surprised. He looked at the phone. He'd been rude and impatient, and the intel puke had told him more than he should have, even over an encryption-enabled, secure satellite-telephone.

"Okay. Is this surveillance mission accomplished?" Jack asked, more evenly.

"In spades. *Ja. Si.* In spades. Yes! It's over, man. Shut it down and come out," The Voice ordered.

"No more?" Jack asked.

"No more killing"—Jack meant. No assassin work.

"Huh? Oh, no, that won't be necessary," as if Jack had offered to sweep out the shack to leave it ready for the next guest. "I already checked on that additional work, and they want you to leave everything just as you—!"

The voice stopped suddenly. Silence. Then—

"You won't believe this! Are you at your monitor? If not, get there now! Now!" The Voice screamed.

Jack ran to the video, and his heart stopped.

There, on grainy video, he saw Consuela in the still-dim, wicker and leather-furnished den, barely dappled by the jungle-dawn sunlight working its way through the canopy and up the channel.

She held a long, wide-bladed, kitchen knife in her right hand. While Jack watched in spellbound horror, Consuela crept up behind a seated, slouching man. The man turned—Jack recognized him as Fats—and began to rise, but not in time. Consuela fell upon him, diving over his back, plunging the knife into his chest, past his upraised arms. He fell back into the chair. Consuela circled around to his front like a jaguar, still slashing madly to stab past his upraised arms, shredding his forearms in deep defensive wounds. The video caught every horrifying detail. It was like watching Hitchcock's most frightening killer at grim work.

Now she stood, astraddle of his knees, knife held overhead, slashing back and forth in tight arcs across his throat. Now with both hands on the knife, Consuela plunged the blade down past the wounded, slippery arms, and into the man's chest, over and over. Jack could hear Fats' gurgling, fading screams on the audio, now turned up.

Then, the rest of the bungalow erupted. The big Iranian Jack identified as Mr. B charged, hitting Consuela in the side of her head with a back-fist blow that knocked her off Fats. Consuela tried to get up but fell back. Mr. B. checked Fats' carotid artery for a pulse, but, plainly, even from the video, Uncle Fats was dead.

Now Mr. C joined the fracas. Mr. B. and Mr. C began screaming Farsi at Consuela all while The Voice shouted urgent orders. Jack didn't hear.

Jack paused only long enough to set the surveillance feed to transmit continuously by the satellite phone. Over the side he went, almost tumbling from the ladder into the river below, almost dropping the phone.

This time, Jack jumped into the longer, green and yellow, covered, motorized canoe, almost rocking it over. After five frantic pulls on the starter cord, the engine sputtered to life. *Damn two-cycle engines to hell!* He wrenched the throttle to wide-open, backed it off just a hair when it faltered, and gave it full throttle again as it fully woke up. Even so, the weed eater-like motor pushing the 16-foot canoe achieved no more than 15 mph. Jack turned the maddeningly slow canoe into the channel, avoiding working his way through the swamp to get to the bungalow. He ran the calculations. South down his own channel, cut back to the left for a quarter-mile, then north up Fats' channel. Still faster than picking his way among the rubber trees and vines, busting the prop on some hidden root, and he would need the speed to get Consuela away—if he arrived in time. The satellite phone sounded.

"Jack, Jack! Answer, damn you! Over!" urgently.

"This is Jack, over," breathlessly.

"Get out fast! Get out —!"

Jack ended the call. He hadn't expected any help from The Voice, and The Voice interfered with the video and audio feed from the bungalow anyway.

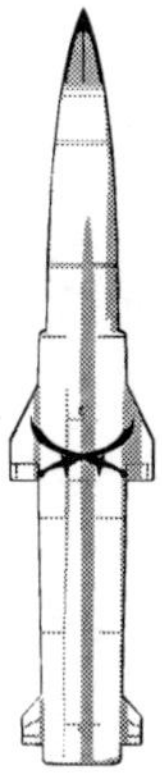

# 16

*Friday morning,*
*surveillance day three*

Decision time. Go in hot and loud? Frontal assault? They could be killing Consuela right now. Jack agonized, gripping the outboard motor throttle, his eyes straining—straining as if to pull the bungalow to himself. He sped straight up the channel with the throttle wide open, but the complacent motor just hummed along.

This was suicide probably. They'd surely hear him coming. Yet, if he slowed the engine even a bit, they might cut her throat in those last, lost seconds. Just like on Basilan Island—just seconds too late. *Not this time! No, God, not this time!*

A diversion. He needed a diversion.

*How do I work a diversion with this weed eater buzzing on the approach?*

He'd have to approach straight in from the channel to the veranda.

The mental sketch gave Jack his diversion: he knew what he would do. Nothing like personal, right there, close-in recon. No satellite photography would show you what Jack had learned, slipping upon, underneath and into the bungalow. It would be tight, but he'd have to make it work.

His plan formed, Jack motored on in cold resolve.

There, front veranda, just hidden! More coming into view. Empty but for swings and chairs.

Jack scanned the structure frantically. They must have heard him. Yes, now two men appeared—weapons drawn—in the front doorway to greet him as he approached within feet of the veranda.

Jack came on far too fast to stop. The last upward glance at the men revealed their surprised looks and wavering pistol muzzles—just as Jack disappeared between the pilings underneath the veranda. Only then did he cut the engine throttle.

Jack aimed the slender canoe for just to the left of the ladder. He rose to his feet, crouching, balancing, keeping his right hand on the motor, using it now as a tiller, and readied himself. As the craft zinged past the ladder, Jack leapt, grabbed the ladder, and swung up and out of the canoe. He had only seconds at best.

In a mad scramble, Jack's feet found the rungs. He hauled himself atop the ladder and immediately sprinted right. He ran the length of the veranda to the corner, grabbed the corner of the bungalow to help swivel himself around, and ran down the side of the bungalow toward its door, hoping to flank the men. In the absence of any better diversion, Jack had become the diversion. If you can't dazzle them will brilliance, baffle them....

Three steps from the corner, Jack spotted his opportunity, pulled up short, and dove through an open window.

Jack's weight tore the plastic mesh screen. He tucked both arms and head, hit the floor on his left shoulder, and forward-rolled. It wasn't pretty but it got him in. He staggered upright out of the roll, right hand going for the Bersa's pistol grip as loud footfalls approached immediately to his left. Mr. B and Mr. C had recovered fast from Jack's strange feint. Jack spotted Consuela tied flat on the floor, spread-eagled, dress torn and pulled up, feet and hands bound to the heavy, leather-covered couches and chairs.

Consuela thrashed to break free. The massive wood and leather couch on one side with the ghastly corpse of Fats adding dead weight to one of the chairs on the other held her fast by both arms.

Jack had the quick carbine coming up in his right hand. No time for two hands on the gun. Left hand braced against the floor as Jack recovered his balance. The unfortunate Mr. B was out in front and appeared through the door first. Jack saw the red dot on his chest and flicked the trigger three times; the suppressed Bersa spat two in Mr. B's chest by habit, then one more to the head. Dead, immediately from the head shot, not the midsection hits.

Training is funny. Training gives you the advantage of acting in patterns without having to pause and lose vital seconds to think out all the steps. The patterns are well thought-out in advance to be effective in a broad variety of scenarios. Experts argue interminably about the interplay between terminal ballistics and gun-fighting tactics.

But, these well-thought-out scenarios and responses represent someone's idea of anticipated combat efficiency. There is always that extraneous variable running around to mess up the equation. Extraneous variables do that. In this case, it was body armor.

Jack's two to Mr. B's chest were good shots. Both struck over the sternum, within two inches of each other. Unfortunately, neither of the 9mm lead bullets hit anything vital, or even slowed the man down, lodging in the plates of the armor. Even as Jack put the two bullets on B's chest, he remembered the advice from the "speed shooting" school instructor, also an ex-Special Forces guy now turned civilian trainer: "Head shots, head shots, head shots!"

In the time Jack took to shift from the chest to the head, Mr. B took one more charging step. The head shot killed Mr. B. It did not stop Mr. B.

By the time the bullet entered his mind, Mr. B had launched his body at Jack in a fury. His corpse still in forward motion, he tumbled into Jack, bowling Jack backwards and down.

Mr. C—unhurt in all of this—followed right behind. Mr. C roared and kicked Jack in the head. Jack—struggling to roll away—pulled back just in time to avoid the full force, but his jaw caught the shoe, and he stumbled back.

The room exploded. Jack wasn't sure what had just happened. Mr. C screamed again but kicked Jack no more. Mr. C clawed instead behind his back. Then, Mr. C's head exploded in a red mist and his husk collapsed.

# Part II: Of Plans, Plots, and Spies

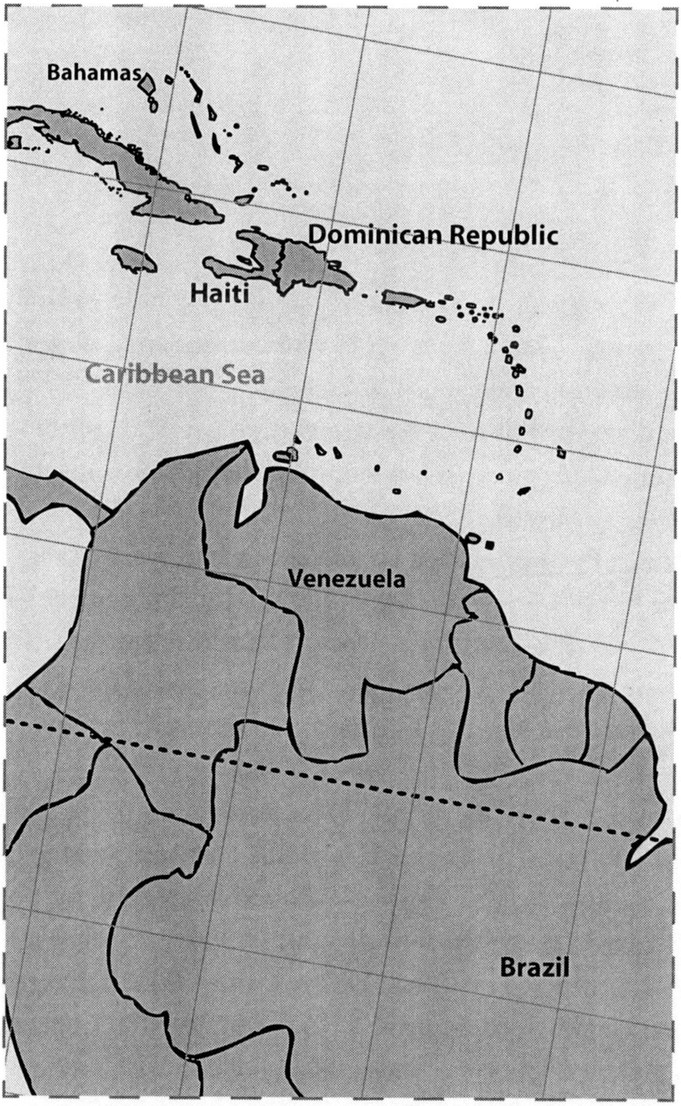

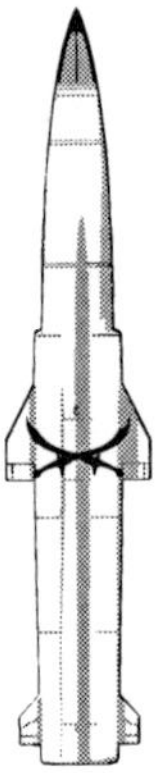

# 17

*Friday morning, after the assault*
*Fats' Amazon Bungalow*

Through the mist and offal strode the most welcome sight. Jack attempted to rise but wavered, dizzy. A strong hand caught his arm.

"I say, we cut this a bit close now, didn't we?" a voice in Jack's face boomed. "And see to her modesty, chaps," the unmistakable British voice ordered.

Richard Pye pulled Jack up and shook him gently.

"Jack my boy—are you daft? Get off the floor, man! What is that? Taking a Transformer peashooter into combat! Tut, tut. Won't do at all. I'll have you court-martialed for this under-calibered offence! Oh, can't do that; you're not Army, now, are you?"

Richard grabbed Jack's shoulders, held Jack's face within inches of his own (to check Jack's pupils for shock) and grinned at Jack from ear to ear. The sandy-haired, blue-eyed, purported diplomat could not resist bursting out laughing. Seeing no penetrating wounds or shock, Richard was relieved. He gripped Jack's arm and helped him stand. Jack staggered to Consuela, now tended to by two medics. She reached for him with red-smeared hands, but one of the medics manhandled him to the couch. Jack turned his head toward her.

In place of her blood-drenched, ripped dress, she now wore a fresh, tan one, pulled hurriedly from the closet by one of the men. Jack heard one of the medics tell her in Spanish she had no wounds or broken bones. She'd survive. Jack relaxed. He assumed something happened that blew it all up for Consuela, and she had fought back for her life. Jack didn't know what Mr. B and Mr. C had in store for her specifically, but she'd narrowly escaped their torture and abuse. Not to mention perhaps captivity and the life—Jack didn't want to even think about it.

Richard tried to return Jack to the immediate tactical situation.

"Unfortunately, Jack my boy, between these Brazilian commando types, now bragging to each other about their shooting, and your own target practice, we have no prisoner."

"What about Mr. A?" Jack asked, searching for the Iranian boss.

"Gone. Left early this morning it would appear. Scheduled departure, I suppose. We might pick him up. We might let him run and see where he goes. Either way, no one else is here. Alive."

"What are you doing here anyway?" Jack asked Richard, through his jaw pain.

"Gordon thought you might need some backing. You already know we were just downriver, taking tea. Just in case, I called on a few of our men to make sure you stayed out of trouble—or at least survived it. We were heading to our own hide a bit closer and saw the video feed and, well, uh—we thought you might be doing some sort of D-Day operation. You Americans can't resist a good rescue, now, can you? Turned the tables on you this time, though! I say, Jack my boy, I believe we have arrived just in the nick of time. We are the cavalry! I give you my permission now to thank Her Majesty—at least her official representative in this far-flung corner of the world—personally."

Richard puffed his chest out, held his hand out, palm down, and looked disaffectedly away, playing Her Majesty's rescue up big time. Not getting his hand kissed, or even the laugh he expected, he checked Jack again.

"Hullo? Jack? Not looking too mellow, there, now are you?"

Richard Pye picked his way through the shambles and the bodies and motioned a medic back to Jack. One of the medics looked up from tending to Consuela. Consuela seized the opportunity, pulled away and ran to Jack's side, kneeling down. Richard motioned the medic to hold.

"Jack, thank you *so* much for not leaving me to these men," she whispered simply, in hushed tones. An embarrassed Richard Pye turned away as Consuela pulled Jack close and kissed him. As Jack wavered on the brink of unconsciousness, Consuela pressed a piece of paper into his jeans pocket.

"What will you do now?" he asked finally.

"I do not know," she whispered, "But, find me." And Consuela was gone.

Jack next came to shaken by the unmistakable sounds and sensations of a chopper ride. He took Richard's offered icepack and held it to his jaw. The helicopter noise prevented conversation and, well, he really didn't feel like talking anyway. Jack didn't even ask where the men were going. He saw Manaus race by below. The chopper descended, turned, and its skids touched down on a pad by a lush lawn. Richard Pye rushed him off the helicopter.

"Where are we?"

"We? You, are nowhere. You were never here anyway."

"Where is it that I've never been, then?" Jack's jaw throbbed.

"We are at the back side of the Marine Police headquarters for this area. They are carefully and discreetly remaining far away. Just look around, enjoy the ambiance, and prepare to say goodbye to Brazil. We'll be here only long enough to collect ourselves, sort everything out, and figure out our next move. Oh, and also to eat. Let's settle in and I'll brief you. I'm told "No One" is coming for you and you'll know what that means. Anyway, I'm to leave but, first, you'll want to know what the bright boys decided about Consuela's blueprints."

Hunger, curiosity, and Lorcet overcame the jaw pain. Jack wondered both what the food and the findings would be. He was invigorated by the chow and astounded by the intelligence analysis.

He wondered where Consuela had been flown to.

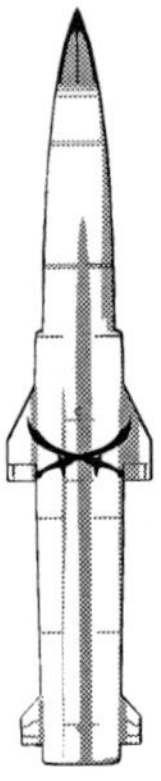

# 18

*Saturday*
*Brasilia, Brazil*
*Cafeteria veranda,*
*British Embassy*

"*Señor*, what do you mean?"

A wary Consuela fidgeted nervously. She sat in a comfortable chair, under a cool fan, far south of the accursed bungalow. She had felt safe with the young American nearby, even in the midst of the evil men. But, not here. She did not feel safe here. She did not feel threatened by Richard, but she sensed some danger awaiting her. What was it? Jack had trusted this man. Perhaps, so could she. They spoke in English, but she continued to express her wariness by addressing Richard in her formal Spanish style, as she had been taught by the nuns, as "*Señor*."

Richard Pye began his pitch.

"Consuela, please be at ease. You are free to leave at any time; you know that, I hope. I have a business proposition for you to consider. A job offer. That's all. For you to consider."

*That's all? A business proposition. Richard! Really*!

Richard stood, hands in pockets, and ambled to the edge of the veranda casually.

"Behold, Brasilia, the capital of your country," he said, gesturing grandly and turning to eye Consuela.

"*Señor*, Brazil is not my country. You know that," Consuela said, pointedly emphasizing the Spanish title instead of using the Portuguese, "*senhor.*"

"Yes, yes, of course, but you've lived here for so long, though. Since you were only a little girl," Richard continued.

"Yes, but my country is Venezuela," Consuela said, looking down and reaching, reaching back so, so far for memories of her parents holding her close. The memories would not materialize, for she had been too young when her parents were ripped from her. Her father. Her mother.... *At least I had a home, once,* she thought. *Where would she make her home now?*

"Oh, yes, your parents. Consuela, do you know what happened back there?" Richard asked.

Suddenly, Consuela felt hot and angry. Richard caught the signs of her discomfort and rushed to correct his mistake and make her more at ease.

"I mean the men—their business—do you know what their business was all about? The Iranians. Guevara. Your Uncle Fats? What were they all on about? Do you know?" He asked, clarifying. Consuela was obviously relieved.

"Somewhat, *señor,*" she replied. Yes, she knew their business, very well. She supposed, though, that the British man meant to discuss their reasons for ordering the strange barge.

Richard pulled up a chair and slid it closer to her, knee to knee. She did not flinch but her eyes widened.

"Precisely, Consuela. We all know *some.* Only some. These men plotted some still-unknown great evil. Thanks to you, we learned enough of their plot to stop it." *Time now for some guilt.* He paused, took on a serious demeanor, then continued.

"Of course, also thanks to you, Fats is—dead—along with

his visitors, so we do not know what mischief they intended. Now, we cannot ask them their sinister purpose for that strange warship." Richard said, trailing off to let that thought sink in, and he smiled knowingly at Consuela.

He saw his shameless manipulation working. It was true, after all. If she had just waited to express her pent-up fury, they'd have either taken the men prisoners already or his teams would be tailing them even now. Had she not murdered Fats and had Jack not intervened.... Once they learned what Fats had done to Consuela, who knows? After the interrogation, they might have done the job for her. Or just turned him over to her.

Richard reddened as Consuela sat, silent, before him. Richard Pye, spy and spy recruiter, was embarrassed by his own callous heart. Had she not killed Fats, and had Jack not intervened, Consuela would have been raped and then murdered or sold into slavery.

He'd been appalled at her conditions. Only a few clothes. No bank account of her own. Nothing, really. Clean and neatly kept, but kept impoverished and utterly dependent on Fats. Fats kept her as a virtual slave of her shame and his twisted cruelty. Upon bringing Consuela to Brasilia, Richard had sent his secretary to the mall on a shopping trip. Now, before him, sat the formerly isolated, enigmatic jungle maiden—Consuela. She had appeared as a peasant girl might. Now, though, sitting quietly in front of him, dressed in comfortable, business-casual elegance, he could see that she truly was beautiful. Even composed, emotionally together. Yet—Richard reminded himself—this same woman now calmly interviewing with him had fallen on Fats like a banshee and shredded her master with that oh-so-personal of weapons:

sharpened, cold steel. Time and again, she'd slashed and plunged the long, Brazilian rosewood-handled, razor-sharp blade she'd used many times to slice mango for breakfast.

Richard Pye eyed Consuela carefully. *Is she crazy*? Could this wild spirit be harnessed? Yes, surely. She had overcome her bondage to Fats. She had connected the Iranian men to Fats' braggadocio, and to all of their hushed conversations. Then, she had connected all of them with even greater evil—and she had stopped them cold. All of this she risked and did for people she'd never seen. Something within this wounded creature answered the call from that relentless taskmaster Richard knew so well, the spirit of *duty.*

She had been repulsed by their evil. Perhaps, she had also been repulsed by her own deeds, but she had risen in the face of the Devil himself, spat in his eye, and prevailed against the gates of hell.

*Yes, oh, yes!* Richard Pye considered, *I can work with this.*

Richard decided to stop trying to manipulate this woman of courage and to get to the point.

"Consuela, I have a job offer for you. You may take it, refuse it, or think about it. If you decline, we will help you get established in a new life. Pay you some money. Get you a passport. British, if you like. U.S.—I'm sure they'd be honored. Brazilian citizenship is yours if you want to stay here. They have already offered. But, if you accept, we'll do all of that and pay you. Well."

Again, Richard Pye pulled his chair close to emphasize what he was about to offer this intelligent and bewitching woman, a woman who spoke three languages, who knew and absolutely hated Carlos Guevara.

"Consuela, I'm not talking about making you a housekeeper

somewhere. I'm talking about making you one of us," Richard Pye began.

"Who are you?" Consuela asked.

"A watcher on the wall. A scout deep within the enemy's territory. A listener. A trickster and sometimes a killer. Always, a guardian of my country. Somehow, you knew this when you came to me at the consulate in Manaus. Yes, I am a spy. And now, so are you."

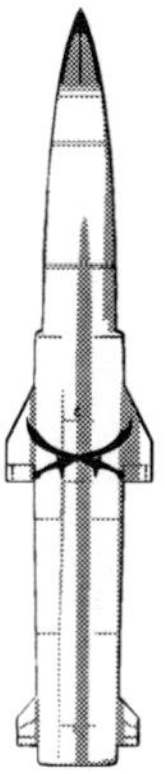

# 19

*Saturday night*
*CIA Headquarters*

Jack's blueprints perplexed Nick Ricollo. There they were surrounding him. All over the walls—projected big. Also on the desktop and table, spread out in the good old, comforting, analog paper form.

The 44-year-old CIA intelligence analyst, aerial photography and diagram expert worked the problem over in his mind. Nice blueprints. Good quality photography uploaded from—God knows who. They wouldn't tell him this time for some reason. There they sat. Good, solid, hard-to-get intel. Looking pretty ordinary except....

*That* was Nick's job. Look at all manner of things intended by someone to look ordinary and sift them for clues—things out of place, things too much in place—these told the true story if you could just extract facts, isolate them, rearrange them, and discern the underlying patterns.

Nick wiped his hand over his brush-cut, graying hair, removed his glasses, and rubbed his tired eyes. So, here sat blueprints for a welded steel barge. Big barge: 100 meters x 60 meters. Bigger than the usual solid aggregate or warehouse barge. Odd, but so what? Not all that odd. I mean, there are lots of barges out there, a few bigger than this one. Still, that size. Odd. *Odd to what purpose?* agonized Nick.

Nick Ricollo. Grandson of proud Italian immigrants from Genoa. Veteran CIA analyst of 20 years. Not as a job—as a calling. As his service to a country in need of someone to listen, someone to make sense out of all of these intercepts, beeps, blips, rumors, planted counter-intelligence hints and downright lies.

As his destiny. As his debt repayment. Duty, as his family legacy.

Nick's grandfather had landed at Anzio and lost his left leg and half his face in the valley below *Monte Cassino* when Nick's own father was only 13. Nick's dad had learned later in life how deficient the intelligence had been about German command of the valley from atop *Monte Cassino.* Nick's dad blamed this lack of intelligence for his father's wounds—and for all of the death in that Italian valley below, on the way to liberating Rome. Nick's own father had dedicated his life to the CIA and died in its service.

Every day reporting to work, Nick passed by the 102 stars on the Memorial Wall at CIA headquarters. Nick's father's own star was one of the 40 whose names are known and spoken only within Langley's walls.

His father and grandfather left Nick his inescapable legacy: this hungry curiosity, with relentless purpose. The urgent stomach-churning sense that The Grim Reaper is on the march and will gather his ghastly harvest again soon—if one doesn't find out fast what he is about and warn the people who can stop him—or at least to delay his arrival for another day, drove Nick on and tied him to his desk for long hours.

Nick took his job personally and seriously, and it accounted for his weight and his ulcer. That, plus vast quantities of strong coffee. Nick's career as a CIA analyst started during the time the Russians gobbled up chunks of thc world and threw them into slave-labor camps. No sooner did the Soviets collapse than the worldwide *jihad* started up.

And now these blueprints. What would these blueprints tell that justified such people risking their life for?

The blueprints. Nick fussed with them for the 20th time and fashioned a stack into somewhat of a different order on his worktable. He stood back and eyed them, scanning for some new pattern to leap out.

"Let me know as soon as you get any hypothesis," the boss had ordered.

Nick had called in shipbuilders from Norfolk, men already responsible for building the hulls and cabins aboard aircraft carriers. They'd volunteered days and he'd pick their brains clean. Now to "process" it all. He compared the odd barge to the more ordinary-looking one sold to NYC by this same barge builder, and now about to be on its way for delivery, behind the ugly duckling barge by a few days.

Down the Amazon, hit the Atlantic, turn northwestward, skirt the coastal countries. Then, somewhere off Venezuela, strike northward through the Caribbean, he supposed. Follow the tanker routes? No, most Venezuelan tankers stop at Mobile or one of the Texas ports. Probably head more northeastward to skirt the Florida coast.

Nick pulled up the slide with the side-by-side data comparison once more and went over the list. What a strange combination of features! Welded steel, tent-like deck over the whole deal with hatches, sealed and airtight. Huge towing brackets in front—and he meant huge. Still, he'd seen other barge plans and barges accessorized all over the place. So, was this one an aggregate barge, a construction crane barge, or maybe a warehouse barge? The inboard profile sheet refused to answer that question. Just what was this barge built to haul? Also, it lacked the usual array of winches, capstans, kevels and bitts, chocks and buttons. What would you tie to this thing? What would you haul? You would certainly haul *something*: the plans showed a deep draft of 4.5 meters! Gold? Lead? That was a lot of barge riding below the surface so it was intended to carry some real weight.

That weird deck. All the deck barge plans he'd looked at showed flat decks. This one rose like a shallow pup tent. You would get extra strength that way. Strength for what? Weight on top? Why? Made no sense. But it had to make sense. Designs had purposes.

Propulsion: none. None. Some barges were self-propelled but, not this one. Those not self-propelled depended on big tugs. Tugs had to tie up.

Crew? No cabin, kitchen or bunkhouse. Therefore, no crew.

Nick flipped to the minor plan details page behind the inboard profile page. *There*, in the guts of the barge, he saw platforms for securing cargo. *What cargo*? Nick puzzled over the powerful hydraulic lifts, apparently for raising cargo through the removed hatches. What would be lifted through those hatches? Why the self-contained hydraulic lifts? Why not just use wharf cranes to lift the cargo out? Those hydraulic lifts below the deck must have been very expensive and they wasted cargo space—if the purpose was hauling cargo. If not, then those on board lifts told a story.

And, again, why were the hull and deck so over-engineered for thickness and strength? Weird! Almost like a—.

"No way! It can't be!" Nick exclaimed.

Yes, it was. Fly with the facts, the unrestrained facts and go where they take you—to the truth.

Nick stretched for his phone, and called his boss with the confidence forged only from experience—and from prior successes. Once the synapses did their work and the neurons pulled the pieces together, they all announced to Nick's brain: *This is it.* Then, Nick *felt* the truth. He did not look back and his instincts had proven reliable. He'd had his hypotheses proved wrong before too, but with those he'd always stated his projections as probabilities far under 100 percent. Not with this one.

"Sir, I am done. Can we talk?"

Nick Ricollo, son and grandson of men whose calling it was to see to it that people did not die because they failed to perceive what lay before them. 9/11 seared Nick's conscience. Even after the first World Trade Center bombing, his country still failed to perceive the evil collecting like storm clouds, only with malevolence—intent—fury. Burning to harm—to kill—his countrymen. Intelligence failures plagued America and cost lives from *Monte Cassino* to the rise of the new Caliphate.

Not on Nick's watch! Nick bundled up blueprints and hustled down the hall to meet his boss in the DD—Intel's office.

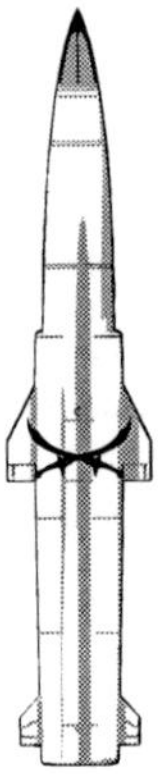

# 20

*Sunday morning*
*Manaus, Brazil*
*Hotel Tropical*

Saya-dar took breakfast on the patio at the Hotel Tropical's courtyard. The shops lining the courtyard were not yet open, and most of the tourists were inside perusing the hotel's buffet or arranging today's tours. The blue, cottoned sky reflected from the courtyard garden's pool surface. Beyond the courtyard's stone tiles and through the white stucco arches, Saya-dar could make out the re-named *Babylon* docked in the Rio Negro by the tour boats. Palms shaded the table area.

As Saya-dar sipped his coffee, Mr. A approached, his countenance clouded, his approach jerky as if he were staggering under a great weight.

He was.

"My men do not answer," Mr. A stated, breathlessly.

"Calm down, my friend, and let us go over what we know," Saya-dar said, staring at Mr. A over the rim of his coffee cup.

"Fats was to call me last night at eight. He did. I called him earlier at five and told him the barge was accepted. I called our men and approved payment. They knew what that meant: they were to pay, celebrate, and go to bed, then get up sometime during the night and kill the man and his whore. They were to leave the bodies to the Amazon, get the money back and call me no later than six this morning. But, I have heard nothing from them since eight last night!" he ended.

"And what did your inquiry of the local police reveal?" Saya-dar asked.

"Just like you said, I called my informant. He runs a little restaurant, several blocks off of the main plaza. Working man's district—not tourist. A few backpackers stray there, but that's all. Small police sub-headquarters there close by. The police eat there all the time. My informant got to know the local police officers well. Here's what he told me.

'The housekeeper had scheduled a grocery delivery, by boat. Deliverymen arrived. Found no one there. No one! But, they found blood all over the furniture and floor! They reported it all. The Manaus police are scouring the whole place. My informant tells me the whole station is abuzz. They don't get much action here in Manaus. For a large city, there just isn't a lot of crime. The DEA and the Brazilian Federal Police run the anti-drug operations and leave them out of the loop. So, they just don't have much to do. Traffic accidents. Complaints by tourists of being ripped off by tour operators. Very few murders. They are convinced Fats and his 'housekeeper' were murdered for Fats' money. Found a secret room broken into. "Murder for money!" They've already reached their conclusions and are quite pleased even though no murderer's been caught, he tells me." Mr. A finished, breathlessly, and calmed a bit just by telling the facts.

Saya-dar sipped his coffee.

"What do we do?" Mr. A asked.

Saya-dar eyed him, saying nothing.

"What—?"

"Silence!" Saya-dar hissed. "I must think. See these other

people about! You must control yourself! Pray for Allah to take the breath from your fear!"

Mr. A's face drained at the veiled threat that Saya-dar might be the one to take his breath from more than his fear, and he collapsed in his chair, drained.

"We will, for now, assume your men murdered Fats and his housekeeper as planned, but it is disturbing that they have not called in. They have all of that money they were to return and meet us with. Surely they have not decided to go out and on their own," Saya-dar said, eyeing Mr. A—the man who had hired Mr. B and Mr. C—grimly. He let the full impact of his suspicion hang heavy. Money and the woman, too.

Saya-dar sat back and relaxed, showing Mr. A that he might do the same. The frightened Mr. A. was coming apart, but he would not die today. Saya-dar continued.

"For now, we have what we came for—the barge—the *Khazir*. The *Khazir* is launching now. The garbage barge ordered by NYC will soon launch behind it. We will check out, board the *Babylon*, and head downriver ourselves just in case the investigation here becomes more intense. Shame. What a charming place!" Saya-dar said, glancing around the Hotel Tropical for show, still evaluating Mr. A's condition and staring at him. Mr. A shifted uncomfortably.

"Go see to our bags and pay the bill. I will meet you on board the *Babylon*," Saya-dar said, finally.

Grateful to still be alive, the no longer so-smooth Iranian complied.

Saya-dar finished his coffee, intentionally taking his time.

This was disastrous! Not because the two goons might have stolen Fats' payment for themselves. That would not be a problem. Saya-dar's reach was long, and he could always find and—chastise—these crimes. They had no idea who they were stealing from, if they were guilty! The return of the money would be a mere bonus. There was no reason to have left it with Fats and taking it created the appearance that the rich hermit was robbed.

No, what concerned the Saya-dar was the prospect that the two enforcers might have disappeared due to some, other, extraneous, intervening cause. What could that possibly be? No, *who* could it be? Who had intervened and why?

Perhaps real bandits had murdered them all. It disturbed Saya-dar that he'd never know. The Amazon could swallow thousands of bodies and none would ever again be found.

That scenario, too, would be fine. Saya-dar had what he'd come for—his barge—his *Khazir*! Bought and now underway, with New York's barge to follow, just as planned. He'd follow the *Khazir* down river from a distance on the *Babylon* and see what else developed.

What else must he do? What if—somehow—this was no mere theft, whether by traitorous fellow-believers or by common thieves?

He could not *know* yet what had happened. He could either abandon operation *Khazir* or proceed.

Abandon his masterpiece? Unthinkable!

Or.... Yes, perhaps now was the time. Perhaps now was the time for his "smokescreen" as the Americans might say. *Maskirovka*, as the Russians still said. Deception. Trickery. Mask your true intentions. The Saya-dar—The Shade—loved deceiving the West! *Sarab—mirage!*

Should he right now set in motion his *sarab*, his mirage—his deception to keep them busy and frantic while his barges and tugs chugged toward New York?

Saya-dar thrilled to such mirages, such deceptions. Certainly this *sarab* would more than suffice to distract western attention. Indeed, the *maskirovka—sarab* he held ready to go stood as an excellent plan on its own merits. Saya-dar's distraction would devastate the West, even if he had to cancel the *Khazir*.

Saya-dar retrieved his mobile phone and prepared to call another mobile phone waiting for his signal on the far side of the world. Initiating his s*arab* required no more. All else had been prepared. With his finger hovering above the Send button, Saya-dar paused. He might need his *sarab* later in the operation. The barge—the *Khazir*—was not yet even out of the Amazon basin and on the way to New York City. Were the unexpected events of last night causing him to panic?

Saya-dar looked around. He saw nothing more than the placid Rio Negro, this quiet, elegant old hotel, a few tourists strolling through the courtyard waiting for the shops to open, and the well-kept riverbank between the Hotel Tropical and the river. His shining yacht, *Babylon*—with the fake name *"Bay-B-Lie"* painted on her transom—swayed gently at the pier. Saya-dar closed his phone. Launching such an elegant s*arab* was premature. He would hold that card. Use it as a future operation if he did not use it as deception for the *Khazir*. Instead, he would, as planned, follow his new purchase downriver from the luxury of the *Babylon* and see what developed next.

Saya-dar arose, entered the hotel, and made for the dark

wood-paneled lobby. He spied Mr. A at the desk with other men, waiting to check out. Saya-dar strode to the concession stand and found an English-language newspaper. He'd catch up on the news.

Saya-dar eyed the fat fellow-Iranian as he passed to the desk. Mr. A smiled thinly. Saya-dar nodded at him. *The man is so nervous! He bears watch* —. Saya-dar bumped into another man turning around from the registration desk.

"Oh, *Desculpa, por favor,*" the man said in poor Portuguese. Saya-dar appraised him in an instant. Obviously an American. Eco-tourist on the way to see giant lily pads, no doubt. Looked a bit hung over. At least he was polite, asking to be excused, thought the Saya-dar.

"No problem, it's quite all right," Saya-dar replied courteously, in perfect English, smiling.

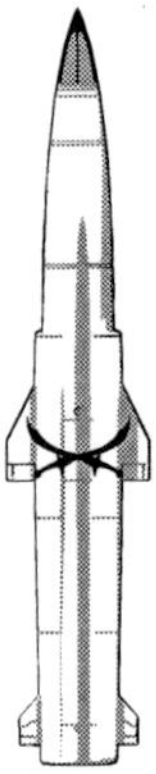

# 21

*Sunday morning*
*Manaus, Brazil*
*Hotel Tropical*

Jack always felt more operational after chow. Bacon and eggs with strong Brazilian coffee breathed new life into a battered man like nothing else. Jack returned from exploring the breakfast bar re-loaded with his favorites and brought fresh coffee to pour for Gordon. Jack sat down across from Gordon Noone, poured Gordon a cup and munched a croissant. Gordon nodded his thanks, saying nothing, in obvious, deep thought.

"Figured out what's next, Gordon?" Jack asked, "I haven't."

"Waiting for orders but, yes, I have a plan. I'd like your thoughts," Gordon said.

"Thoughts? Simple. The U.S. is in no immediate danger that we know. The weird designer barge is underway. We don't know the destination for sure although the second barge—the garbage barge—is slated for delivery to the Port Authority of New York. Forget the PATH garbage-barge for a minute. Here's what we want to know about the strange barge ordered by these Middle Easterners: destination, design and purpose, cargo, and the identity of the shipper sending that cargo.

'Once we know these things, we'll be ready for action. That

is, I suspect I'll be getting further orders. Until then, we wait. Right? As far as you and I can tell, the situation tells us nothing that is definitely actionable. We track the barges from the *Arcturus* and continue the surveillance op from the yacht. Can't think of a better place. I see no better course of action right now. We wait. We track. We lay our trap," Jack ended positively. "Of course, that's my limited viewpoint. We've reported to the S-2 and I'm sure the intel shack has the bigger picture," Jack ended, using infantry verbiage to express his hope that somebody had more puzzle pieces, and that his had added to the intelligence picture.

Jack had saved Consuela, found valuable intel, and had spread before him a fine breakfast with good coffee, all as the sun glinted off the river. He felt pretty good, despite the aching, swollen jaw.

Gordon Noone looked across the table at Jack. He'd recruited the 30-year-old, ex-Army Ranger captain well. He watched the younger man, obviously in a good mood. There sat a man immersed in either rough training or combat since he was 21. Jack had saved all of their lives during the *Arcturus* adventure, had been wounded, and had lost his best friend, Bobby, killed in action. Gordon knew from reading Jack's record that he had killed many men and had lost a score of comrades. The kind of combat Jack had led and done left behind a train of ghosts. Yet, here he sat, obviously quite pleased with himself and enjoying breakfast. Gordon marveled.

"Jack, there's something besides the operation I need to discuss with you," Gordon began.

*Uh, oh, here it is,* thought Jack.

"Jack, you just witnessed a brutal killing on video and killed a man yourself. Does that not affect you? How do you feel about that?"

Jack took another bite, poured more coffee, and eyed Gordon, quizzically. *What is Gordon getting at?* Jack had expected Gordon to criticize him about Consuela.

"How do I *feel* about it? Oh, I get it. It's the new touchy-feely administration's idea of showing that management cares. Look, I don't know what you're getting at, but this is a beautiful day. Mission accomplished. Agent rescued. We are at a fine old hotel, in an exotic location I've never been to before, and you're not ruining my morning with all of this grim talk."

"No, seriously. How do you feel about all of this?"

"What, have you been taking some kind of new human relations course? Ortega sending you to sensitivity training, Gordon? Course title: 'Feelings for Soldiers.' 'Feelings for Killers.' Is that what's going on back in the states while I'm out swimming with the crocodiles? That's it, isn't it? See, if I were teaching that course, it would include stuff like taking a light twig between your thumb and forefinger, and ever so gently *feeling* your way along a trail, learning what it *feels* like when you touch a tripwire with the end of the probe in the middle of the night. That's how I explore my feelings! How do I *feel* about it, Gordon?

'You know how these things are, Gordon. You know much more about me than I know about you. I assume you've been in the same kind of business. Are we not of like mind? You do what you *have* to do. I don't *like* killing people. But, if you're going to *resist* evil people, you have to decide up front you're going to *kill* evil people. They just don't like to be *resisted.* So, sometimes, just sometimes, you have to kill them. I'm a point man for my country, Gordon. Others enjoy the luxury of debating such questions in seminars on feelings. I don't.

'You and I are on the front line. I pray to God he gives me the wisdom to see the situations for what they are, and accompanies that wisdom with the will to act. If I don't, others die. Good people are safe from Jack McDonald. Evil people are not. It's as simple as that," Jack said, sitting back, sipping coffee and eyeing Gordon.

"What a curious question for you to pose to me on this bright, sunny, and—I might add—successful morning, Gordon" Jack ended, cheerily, holding up his coffee cup in a mock toast.

Gordon was not to be deflected.

"I know it all happened very fast. I was listening and watching the surveillance video. When CIA alerted you and you saw the video of Consuela about to be raped and murdered, you didn't hesitate. You loaded up and went to her rescue. Yet, Jack, you were ordered to get out.

'My question to you, Jack, is this: did you consider that, after her murdering Fats, her *being* murdered helped keep our surveillance cover intact? You could have watched; you could have just reported. Later, we'd all have checked the bungalow and cleaned it up. Your intervention made known our presence. Otherwise, they'd have left the bungalow amazed at Consuela's revenge and we could have tracked them to whatever devilment they might get into next. As it is, they'll tell no tales. But, I'm sure their controller—whoever and wherever he is—must be wondering where his children are.

'Did you *think* about that Jack? If you did, if you actually made a choice, why did you choose to save Consuela and jeopardize the mission?" Gordon ended.

Gordon did not indict Jack. Nor did he mean to. As a matter of training and tactics, it was a fair question. In the cool calm of post-operation de-briefing, it was worth exploring. Besides, Gordon had been there and had worked with other young professional killers. He knew it was best if they talked about it to someone else who had washed the blood from his hands.

*So that's it.* "Gordon, I'll answer you straight, but, first, I want to know: Why are you asking me?" Jack responded.

"First, Jack, I have to know whether or not you saw the options. You cut the CIA controller off and immediately tore out for the bungalow. Did you consider—even see—the threat your own actions were to the mission?" Gordon said, ending his first question.

"I'll field that one. It's a fair question. Yes, I knew slipping out, never having any interaction with the targets was the most secure bet for the operation. I didn't have to think about that. That's just true for any surveillance or recon op. I knew when I loaded up and headed for the bungalow I was converting the recon patrol to a combat patrol. Recon to raid, right? I knew it would blow our surveillance. Besides, I had more time to think about it in the boat—during the approach. I put such second-thoughts out of my mind," Jack explained.

"Okay, then why? Why did you choose to save the life of our agent, why? What's Consuela to you?" Gordon pressed.

"Is that it, Gordon? You think I put my emotions—my *feelings*—in the way of the mission? That's it, isn't it? You think I'm missing Donna and saved Consuela because I couldn't save my wife?" Jack was getting a bit angry at this point.

"I don't know. Did you?" Gordon asked, sighing. "Look, Jack, you and Donna had started a different life, a real life. I know you loved my niece. While I hated to lose my prize recruit, I was thrilled for you both. I mean that. I was very happy for both Donna and you, and for what you had found together. I just wanted you to be happy. I certainly did not want you back aboard Team *Arcturus* because my niece got killed in a car wreck," Gordon said.

The men sat. The awkward moment hung between them. They lacked the luxury of time to deal with all that had happened, so Jack got to the point.

"Here it is, Gordon. Anyone else, I'd not even answer. I'd tell him to—well, never mind what I'd tell him. You, though, you are not just my recruiter. You are my wife's—my deceased wife's—you're Donna's uncle. We've been through a lot together. I *trust* you, Gordon. I *have* to trust you. My life is literally in your hands on these operations.

'I'll admit Consuela stirred emotions I'd not felt since Donna. Working for you, Gordon, serving the country in this capacity, man, this is a lonely proposition. Consuela shattered my isolation. She risked her *life* to help us. She is not an American. Here she is, thousands of miles from the United States, having nothing to do with us, and yet she saw evil being spawned right before her. She had the goodness in her heart to act. That's the very definition of selfless courage. At the same time, and much more immediately, she literally held my life in her hands, too. She could have betrayed me at any second. Likewise, I could have just left her to whatever fate those guys had in mind for her. The two of us were thrown together. No, Gordon, *you* threw the two of us together.

'So, know this, Gordon. I really had no choice. Would you have rather I just sat at the video and watched this woman who came to our aid be raped, tortured, and murdered? Maybe hauled away into sex-slavery? I could not just sit there and you *know* it. More than that: I know you wouldn't have either, would you?" Jack ended with his own challenge.

Gordon took his time, and replied quietly.

"I do not question your decision at all, Jack. I respect you for it. I confirm you in it. Here's what I guess I'm really saying. This 'work' puts you out on the edge in many ways. You are thrown into situations that demand choices that normal people never have to even think about making. And, you get no guidance from your government. The things you—and I—are drawn into strain the limits of a man's ability to know what's right from what's wrong. Not to mention straining the limits of the law! How do you handle that, Jack? That is really what I am getting at," Gordon said.

Outside, over the reddish-orange, tiled rooftops of the hotel's courtyard shops, a seaplane bobbed at its moorings, waiting for the tourists who chartered it that morning. People began to board a brilliantly-colored red, white, and blue tour boat to head down the Rio Negro to where it joined the Amazon—the "Meeting of the Waters"—where the black Rio Negro ran for miles visibly distinct alongside the less acidic, chocolate-brown Amazon River. Guests lounged on the patio, enjoying their mango, pineapple, and delicious breakfast in the tropical sunshine and leisurely comfort of this fine old hotel, the Hotel Tropical.

*None of those people out there,* Jack thought, *can possibly understand what I am up against. What I must do.*

He knew how to answer Gordon.

"Gordon, I knew already from my Army days that these decisions would get in my face. They confront all soldiers. I am not special and neither are you. It's just that covert soldiers confront their own kind of moral crises, usually alone.

'So, here it is Gordon: in this sinful world, you cannot insulate yourself from having to make these horrible choices. Here's what makes Jack McDonald take a lickin' and keep on tickin.' You can kid yourself. You can shield yourself from some hard decisions, for a while, by checking out of the fight. Maybe, you can even get by with living your entire life without personally lifting a finger against evil. Just because you get to live in personal peace, that doesn't mean that evil in the world just goes away. It's just out of your sight. Someone else has to suffer. Someone else has to deal with it. So, some of us choose to show up, suit up, arm up and go looking for that evil. Go looking for those evil ones. And kill them.

'Choices, Gordon. Everybody makes choices. Many choose to live as though others aren't being raped, tortured, starved and murdered. Some of us get into the fight. When you do, it becomes personal. Either way, a man must make the choice. Acting or declining the Evil One's invitation to battle. 'To be or not to be, that is the question. Whether it is nobler in the mind to suffer the slings and arrows of outrageous fortune, or, to take arms against a sea of troubles, and—by opposing—end them.' Dithering around like Hamlet is fake, false, an illusion. You end up just letting evil ones have their way. Both getting into the fight and staying out of the fight are choices. Either way, people die. I nominate the evil people for the grave, and I'm stepping forward to send them on their way.

'Gordon, I saw this good woman about to be raped and killed. Really Gordon, the choice was not difficult, now was it?"

"No, son, I suppose not," Gordon agreed.

"Are you satisfied?" Jack asked.

"I'm more than satisfied."

Jack thought Gordon might cry. *Can't have that*! He made another decision.

"Let's check out and get the *Arcturus* going, Gordon. I'm eager to be back on board her. I'll pay the bill and meet you out at the dock. Okay?"

Gordon smiled. "Yes, okay. Jack?"

"Yes?"

"You're a good man. You did the right thing with Consuela.

I'm proud of you."

The men pushed their chairs back. Jack picked his way through the tables where other patrons sat. *They are just heading out to enjoy the city, or to enjoy one of these excursions*, Jack thought. Down the dark wood stairs, through the stately white-stucco corridors and archways. As Jack entered the lobby, he determined to return here someday when he, too, could simply enjoy the hotel's jungle wood and colonial ambience.

His thoughts were so occupied when he bid the concierge *Obrigado* and *Tchau*, trying out his limited Portuguese for "thanks" and "goodbye." As Jack turned, he bumped into another patron passing by.

"Oh, *desculpa por favor*," Jack said, in rough Portuguese.

This man also looked pre-occupied. For a second, Jack thought he'd made the man angry and there would be a scene. Jack was forming his defensive plan to humbly disengage without a drama but, instead, the man smiled and replied in perfect English:" No problem, It's quite all right."

*How'd they always know he was an American?*

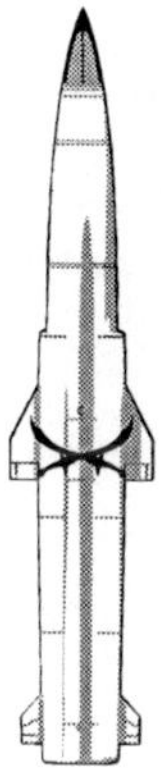

# 22

*Sunday morning*
*On the Rio Negro*
*Fourteen miles from the Amazon River, above Manaus, Brazil*

The *Arcturus.* Last time Jack had been aboard the yacht, Donna was still alive. His wife. They'd met right here, on board. She'd brought him coffee there at the rail. Right there. Jack touched the steel rail where they had faced the sea and unknown adventure together. *Right here's where I fell in love with her. The Caribbean, the adventure, the salt smell of the sea. And Donna. I had no chance.*

And his best friend and old combat comrade, Bobby. In quiet moments, Jack still experienced pangs of guilt. Bobby, Jack's old executive officer from Charlie Company, 1st Battalion of the 506th infantry, 101st Airborne Division had shipped aboard the *Arcturus* with Jack, at Jack's invitation. Jack had insisted on getting Bobby to help guard the *Arcturus* and its people, and guard them he did.

"Ask your doctor if *Arcturus* is right for you," Jack had joked. "You need this mission more than they need you," he had told Bobby, pointing his finger at Bobby for emphasis, but really speaking about himself. Classic Freudian projection of your own angst onto someone else, Jack decided later.

What would Bobby have done, once he was out of the Army?

Watch TV and grow fat? Bobby had needed *Arcturus.* But, it cost Bobby his life, killed by the Cuban pirates while Bobby and the *Arcturus* crew held out at that old Spanish mission on top of the island. While Jack was knocked out cold. *Maybe if I'd stayed conscious I could have ....*

"A few old memories coming back, Jack?" Gordon interrupted.

"Yeah, a few more than a few," Jack admitted.

"Well, get squared away. (*Sounds like a Ranger counseling session*, Jack thought.) It's a three-day haul back down the Amazon to its estuary and that's if our friends don't stop for some reason or drag along. Might take them—and, therefore, us—four days. We'll tail the barge from way back here. On the official side, our friends with the Brazilian Marine Police have agreed to watch the barge along the way and post the DEA from time to time with her passage. They cooperate with the DEA all the time on drug-running investigations, so DEA participation in this adventure won't look unusual. Now that the Patriot Act specifically permits it, DEA will share the intel with CIA. CIA will talk to Ortega. Between their updates and our own satellite surveillance, we'll not have to chase her so closely. We're going to hang back, out of sight. You might even get a chance to give that sore jaw a rest."

"I have to admit, I could use some sleep," Jack said, rubbing his jaw.

"Your cabin is your old one. Hope it makes you feel at home," Gordon said.

Jack climbed down the gangway, stowed his scant belongings, and tried the bunk. Troubles made a futile effort to deny him sleep as the duty and tension of the last days melted away and Jack McDonald rested. Far too soon, he heard a voice calling his name. From a fog, he recognized the voice as Gordon's and was up in an instant.

"Trouble?" he asked once on the deck, peering around, trying to scrape together his full faculties.

"No, not at all. All's well. I am sorry to awaken you so soon, but we are about to pass something I want you to see. Why don't you come topside?"

Jack followed Gordon, rubbing his eyes. On the deck, the day shone bright and hot. The Amazon's seemingly always-present breeze cooled the river travelers mercifully. Gordon offered Jack water and pointed to the afterdeck lounge chairs. Jack eased down into a lounge chair next to Gordon and hoped he didn't instantly fall asleep again.

Settling in, Jack looked again out on the mighty, wide Amazon River. This time, he was cruising east—downriver—passing Manaus on his left. Jack marveled at the bustling shores and high buildings. His earlier passage had been further downriver where the city had already tapered off, and at night. Here, the shores teemed with commerce. The colorful three-decker ferries bobbed everywhere Jack could see. The slender canoes with the "weed-eater" outboard motors raced in and out among them, sometimes filled with bananas, sometimes just carrying a couple of people. Jack spied Maersk container ships, huge oil tankers, barges, and gunmetal gray cruisers run by the Brazilian Marine Police. This city—1,000 miles upriver—bustled. Gordon pointed down to the oddly striped water where Jack saw a distinct line—black next to light tan.

"The Meeting Of the Waters" Gordon announced, tour-guide like. "You're looking at the Rio Negro still not mixing with the Amazon even this far down from where it flows into the Amazon. You can see it from miles high."

Leaving the taller buildings behind, Jack spied hundreds of shacks painted in all colors, packed together like a stack of building blocks, clinging to the riverbank on stilts.

"We're coming up on what I awakened you to see," Gordon interrupted. "Take these. I want to know what you think. Over there, see the barge-building yard?"

Jack raised the offered binoculars and could make out what looked like soccer fields with men moving about on them. These occupied a scraped-bare portion of the red-earth bank, with corrugated, shed buildings arranged beside and behind. Jack zoomed in the binoculars and the activity became even clearer. These were not soccer fields. Jack plainly made out three, flat, steel barges. On each, about 25 men worked atop the deck. Where a fourth had been, immediately by the riverbank, lay a patch of reddish, bare earth. Plainly, the men had recently launched one barge from the bank into the Amazon, rolling it down the slope into the still black water from the Rio Negro, not yet mixed with the coffee-colored Amazon.

"That's Fats' operation, Jack. He built NYC's barge and the odd one you saw blueprinted."

"Is that blank space any indication of the blueprinted barge's size?" Jack asked.

"Good observation, and yes, it is. There seems to be a standard size for these others—all built from the same design. The blueprinted specialty barge is half again as big," Gordon answered.

Soon, the banks showed more green and fewer houses until only a house or two dotted the banks. They came to the channel leading back toward Fats' bungalow. Jack thought of Consuela and her whispered secret. *Find me.* She would start a new life. However tragic he thought her past might have been, Jack foresaw a bright future for Consuela. Was that realistic, considering her display of slashing violence? Would the strength of her heart and the power of her will carry her out of this dark, isolated jungle of her past, and into.... What?

Jack felt good about his part in fighting for her. Consuela's decision to contact the Brits started her personal revolution. He still did not understand what set her on Fats but stabbing Fats was dramatic liberation. No, her courageous decision to break with him and pursue what was right marked her liberating moment. Murder? Was Consuela guilty of murdering Fats?

*Maybe she could have escaped*, Jack conceded. Revenge? For what? Why was it necessary for her to ambush Fats and cut him up? The gentle housekeeper who came to their rescue had turned homicidal overnight! Must have been a reason. Jack sorted Fats into the category of "evil," convened a benevolent jury-of-the-mind and returned a verdict of "justifiable homicide by self-defense."

Another 15 minutes and only the green banks lined the river. Jack saw little else to be accomplished now and excused himself. This time, he collapsed in the bunk and slept like a rock.

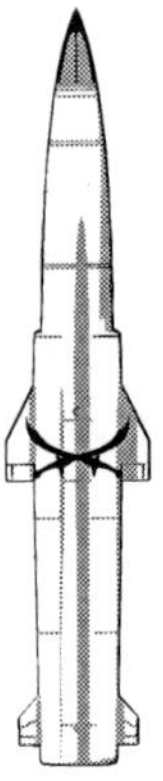

# 23

*Sunday, lunchtime*
*Aboard Arcturus*
*80 Miles Downriver from Manaus*

Hunger pulled Jack out the bunk around noon and he climbed topside. He found Gordon in the main lounge, on the phone. Leaving Gordon, Jack toured the *Arcturus*, re-familiarizing himself with the Burger Flush-Deck Motor Yacht's layout and appointments. He saw no changes, but for faint evidence of the repairs made to the bow where the Cuban pirates had attacked the *Arcturus* with RPG-7 anti-tank rockets. Jack wondered who owned her. Gordon caught up with him.

"I ordered sandwiches from the galley. Let's sit and plan what's next," Gordon said. The men arranged two chairs in the *Arcturus'* luxurious main cabin.

"We'll have to follow orders, of course, but I'd leave us right here," Jack said. "No one knows what's up so why deploy us elsewhere? If anything develops with this barge business, then we are right here in the AO," Jack said, referring to the Amazon as their Area of Operations.

Gordon munched his sandwich, and thought. Jack scanned the far banks of the Amazon.

"Gordon, this work you got me into, it sure has its highs and lows, just like combat," Jack said.

"Yes, one minute, you're fighting for your life and the next you have nothing to do but sit on a lounge chair, basking in the sun like a tourist, but feeling really out of it and useless. Is that what you mean?" Gordon asked.

"Precisely," Jack agreed. "This leg of the mission at least makes sense. Consuela's instincts about the danger to America are right. Guevara, the Iranians, and the now-knifed Fats were up to something and that secret is welded into the steel in that mystery barge," Jack said, pointing vaguely over the bow even though both barges were miles ahead, out of sight. "I guess you could say we're on stakeout. Not bad digs for a stakeout hide site," Jack joked.

"It's the coming together of these men for the purpose of creating some new terrorist attack that worries me," Gordon said.

"Where is all of this going, Gordon?" Jack asked.

"What do you mean? All of this what? Killing? The return of West-hating Islamic nut cases? Your own future?"

"This terrorism, Gordon. You ever read the story of Theseus and the Minotaur? The Athenians bought their peace with King Minos by sending a ship load of their finest young men and women as tribute. This human tribute was really a human sacrifice to the Minotaur—a monster living in the labyrinth."

"I'm impressed Jack. I didn't know you were such a student of Greek mythology," Gordon laughed.

"My mom and dad had bookcases filled with old books and this book on Greek mythology was one of them. I read it and reread it and I can still remember some of the pictures. I find the myths instructive from time to time and this is one of those instructive moments. Care to switch roles while Jack becomes the professor?"

"By all means Prof, please continue," Gordon invited.

"One year, Theseus volunteered to ship as one of the intended sacrifices. With help from King Minos' daughter—love is always involved in these stories, you know—Theseus made a plan. No dithering Hamlet, that boy! He killed the Minotaur and escaped from the labyrinth, ending the ghastly tribute," Jack concluded.

"I see your point. We—meaning almost all of us in the West—could go about our days and ignore the raids against us. So what if a trainload of commuters gets blown up? So what if an American reporter overseas gets kidnapped and they cut his head off? So what if an old, wheelchair-bound Jew is shot and thrown overboard the *Achille Lauro*? These are just little sacrifices. Like those nature shows where some animal on the edge of the herd gets picked off by the wild dogs. If you're in the herd, the risk of being a terrorist victim is so, so low. Why not just write newspaper articles about it and let our bloody tribute appease the voracious monster?" Gordon asked, ending his rhetorical question.

"Exactly. However, unlike the half-man, half-bull Minotaur, there are many Islamic Minotaurs, and they emerge from their labyrinth and come hunting for us. The easier we make it for them, the more of us they kill. Unlike King Minos, there is no amount of tribute we could pay to buy our peace, even if we were cowardly enough to try," Jack said.

"Well spoken!" Gordon said, clapping. "I'll swap you a modern parable in return Jack, the Greek scholar," Gordon teased.

"I am all ears. Shoot."

"Did you see 'Independence Day' with Will Smith?" Gordon asked.

Jack was surprised. He didn't picture Gordon as the movie-going type. "Yeah, sure, it's been a few years though. Please refresh my memory," Jack said.

"Well, Will Smith is this Air Force fighter-jock. Aliens attack Earth. He shoots down and captures this one alien fighter pilot. Punches him out! He brings home his dazed outer-space prisoner and the leaders and scientists lock the alien up. They want to *talk* to the alien. Some want to *negotiate.* Well, to compromise and parley, you have to know what the person you are afraid of *wants.* So, they asked him straight up: 'What do you want of us?'

'Do you remember, Jack, what the alien said in reply? Do you remember what they wanted of us?" Gordon asked, growing more animated.

"No, can't say I do. What?" Jack asked.

"To *die*, Jack. The aliens just wanted us all to *die*," Gordon answered, shaking his head.

"There is no appeasing these *jihadists.* The other Muslims cannot appease them, either. Islamic terrorism is first a civil war within Islam. The bloodbath sloshes over onto us because we exist. How can the West appease such men? You can't negotiate with them because they simply want our eradication. They have de-humanized us as infidels. Their sole goal is for us to die," Gordon ended.

"Allah is for the world," Jack said.

"Huh?"

"Allah is for the world," Jack repeated. That's what one young terrorist told the missionary woman we rescued in the Philippines when she asked him what it was he wanted. Not just his own island. Not just the nearby islands, too. Not just the Philippines. Not just a cleansed Muslim world. There was no end to it until the entire world was conquered in The *Jihad.* You had to either kill the infidel, or conquer the infidel, convert him, and make a slave of him."

"Oh, I know who you are talking about. What was that like, Jack, working with the Philippine Marine patrols hunting Abu Sayyaf?" Gordon asked.

"In a word, very rewarding. We knew the Abu Sayaff had the Americans—the missionary pilot and his wife—and others. We spent months in the field. I got close to my Philippine Marine Light Reaction Company. They are tough, dedicated men. It broke their hearts that the husband was killed in the final battle. All that work and misery! Finally, we tracked them down and freed the wife—and her husband gets killed!" Jack said. "To this day, his death haunts me."

"Any idea whose shot got him?" Gordon asked.

"None," Jack said. "Once it was over and we killed or captured all of them, we searched and found him wounded. No way to know. His wife could not see him during the battle. No witnesses. We suspect they assassinated him, but we'll never know. Truth is, we were all shooting at their captors. You know how it is. Chaotic. It could have been friendly fire. We so badly wanted them both freed. We followed the Abu Sayyaf for over a year, you know? They had cut heads off and raped some of the women," Jack ended.

"I know," Gordon said. "I know. The teams did a great job. Great job training the Philippine Light Reaction Companies and super job staying in the woods with them all that time."

"It paid off. Besides, it makes me feel at home here in the Amazon," Jack added. "I tell you, though, it will always haunt me that we couldn't keep that man from getting killed. No way to know if they murdered him or if one of us shot him accidentally in the crossfire. Gordon, it could have been one of my rounds," Jack said.

Gordon gripped Jack's shoulder.

"Don't worry, Gordon, it doesn't keep me up at night. None of this does. I resolved long ago that being a soldier is more than joining some outfit. In a way, you also have to 'check out.' You just have to accept that even justifiable—moral—violence is a messy business and you'll get yourself bloody doing it. I am doing what I think is right, and I know the cost is high. High in ways I probably can't even foresee. The alternative is to wave good-bye while our young men and women sail to King Minos for sacrifice," Jack said.

"One of those costs is what most people would call an ordinary family life. Do you know what I'm talking about, Jack?"

Jack got up, walked to the bar, and opened the compact refrigerator.

"Want anything, Gordon?" Jack asked.

"I'll take iced tea if there's any left."

"Sure."

Jack poured two and returned.

"Yes, I know what you're talking about. I know w*ho* you are talking about. Donna," Jack said, flatly.

"Yes, Donna," Gordon affirmed.

"I don't know what to say, Gordon. She and I had a chance—a time—and I'm thankful for that. For her. She is dead, though, and Jack McDonald is still here. Yes, I'm lonely. Lonely in a way I've not experienced before loving Donna. But, she's gone and there are so many enemies wanting to destroy us. I feel—compelled—to fight back."

"How lonely are you, Jack?" Gordon asked.

*Uh, oh. Consuela.*

"I'll be okay, Gordon. It's just going to take a while," Jack insisted.

"Well, while it's taking a while, you be careful. I worry about you," Gordon said.

"You mean about one of your recruits being rendered combat-ineffective?" Jack asked.

"No, son, I mean much more than that. You be careful."

The men left it there. Indeed, they were both lonely. Jack got up, walked out of the lounge, and stood at the rail—like he had done when he first fell in love with Donna.

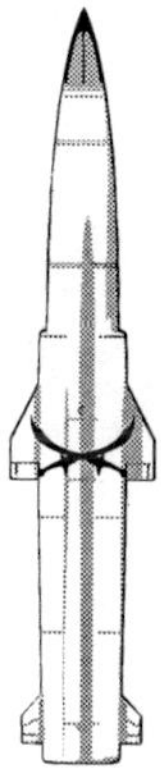

# 24

*Washington, D.C.*
*White House Secret Service*
*Operations Office*
*Sunday afternoon, two days after the bungalow*

Grant Gammon hated these moments. He'd tried to order this president—tried to refuse the president's request. That didn't work. President Robert Bullington had only laughed, clapped him on the back, and called him a "good soldier."

"Throw 'em off! Be unpredictable! Never return by the same route! 'Random' will be our Chief of Security on these little jaunts. Besides, they'll keep us all alert, right, Grant?" the president had cajoled. Unconvincingly—but he was the president.

Besides, there was some logic to it. Get out the door and grab one of the president's personal cars. He traded often and owned several. Then, with the president driving, he would hit the streets. Flanked by the best—now very keyed up, very alert Secret Service agents—they'd go somewhere known only to President Bullington until the last minute. The "flankers" as the president called them would secure a perimeter. The "recon team," as the president labeled them, would move out to do a recon at the destination (the "objective" the president called it). Then, unless there just happened to be some odd rock concert or something going on, the president would stride in like any other citizen—only with his own personal security close at hand and a professional perimeter posted all around outside.

So, would this be one of their little adventures? It usually was when the president himself called to set it up. Thirty minutes' notification!

Grant had to admit even further though: the Secret Service agents had grown to the task and gotten good at it. They were more flexible now than ever before. They were, in fact, up to the mission. And, it did keep them at high-ready.

Let's face it. With the destination and the departure vehicle known only to the president, by the time any news dog or assassin figured it out, there was just no way to get to the man. President Bullington even had his assistants take out his various cars for random drives. Secret Service agent Gammon chuckled. He'd recommended to the president that agents sometimes take the cars out and see who followed. So, the agents enjoyed joyriding in the president's vintage roadsters and souped-up muscle cars, but it drove the press corps mad. "Chasing their tails" they complained.

This president didn't care. But, he wasn't stupid, and he wasn't reckless. He wasn't exposing the agents to risk just to create a photo op being seen grabbing a hamburger like an ordinary guy. Indeed, once spotted, and once the curious started coming around, the president would wave goodbye and leave a big tip for the hassled proprietor before heading out.

It wouldn't work for every president, but this one thought like a Secret Service agent. No, this president thought like the ex-infantryman and Airborne Ranger he was. Learned his caution and tactics the hard way: running long range reconnaissance (lurp) patrols late in Vietnam as a staff sergeant. So, this time, agent Gammon wondered at what "LZ behind the lines" they would all be "dropped in" to "recon" as he knocked on the president's door.

"Grant! Come in!" President Bullington said, brightening into a big grin. The president made it hard for Gammon to begrudge him these little outings. Besides, they all had fun once they got over the radical change from the last president.

The President of the United States downshifted into second and turned some heads as he pulled his onyx black, 1964 Super Sport 396 Chevy Nova two-door coupe into the parking lot. Here, he paused in a parking space for 10 seconds, then moved to another. (This, he called a "false insertion" adapting chopper pilot lingo and tactics.) He and the close-security Secret Service entourage then jumped out and entered the timber-framed door to the bar. At three p.m., only a few patrons sat about. The president's fake beard and ball cap made him unrecognizable in the dimness. The whole patrol looked like it might be a bunch of golfers in for some refreshment, except the agents looked so—serious! The president had chided them trying to get them to act—to pretend to be joking and ribbing each other over golf scores, or wives, or something—but he'd finally given up on it. They were just too—professional.

President Bullington strode over to a room in the corner and stopped Agent Gammon.

"You only from here, Grant," the president said.

Agent Grant Gammon knew not to argue. He signaled the inside close-security detail to set up a perimeter, and then he followed President Bullington inside.

"Get yourself a beer, too," the president joked.

"Real funny, Mr. President," Grant said

"Now you order for us all will you? So I don't have to show my face to the bartender. I'll be over there."

President Bullington pointed to a table where a man sat alone, back turned to them, reading a newspaper. Big man, like a linebacker. Civilian, casual clothes. Black polo shirt, dark pants. Civilian but tactically sensible, too. Who was *this* who the President of the United States was meeting in a bar in suburban Washington?

Agent Gammon sighed. He knew President Bullington wouldn't say. "For your own good," he would say, transmitting a somewhat pained expression like a father might. This was the strangest presidential protection detail.

But, it was fun. And Gammon would follow this president anywhere.

Agent Gammon ordered two Paulaner drafts for the president and his mystery guest. *Uh, oh. Got to keep the innkeeper in check.* The innkeeper was no dummy. He had obviously "made" the president despite the disguise. Probably the detail spooked him and he figured the president was some VIP CEO. Anyway, Gammon spoke into his mike and summoned an agent to tail the innkeeper and prevent all phone calls and all conversations during the visit. The agent would apologize, ask for the man's willing cooperation, and explain. At the end, the president himself would walk over, shake the innkeeper's hand, thank the man for his hospitality and his "keen ability to keep a secret," and slap him on the back. Then, President Bullington would hand the charmed innkeeper an invitation to tour the White House with his family and press the presidential bronze coin into the dumbstruck man's palm.

Agent Grant Gammon, Secret Service veteran of three administrations, smiled. He'd admit it. Best presidential protection detail duty ever. And, he learned things about security from this president that he had never thought of before.

President Bullington approached the man seated in the corner.

"Paul, glad you could come," President Bullington greeted Major General Paul Ortega, Deputy Commander, Special Operations Command. "How did the move from Tampa to Fort Bragg go?" the president added, hinting at General Ortega's recent promotion to two stars.

"Fine sir, just fine. Been there before. Started there. Know it well. Pine trees and sand. Had my first rifle platoon there. Good men. Good men. Good to see you, sir," Ortega said, rising and shaking his friend's hand. "And, sir, when the President of the United States—and a fellow Ranger calls—I come."

The men sat.

"I like this place, sir. Too bad we can never come here again," Ortega said.

The men settled in. The president smiled as Agent Gammon returned with beer for both, but not for himself.

"Thanks Grant," the president said, more seriously. "I really appreciate your working with me on these forays out. I go nuts cooped up all the time. I know this is outside of your usual security plan, and I really appreciate your adaptability."

*How can I hold that against the guy?* "No problem, sir. I'll be right there," Gammon said, indicating the door with a nod.

"Got a man outside there?" The president asked, indicating a back entrance door.

"Two, plus a sniper team on the roof and teams securing each end of the alley, sir," Agent Gammon responded. We have two cars on constant patrol in the surrounding neighborhoods.

"My cars?"

"No sir, yours attract too much attention."

Agent Gammon had resented these questions at first, like the president didn't trust him to do his job. Later, he realized the president was not questioning his ability. Indeed, this president had more respect for the nuances of the security detail than any he had guarded before. When he realized this, then Agent Gammon felt more appreciated. It was like the president was a member of his own team.

"Paul, I am handing a mission to you. No, I am keeping you on a mission," the president spoke. "I want you to keep McDonald in the field."

"Piranha?" Ortega asked. "I hope so."

"Yes, Operation Piranha," the president affirmed. "It started as just oddball surveillance. I thought we could keep McDonald out of trouble for a while, but there's more now. Here's what we know. This morning, the DD CIA—Intel came to my office and brought with him an analyst. Now this analyst carried in the oddest set of blueprints, all rolled up underneath his arm. The DD wound the analyst up and turned him on. This man—an Italian guy, Nick Ricollo, very experienced—told quite a tale. Very logical. You'll be impressed. I looked at Ricollo's file. He's solid. Call to duty goes way back."

"Blueprints? You mean the blueprints Jack took from the

bungalow in the Amazon?" Paul asked.

"The same. Here's what this super-analyst Nick thinks they are. You won't believe it, Paul! We play this right and we're gonna take care of several problems all at once. Kicker is, we may end up in U.S. waters or even on land, along the east coast at some point. You know what the lawyers say that means. First thing I know, some foreign intelligence operation becomes a domestic legal problem. However, I will not limit my options on this one. Regardless of who else gets in on this, I want you and your *Arcturus* team staying on this job for now. If I can, and as soon as I can, I'll pass it to the FBI, but for now, you're on it. It's tight, and off the books. If this plays out like I think it's going to, I will be making a finding creating an exception to a particular executive order," the president ended dramatically, sitting back and taking a sip of beer.

General Paul Ortega—59 years old—at an age when most military men were long-retired, delighted in what he was hearing. He didn't want Jack pulled from the job. Something told him they just scratched the surface and they were all over this one. He knew what executive order the president must be referring to, and, so, politely, refrained from asking. No sense mentioning assassination yet.

"Okay. Got it. Jack's okay. Got roughed up a bit in a surprise takedown but he's okay—fit for duty. He did a hell of a job down there. I'll tell you about it sometime, but why don't you tell me what all of these Iranians and Venezuelans and barge-builders are up to?" the Deputy CG of SOCOM asked next.

At the end, General Paul Ortega sat back, impressed. He'd thought he could not be surprised after 35 years in special operations. Part of him enjoyed the enemy's sheer genius. Now that he'd been told, it all seemed so obvious. But, only now.

"So, we give him sufficient rope —"

"To hang himself," the president added, completing Paul's thought. President Bullington raised his glass, and the men clinked their glasses together.

"So, where are Jack and Gordon now?" President Bullington asked.

"Heading downriver tailing the mysterious barge traffic, and awaiting further orders," Paul Ortega replied.

*Arcturus* was on the job for the next phase, and what a catch they planned on this fishing trip!

# Part III: Seeking My Fortune

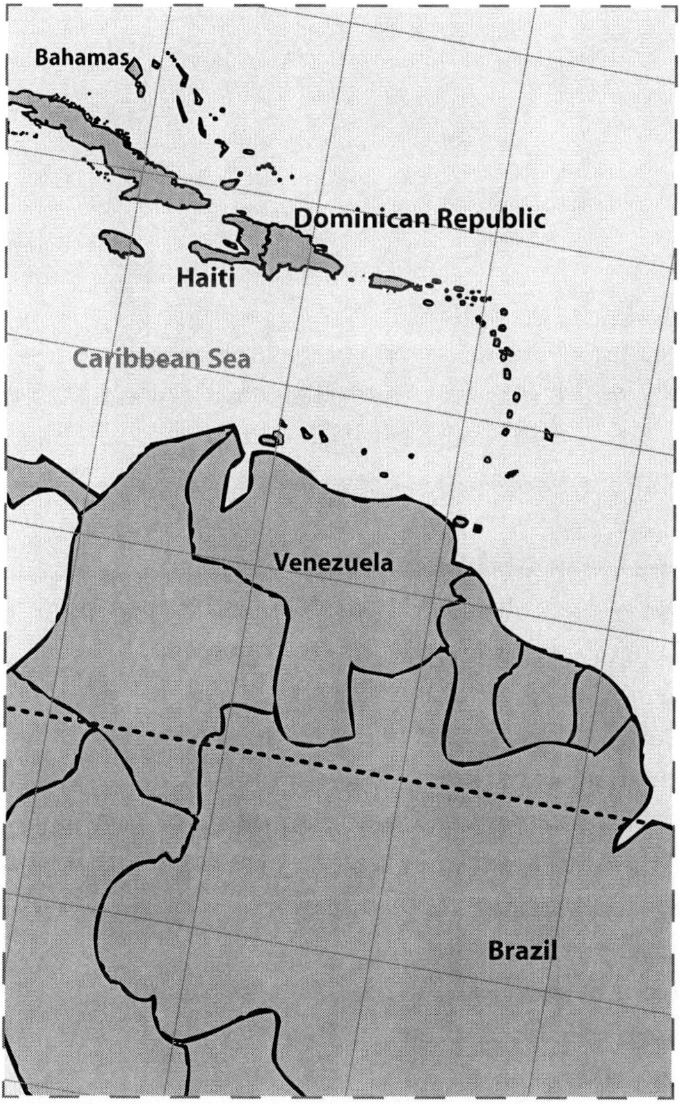

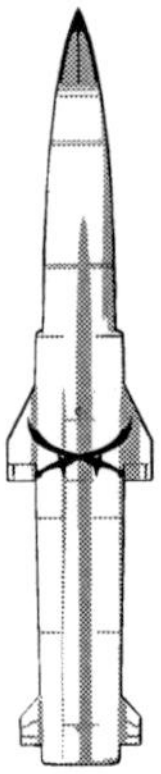

# 25

*Sunday*
*Aboard the Bay-B-Lie*
*Amazon River, 200 miles downriver from Manaus*

Shortly before sundown, Saya-dar noticed her.

"Bring me my telescope," he ordered his servant.

The quiet, slim man, dressed in white, fetched a brass-and-ivory telescope and handed it to his master.

"How long has that yacht been back there?" Saya-dar asked him.

"Since we left Manaus, master."

"Since we left Manaus? Hmm. We shall have to know more."

"Captain," Saya-dar spoke into the intercom.

"Yes, sir," came the immediate reply.

"Change course toward that creek mouth you see on the left—and slow to no wake speed," Saya-dar ordered.

Yet, the gleaming yacht continued on as the *Babylon* angled toward the north—toward a tributary creek pouring its contents into the ever-widening Amazon.

Probably a coincidence.

*There is no coincidence,* warned Saya-dar's mind.

"Sometimes, it's just chance."

*Not in Allah's world,* his mind countered.

"Yes, not in Allah's world," Saya-dar spoke, causing his servant to wonder.

"Do you enjoy fishing?" Saya-dar asked suddenly, causing his servant to wonder more.

"Why, yes, I have, master, I mean, I used to," stammered the now wary man, who grew up along the shore of one of Iran's northern lakes.

"Splendid! Quickly, now, fetch two outfits and join me at the bow!" Saya-dar commanded, delighted at his game.

The man complied, albeit nervously.

"Now, you and I shall see what we will catch," Saya-dar said when he returned.

Together, they threw in their lines over the anchored bow. Soon the anchor rope drew taut as the Amazon pushed to move the yacht on downstream and into the ocean. The *Bay-B-Lie* swung, coming about, pivoting on the anchor line until the bow faced upstream—toward the oncoming vessel.

"Stand here, please," crooned Saya-dar, directing his servant in front of him.

Saya-dar, the terrorist financier, the terrorist strategist, the terrorist mastermind, delighted in his ploy. He would respond to Allah's prompting and see what Allah had to offer him. Besides, one could not be too careful. The debacle at the bungalow below Manaus plagued him. What had he missed? Contract—purchase—inspect—pay—accept for delivery—launch. Simple. Nonetheless, someone murdered Fats and stole the payment money, injecting utter chaos into what should have been a straightforward business transaction. Just a home-invasion robbery? Did someone know about the money or was the robbery timing purely a coincidence? What could possibly have intervened to wreak havoc with such an elegant plan?

The servant actually caught one. A big peacock bass. Not exactly in the plan. Saya-dar waited impatiently for the excited man to reel in his catch. He posed with his proud servant for the benefit of anyone who might be watching. Now, with the servant again turned to the rail, Saya-dar positioned himself behind the man.

"Remain very still now. Just hold your rod out there, no casting," Saya-dar instructed.

Saya-dar extended his telescope and propped the end on his servant's shoulder. The sparkling water rippled into view, the setting sun shimmering the image in the scope's eyepiece. He could not find a white speck in the field. Saya-dar lowered the scope, looked again, found the yacht, and raised the scope carefully, sighting over the tube so he would not lose the yacht again in the low sun. This time, he found it.

*Nice,* he granted. About 80 feet he judged, comparable to his own. In minutes, the yacht's name began to come into focus. Saya-dar turned the variable power-ring carefully, keeping the approaching yacht in the telescope's field of view even as the field narrowed. The gleaming yacht grew. It rocked slightly. A minute or more perhaps before he could read the name. There.

Saya-dar fiddled with the focus ring, sharpening the image of the letters coming into view. The servant, growing weary, shifted on his feet. Saya-dar chastised the man bitterly. Once again, the telescope settled. With the yacht closer now and more squarely in front of the anchored *Bay-B-Lie,* the name came more plainly into view.

A cry escaped Saya-dar's lips. Saya-dar staggered backward in disbelief. *No! It is not possible!*

"Turn around, fool!" Saya-dar commanded his astonished servant. "Fish!"

The doubly-astonished man resumed what had been fun.

Saya-dar regained his composure quickly. From somewhere within his fears, *the name* had arisen. He was in the bowels of a vast jungle, far from the West's centers of power. Brazil mostly sat out the "war on terror" did it not? Thought itself outside the pulsing supernova of Islamic *jihad*—for now anyway—it thought. From time to time, some even made noises like gloating in the misfortune of its powerful neighbor to the north. Less of that lately. *The infernal Guevara*! Useful as a gadfly but—noisy! "Poke your spear only at the starving lion," Saya-dar recalled the saying. Guevara insisted on taunting the muscled beast to his north from the position of his own bloated impotence. Oil was the ironic joke played by Allah on the infidel. Like all jokes, it would fade. The infidel Guevara rode his oil like the crest of a never-ending victory wave. That wave, too, would someday expend its power.

No, Saya-dar shook his head as if to shake off the reality he had just seen. It simply could not be. The rippling light scattered by the vast river must have tricked him.

Saya-dar seized the servant and bade him be still again. Again, Saya-dar propped the scope on the servant's shoulder and peered through the eyepiece at the impossible apparition, growing in size. The name on the bow was, indeed, unmistakable.

*Arcturus,* Saya-dar read, as if reading his fate.

Saya-dar dropped the scope quickly down. How could it possibly be so? What did this mean? Was Allah playing a cruel trick? Punishing him for indiscretions? Saya-dar didn't really believe in all of that, but now *the name* forced him to more seriously entertain the notion that, despite his *jihad,* he did not stand in favor with Allah, whatever that meant. Saya-dar's calculating mind resumed control over the sick feeling welling up inside him.

Two years had passed since he'd gone after the *Arcturus*—gone after her captain. He'd failed, and only narrowly averted capture! He'd heard nothing of her since and never found anything about the incident in the local newspaper. He'd scoured the *Knoxville News-Sentinel* online reports for days, sure that such a fracas must have attracted swarms of law enforcement officers and reporters. An automatic weapons firefight in the middle of the night usually did that, even in the American South. Yet, Saya-dar had read nothing of it in the paper.

Saya-dar had his assistant check the local news for another year, but life had gone on in the hills of the Tennessee city by the river as if nothing had happened. Saya-dar reckoned his entire team had been killed during the assault on the lodge. At least, he *hoped* they had been killed. The thought that one of his men might have been captured terrified him. Still, there had been no repercussions that he could discern. Saya-dar had been relieved, finally relaxing. Now, that silence struck him as deceptive, and his own relaxation struck him as premature. Saya-dar cursed his own stupidity. There could be only one explanation: the power behind the wheel of the *Arcturus* sufficed to impose silence even on the noisy American news.

And now, here she was! Less than a quarter of a mile away!

Saya-dar shuddered as the *Arcturus* cruised languidly by. She seemed not to even know he was there! *This is insane*!

*The barge! She tracks the barge!* Somehow, she knows! Somehow, too, she had been guided to the northern Bahamas where he'd planted his Urns of Judgment two years ago, and now, somehow she had been guided here, deep within the Amazon jungle.

*The hand of God is against me*!

But to what purpose? Allah condemned the *infidel*, not his *Protector of the Faithful*. Why would Allah send this *Arcturus* across his path unless….

"Yes! Of course! Praise Allah!" Saya-dar stiffened and said, now bold. He laughed. His servant glanced around, nervously.

"You may stop fishing now, or you may continue if you like. Do you enjoy fishing?" Saya-dar asked.

The servant, Hamid, was born northwest of Teheran, in Rashakan, by Lake Urmia. Hamid often wondered why he had ever left to serve this irreverent madman in steamy, God-forsaken corners of the world. He prayed he would give the right answer. Hamid opted for simple honesty.

"Yes, master, I enjoy fishing!" Hamid replied.

"So do I! I enjoy fishing very much!" Saya-dar proclaimed.

*Odd, I've never seen you fish before*, Hamid thought, but did not say.

"We will fish! We will rise from this river like its anaconda, and we will crush our prey. We have entered this mighty river at Allah's will. We have set into motion His holy plan and He has rewarded us by sending our enemy to us! Allah himself hands us our enemy and we need only to cast out the line and hook, and accept His great gift. This *Arcturus*—this false Keeper of Heaven—insults Allah and Allah graces me—His true Protector of the Faithful—as His instrument—the instrument of Allah's own revenge! I am *Jabbar: The Avenger*! Allah appoints me as His Avenger! I shall add this title. I am now *Allah's Avenging Protector of the Faithful*! *Jabbar, Saya-dar*!"

*Arcturus* steamed on into the early evening, the name painted on her stern burning hatred into Saya-dar's eyes, mind, and evil heart.

# 26

*Same Sunday evening*
*Amazon River, aboard the Arcturus*

"Nice yacht," Jack said.

"The *Arcturus*? Yes, she certainly is," Gordon said.

"No, I mean that one," Jack said, pointing to the north at a long, shapely, white yacht anchoring just off the riverbank.

"Our companion, you mean," said Gordon, referring to the fact that the yacht had been mostly in their sight since they embarked from Manaus." Yes. She was docked at the Hotel Tropical, you know. I took a couple of digital pictures of her there this morning, Gordon said."

No, Jack didn't know. He should have. He should have made the same observation. *What is wrong with me?*

"You worried about it?" Jack asked.

"No, no reason to be. However, I am—curious. She's quite a luxurious yacht for cruising the Amazon, is she not? Getting in some fishing? Nothing really unusual about that, really. Eco-tourism has boomed here. That might account for it." Then, Gordon added, "However, that yacht has motored ahead of us all day. I cannot help but wonder if that yacht is also tracking the barge."

"Not anymore. Our shadow is falling behind," Jack observed.

"Why? To fish? Collect eco-samples. Maybe to check us out or throw us off. The *Bay-B-Lie*," Gordon noted, sighting through his binoculars. "I'll run its name and registration and check it out."

Gordon and Jack stepped off the deck and into the teak-lined pilothouse. From the wireless work-station by the wheel, Gordon sent an email inquiry.

Saya-dar tore open the package, carefully broke out the pre-paid SIM card, and inserted it into his mobile phone's SIM card slot. After tolerating the usual power-up glitz, he keyed in a number from memory—his memory.

"*Señor*, it is I. We must meet. Are you yet in Manaus?" Saya-dar asked Carlos Guevara, the dictator of Venezuela, his ally, and his new business associate.

"Why, yes, I remain in Manaus for now. I return home tomorrow. Where, and when might we meet?" the dictator asked.

"I am returning to Manaus and could meet you there at once. In the morning or late tonight even. Would you be able to extend to me this kindness?" Saya-dar asked.

The man on the other end of the call considered. He weighed the risk but so foolishly flirted with his own destruction anyway. Mostly, Carlos Guevara weighed the money. This caller *paid.* Paid very well. He also weighed their common currency: hatred for the Americans. With some fear, he also weighed what this wily Persian already knew about him—enough to bring the *Yanqis* after him—if they dared! Already, he'd thought he'd taunted them enough to at least provoke a reaction, but they largely ignored him. Him!

No, they did not ignore him; they *insulted* him. They would not treat him with such disrespect for much longer. The Americans had made the wrong enemy!

Thus, the foolish Guevara, who should have run from such a dangerous liaison, instead agreed, flouting both the Monroe and Bush Doctrines.

Still, he did not trust Saya-dar. He'd have to think about this. He'd have to plan for this meeting.

"Certainly, for you my friend—my brother—I will wait. I will meet you for breakfast in the morning. I welcome your return," Guevara responded.

"You are a most gracious friend. I will see you on the patio of the Hotel Tropical for breakfast at 7:00 if that is satisfactory," Saya-dar ended, hoping the early hour did not suggest desperation on his part.

Saya-dar felt sickened by the man. *Brother*! The puffing, godless fool! *Brother*! Yet, Saya-dar needed him for now. Needed his friendly ports. Needed the fire of Guevara's anger. Needed his—connections in this part of the world, so close to the United States. Saya-dar ordered the *Bay-B-Lie* to weigh anchor, reverse course and return to the Hotel Tropical where he'd have to meet with Carlos Guevara, the President of Venezuela, once again.

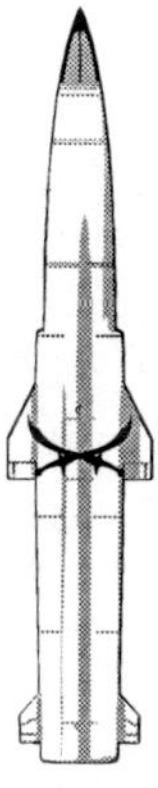

# 27

*0600 Monday morning*
*Fort Bragg, North Carolina*
*Headquarters,*
*Special Operations Command*

In Fort Bragg, North Carolina, Master Sergeant David Burnell returned to his desk from the coffee-maker and checked his email. By now, he knew better than to try to plan his day. Just be ready for whatever. "Stand by and help these boys in the field however I can," was Sergeant Burnell's mission, now. So, the email message from "nix-x-ist" did not surprise him at all, but it commanded his attention. Gordon "No One" Noone communicated only when it was life or death, or when he was hot on the trail and he and Jack were closing in, just needing a little discreet investigatory work on Burnell's end.

Part of Sergeant Burnell's job was to know where to go for answers to these odd inquiries. Eighteen years in special operations, the last several as General Paul Ortega's Operations Sergeant, thickened his book of intelligence and operations contacts. It was easy enough. He'd eaten dust and dodged lead with most of those "contacts."

Burnell bypassed the usual suspects—CIA analysts and those in official channels—and simply called Mr. Hale.

One of those guys who got into computers early, before there was a Computer Science major or any recognized education track into the field, Hale had carved his way in on skill. A commo-sergeant in a Special Forces A-Team by day and cross-trained in combat medicine, Hale latched onto an early "hardened" laptop and made it his constant companion. The laptop launched his new career.

The Army embraced IT along with the business world, thirsting for timely intelligence it could share with line troops quickly. At SOCOM, like everywhere else in America, dependence on computers made it clear that you needed someone around to fix the accursed things. You either had to have a reliable little company down the street or a teenage son. Lacking a teenage son with a Top Secret clearance, the Commanding General of SOCOM at the time hijacked Mr. Hale from his A-Team and made him SOCOM's IT guy—the General's "Special Assistant for Digital Affairs" they named him over guffaws. Everybody thought that was funny and they razzed him mercilessly—at first. Then, troubling things began happening to their bills, their bank accounts, and their computers. Mr. Hale made his point and the bawdy jokes stopped.

Knowledge is power.

Naturally, serving such Army clientele under the SOCOM "cloud" as Delta Force, Special Forces, SEAL teams, and the Ranger Battalions, Mr. Hale's duties grew beyond guiding frustrated users through using PowerPoint, or through the occasional processor upgrade or cooling fan replacement. From time to time, his customers found it convenient to hack into someone's computer. When no one wanted to bring an investigation to NSA's attention, or when no one wanted to wait to be shuttled among other priorities, the SOCOM commander just had Mr. Hale do it. "Give 'em Hale!" became a common command at Fort Bragg's SOCOM HQ.

After one of Mr. Hale's intrusions into a European bank's system took only 20 minutes, the Commanding General woke up in the middle of the night in a panic and called Mr. Hale at home. "How vulnerable are *we*?" the general had demanded to know.

This hurt Mr. Hale's feelings. He calmly explained to his boss that everything he learned, he put into practice guarding their own system. He had his counterpart at NSA trying to hack SOCOM. He had his counterpart at Eglin Air Force Base in special air operations trying to hack SOCOM. He had his brother-in-law trying to hack SOCOM. They all tried to hack each other. "Like the Bible says, 'Iron sharpens iron,'" he explained.

Now Hale had the CG of SOCOM fully awake.

"Your brother-in-law! Hale! What does he do for a living?"

"He keeps books for a string of car dealerships in the Virginia Tidewater area," Mr. Hale told him.

The general had yelled, rather ineloquently Mr. Hale thought, but, then again, it was 2:45 a.m.

"What if some civilian breaks into my computer? Can you imagine the repercussions and the press?" the general had exclaimed, panicking.

"Repercussions?" (Here, Hale utterly failed to suppress an impolitic laugh. Aren't those IT guys like that?)

'I'll tell you the repercussions, sir. He'll tell me, sir. So will my buddies if they succeed. If you run this through official channels, they'll tell the Inspector General and shifty dweebs in suits who think a mortar tube is what you grout bathroom tile with will knock on your door trying to end your career. Bringing down a barrel-chested 3-star will be their shining achievement in life. Some Army-hater will leak it to a congressional staffer. Some Marxist agitator in Congress will smell ink mixed with your blood and, next thing you know, you'll be Ollie Northing in front of Congress. Ollie pulled it off, but do you even want to have to contend in that arena? Sir?" Hale added.

The general got the point and did not fail to note that Mr. Hale had covered his ass without his even being aware.

When Mr. Hale retired, he formed his own company and offered the Department of Defense information security services. DOD was "Ho-hum" unimpressed with this former sergeant's overtures. Then he hacked into DOD's system and wrote the code that automatically re-submitted his proposal as the head of their IT department's screen saver. This time, they not only ignored him; they tried to bury him. So, Mr. Hale sighed tiredly, and played his cards to his former commander, now the Assistant Secretary of Defense for Special Operations. After they both finished belly-laughing at how simply the former Green Beret IT "hobbyist" had cracked the Defense Department, the general made some calls and—*voila*!—the new Harmony Church Security Services Company was in business with a lucrative contract. In no time at all, Mr. Hale was, indeed, buried—in more work than he could handle.

The nondescript but deadly, brilliant, and patriotic Mr. Hale had never let the United States down. He wasn't about to now, either. Burnell had seen him last year on Dupont Circle at Fort Bragg, North Carolina, chewing Bar-B-Q (that would be pork) and drinking cold beer at the Deputy SOCOM Commander's house after the general's retirement ceremony. Old Hale still looked the computer-guy part, but Burnell saw his muscles were still hard, and he knew the man's combat record and wounds. Two Purple Hearts and the Silver Star for action in the Balkans where he wasn't supposed to be.

Mr. Hale emailed back a characteristically simple, mid-morning reply:

The *Bay-B-Lie* is owned by a Saudi oil-drilling support and oil transport company. The company has no known—I emphasize *known*—connection to any terrorist or terrorist suspect. More? Just holler, Bernie.

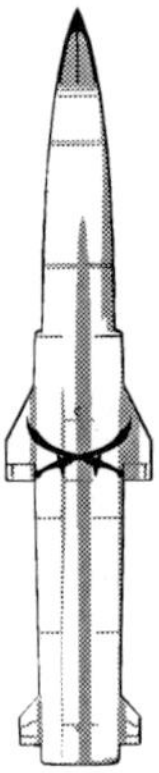

# 28

*Monday morning, 7:00 a.m.*
*Hotel Tropical, on the patio*
*overlooking the Rio Negro*
*Manaus, Brazil*

"I must be quick. Thank you for delaying your departure and meeting with me," Saya-dar said to Carlos Guevara.

"You're most welcome. Please tell me what urgent business cancelled your cruise and compelled your return to Manaus?" Guevara asked.

The two men arose and strolled through the hotel's courtyard. Neither fully trusted the rooms. Guevara still had his rented and they could have conversed there, surrounded by dark-paneled woods reminiscent of the jungle that lay just beyond the hotel. Guevara understood that Saya-dar would also not fully trust him—the table on the patio might be bugged, or surveillance might be set up, with listening devices aimed at the table. So, they each chose a random stroll about the grounds and down to the grassy, carefully mowed bank of the Rio Negro.

"We might have been followed," Saya-dar said.

"Followed?" Guevara repeated, alarmed. "By whom? The Marine Police? The Federal Police?"

"No, by an old acquaintance. An old enemy. On a yacht named *Arcturus,*" Saya-dar said, cryptically.

"Who is on this yacht? The Americans?" Guevara demanded.

Carlos Guevara, the mouthy dictator, strained to contain his alarm. His destruction seemed a bit closer. His personal poltergeist that always whispered, whispered into his ear, urging him to new heights in mocking the Americans loosened its grip for just a moment. He remembered the scene from "Clear and Present Danger" where the missile falls from the sky, and looked up.

"No, not the government. A man. Look, Mr. Guevara, I need you to arrange for this man's demise—if he is, indeed, following us. If not, we may let him be for now. Perhaps he sold the yacht. Perhaps there is another of the same name. But, perhaps his presence here is no coincidence. If he continues to follow the *Khazir*, then I need you to take him out, as the gangsters say. In a manner not pointing back to me or to you. I think you know such men who could do this task." Saya-dar said, coming to the point.

"Yes, it could be arranged. How will we know whether you and I must do this job?" Guevara asked.

"In one more day, the *Khazir* will reach the Atlantic Ocean. Before that, it passes through the estuary." Here, Saya-dar became more excited. "The Amazon's estuary is vast, I am sure you know. I looked; it is nearly 100 miles wide from north to south." Saya-dar began.

"Yes, that is so, but almost all traffic passes down the northern channel by Macapa—using the *Canal do Norte*," Guevara pointed out.

"Exactly! We will re-route the *Khazir* to leave this North Canal, turn south, pass the Island of Serraria and then continue westward toward the Atlantic through the Southern Canal—the *Canal do Sul*. There would be no reason whatsoever for the *Arcturus* to follow unless it intends us harm. If *Arcturus* continues on its way without following us, then we assume it is no threat.

We leave her be. If, however, it follows the *Khazir*, then I am certain that it tracks us! If so, it must be eliminated before the *Khazir* enters your port at Maiquetia," Saya-dar said, slowing to emphasize the critical timing of the kill.

"Yes, I would not want your barge traced to my port," Guevara agreed.

"Will you do it?" Saya-dar pressed.

"Do what?"

"Prepare a way to remove the *Arcturus* if she follows the *Khazir* into the *Canal do Sul*?" Saya-dar said, straining to preserve his patience. "Can you?"

"Yes, of course," Guevara said

"How?"

"How? Do you care? Do you really want to know, Saya-dar?" Guevara asked.

"Yes, I must know. I must make certain that your means looks like an ordinary crime or accident," Saya-dar explained.

Guevara laughed. "Pirates still ply the waters of the Caribbean, my friend. They lack the glamour and romance ascribed to them by Hollywood, but they surpass the old buccaneers in boldness and cruelty. Alas, their small but very fast boats are not the grand galleons of the past, but these overpowered pirate launches are more like the Americans' famous PT boats." Guevara laughed again. "Look, Saya-dar, I have arrangements with men who captain such crews. They frequent my border with Guyana. The law in those coastal border regions is—loose, shall we say? I find that convenient from time to time and do not molest the pirates who operate there. They return my favor and remain at my service to perform certain jobs as I request. They are very effective. I assure you, this could be arranged," Guevara bragged.

"Excellent. It is so arranged, then?" Saya-dar pressed to close.

"No."

"No? I do not understand," Saya-dar said.

Carlos Guevara looked hard at Saya-dar. In Saya-dar's eyes, he saw the dangerous kind of madness induced by hatred but not clouded by stupidity. Guevara briefly fretted that his own hatred for America had not crossed a line with this operation he plotted with Saya-dar. He resumed more soberly, more slowly, more confidentially.

"Saya-dar, my shady friend, I note that while you and I plot destruction on the Great Satan, neither you nor I drove one of those 20 suicide-bomber trucks we slipped into the belly of The Beast. We have remained discreet—distant—or at least we thought we had. The imperialists have a long reach. They leave me alone, and I've tried hard to make them believe I am but noise. I tweak their nose, but we do business. I am pushing it already by inviting the Russians to visit me. America is too pre-occupied with its politics and economy right now, but someday, somebody there with some balls will read some report and will not like it that I invited the Russian Navy to lob pot shots at their Monroe Doctrine.

'From time to time, you may have noticed, they wake up unpredictably, become agitated, and send down destruction on the enemy *de jour.* Libya. Iraq. Afghanistan. Even Granada in my own part of the world! And Noriega! I must never forget what they did to Noriega! If the imperialists suspect your *Khazir* as having anything to do with any threat to them, they may turn their attention to your barge and begin studying it. They may guess how we worked out our plans. If so, they may trace the barge back to Manaus and *Señor* Fats there. I am connected to Fats and you to me. Agreed?"

Saya-dar had to agree.

"If you must pirate the *Arcturus*, then we must interdict the *Americanos* on the *Arcturus* well before they or your barge reach Venezuelan waters and keep all of this action away from my country's coast. So, yes, I will arrange this thing for you," Guevara said. "But, no, you must find another port for your—cargo—to be loaded onto the *Khazir*."

"But, —," Saya-dar protested.

"That is final."

Saya-dar stared at the man, his ally. The Shade, The Protector of The Faithful, was not accustomed to being told no. What would it take for this, this anachronistic Marxist dictator to see it his way? What was wrong with Guevara?

Saya-dar saw fear in Guevara's eyes. Fear. *Fear outweighs the fool's blustering ego!*

Fear also freezes men into inaction. Saya-dar sifted the tyrant before him and saw that—for now—Guevara's fear paralyzed him; Saya-dar perceived that no threats or reasoning would move the dictator to change his mind. Saya-dar over-rode the fierce anger within him toward the man and chose a new course. He had time while his navy steadily plied the waters toward America. He would find a way to achieve his aims and change the dictator's mind, but that would not happen this sunny morning.

Saya-dar thanked Guevara and bade him good day. Saya-dar left his newspaper with Guevara. Saya-dar had already read the news and knew the paper's contents.

Carlos Guevara checked around the grounds. He spied all four teams of big, tough men—his bodyguards for the day. He knew them all and had handpicked them. Every one of them had killed. He sent each recruit to one of his prisons where the warden handed the recruit a letter. The letter was written by Carlos Guevara himself. In that letter, Guevara ordered the recruit to torture and kill a particular prisoner. Those who balked lost the job. Those who completed this final interview passed the test and joined a very well-paid and well-entertained crew of bodyguards. In this way, Guevara knew the men would not hesitate to kill on his behalf. They already had.

The bodyguards looked back expectantly, trying to discern their boss's next move. Guevara nodded to the chief bodyguard. His chief nodded to one of his subordinates, and that man moved his team inside the hotel. Less than a minute later, the man returned to the door and nodded to Guevara. He had checked the bar area and assured his boss the bar was safe for him to enter.

Guevara moved from the patio, already beginning to bake in the Amazon sun, then paused and stood between two white-stucco columns at the entrance to the hotel. He looked overhead. Was that sound the hum of a boat engine on the river or a predator drone—one of those with the Hellfire missile attached, sent by the CIA? An aluminum fishing boat emerged from behind the palm trees on the bank by the seaplane dock and Guevara breathed again.

Guevara turned, made his way through the lobby, and stepped down into the wood-floored bar area. Guevara picked the table indicated by his team and sat down on one of the wicker chairs, by one of the palm trees in the bar. The waiter immediately brought a Caipirinha. The sweet, strong, Brazilian rum-like drink and lime soothed his nerves. Guevara downed it and ordered another. His bodyguard looked just a bit too long but obeyed.

Two years had passed since the modified Iranian tanker

delivered 22 young Middle Eastern men—20 bombers and 2 spares—to his docks at the port at Maiquetia, just over the mountains and a scant 10 miles from his palace at Caracas. He'd housed them only fleetingly before they filed aboard his own modified tanker, the *Mi Fortuna,* under cover of darkness. Sayadar's agents had supervised transferring the men from the sleeping quarters he had provided at the docks to the *Mi Fortuna.* Guevara had watched from a distance.

Really, all he had done was order the modifications to the tanker and let these young terrorists sleep at his wharf for a few nights.

No, his role was greater than that. His own *Mi Fortuna* brought the terrorists to America. They'd made their journey across the Caribbean and then the Gulf of Mexico hidden in the concealed quarters Fats had built into the hull.

After they blew themselves up in 20 trucks (Guevara wondered what the spare two felt.), Guevara had intended to undo the secret chamber and its only visible sign—the cut-steel, removable hull patch that served as the exit for the secret cargo. But, he had so delighted in the havoc he'd helped wreak, he just couldn't do it. *Might need it again someday,* he'd thought.

Perhaps he'd been too bold. Yes, two years had passed, but what if some unforeseen clue created that one little trace back to him? What if the Americans began to construct the pieces into a picture and the image that began to emerge from the mist of clues and secrets was his own image!

But how could they? He wished he'd de-constructed the chamber on the *Mi Fortuna* now, but nothing connected him to Fats and his work far up the Amazon. That was a cash and gold deal with no records. Were there? Had Fats made records that he had not said anything about, despite their agreement to keep nothing in writing? Had the Americans found the money? That would not help them. Guevara had paid Fats in dollars! And so what if the Americans discovered that Guevara was a customer of Fats, so what? Many were the legitimate customers of the butchered shipwright. Nothing could connect the job Fats had done with Guevara's helping to infiltrate 22 Islamic terrorist suicide bombers into Mobile Bay.

Yet, what happened there at Fats' home that night? Guevara had been shocked to read of Fats' murder in the local paper.

*The paper. Where is it?*

He must have left the paper on his table outside. Guevara motioned for the waiter, who appeared immediately. He ordered the newspaper retrieved to see if more news had developed about the murder. It came with the second Caipirinha. Guevara spread one and lifted the other.

*Ah, good! My invitation to the Russian Navy has captured the headlines!* Momentarily, Guevara forgot about the local reporting on Fats' murder and delved with relish into the article announcing his own grand theater performance with the Russians.

> The United States Navy re-activated its 4th Fleet to patrol the Caribbean waters, and this did not go unnoticed by the U.S.'s chief critic in the region, President Carlos Guevara. The Latin American dictator invited the Russian Navy for a visit. Soon, Russian naval vessels and even Russian soldiers will conduct joint military exercises off the coast of Venezuela.
>
> As if this provocation were not enough, Guevara offered the Russians a landing strip for their strategic

> bombers, capable of striking the U.S. mainland: "Why, yes, if Russian long-range airplanes [Here, Guevara had winked at the reporter.] ask for a place to land, I will gladly oblige my strategic partners," President Guevara told reporters.
>
> At a news conference Tuesday, a Pentagon spokesman responded: "The Russian Navy is a blip on the radar screen compared to our naval forces, and Guevara is a posturing buffoon."

*Buffoon! A posturing buffoon!*

Guevara reddened, and not from the increasing sun piercing the glass roof, lighting the palm and jungle-wood bar. He forgot all about the murdered Fats, the vanished Iranians and the disappearance of Fats' exotic housekeeper. He forgot about Muhammar Khadafy, about "Clear and Present Danger," and he forgot about predator drones. He even forgot about Manuel Noriega now languishing in an American prison, courtesy of American special forces troops. With hands trembling from rage—the rage that surpasses protective fear—Carlos Guevara reached for his phone, flipped it open hard, jabbed his stubby fingers at his contacts, and called Saya-dar.

Saya-dar found Guevara still in the bar. As Saya-dar stepped down into the wood-floored bar area, he noted two empty glasses on the table and the edginess displayed by Guevara's security. Saya-dar strode toward the table, but Guevara did not get up. Instead, Saya-dar noted, Guevara gripped the newspaper Saya-dar had intentionally left, unfolded to an article Saya-dar had thought Guevara might be interested in.

"I am grateful, my friend. What do you ask in return?" Saya-dar asked, not particularly surprised at the sudden change of heart—and hardness in Guevara's voice.

Guevara leaned in to make his appeal, now the eager buyer, not the disinterested seller.

*A far cry from his cautious rebuff of only a few minutes ago,* Saya-dar observed. *Took less time than I thought.*

"A diversion. Merely a diversion! Can you draw them from my coast? Can you draw their attention to some other place, some other harbor? Draw this *Arcturus* away from Caracas. Get them to move away, to the north and east. Do that and I invite you to Maiquetia Port where you may do your business." Guevara said.

Saya-dar smiled and made a bowing gesture. "You are so kind. Truly, a man with the heart of a lion. This is why I so respect you, *Señor* Guevara. I knew your courage. It is already done. I will take care of the rest."

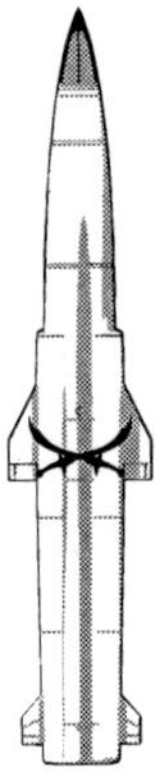

# 29

*Monday*
*Downriver, aboard Arcturus*

Two hours later than at Fort Bragg, considering Burnell's reply over mid-Monday morning coffee, Jack asked Gordon: "Rich Sheikh touring the world?"

"What do you think, Jack?"

"I think we lack sufficient information to surmise anything other than noting that the 19 hijackers came from the homeland of *Wahhabi* Islam—same place that yacht came from. I think it's a connection to be explored further and—hopefully—eliminated."

"Eliminated? You are that ready to kill them? My, aren't you bloodthirsty? What was that Jack Nicholson typed at that lodge in *The Shining*? 'All work and no play makes Jack a dull boy'—over and over. REDRUM!" Gordon teased.

"No, I'm too sore to off somebody today. I want this *Bay-B-Lie* eliminated from our threat list by the twin barrels of facts and logic," Jack replied. "After all, the mind is your most powerful weapon."

"How Zen. Been reading those military motivational posters again? Agreed, then. But, explored further how?" Gordon asked.

"I want its customs check-in log for the last three years. I'd like to know where—at least on record—this *Bay-B-Lie* has been," Jack said. Then, Jack added one more request.

"Gordon, this Saudi yacht's appearance here, coinciding with Iranians and Guevara reminds me of something. You remember what Colonel Casteńeda told us? He was visited in Havana by a rich Iranian playboy type who cruised in on this luxurious super-yacht, the *Babylon.* Instead of bearing gifts, this wise man from afar came to buy radioactive material for a dirty bomb. Instead of riding in on a camel, he rode in on a super-yacht. He called Casteńeda and cancelled the planned infiltration, but—it just looks so, so similar. We never saw the *Babylon,* but here is this other Middle Eastern yacht—grander than the *Arcturus*—named *Bay-B-Lie. Bay-B-Lie.* I wonder what that name means, if anything. It seems odd. Of course, so many of these yacht names are contorted takeoffs on some business success or some misadventure. Like the *Monkey Business.* I don't remember that one, of course, but I bet you do," Jack teased. "Anyway, Gordon, I don't like it at all."

"Agreed again. I'll see if Sergeant Burnell can get us the answers to both lines of inquiry. He's a Farsi expert; he'll probe the name significance personally."

Gordon tapped out another inquiry to Burnell, adding the request that he examine the name specifically. "Play with it phonetically and check it in various languages, particularly Middle Eastern languages. I know this is a long shot, but let's see what we turn up." Gordon wrote in his email from nix-x-ist.

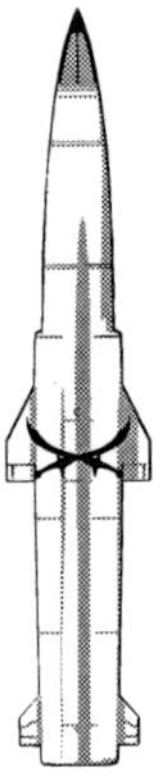

# 30

*Monday*
*Special Operations Command*
*Headquarters, Meadows Field*
*Fort Bragg, North Carolina*

Master Sergeant David Burnell read Gordon's new questions, and sat back, munching his tuna sandwich. He had already looked up *Bay-B-Lie.* Cryptic. Clever. It had taken some thought and research. Though steeped in Persian history, the significance and identity of the *Bay-B-Lie* were plain.

Sergeant Burnell swiveled, arose, and walked to his window, overlooking Meadows Field. He shifted his weight off his aching left leg and peered out the window onto the field lit by the noon sun.

Burnell did this a lot. "Bronze Bruce" looked back Burnell's direction, but from off to Sergeant Burnell's right. The Bronze Bruce wasn't looking at Burnell, though. The Vietnam era, Special Forces Sergeant First Class statue attended to the mission, not the headquarters, weapon ready, leading. On the field of battle. And, Bronze Bruce looked toward The Wall.

The Wall. The special forces soldiers represented there. Fallen. The names there on that plain, brown brick wall faced away from Burnell. While from Burnell's office window there at Special Operations Command HQ he could not see them, he did not need to see them. They were etched into his mind. Never, never were the names, and the living whose names might one day appear there, far from Sergeant Burnell's heart. He had known some of them.

For the thousandth time, Burnell watched the unmoving memorial statue. He thought about what happens to field operators when too many people know their whereabouts. He worried about Gordon and Jack, and how Saya-dar had come to be in the same waters in a most unexpected location. Why was the Iranian terrorist mastermind who had tried to kill Gordon and Jack before, now shadowing them now in the Amazon? Who had been careless and let out knowledge of their operating there? Plenty of people knew about it; too many, from Burnell's point of view.

The British knew. The Brazilians knew. That housekeeper knew. As operations go, this one might as well have been splashed across the Associated Press, as far as Burnell was concerned.

Sergeant Burnell returned to his desk and his worries on the men's behalf. He wondered if the appearance of the *Bay-B-Lie* signaled another attack on Gordon and Jack—another raid to kill them.

This was not theoretical to Master Sergeant David Burnell of 24 years' service in the Army. The pain in his left hip constantly brought his failings before him. Or at least his doubts, for he would never know if he'd failed to secure his own operation and caused the deaths of an entire Iranian family. Sergeant Burnell returned to Iran, often, in his deepest agony. He returned to people, faces, names that would never be memorialized, but names of the brave, nonetheless.

The younger Staff Sergeant Burnell had first met the couple from Iran when all were students at Ohio State University where he was cadre with the ROTC detachment there. He made friends with the husband, just drinking coffee at the Ohio Union. Casual conversation at first. Then, they met regularly to socialize, becoming fast friends with both the man and his wife, though from different worlds. As part of his routine reports, he had reported the foreign-national contact to SOCOM, where he knew he would return after the ROTC assignment.

He had talked hours into the night with his friends. America. What was right. What was wrong. The glory of man freed from tyrannical government. The bizarre degeneracy of this same freed man, reveling in license. The foolishness of religious rules, burdening down people's souls with guilt and shame. The absurdity of legal rules run amok, grounded only on the shifting sands of human whim. The wonders men wrought when liberated. The emptiness of their grand accomplishments when weighed against their depravity.

His Iranian friends had wanted to stay in the United States but could not. Visas approached expiration, and it was time to go. Burnell saw them off at the airport. Couldn't say much; the local informant had come along, too.

A few years later, Burnell was called in for a mission briefing: infiltrate, establish contact, recruit his friend as an agent. No agents in Iran. No, not one. Yes, yes, we know, pathetic intelligence failure. The Army can't wait for the politicians to get their heads out of their collective ass. Let CIA deal with them. You're going in, Burnell. That's the mission.

Burnell knew the importance of the mission. Every special

operator with any age on him at all ached over the catastrophe that overtook Operation Eagle Claw at Desert One. A young Ranger corporal then, Burnell watched, horrified, as tragedy compounded upon accident, killing his friends and breaking his commander's heart. His own heart broke as he hauled in the last man to board the C-130 Combat Talon transport, the newly-formed Delta Force operator in jeans, running madly to catch the Talon, already beginning its takeoff run. In the flames, re-shuffling among the available transports, and with the general FUBAR, they had almost left this man behind! What a fate that would have been! What would the Iranians have done to him?

Major Paul Ortega had never forgotten Sergeant Burnell's strong hand, stretching out to grab his equipment harness, heaving him aboard that rolling Talon as the wheels left the sand, and saving his life. The flames roaring behind him lit the young corporal's face forever in Ortega's memories.

Because they lacked agents inside Iran, Jim Ryan, John Carney and "Bud" had infiltrated into Iran to set up Desert One and the rescue, a behind-the-lines secret mission against suicidal odds. How did they summon up the guts to do that? Had the U.S. recruited and run a network of agents inside Iran over decades, that kind of high-risk, outlandish bravery would not have been necessary. But, Congress had cut back the CIA's funds and operations after Vietnam, and the president at the time showed no inclination to be strong abroad, so the Iranian hostage crisis caught the country off-guard and unprepared. "No agents, no not a single one," they told Burnell.

Good men die when their political leaders cower before the press and the public, and fail to prepare to defend the country. They should *lead* despite the odds and criticism. It's the military that bears the brunt of political cowardice.

So, Burnell knew that recruiting his friend—if possible—was as important as it was dangerous. Iran was full of people who admired the U.S. Getting to them and keeping regular contact was the problem.

Burnell infiltrated through the former Soviet Union, into the mountainous region far north of Teheran. He'd done it. He'd found their home. He'd stayed with them, talked with them, and recruited the husband—his friend—to befriend his country, as well. He would gladly serve as an American agent. He was destined for mounting success in his academic field and would work his way toward a professorship at one of the several Teheran universities, then, into government, or into some sensitive technical field. From there, he would work to free Iran from the grip of the Islamic Revolution, and he expected America to help him. To help Iran. Iran would face the same complex but wondrous task as America: creating a country where people at liberty exercised self-restraint instead of top-down oppression to keep them in line. An Iranian Republic instead of an Islamic Republic.

At least, that was the plan. The explosion in the middle of the night. RPG probably. Followed up by cursing men kicking in the door. Picking through the rubble. Bayoneting the children and the wife. Burnell watched it all—stunned and horrified—from underneath the stone and timbers that fell on him, pinned him, and choked him, nearly suffocating him. Watched his friend being dragged from beneath the kitchen table lying broken on top of him. Watched them kick him, beat him, and laugh. Heard them congratulating each other on the capture on the way out the doorway. Miraculously, in their excitement he supposed, they neglected to search for him. Neighbors waited until the killers left and dragged Burnell out from under the imprisoning rubble, hiding him at another house that night. Instead of turning him in, that frightened family had treated his broken leg and helped to smuggle him back out. Burnell prayed for them every night, hoping that God had protected them.

*I wonder what happened to them.*

*So, so many names. So, so many people.*

Had Burnell been seen coming or going? Had he been careless? Had his rescuers also been discovered and killed—or worse?

Had he messed up?

Master Sergeant Burnell, who owed his life to ordinary Iranians who risked it all to save him, would never know, but he thought he must have made *some* mistake that exposed the mission to discovery. The specter of his failure haunted his nights.

Now, here was this operation General Ortega and he were running down in the Amazon. Put together fast, it bore all of the risky marks of hasty planning. Operational security—OPSEC—took a back seat to expediency. No way to avoid getting on-the-ground help from the Brazilian government. No way to contain it after that. Jack ended up staying with a Brazilian Amazon fisherman on the government's payroll! Had someone talked? Had Burnell opened Death's door to yet another loyal friend of America? Somehow, all of this didn't seem to bother Ortega, but it bothered Burnell. A lot. Desperately, so desperately, he wanted no more ghosts. He did not want to add the face of young McDonald to his graveyard ghosts.

General Paul Ortega watched Master Sergeant David Burnell, his Operations Sergeant and friend. His rescuer. He knew Burnell's past. He knew what lay behind the thousand-yard stare on Burnell's face. Somehow, Ortega had long ago gotten over anguishing over whether his decisions sent others to death; of course, his plans and orders sent men to die. Ortega could name and count the men he knew had so died, and he knew there were others whose names he would never learn. Some, he had known would die when he relented and gave permission for them to go and do their urgently requested suicide missions. Mogadishu. Yet, somehow, Ortega knew that they died because they chose to fight, not because of his orders. They needed his official permission, but these were mature, trained-up, professional soldiers, eager to descend into the streets and exercise their skills to protect the pilot. They were fighters; they *had* to go. His authority released them, but their orders came from their hearts. So, Ortega never forgot, but he never blamed himself. Otherwise, the burden of command hindered you from commanding. And the men needed commanders, not emotional mincemeat. General Paul Ortega did the job: he commanded.

Even had Ortega stayed with the 82nd Airborne Division and declined the strange invitation into "this new unit" Bucky Burrus was forming, he would have lost men to the god of war. Wouldn't have mattered. If you are a combat officer, NCO, or soldier, you will hold the lives of others in your hands. You will make split second decisions—if you hesitate, then others will certainly die. You are not perfect, and you don't operate from perfect information.

Somehow, Paul reflected, as Burnell stood quietly across from him, at the window, waiting for the word, he, Paul Ortega, had the gift. Maybe someday it would all crush him, but he didn't think so. Hell, he loved it! Wouldn't trade…yes, he would. There were moments he'd re-live and do it better, but he'd still be a soldier. Someday, God would make it all right but right now, in the world of jungle, sand, and sin, an infantry division could sure solve a lot of problems. Ortega saw himself—and his men—as called. *Yep, that's a pretty high calling,* General Paul Ortega thought. *Enough! This calling means action. Continue the mission.*

"Bernie, you with me, man?" he asked, breaking Sergeant Burnell's reverie.

"Yes, sir! What are your orders, sir?" Sergeant Burnell snapped back.

"Send a five-man team south into the Caribbean by boat. Stage them where you think they will be in a convenient place to support Gordon by boat if he needs help. Disguise them as—I don't know—sport fishermen I guess. Tell Gordon we're sending reinforcements. Tell the Coast Guard to leave them alone. No more than we know now, that's about all we can do.

'Oh, I'm sure he's made some connection or he wouldn't have asked you about the name, but call Gordon and tell him you think this *Bay-B-Lie* is nothing more than that fiendish Shade's *Babylon* in sheep's clothing. Tell him looks like our potential catch just got even bigger."

"Roger. General?"

"Yes?"

"These names are important. Did Jack or Gordon tell you the name of the barge they are tracking down the Amazon?"

"No. There's no name on it."

"Odd. If, somewhere along the route, someone paints a name on it, I want to know," Sergeant Burnell said.

"Tell 'em," General Ortega said. "We can use all the clues we can get."

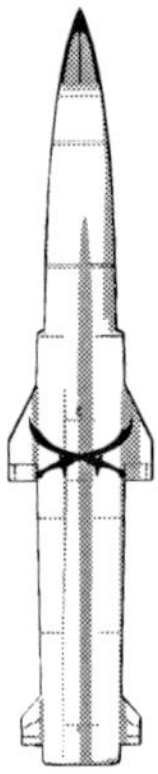

# 31

*Monday,*
*mid-afternoon Brazil time*
*Amazon River*

Jack printed Sergeant Burnell's email attachments and spread them out on the circular, glass-top table in the lounge.

"We have a problem," Jack said.

"What do you mean?" Gordon asked.

"The registration has been doctored. The yacht was manufactured five years ago. However, it's registration history is fresh, dating back only about one year. It has no registration history or customs check-in history before September of last year; yet, the boat is five years old. There's more."

"More?" Gordon did so enjoy the suspense.

"More. Burnell deciphered the yacht's name, or at least he has a solid theory. Man, when you ask an expert, you always learn more than you wanted to know. Here it goes." Jack drew a deep breath.

"Farsi is the modern Persian language spoken in Iran, Afghanistan and Tajikistan that developed from ancient Persian. They really are the same language, just modernized like English has been. This is where Burnell's study of ancient Persian helped.

'The name '*Bay-B-Lie*' could, of course, refer to some

playboy's secrets, or his wish that his favorite squeeze of the hour might recline. However, phonetically, it sounds the same as the Persian word 'babili' which means—drumroll please—'of or belonging to Babylon'."

"Oh. Oh, oh! *Babylon*! Not again!" Gordon exclaimed, absorbing the ramifications.

"There's more, Gordon. The name also may mean 'poison,'" Jack added. "Isn't this stuff interesting? So, if this Saya-dar, the owner of the *Babylon* wanted to disguise the *Babylon's* name, but just couldn't bring himself to abandon its significance to him...?" Jack pondered aloud. Gordon supplied the answer.

"He might try to hid it underneath one of these crazy yacht names that would look English to most people. Pretty clever, actually. In reality, he did not get far from his original name, *Babylon*, at all. *Babili*: of Babylon," Gordon said.

"Gordon, this is just unbelievable. No. It's the most logical explanation. Our enemy—whom we never saw—who eluded us before, was with us here in this far-flung corner of the world, fishing a few hundred yards from us."

By now, the *Arcturus* had plied the Amazon miles downstream from the *Bay-B-Lie*, now rocking again, tied to a pier north of Manaus, as Saya-dar worked his current plan for Jack's and Gordon's destruction.

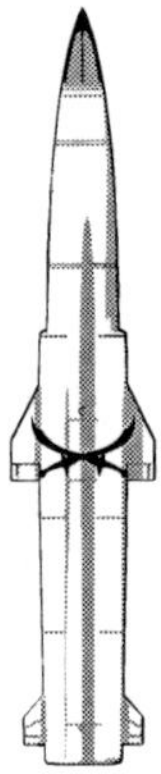

# 32

*Monday afternoon*
*Havana, Cuba*
*Office of the Cuban DGF*
*Deputy Chief*

Colonel Casteńeda flipped his cell phone open, checked caller ID, but did not recognize the number. He almost let it go to voicemail but jabbed at "Send" to answer and take the mysterious call. Knowledge of this number was restricted to the family, the Cuban government intelligence community, and Casteńeda agents. This might be an agent needing hand-holding.

"Colonel Casteńeda."

"My Cuban fisherman friend, how are you?" crooned Saya-dar.

The answering voice almost made Casteńeda drop the phone. *No! Unreal!* Casteńeda glanced around, then outside his window.

"Sa—, my fr—, I am so surp—pleased to hear from you," Casteńeda groped to recover. Saya-dar laughed. "Are you—in town?" Casteńeda asked, still trying to overcome his disbelief, but now moving to take tactical advantage of this unexpected gift.

Saya-dar laughed again, disarmingly.

"I'm out and about as you might say," he replied cryptically, calling from his room at the Hotel Tropical.

"Of course," Casteńeda resumed, "I ask only to know when I might enjoy your most generous hospitality again. I have not heard from you since our—adventure—in the northern Bahamas. Once you departed, I was forced to revert to the sorry excuse for rum we produce here. The quality of my lifestyle dropped dramatically! I had hoped you would return soon. However, I could not help but note the explosions across the *Yanqi* landscape after you sailed off, and I wondered if those had something to do with your sudden departure and disappearance," Casteńeda said, beginning to fish again.

"Oh, while I wish nothing but ill upon our mutual enemy, I was, of course, shocked to learn of the 20 simultaneous truck-bombings in places they thought they were safe. I cannot imagine who could have wreaked such clever havoc on your American neighbors," Saya-dar lied. Not giving Casteńeda time to question his integrity, Saya-dar resumed immediately.

"To answer your question, I remain in the Mediterranean, but do have certain business ventures in your area of the world. I expect to return to your beautiful Havana Harbor someday and eagerly await the time you walk up my gangplank to join me in savoring the world's finest Scotch whiskey—and rum. I do hope all is well with you. For now, I have a humble request," Saya-dar said, lying on all points, except about the quality of his bar stock and having "certain business ventures."

That made Casteńeda pause. The last time Saya-dar presented Casteńeda with a request, Casteńeda's men had died helping Saya-dar attempt to smuggle nuclear poison into the United States. The gravity of Casteńeda's drunken complicity led Casteńeda to sobriety, repentance and to Special Operations Command—Central in Tampa where Casteńeda had sought out General Ortega and offered to help. Casteńeda and Ortega had attempted to lure Saya-dar into the United States. For reasons Saya-dar never explained, he had cancelled his infiltration and bade "good bye."

What could the fiend be requesting this time? Whatever it was, Casteńeda had no doubt the Americans should know about it. He decided to play along, extract what he could, and report to General Ortega as soon as this call ended.

"Havana Harbor and my services are at your disposal. I do hope you will visit me again soon. Until we meet again, how may I help you?" Casteńeda asked.

"This time, my friend, I have a request for your services—for the services of men like those in your hire. As before—but not as before," Saya-dar ended, acknowledging the disaster wreaked on Casteńeda's men by the *Arcturus* team.

"My Persian friend, we both lost so much. You forfeited that fine Italian helicopter and I—I lost so many men. It was not easy to explain this to their mothers. Having said that, it is my earnest desire to help you if I can. So, please go on," Casteńeda said.

"Oh, my friend, I would not so presume to ask you to loan me your relatives again. Neither does my business require such men for such action. This is a much smaller favor, yet one of vital importance to my business interests. Also, any assistance you furnish would be much more—distant from yourself this time.

'Neither you nor your men would be involved in any way. I simply need some help in your region and want to ask you for a—referral. I know you know many men in the Caribbean and in the Americas. You are a man of great influence and far-reaching knowledge. I trust you will find this request to be humble.

'If one were to need a crew of rough men to do rough work in your part of the world, at sea, then whom would you call upon to assemble and dispatch such a crew? I seek only your recommendation in the form of a few names and telephone numbers, perhaps?" Saya-dar purred.

*Pirates! Saya-dar wants to hire pirates again!*

Then, Casteńeda saw the opportunity: *Despite his insistence, he is at mischief targeting the Americans again! How fortunate that he has called me!*

"I see. Let me consider. There are, as you might imagine, several contractors suitable. Perhaps you might help me narrow my recommendations down a bit. While the Caribbean Basin is largely forgotten by the capitalist pigs who think of it as a single beach at Cancun, you, my friend, you know it's wondrous size and variety. Perhaps you could give me some idea of where you might need this kind of work done. Perhaps, also, you could tell me what kind of work you require so that I could match you with the appropriate—subcontractor," Casteńeda said, now angling skillfully for specific intelligence with which to warn the Americans. Would Saya-dar take the bait?

"But of course! (*Yes!*) I would need this work done just east of your own island on the north side of your neighbor island named Hispaniola by Christopher Columbus," Saya-dar said, notably avoiding any reference to the nature of the work he planned.

"Haiti?" Casteńeda asked, surprised. *What could the Saya-dar—The Shade—possibly want with poor Haiti? Hadn't Haiti suffered enough without getting Saya-dar's attention?*

"No, a bit further east. At the border between Haiti and the Dominican Republic lies a national park. A most uninhabited area it appears from the map. Border areas tend to be a bit—ungovernable, don't you think?" Saya-dar responded.

"Yes, indeed, that is true. Such border zones garner the least official presence and, therefore, they attract the lawless ones," Casteńeda agreed, hoping more information would be forthcoming. "That park is on the north coast of the DR, away from the busy traffic of the Windward Passage and away from the resorts," Casteńeda said. "I know it well. And, yes you are wise to avoid the Windward Passage. The Americans patrol it constantly. I will have to check my own black book as they say. I am even now at sea, my friend. Can I get back to you tomorrow?"

"Yes. However, after tomorrow, this cell phone will no longer work. So please do call me by three o'clock your time. Can you do that?" Saya-dar asked, playing along.

"Certainly. I will provide captains for your consideration," Casteńeda promised.

"Then, until tomorrow, and until we speak again," Saya-dar spoke, sinking the hook into this fisherman.

Saya-dar did not *know* Casteńeda would tell the Americans but, he knew this: His assassination attack on Gordon's lodge had ended in disaster. He had worked with Casteńeda to acquire dirty bomb material, and to arrange for his own infiltration. Even though he did not use Casteńeda for the infiltration into the United States, nonetheless, Casteńeda knew of him. He did not trust the rum-soaked, womanizing, Cuban intelligence chieftain—but found him useful. Saya-dar had just spun Casteńeda into motion. Now, Casteńeda might spin the Americans into motion. Let the Americans chase their tails in the Atlantic. If Casteńeda were, indeed, trustworthy, then, no harm was done. *Maskirovka*!

Saya-dar ordered a business-class ticket for Manaus' Wednesday Delta flight through Atlanta to New York City.

Casteńeda shook his head, as if to make sure he was awake and he had just spoken to Saya-dar. He had no idea what the man might be up to, but he was confident of three things: that Saya-dar hated the Americans; that he planned some operation in their sphere of influence; and that Paul Ortega should know immediately that Saya-dar had called. The Cuban intelligence chief—working toward the day his poor country reconciled with America—called.

The Cuban's afternoon call amazed and alarmed General Ortega.

"Yes, General, I am sure he plans some mischief off the north coast of Hispaniola, east of Cuba. Of course, we can never know what portions of Saya-dar's statements are true, and what portions are deception," Casteńeda pointed out.

"Colonel, once again, I am grateful you sought me out two years ago and offered to help us. We knew about you, of course. I mean, we knew who you were, what your position was within the Cuban Intelligence service, but we had no idea about your wrestling with whether to continue defending your country's dictator—and his system. You were our only link to this Saya-dar—our first source of information. Say, we almost trapped him, did we not? That call he made to you cancelling his infiltration stopped our plans. Do you think he was on to you? Do you think that's why he cancelled? I know we've talked about all of this at length before, but I wonder if you've processed any more thoughts about it since we last spoke. I mean, here he is again," Ortega found himself running on.

It was unlike Paul Ortega, but excitement revved up his thoughts and propelled his words. He also wondered why Saya-dar had attacked Gordon, Jack, and Donna LaRue at Gordon's lodge, but saw no benefit in mentioning the three to Colonel

Casteńeda.

"Yes, general, we will never know, but I must suspect that he used me to plant the suggestion that he had "gone to the house" as you say. And, I cannot help but wonder if he is using me to plant disinformation—*dezinformatzia*, as my former Russian colleagues called it—even now. Nonetheless, here I am, carrying out his wishes like a—like a zombie," Casteńeda said, amused at his own reference to the legendary walking dead of Haiti.

"You and I both, voodoo brother, you and I both," Ortega agreed.

The men could not help it. They shared a laugh over the image of them both stalking Haiti, Washington, and Havana, in a trance, eyes bugged out, arms in front like Frankenstein in the movies, ever searching for Saya-dar.

"Well, we must be fast zombies instead of slow zombies, then," Ortega said.

They laughed again, said their "good-byes" and ended the call, figuring what to do next.

Ortega looked at Burnell. "Bernie, did you get all that?"

"Yes, sir. Here's the Hispaniola map sheet. "Right here, sir," Sergeant Burnell said, jabbing his finger roughly at *Monte Cristi* on the north coast of the Dominican Republic.

The two nations of Haiti and the Dominican Republic uncomfortably share the same island, Hispaniola. Haiti harks back to the days of its French colonial masters, still heard in the *Creole* and echoed in the place names. The DR's history dates proudly back to the Spanish conquistadors. Santo Domingo's streets at night transport the visitor to a time of wooden ships, steel armor, horses, and bold conquest. But, when the world found cheaper ways to produce sugar, both former colonies lapsed into poverty. The DR emerged from dictatorship into democracy and exudes hopeful enterprise and promise. Haiti, though, churns in spasms of violence, corruption, poverty, and the manifold curses that bad government spreads onto any people unwilling to overthrow it. The DR tries to guard its rugged border with Haiti, but nature rules. Mountains join the two in the middle of the island. An alligator-infested lake and near-desert hold down the southern border. The northern border zone near the coast is miles of wild swamp. The armed forces of both countries—few in number—avoid this swamp if at all possible.

So, hard men fill the swampy void. Mostly, these prey on the poor of Haiti, unable to defend themselves. No western country really wants to—once again—intervene in Haiti's morass of corrupt dictatorship and gang violence. The task seems utterly resistant to lifting Haiti up from its wretched condition.

And so, a man needing to hide away or conduct mischief might well choose this particular forgotten corner of the world to start from. Saya-dar's announced intention—left a bit vague as to operations but not as to locale—struck both Ortega and Burnell as plausible.

"Divert the *Arcturus* Team to *Monte Cristi*," General Ortega ordered.

Their assumption—so carefully crafted by the master terrorist, Saya-dar—The Shade—the Protector of the Faithful—was dead wrong.

Saya-dar did not trust Casteñeda.

He suspected Casteńeda would run straight to the Americans and tell. If he did, Americans would show up and find no pirates. If, though, Casteńeda were true, then the band of armed pirates would show up with no Americans to harass.

Saya-dar didn't care how many western criminals slaughtered each other. Saya-dar opened his Contacts folder and retrieved a number given him by his "brother," Mr. Guevara. A fine referral source, that Mr. Guevara.

The name, "René," Saya-dar read. Guevara included his own notes: "Port-au-Prince, Haiti. Makes small fortune smuggling poor Haitians into the Dominican Republic. Sometimes, puts them afloat toward America in leaky boats. Hopes high, chances slim, money good. In other words, he knows seafarers—captains with boats, willing to take on odd jobs. Sometimes, when they need a new boat, they take that, too," the notes read.

It was so easy. Saya-dar called the number and was pleased to reach René immediately. Hearing Saya-dar drop Guevara's name and referral code-word, René accepted Saya-dar's guarantee of payment without even asking for any other identifying details. Just deposit the money. René would take it from there. No further questions asked. No need for any. Don't need to know more about you and don't want to. The deposit answered all the questions René had.

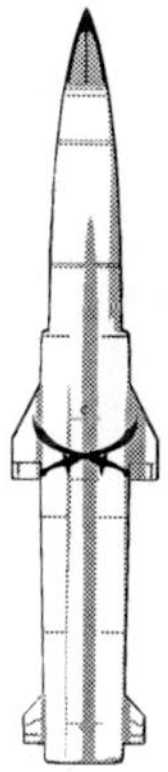

# 33

*Monday, sunset*
*Amazon River, two days downriver from Manaus*

*Arcturus* chugged casually down river, still a day from the Atlantic, keeping its distance from the barge.

"Hey, guess who's no longer our neighbor," Jack said to Gordon.

The two men had resolved to relax. Nothing else to do at this point.

"The Babylonian mystery man—he's nowhere around. Either staying at his fishing spot or hanging back, I suppose," Jack said. "Can you get a sat shot to show all of our relative positions? I want to make sure the mystery barge doesn't disappear, too."

"Ordered it this morning," Gordon said.

Silence for a few minutes.

"So, what do we do now?" Jack asked.

"Ha! Getting impatient, we are? Too much sitting on your duff?" Gordon asked, referring to Jack sitting on his duffel bag—slang for just more sitting and waiting.

"Yes. Although, every op needs an HQ—a base. I must say, the *Arcturus* is as good as they get."

By, now, Gordon and Jack watched the sun go down on their second day out of Manaus. They'd not seen the *Bay-B-Lie* since she stopped and *Arcturus* passed by. Jack didn't like it.

"I'll be interested in seeing that satellite shot when you get it. In the meantime, can we put together what we absolutely *know* and see where it takes us?" Jack asked.

"Sure. Want to start, I take it?"

"OK. Here's how I see it," Jack began.

"First, Gordon, let's start two years ago. No *jihadist* success against us since 9/11 for years. Then, these 20 suicide bombers detonated themselves and their delivery trucks. Trucks expertly loaded with a special blend of nitrogen-based explosive. Fertilizer and diesel fuel, basically, but compounded with a dash of extra explosive expertise, and tamped cleverly to turn the truck into an aimed, enhanced explosive delivery system. Simultaneously, 20 stores all across America blow up on a busy Saturday afternoon.

'We never caught the terrorist who commanded this op, assuming the commander remained outside the group of bombers and, thus, is still alive. We got some help from loyal American Muslims who had been recruited into the plan, but chose, instead, to be Americans. Trouble is, the commander had this whole operation so well compartmentalized that each knew only his little piece of the plan. No one was able to lead us to the commander. No one we caught knew how the bombers got into the states.

'We suspect the bombers came in through a southern port, perhaps the big port at Mobile, Alabama. That suspicion is based on the roughly fan-shaped cone formed when you plot the bombing sites. Mobile's at the point or the tip of the cone. From lower Alabama, the cone extends northward and spreads out. No bombers reached further west than Colorado, no further north than Oswego. We think that's because of the extra travel time required. We know the detonations were nearly simultaneous. To achieve simultaneous detonations, the nearer bombers had to sit and wait, exposing them to additional risk of discovery. Sending bombers out toward the Pacific Northwest would have meant that the nearest bombers would be waiting maybe three days. But, if the bombers all traveled within say 15 hours driving time from their insertion point, then the sit-and-wait discovery risk was limited to under that 15-hour window. So, as the bombing locations narrow and grow closer in the cone, that pattern points toward the origin.

'We know that the Turkish informant told us that his only contact with the commander was by email. The Turk was planted long, long ago. His motivation was Marxism. The Turk was a communist, not a committed Islamic *jihadist.* Over time, the gloss of Marxism wore thin, and he grew to respect the freedom he enjoyed in the United States. When finally called on by his handler to activate, he just couldn't see any reason to start blowing up the new home he loved. So, he came to us on his own. We should presume others were—are here as well. He tipped us off but knew only his compartmented portion of the op."

Here, Jack paused, thought some more, looked to see if Gordon was game for more analysis, and continued thinking out loud.

"We know from Colonel Casteńeda that a wealthy Iranian named Saya-dar visited him on the *Babylon* a few months before all of this went down. Buying radioactive material—polonium—from the Cubans, for a dirty bomb.

'We know the *Arcturus* was attacked by pirates at the island—same island where Saya-dar secured his canister of nuclear nasty. We know any dirty bomb attack was foiled. But, we have nothing connecting this Saya-dar to the 20 bombings other than the correlation in time between the explosions and his shopping trip to Cuba.

'Now, here is this same *Babylon*, we think, on the Amazon with us at the same time Iranians are buying a custom-fitted barge. Buying it from a man who associates with another of our enemies, Mr. *el Presidente*, Carlos Guevara, himself," Jack ended.

"OK, Jack, what are you getting to?" Gordon asked.

"There are common points that cannot comprise coincidence. Here's something we need to know. We checked on all the shipping into Mobile the weeks before the bombings and nothing stood out. Usual stuff. Containers, barges of raw materials and oil tankers. But, that was before we learned through Consuela of this Fats—this custom welding shop. Now, we know Fats' customer list—his guest list—includes Guevara. And, Consuela overheard them hinting about smuggling men into the U.S.!

'So, I say let's return to the list of ships porting at Mobile Bay shortly before the bombings and look behind those vessels. Where did they embark from before making that run to Mobile? Who built them? Who outfitted them and when? More precisely—drumroll, please." Jack paused for effect.

"You're on quite a roll here, Jack. I'm all ears," Gordon said.

"I want to know if any of those vessels has any connection to Manaus. Had any one of them ever been outfitted or modified by Fats in Manaus and, if so, when? If Fats modified any one of them, then that vessel is suspect. We would have a solid theory explaining how the bombers got in, we would know who helped them and,—Whoa! These connections could be politically explosive," Jack said.

"What?"

"It's looking like this trail leads up this river to Manaus—to the bungalow. Does it lead further?" Jack asked.

"You mean to Guevara?" Gordon said, not really asking.

"Yes, to Guevara." Jack answered. "Think about it. Fats outfitted. He didn't own or build tankers, but he outfitted them. He doesn't do shipping. This Saya-dar—if he planned the truck-bombings—needed a shipper. He couldn't very well show up with an Iranian tanker or container ship. That would get too much attention. He needed routine shipping to mask his infiltration," Jack said.

"Oil. An oil tanker. Venezuelan, outfitted by Fats with a secret passenger compartment! Big enough for 20 drivers, whoever else they might have had along to help, and their minimal equipment," Gordon concluded.

"Exactly. That's how I see it. Consuela supplies the key missing piece to let us see that. Right now, Iranians who hate us are buying a custom-outfitted barge from Fats. Fats is—make that was—connected to Guevara who hates us: they knew each other personally and did business together. All three men are here, in Manaus, at the same time. We never discovered how the 20 truck-bombers infiltrated, but we theorize Mobile as the insertion point. That implies insertion by ship. Tankers frequent Mobile Bay. Fats outfits tankers," Jack continued, summarizing the evidence.

"What are we lounging around here for? Let's set some inquiries into motion and find out if any ship on that list of Mobile Bay visitors stopped through Manaus for modification before the bombings," Gordon said.

Both men paused and looked at each other.

"Jack, this is big. They plan something having to do with that strange barge. On top of that, we are on the trail—finally—of the man who planned those 20 truck-bombings. All thanks to Consuela. By the way, she did a great job. Particularly for an—emotionally-involved amateur. Don't you think?" Gordon asked.

"Yes. Yes, Gordon, she is truly remarkable." Jack let it go at that.

Sifting Fats' records was easy enough. Fats had stored his books in the secret room Consuela found. Gordon called Sergeant Burnell, who caught Richard Pye waiting at the airport in São Paulo, Brazil on the way to London. Richard relayed the request to his man in Brasilia, who was already going through all of the documents found in the bungalow. An excited but flight-delayed Richard called back within two hours. Burnell patched the call through to Gordon, who put it on speakerphone.

"Found it! Fastidious record-keeper, he was. Thought it'd all remain hidden, I suppose. It's all right here," Richard reported. "In early 2006, Mr. Fats received an order from a Venezuelan shipping company to outfit an oil tanker. This company is owned by Guevara, personally. Guevara ordered the tanker modified." Richard said.

"Modified how?" Burnell asked as the others listened.

"That we don't know—at least we've not come across any plans showing the modification yet. We just know that this Venezuelan tanker named the *Mi Fortuna*—'My Fortune'—arrived in Manaus in November, 2006, was outfitted by Fats' welders and shipwrights by March, 2007, and left in May, 2007: only 3 months before your countryside exploded," Richard pointed out.

"This Venezuelan shipping firm. How distinct is the trace between the company and Guevara?" Gordon asked Richard.

"Guevara is the owner. The sole owner," came Richard's reply.

"Is the company otherwise legit? I mean, does it actually ship anything—other than terrorists? Is it involved in routine business?" Gordon asked.

"Oh, quite. It's a money-maker. But, with some twists. The company specializes in custom, specialized deliveries to places where no big shipping company runs. It mostly delivers oil using its small tankers, but it does other shipping as well. We're looking at some of those other destinations now. It looks like Guevara uses the company to prop up places he wants influence, like Cuba. Guevara is making money on the company, too. It's not a big player, but it's important in its niche market. Right now, it owns five tankers," Richard said.

"Where is the modified *Mi Fortuna* now? I mean, where did she go after Mobile, and then where is she now?" Jack asked.

"Good questions. The Brazilians had record of its docking in Manaus and leaving. Don't know yet where her next port of call was. We'll find out. This will take some time," Richard said, thinking about all of the photography and records to be sifted. "I've got to go. They're calling my flight."

Gordon kept his phone connected when Richard hung up.

"Did No One get all of that?" Burnell asked.

"No One copied Lima Charlie. Lickin' chicken," replied Gordon, reverting to dated Army slang (for "loud and clear") like Jack had noticed he sometimes did when excited and on the hunt.

"Anything else? Want me to report anything else to the boss?" Burnell clarified.

"Not yet. We have a theory but we need that last piece of data before publishing it in the scientific journals," Gordon said. He added, "This may be time-critical. Critical."

"I understand. I'll tell the head of the lab. Out."

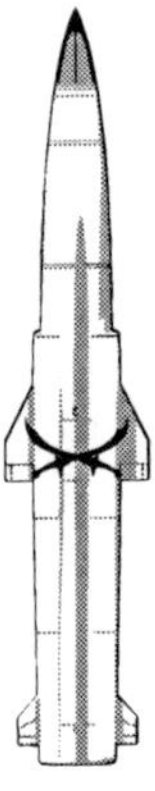

# 34

*That Monday night, late*
*Aboard British Airways Flight 246 from São Paulo to London*

Richard stretched back, trying hard to get his feet into some position other than contorted. *Bloody passenger class!* The coast of Brazil disappeared off the navigation map tracking the airplane for the passengers. His long legs ached already, but his brain spun. Just look what was coming together! All because of this one woman—Consuela. He considered her history—privation—sexual abuse. How remarkable that her intellect and conscience remained intact and combined to send her to him in Manaus!

Richard Pye didn't pray much. He still attended the Church of England once in a while. He planned to make a point of it this trip back, if he could get back home. Regularly though? No, a liberal education and a cynical line of work had battered his faith for a long time.

Richard went to his faith now, and prayed a short "thank you" to God for working in those mysterious ways said to characterize Him. A jungle beauty, orphaned by her parents' murderer, and then sexually kept by the same murderer, is in just the right place decades later to tip them off to a planned mass murder!

Then, she murders her parents' murderer. *Bloody hell!*

The extra miracle is that this damaged spirit saw the evil and had the will and courage to help. No, not just to help. To kill. To kill evil. Consuela proved she had the will and courage to confront evil, even to the death.

*Yes, a miracle, indeed,* Richard Pye concluded. He fancied that he had satisfied Vauxhall Cross and that C would be more than pleased.

Richard Pye, MI-6's Chief of Station in Brazil despite his protestations, puzzled. Where to start? Venezuela was not on the U.S. maritime watch list. The U.S. still had no consistent long-range tracking capability, although it tracked ships once in U.S. waters. He wondered why Venezuela was not on the watch list. Richard wanted his own boys at Vauxhall Cross in London to work these data to conclusion. So tempting. However, he had his instructions: "You keep up the U.K.'s distance from whatever is going on down there."

The "distance" seemed pretty scant to Richard right now. Here he was, the MI-6 Station Chief, smack in the middle of whatever the Americans also wanted distance from: The *Arcturus* Team, his Director had told him. The Americans are using the *Arcturus* Team for distance.

*Bloody hell of a way to run counter-terrorism operations!*

Richard marveled at his traveling companion, already peacefully asleep.

*How does she sleep with such a clean conscience?*

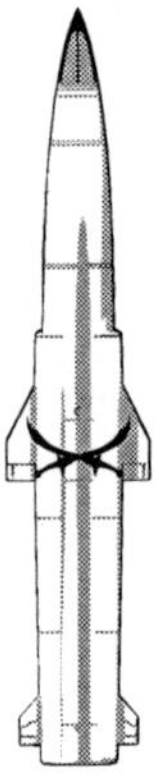

# 35

*2006*
*London, Vauxhall Cross Bridge*
*Office of the British Secret*
*Intelligence Service (MI-6)*

"You'll be our liaison to this team the Americans have formed," C told Richard. "Only, it doesn't exist, you see. It's all off the books, you see. Has to do with limits on their ability to run around in their country, or some such rot, you see?"

Apparently C saw. Richard heard C, but did not see, and said so.

"No, I don't see, C. Their Army—Special Operations Command, actually—is running this. How much more official can it be? And, if it were legal, would it not be official?" Richard asked, pointedly.

"Ah, my boy, you are so smart. Plus, you were such a bored lad! That's why I recruited you away from your owning that football team. Why, you would positively have shriveled up! All that press, and all those parties! Fast cars and fast women! Beer sloshing around all over the place! Bad for the health! So, here you are, Richard, in the service of Her Majesty. Wanting for nothing. Wealthy, handsome, charming, stationed away from the Island, but in a warm, wonderful country. The tropics! Just not a great deal going on down there, in Brazil. Not exactly the Berlin

Wall in the '60s, now is it? I wager you suspected I thought ill of you when I posted you down there. Did you? Never mind.

'Fact is, my boy, Paul Ortega and I go way back. He asked for my help. I am nothing if not grateful. How could I decline? Trouble is, if it would look bad in the press for the G.I.s to be running around killing terrorists in the U.S., what would it look like for a foreign country to be caught with its hands in such shenanigans? That's what I said to him, Richard. 'Shenanigans! Outlaws!' I told him. Outlaws! You Yanks have these romantic notions about outlaws and highwaymen; we British know what happens to outlaws. They hang. Remember your poetry? 'Shot down like a dog in the highway…,' and all that. Noyes. 'The Highwayman.' Oh, never mind.

'Paul says to me, "We are organized to fight identifiable enemies, overseas. We are not prepared—either by intelligence, manpower, political will or law—to hunt down and kill terrorists in our own country. I have no doubt that a hodgepodge of statutes and regulations, with supposedly clarifying memos, will be cobbled together some day, but, in the meantime, our enemies use our freedom and our law against us. We've always had people coming to the states to *start* their new life, not end everybody else's. Until we figure out how we remain constitutionally free and still live, someone must fill that gap in the wall."

'So, Richard my boy, he stood up—in that gap. Found he needed some support. They do always call on us, you know. Couldn't try to run the world without us. Called in some favors. Here we all are! Simple as that, you see?" C concluded, as if he had explained it all.

Richard held his fingers to his forehead and closed his eyes, raising his face to the sky outside the window. He felt a headache coming on and eyed the bottle of Scotch in C's fine cabinet.

"What I see, sir, is being recalled to London in disgrace, and—once the Parliament and the press are done with me here—handed over to the Yank Congress so they can posture before the tellie," Richard said, absent his usual good humor.

"Tut, tut, my boy. Tennyson! Tennyson, man! 'Ours is not to question why,…'" C began.

"And Pye's arse is the one to fry!" Richard ended the poem with his own apropos twist on 'The Charge of the Light Brigade.' "Besides, sir, you do recall how the charge ended, do you not? Indeed, I do believe that you ride at the head of the fated Brigade, sir," Richard had said, "together with cannon to the left of us and cannon to the right of us. You and your poetry! Sir."

Sir John Oxley-Bedsford, now head of the Secret Intelligence Service's MI-6 branch, smiled, left Richard on the plush, leather couch, mixed a whiskey with soda, and walked to his window, overlooking the Thames. The first tourist cruise boat of Tuesday morning passed beneath Vauxhall Bridge. Sir John checked his watch. *Still quiet in Washington, at least for the next few hours.*

Downriver, in the distance, he took in the Parliament and then the grim heights of The Tower beyond. The order of things was not lost on Sir John. First, spy for your country; then get crucified by Parliament; then get thrown in the Tower, as of old. Hauled in like a mad dog at Traitor's Gate?

London lay before him. Sir John sighed, for he had endured the scorn of his city—his country—and yet, somehow, survived and returned. Here, he remained, ensconced in new quarters, the current "C" in a long line of heads of the Secret Service over the last 100 years. The Service had achieved its glorious moments and suffered inglorious shame and invective, as well.

Iraq. The country wanted out. More so because of the accusations that the Secret Service had "cooked" the books over intelligence pointing to Saddam's having nuclear weapons of mass destruction.

*It's not as though the Devil sends you regular briefings on what mischief he plans,* Sir John reflected bitterly. You took what you got, cobbled together from all manner of sources, dubious, doubtful, and undisputed all mixed together in a pudding of damnation. Unfortunately, this one turned out to be Four-and-Twenty Blackbirds, and the empire had blackbird poop on its face. Poor Blair! And the scandal reported in the press—that Sir John himself had either been involved or had ordered the intelligence cooked to help make the case for war in Iraq.

Yet, somehow, Sir John endured. He made it past the inquiries and the public anger, and here he still stood. It seemed his beloved Kingdom gritted her teeth and grew more determined over time. Little talk now of cutting and running. Blair stubbornly giving them what for. It appeared to Sir John that he and the war had both weathered a close call.

By all rights, any operation with even the hint of scandal should go into the bin immediately.

Yet, Ortega called him, and here Sir John was, offering British help. Unofficially.

Sir John turned from London below, looked at Richard and smiled. Richard wondered what he was thinking.

"'British troops operating on American soil? Last time we did that, we burned Washington,' I said to Paul Ortega, Richard. That's what I told him. By God, you should have seen his face! 'They find this out, and your Washington will have its revenge. They will, by God, burn the troops, and we are the troops,' I told him," Sir John said, pointing to Richard and to himself.

"How sometimes I wish I could operate with the bold hubris of those British soldiers sailing up the Chesapeake in 1814, lighting fire to Washington's capital and even their White House. By God, that must have felt good after the humiliation of their 1776 upstart brouhaha. Now, times have changed. More Americans than Brits would like to burn Washington, D.C.! This tea party in Boston Harbor has come back to haunt Washington, has it not? Serves 'em right, I say, Richard.

'Must admit, though, the Yanks make pretty good chums. Prone to plunge headlong where others would tread lightly, perhaps, but there is something to be said for bold action," he said, turning away from Richard once again to look out upon the heart of England.

Indeed, Sir John thought, there was something very British about bold action. He turned away from Richard, looked out on London again, trying to imagine the city as a rude log camp with the stone foundations of the tower going up. He thought about the Tower's dungeons, and he thought about Peshawar, 1982.

*Tricked me, they did. Didn't see it coming.*

At the time, *jihadist* kidnapping wasn't all that common. Hijacking airplanes, certainly, but kidnapping a British intelligence officer was considered beyond them. Sir John shuddered: His own "Black Hole of Calcutta" experience still returned to him in nightmares.

Then, it all ended. A tremendous explosion shook him from filthy exhaustion. Then, spurts of automatic weapons fire, each burst closer and closer to his own dirt-floored cell, brought him to his still-chained feet. Then, the voice in English (American-accented) yelling at him to stand clear of the door, which blew off its hinges seconds later.

Through the smoke and dust cloud came a big bear of a man, blue jeans, black sweatshirt, flanked by intense-looking, younger and similarly-clad boyos securing the room.

"Sir John, let's go have a pint and some fish-and-chips. I'll leave off the mushy peas, if you don't mind," the man said to him, grinning crazily like only an American can, face no more than six inches from Sir John's.

And so, Sir John Oxley-Bedsford met Major Paul Ortega, special operator with the young Delta Force. That was 25 years ago. Their personal and professional friendship was for life.

*Well, if you had to get in trouble with the legislatures on both sides of the Atlantic, you might as well stand in good company,* Sir John had concluded when now-General Paul Ortega called for his help. Yes, he would support Ortega's *Arcturus* team and the Devil take the hind parts! While the MPs and Congress dithered and politicked, men who loved their countries would take up arms. Let the law catch up to them later, perhaps in both opposite senses of the word. It was only a matter of time, but what a run they would give the *jihad* in the meantime!

Sir John twirled his whiskey absently as his thoughts returned to London, to now. He turned, and looked at Richard Pye.

Well-dressed, casual. Had to be exhausted after the all-night flight to Heathrow, but there he was, always that air of being just beyond and above the fracas, as if it were all a lark. Sometimes,

Sir John thought of Richard as The Scarlet Pimpernel, but less the dandy and more the suave, cool, rich businessman Richard really was. Sir John's instincts about the promoter personality behind Richard's successful soccer team were right. Richard turned on that same aristocrat playboy dazzle to recruit agents everywhere he went. Richard had more agents lined up than MI-6 could put on the payroll. He hoped, when all of this came to light, Richard would remain unscathed. He doubted it.

*So, just what does "distance" look like under these unusual circumstances?* Richard asked himself while Sir John stood, lost in thought at the window. Richard bet Ortega had already sent Jack's and Consuela's intel into someone he was working with on the sly at CIA.

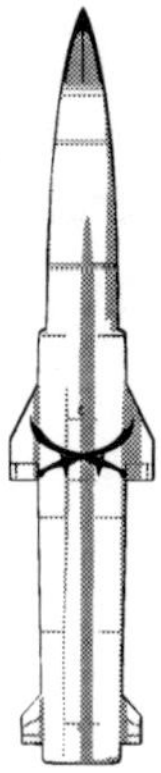

# 36

*Tuesday morning*
*Langley, Virginia*
*CIA Headquarters*

"That's the job," the DD CIA—Intelligence said, somewhat flippantly, Nick Riccolo thought. Nick chose his next words carefully, attempting to avoid sarcasm.

"Mission: look back into 2007—into the months before the simultaneous truck bombings. Pick up this *Mi Fortuna*, a Venezuelan oil tanker calling at Mobile in August, 2007. Then, work backward and spot its ports of call between leaving Manaus and arriving in Mobile. Your theory is Caracas. You're looking for evidence that the President of Venezuela, Carlos Guevara—the tanker's owner—ordered his captain to pick up a crew of Islamic homicide-suicide bombers in Venezuela and gave them a ride on an otherwise legitimate oil run to Mobile. Right?" Nick summarized.

"That's it," the DD agreed.

"And this is urgent?" Nick asked.

"Right. The Brits say so," the DD replied.

"What if the maniac Guevara didn't register the vessel's arrival or departure in Caracas—actually at his port at Maiquetia since Caracas lies inland—and won't cooperate with us—which he didn't and won't?" Nick asked. "He's not on our maritime watch list and we have no agreement with him that he will report all ships bound for the U.S. stopping in Venezuelan waters. This fits into the category of needles in haystacks," Nick said. "Searching for *My Fortune* in a haystack."

"That's where you come in. Hell, if it were easy, I wouldn't need you, would I?" the DD CIA—Intel asked, defaulting to both his natural impatience and reflex flattery.

It didn't work, but Nick would. The DD knew that. Nick arose from across the DD's desk, his mind already exploring sources of information. Wordlessly, he walked out. Nick Ricollo was already absorbed in the problem, spurred to action by the ghost of his grandfather: *Cassino, boy! Remember Cassino! You can't let that happen again.*

But it did happen. Over and over again. Not this time, if Nick could stop it.

*Wind him up and let him go*, the DD thought, watching Nick walk out his door.

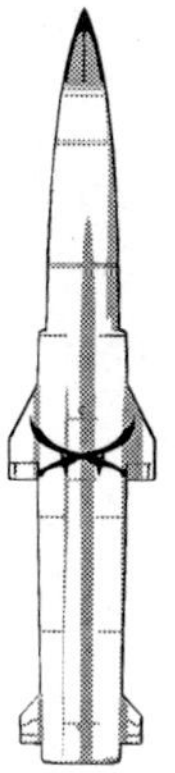

# 37

*Tuesday morning*
*Amazon River estuary*
*50 miles from the Atlantic Ocean*

Jack scanned the barge for the thousandth time since they had closed on it. "That's it," he announced.

"What's it?" Gordon asked.

"That is the barge in the plans—the one built there outside of Manaus. You know, it reminds me of the Merrimac. Low. Squat. Covered completely in what appears to be armor—although we know from the blueprints that the steel is not heavy enough for armor. This steel capped deck serves some other purpose," Jack said. "Whoa! That's odd!" he added.

"What's odd? It's all odd."

"It's turning south, Gordon, away from the Atlantic. Let's check the chart. Would you lay it out? I want to keep my eye on the barge," Jack said.

Gordon grabbed the chart and held it for Jack to explain himself.

"Here, look here," Jack said, grabbing a section of the rustling chart, folding it and showing Gordon. "This makes no sense. It's taking the *Canal do Sul*—the South Canal. You can get to the Atlantic doing that, but it's a roundabout way. Know what this looks like?" Jack asked.

"Yes. It looks like they might be trying to shake surveillance. We have no choice. We have to keep going straight. Pye's surveillance operation and NSA will have to take it from here," Gordon said.

Jack turned gloomy, that familiar failure feeling crawling back, as the *Arcturus* plowed straight ahead east through the estuary while, to his south, the barge's stern disappeared. Gordon's orders betrayed no such doubt, Gordon's calm reminding Jack that rotating surveillance teams in and out to avoid detection was just part of the job. Still, they were breaking chase.

"Chief, take 'er northeast out to sea 40 miles and then cut due north. Keep the boat within radar range of the coast so we can watch any traffic coming out to meet us. No point in staying in close in these coastal waters. I'm not crazy about cruising through Venezuela's dominion, anyway," Gordon ordered. "Put in at Georgetown for fuel and water. There's an international airport there, too, in case they want us to fly out somewhere fast. Fact is, boys, we're off the job right now. We'll sit tight there for a day until everybody figures out what's next," Gordon added.

Gordon looked at Jack.

"Don't let it get to you, Jack. Haven't you learned by now you'd better take advantage of these breaks in the action?" Gordon joked, properly reading Jack.

*Arcturus* left the vast estuary behind and headed out into the open Atlantic for her run north to the Guyana capital, Georgetown. After that? They just didn't know. Who did? Once again, waiting for orders.

Jack cased his binoculars and turned to check the shotgun cabinet—for the tenth time. He hated being out of the action.

"I hope Langley comes up with something fast," Jack groused.

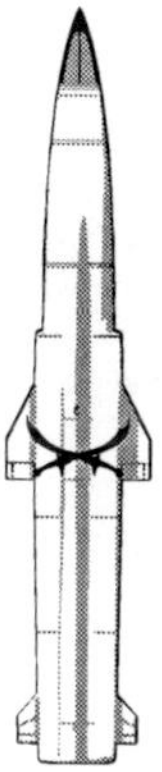

# 38

*Tuesday*
*CIA Headquarters,*
*Langley, Virginia*

Facts.

Religion to Nick Riccolo.

You must follow.

You must follow where the facts take you.

The facts.

Not your pre-suppositions. Pre-suppositions are not facts. Pre-suppositions limit your thinking. Those invite you onto false trails.

Not your boss's expressed or implied wishes.

Not the blathering din from the press one way or the other.

Action is where the operators live. The *evidence* is the analyst's operational reality. History. The trail. What did it all mean?

Nick sat behind his closed door. He'd grabbed a fat Sharpie and scrawled a rude sign, emerging only long enough to tape it askew to his door: "Stay Out!" He unfolded a large artist's sketch pad, wiped his desk clean of everything else, and began writing down each fact he knew about these infernal Amazon River barges.

In the end, it had been simple. He drew lines connecting each fact. After about 30 minutes of letting his mind make these connections, he saw it. Nick sat back and put his pen down. He started to reward himself with a cup of coffee, but the half-cup left in the bottom of his thermal urn had chilled to lukewarm. He drank it anyway.

Oil tankers—even the mid-sized ones operated by Guevara cannot be raced. A journey from one of Guevara's ports to Mobile covered nearly 2,000 nautical miles regardless of which route the captain chose around Cuba. At a realistic 15 knots, that required at least 133 hours of travel. So, when the *Mi Fortuna* sailed from Venezuela, she lumbered across the Atlantic exposed to blue sky and the eyes of the United States for about 5½ continuous days. That's nearly a week.

Nick identified the *Mi Fortuna* from The Alabama State Port Authority records kept in 2007. There just weren't whole fleets of Venezuelan oil tankers coming and going at Mobile Bay—fewer tankers from Venezuela than he had thought. Most oil coming into America through the Gulf of Mexico came in through the big Texas ports. Lots of container ships coming into Mobile, but not so much oil. Regular traffic. Business goes on. The Supreme Dictator didn't seem to mind doing business with America.

*So, now, where did the Mi Fortuna come from before Venezuela? And where before that, earlier in 2007, before the truck-bombings?*

The pictures told the story. More precisely, the KH-11 Crystal satellite photography archived over the relevant time span told volumes. Too many volumes to go through. Massive data.

Once the *Mi Fortuna* was imaged, Nick determined the next task to be data-crunching.

Nick recruited Colin Ferguson from the University of Tennessee's Computer Science Department. Colin caught the CIA's attention when he co-authored a paper writing up the exotic data visualization laboratory projects conducted jointly by UT and the Oak Ridge nuclear weapons plant nearby on the Cray *Jaguar*—the most powerful supercomputer in the world, jockeying back and forth with the Chinese, who were fast emerging as top computer competition.

Nick's first recruiting pitch landed Colin's "Hmmph, I'll think about it. Why would I want to leave Oak Ridge National Laboratory?" Nick just smiled: he now knew the hook. Whispering in Colin's ear about just who the first and second most powerful computers worked for convinced Colin to make the jump. Then, Nick took him to the intelligence analyst level by sending him to the George H. W. Bush School of Government and Public Service at Texas A&M. And, a few other places.

Nick hit the intercom button for Colin Ferguson.

"Seeing beyond the bounds, Colin Ferguson here."

"Cute. Colin, got a job for you. Needs Mr. Viz Lab himself. I have one of those too-much-information problems," Nick said and coughed. "Right now," he added.

"Delightful. It's Thursday. I'm racing my modified BMW 320i this weekend. I've spent a lot of time on the suspension and engine. Trying out my new Vacarro seats. Will your excess information get in the way of my getting my rebuilt BMW up to excess speed?" Colin asked.

"Your dedication to the service is noted. Seriously, come on down here, will you? You will like this spy work. Besides, this may fit into the saving the world category. Some guys in the field are counting on us," Nick finished. Hook sunk again.

Data collection and storage capability outpaces the ability of humans to observe, manipulate, and interpret. This is a problem with all manner of data, not just intelligence data. Graphs and charts help illustrate the relationships between numbers, but these 2-D representations are confined to their X and Y axes. They are so, well—flat. So bland. So, yesterday. They just cannot adequately represent complex data sets.

The Viz Lab project literally exploded these imprisoned numbers into brilliantly creative displays of light and color. The Viz Lab makes graphs supercool. And we humans do so like light and color. Light and color get attention—and grant money. You can put it all to music, too. Just ask *Kraken*, paired with the *Jaguar* at Oak Ridge where Colin still worked out doing data heavy-lifting.

Minutes later, Colin appeared in the door, coffee cup in hand, tie loosened, looking casual as always. Nick explained the problem. Colin left immediately to get to work on it.

He appeared mid-morning the next day, smiling.

"Boss, I've got it," Colin said.

"Took long enough," Nick groused.

Colin reddened. Temper, not embarrassment. He started to ….

"Relax, Colin, I'm joking," Nick chuckled. "You traced the *Mi Fortuna* out of mountains of data and came up with the answer in under a day. That's amazing really. I knew you'd squeeze every bit of ability from our image-processing software. Whatcha got?"

Now, Colin flushed with embarrassment. "Actually, boss, that really wasn't hard. The task reduced to—."

"Oh, don't be so modest. Now, give me just a minute to think before you launch into what I know will be way more explanation than I need. Ha! What will be the next question? These questions never stop with just the one you answer, you know. Get yourself a chair. Help me with this. You tell me, Colin, now that you have answered the query I handed you, what will Ortega and his merry band of men next tell me they want? What will be my next data query for you to run?"

"Easy, Boss," Colin answered.

"What do you mean?"

"Well, I ran that already."

"Ran what already?"

"I ran the next question already. They—you—I—want to know all stops the *Mi Fortuna* made right before the truck-bombings, even between Manaus and Mobile. They know it was modified in Manaus and that it made port in Mobile. So, what did it do in between? Answer: The *Mi Fortuna* came to Mobile from the Venezuelan port at Maiquetia," Colin began.

"So what? We figured the Venezuelan oil tanker came from Venezuela." Nick interrupted.

"I checked. They don't load oil at Maiquetia," Colin said. And, the port paperwork at Maiquetia does not show that the *Mi Fortuna* has ever been there at all."

"Oh. Oh! O-Kaaaay.... Why would a Venezuelan oil tanker visit a port with no petroleum transport facilities, and avoid registering its visit? Indeed, how *could* it avoid port control without the cooperation of the Venezuelan government—and we know who that is?" Nick asked himself, aloud.

"It gets more interesting, boss. Before Maiquetia, the *Mi Fortuna* stopped just around the corner, in Venezuela at the port there at Point Cardon. *Puento Cardon.* There, they do load oil," Colin pointed out. "We checked on this. The paperwork's in place on that stop. No surprises there. It's the stop at Maiquetia that looks fishy. Why would a Venezuelan tanker, picking up oil to deliver to Mobile—a perfectly legitimate stop—dart around the corner and disappear for a while and stop at another port where it has no business? Ships stop at ports for a reason: they pick something up, they drop something off. Well, maybe maintenance, but Maiquetia is out of the way for a ship making the run to Mobile with oil."

"Where is Maiquetia?" Nick asked, his own suspicions growing.

"Literally, just over the hill from the capital at Caracas. Here, look at the map. It's less than 10 miles from *el Presidente's* palace! If you are the Venezuelan dictator, and are up to no good, and in need of a maritime port for your mischief-launching, then Maiquetia is just next door. This pier right here is somewhat remote too, not exactly situated in the center of things," Colin added, pointing out a pier jutting out into the bay. "So, the *Mi Fortuna*, a Venezuelan oil tanker, sails to Manaus for modification X, then to the oil terminals at Point Cardon to take on a legit cargo Y, and then on to mystery run Z at Maiquetia. We may assume that X and Z are connected. The modification had something to do with the secret port call. And, there's more," he said.

"More!"

"Yes, that's what required the extra three hours," Colin said, playing his best cards. I can solve the equation with the unknown variable Z."

Nick stared at his assistant. *I am getting behind the times. I don't even know the lingo anymore.*

"Anticipating your next line of inquiry, I asked myself what ships might have docked at Maiquetia shortly before the *Mi Fortuna.* In other words, looking for additional variables—additional connections—*what* might have been unloaded at Maiquetia first, and then re-loaded onto the arriving, modified *Mi Fortuna*?

'Specifically, let's devise a hypothesis linking Guevara to the 20 truck-bombings. Let's test the hypothesis. So here's what we ask: 'Did someone smuggle in the 20 bombers to Maiquetia where they transferred to the *Mi Fortuna*?' That is the question, the answer to which, damns Guevara!" Colin said, raising his voice in a manner he usually reserved for "poning" opponents in video gaming.

Franz von Suppe's *Light Cavalry* overture built toward crescendo on the MP3 player. Colin charged and lowered his lance-like logic, crashing horse-and-headlong against the enemy's maneuver.

"Boss, equation solved! The *Mi Fortuna* originated from *Iran,* not Venezuela. She first sailed late 2006 from Iran—then Manaus—Venezuela—and then on to Mobile. Think about it! Owned by someone in Iran, sent to Manaus for modification; then to pick up a cover-load of oil in Point Cardon; then on, as-modified, to pick up the bombers at Maiquetia. The oil was a convenient cover to get the bombers in. She had been sold by the Iranian owner to Guevara's company, reflagged as Venezuelan and looked like just another Venezuelan medium-sized tanker after that. After those runs, then she sailed on into Mobile and we know what happened after that," Colin said. "Boom! Twenty places at once."

"The theory works," Nick said.

"There's more, and you are not going to like this. It's probably not what you think," Colin said.

"Please, just give it to me. I think only when I have data—information—evidence from which to think! 'Data, Watson! I must have data!' That's from *Sherlock Holmes*, you know. You really must read *Sherlock Holmes* if you have not already."

Plainly, Nick was excited. They were on the hunt and fast-closing on their prey. Looked like that would be prey, plural, multi-cultural. Colin stepped to the MP3 player and selected the BBC's Sherlock Holmes theme.

"So, data!" Nick demanded dramatically. "Where did our enemy's ship dock next?" Nick asked, expecting Colin to say "back to Iran."

"The *Mi Fortuna* is a busy little tanker. She continues to ply our seas. But first, after discharging her deadly cargo in Mobile, she returned to Manaus," Colin announced, pausing.

"Huh? Manaus? Why back to Manaus? Wait! Oh, oh! I can think of only one reason," Nick said.

"Right. Chief, we must reason this was for other modifications, necessary to carry some other cargo. This second outfitting for new cargo was for another attack. A different form of attack. Now underway," Colin added.

"I agree. How long was the *Mi Fortuna* in Manaus the second time? I assume by "Manaus" you mean she went back to Fats' shipyard on the river bank," Nick said.

"Oh, yes. I left out that detail. All that work must be done outdoors. These barges look like football fields lining the bank of the river. Passing by on a boat out in the Amazon, you can see crews of men walking about on top of them. We have a series of photos spanning months. Fats also had a dock where he could modify ships. I request you task a team to analyze the series to see if we can identify the purpose from the modifications shown on the photography," Colin recommended.

"Yes, of course. Good idea. We'll need to call in some outside expertise on this one. Some civilian expert in shipbuilding from Norfolk or Hampton Roads maybe," Nick thought out loud. "In the meantime, where is the *Mi Fortuna* now?" he asked, getting worried.

"Then, she sailed for Iran."

"She sailed back to Iran?" Nick asked Colin to clarify what was a murky picture striving to emerge.

"Yes. But, she avoided the scrutiny she'd get passing through the narrows in the Straits of Hormuz. She stopped right here," Colin said. He turned his opened laptop computer around so Nick could see the screen, and zoomed in on a no-name port on the Gulf of Oman, with no apparent reason for its existence, surrounded by desert.

"What did she take on there, at that port?" Nick asked.

Colin closed the laptop. "We don't know," he said, downcast.

Nick looked at his assistant. Earnest, excited. More. *Loves his country. I wonder why. Where does he get that from?*

"Brilliant analysis," Nick said. He got up from his desk and did something that shocked Colin. Nick Ricollo, a legend within the CIA, the man Colin aspired to be some day, bear-hugged his understudy, stepped back, wiped his eyes, beamed and said in Italian: "My grandfather would be proud of you; my father would be proud of you. And, I am proud of you."

"Uh, thanks, Chief," was all the surprised Colin could muster, catching the various forms of "*grazie*" and the drift.

"OK. Where is the *Mi Fortuna* now?" Nick asked.

"Once again—just as before—from modification in Manaus, to pickup at the port in Iran. From Iran back west. Right now, even as we speak, she's headed this way, approaching the Caribbean."

Nick jerked involuntarily. *Right here on our doorstep! Time to report.*

*Now.*

Colin had just implicated a head of state of a foreign country in the 2007 simultaneous truck-bombings and spotted the probable next attack inbound. This one was going all the way to the top, for sure. Nick could see those black operators down there in the Amazon cleaning their weapons, sharpening knives, and drawing equipment now.

"Very good, Colin. I've got to report all of this now. You write it up later. First, here's what I want you to do for satellite imagery. Prep a request for me to coordinate with NSA to make sure we track in real time and don't take our eyes off of the *Mi Fortuna* at all. Request Navy recon patrols too—with no break in surveillance. You be sure to tell the National Reconnaissance Office that, too. Between satellites and planes, real time, no break in surveillance. Find out what the Navy has along the possible routes through the Caribbean. Ops will want to start making plans to take her out. Man, if that devil-ship is steaming for Venezuela again…,"Nick said, thinking of the Bush Doctrine: "The United States will consider nation-states sponsoring terrorism as at war with the United States." He didn't know if it applied anymore, but it looked like they were going to find out.

"I gotta go see the DD. Let's get to it," Nick ended.

# Part IV:
# Storms Converge

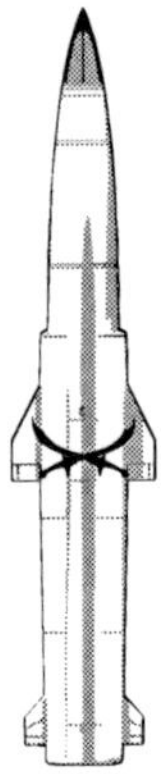

# 39

*Tuesday*
*Aboard the Mi Fortuna*
*Mid-Atlantic Ocean*

The Islamic Republic of Iran Maritime Cargo Line is nothing more than the mullahs' covert terrorism export navy, said a spokesman from the U.S. Treasury Department. On this historic day, we are formally accusing Iran of using this supposedly private shipping line to smuggle nuclear material in and out, and to ship missiles for mischief launched overseas—against the United States. IRIMCL is the 'shipper of choice' for Iran's export-to-terrorists missile business.

*--World Commerce Journal, 9-11-2008, "U.S. Accuses Iran Shipper of Nuclear Smuggling."*

Greece's blue and white flag snapped and jerked in the still-strong, tail-of-the-hurricane winds. The *Mi Fortuna*—registered and flying the Greek flag of convenience, lost two days making sure that Tropical Storm Fay had cleared out. Captain Kiani stood at the rail, taking in the freshening salt breeze. Twenty-two years of sailing for his native Iran, and he still loved the sea. He breathed in deeply. To Kiani, the sea smell was the fragrance of freedom.

This trip was different, though—different from any Captain Kiani could recall. For one thing, there was his "passenger." Captain Kiani couldn't place the accent precisely, but the features and accent together suggested to him one of the fragmented, fragile lands on the sub-Russian steppes—Georgia perhaps. Maybe Chechnya.

The man behaved himself. Pleasant enough. Indeed, you'd hardly know he was aboard. He watched, checked the ship's position constantly, carried his own satellite phone, and reported to someone every night. All of this suggested to Captain Kiani that this passenger wanted more than just covert passage from Iran to Venezuela.

When Captain Kiani had announced the weather-caused delay, the guest had exhibited the first, but only slight, sign of agitation. The news prompted several minutes of satellite phone conversation. Why? Oil moved all over the world all of the time. Iran traded crude to Venezuela for refined gasoline—since Iran had only the most limited refinery capacity—and their ships passed back and forth all the time. Captain Kiani had picked up gasoline with the *Mi Fortuna* from all over Europe, India, and Venezuela. What was special about this run?

Of course, he had his suspicions. Often, the government ordered him to take a short leave, to put his entire crew on leave, and to return to ship only when ordered. He'd return to find sealed shipping containers stored in "the special hold." While Captain of the ship, Kiani was smart enough to know that he was not captain of his fate: he kept his mouth shut and stayed well away from the "special hold" cargo, never mentioning it. Besides, he was afraid of it. Afraid it would poison him.

Afraid it would radiate.

And where were the Greeks? Kiani had sailed flagged Greek many times, but he knew the Greek laws on this point. Had to have some Greek seamen aboard. Easier and cheaper to sail flagged as German, but the Germans required inspections.

Why not just sail Iranian-flagged? Captain Kiani could think of a few good reasons.

But this time, he'd dismissed his suspicions and then returned to them several times. Had the destination been almost anywhere else in the West, he'd have been reassured, knowing his passenger would have to clear customs wherever he would alight. Then, he checked and discovered that the crew's manifest did not list the man. At least Kiani would not have to hide the man or pretend he was a sailor. He would put the man ashore and be done with him.

But, this shipment was bound for Venezuela.

At sea, Captain Kiani received all manner of Internet news. What an unholy alliance! The Godless Russians, the insane dictator-come-lately Guevara, and his own beloved but troubled Iran. Strange friends, united only in their common hatred for the Americans, and in their mutual ambition to rise to greater power.

And so, Captain Kiani sailed on, making his uneasy passage, eager to find a gap between the tropical storms and hurricanes that assaulted the Caribbean. Captain Kiani breathed deeply of the sea air, trying to breathe the tension out. Soon, they would make the Mona Passage, leave the rough Atlantic and enter the Caribbean. If more storms disrupted his planned route, he'd cut south by Trinidad and Tobago, avoiding Hurricane Alley. If all went as planned, in 36 hours, he'd make port, dock at Maiquetia, discharge his passenger and be done with it. This time. Still, what was the Russian's business in Maiquetia, and what cargo sat in that hidden "special hold" he was warned to stay away from this time?

Captain Kiani prayed for the end to this accursed voyage.

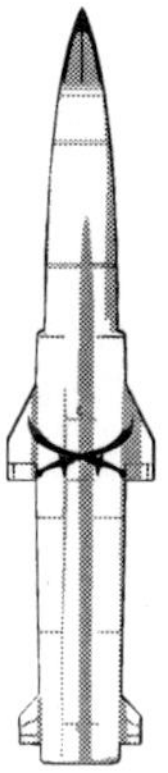

# 40

*Tuesday, just before sunset*
*Port La Guaira*
*Maiquetia, Venezuela*

Captain Emilio Vasquez long ago got over marveling at the odd whims of his president. He hunched over his rum-and-Coke and eyed his sullen tugboat crew sprawled about the far corner of the bar. Clouds of cigar smoke floated. Crazy beat out his hit "Phone Card" over the boom box. Free, energy-saving bulbs passed out by the UN dimmed whatever atmosphere the sailors' hangout held onto, the bar-keeper had explained, apologizing. Two of the crew burst into competing profanity. Two sang at the top of their lungs with Crazy, like Karaoke, but substituting X-rated lyrics.

"Getting restless, like me," he observed to his first mate.

"I'm ready to get the hell out of here, too," the Mate avowed, fidgeting. "Why the hell are we sitting here?" he asked, not expecting an answer. The Mate returned to his drink. Rum. Brugal. On ice. Nothing else. No Coke. Just the smooth Dominican rum. No "*Cuba libre*!" mixture with Coke, the Captain noticed.

The Mate's heart ached and he desperately needed to be home. Last time he'd been to Caracas, he'd gotten the bad news. "Another man," his cousin had whispered.

His wife had admitted it—been defiant—cursed him and his long voyages. Bitch! No gratitude for the regular income his job as an oceangoing tug's First Mate gave them both.

The Mate gave his captain no more response. Instead, he turned inward to the brooding dark thoughts within.

Emilio Vasquez eyed his troubled First Mate. Emilio wished for the First Mate, and for his own reasons, that this next voyage was already over.

Sitting still, with nothing to do in port other than drink was the bane and downfall of sailors the world over. They'd been stuck here in Maiquetia for three weeks, just waiting, waiting. Why? For what? "Tow a barge to New York City. Wait until you are told to embark." No more details than that. Normally, the seller-shipper pressed them to get aboard their tug and hurry, and the buyer wondered why they were not entering the harbor already. Instead, here they sat, ahead of schedule, delaying for what reason? The possibility of hurricanes? True, those storms were building and heading this way, but they boasted a full complement of experienced, ocean-going tug boat crew—his Chief of the Yard had personally seen to that. *Good men, too,* Emilio thought, perusing the now boisterous crew again.

*Let's go!* He sighed.

When you worked for the government—the "neo Marxist" government of President Big Mouth (as Emilio called Carlos Guevara, but only secretly in his thoughts), you played your role, blown about by the winds. Someone wanted them sitting. So, here they sat in a bright yellow-painted, sawmill slab-sided, tin-roofed, concrete-floored bar, only 100 yards from the port gate, awaiting orders.

Why complain? Many would enjoy the break. However, these orders made the break like house arrest: "Do not cross the *Avenida Soublette,*" they'd been warned by the Venezuelan Army major. Not even permitted to take the train over the mountains, the mere 15 miles into Caracas? Not allowed to call? Cell phones taken up? Now, that was different, and alarming. *We are virtually confined to quarters. Most unusual orders for delivering a garbage barge!*

They'd all strolled the piers. They'd fished. Watched from afar as the tourists boarded and toured the *Libertad* sailing ship, visiting in the distance from the Argentine armada. Some of his crew had started toward the three-masted sailing ship to join the tour, but helmeted guards from the military base at the port had rounded them up, aimed short, ugly, fully automatic weapons at them, and threatened them with jail, beating at them with nightsticks until they returned to their own sequestered, extreme eastern end of the port.

Without getting across the mountain into Caracas, all they could do was drink. The 30-foot high poster advertising Regional Light beer across the street showed a beautiful blonde's nearly-naked backside. They'd gawked and all lustily agreed she was "truly delicious," as the double-entendre advertisement showing both blonde and beer boasted. They fought over naming her. They competed in fantasy-land, and laughed when the cook won the contest. But, the butt poster just did not substitute: its enticements remained out of range.

"Emilio Vasquez?" sounded the high, strained summons from toward the open air front of the bar.

Emilio Vasquez and the Mate both swiveled. So did every crewman. All expectant. All ready to get a move-on.

The late afternoon sun backlit the bar's front door. From the glare stepped a smallish figure, black pants, white shirt, fedora. Tie. Patch sewn above the shirt pocket. The new arrival stopped abruptly. The attention—the hostile eyes riveted on him—the taut faces—startled him. He was already scared enough by what was going on out on the docks.

"I am searching for Captain Vasquez," he announced, nervously. Emilio rose and came to greet him, almost feeling sorry for the man.

"I am Captain Emilio Vasquez. Do you have word for me? Orders?"

"Yes. I am from the Harbor Master's office."

*Yes, idiot, I can see that by your uniform!* Emilio thought but did not say. *Get on with it!*

"And your point is?" said Captain Vazquez, instead.

The man coughed, and his voice quaked a bit: "You are to report, with your crew, to the Harbor Master at dawn—at 0600 hours."

A throaty, loud cheer chorus erupted from the corner.

Emilio Vasquez turned and smiled at his eight crewmen. They returned the expressed emotion.

The Mate did not smile, but some of his tension lapsed. The sooner they departed for New York City, the sooner he could go on leave and go home. Perhaps yet, in three weeks, he could regain the love of his errant and bored young wife. *If not…* He let the black thought hang.

Be careful what you wish for. In truth, he'd return unexpectedly the next day to find her in his bed with her lover. He'd knife them both, leave his home drenched in their blood, be tried for murder, and spend 20 years in jail.

The enlivened and now-cheerful crew reported to the Harbor Master Wednesday morning, more than ready to cast off. Imagine their surprise when the Harbor Master stood from his desk, addressed Captain Vasquez, and said, "Your crew is free to go home. They are released."

*This new-Marxism might not be all tragic,* thought Emilio Vasquez upon receiving the news.

No explanation. No request for an explanation. The somber, quiet man seated in the back of the Harbor Master's office said enough without speaking a word. The man's stare unnerved Emilio. Plainly, the man had walked in from President Guevara's world of intrigue and control and announced to the Harbor Master the change of plans. The Harbor Master smiled nervously, his eyes darting around, signaling he would like to be somewhere else.

*Not a time to ask questions.* Emilio was in the course of thinking *Do not look a gift horse in the mouth,* when the Harbor Master interrupted his forming plans for the unexpected holiday: "You, however, shall accompany this man aboard your tug. He will explain," the Harbor Master said, pointing to the mystery man.

The crew, other than the First Mate, would savor their vacation. However, Captain Emilio Vasquez, age 46, lifelong tugboat sailor and grandfather already of three, would never again return to the tropical paradise shores of his now accursed country. The neo-Marxist intrigue of President Guevara would swallow him alive at sea.

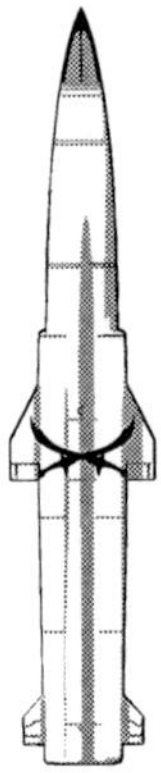

# 41

*Wednesday morning*
*Washington, D.C.*
*The White House, The Oval Office*

President Bullington heard his assistant but didn't hear. He interrupted the prattle—the recital of the day's schedule. "Cancel the morning and get Ortega on the line. Better yet, is he still in town? If he is, let me know and tell him to hold fast where he is. Tell him I want to meet with him, again," President Bullington told the flustered assistant. "Today."

Grant Gammon watched and chuckled inwardly as the assistant stopped and stared blankly. By now, Grant Gammon, head of the president's Secret Service security detail, had learned that this president was anything but predictable. He'd learned, too, not to expect explanations for abrupt changes of direction. Agent Gammon simply altered course and mustered the detail to travel with the president—wherever that might be. Agent Gammon had also learned, by now, that the president had reasons for these changes.

"Bryant Point LZ, Chief," President Bullington shouted to Agent Gammon as they climbed aboard Marine One. Gammon and the pilot exchanged a glance. President Bullington immediately said: "I saw that," and all three men laughed.

This was one of the president's favorite jokes. President Bullington had arranged privately with a dozen landowners around Washington to land Marine One whenever he wanted. He tried to rotate among the locations at random, but Gammon knew that Bryant Point had emerged as one of the president's favorites. The estate owner there, a friend, kept a field mowed and maintained—and guarded. From the "Bryant Point Landing Zone," as the president insisted on calling the designated corner of the field where Marine One would land, a short walk over the grass, and a climb over a fence brought the party to the high south bank of the Potomac River. From atop the bank, the president would stand, looking across the river at the shining white face of Mount Vernon in the distance. Gammon thought the president drew inspiration from the privations endured by General Washington at the fickle hand of Congress during the Revolution, and from the great general's tribulations as president afterward.

The detail fanned out as the rest choppered in and formed a perimeter watching over the president. Across the field stood a man leaning against a car, watching them. As the president began walking toward the man, a team started to jog across the field to get there first, but President Bullington ordered Gammon to stand the detail down. They would not check General Ortega and there would be no log entry of General Ortega having rallied with the president at the Bryant Point LZ.

"Thanks, Paul, for the change of plan. I know you have your

own life. I know our—little arrangement—must be causing you fits," the president began.

"Causing me fits? You should see what it's doing to the Commander of SOCOM—my ostensible boss!" Ortega said. The president stopped.

"I know, I know. I'll speak with Max myself—someday. If your career starts to take hits, let me know. I have some clout, you know."

"Sir, I'm a two-star general. I've been in the Army 35 years. I've been in special operations since after I was a two L-T platoon leader with the 82$^{nd}$. I've been on borrowed time career-wise now for years. I never expected to get this far. Besides, you know Max. He is a super commander. He understands that he doesn't have to understand. He's just envious he can't—at this juncture in his own three-star career—get his pistol into whatever banditry I've gotten myself into. Those were his words, sir. 'Banditry,' he said. He wants to do more than just provide passive concealment for us, whatever it is we are up to. He wants to provide shooting cover."

Paul Ortega always tried to lighten his friend's load. He could not imagine the daily stress President Bullington must operate under. What was it this time? The resurgence of the Red Army in the resurgent Soviet Empire? Their offensive missiles aimed at the rest of Europe to "offset the United States missile shield?" Threats of impeachment for torturing terrorists at the persistently open Guantanamo? Iran's nuclear weapons program about to hit the market? Another graft and corruption expose'?

President Bullington nodded but said nothing, instead pointing to a concrete bench.

"Officially, call Gordon and Jack and stand Operation *Piranha* down," he ordered.

"You're hitting me with DC-speak, sir? Why, and what does it mean that you qualified the order with 'officially?'" Ortega asked.

"It means this little recon patrol you ordered Jack to do down there in the Amazon has developed into something big. Big enough that I have to approve actual, official surveillance requests from the National Reconnaissance Office. CIA has got NSA re-directing satellite surveillance. It's beyond your boys in Brazil, now," the president explained. "Jack uncovered quite a little conspiracy, there."

"What's going on?"

"Two things—at least two, maybe more. First, we've learned that Carlos Guevara almost certainly was complicit in the truck-bombings two years ago. Guilty as sin, Paul! The one-two punches of Monroe Doctrine and the Bush Doctrine are about to take that tinhorn from the doctrines to D-Day!" the president said.

Raised eyebrows. Silence as Ortega thought through the ramifications. He decided the president was at least somewhat blowing off steam and let the president continue with the real plan. With operations ramped up in Afghanistan again, he didn't see opening up another invasion.

"I can't do all of this alone and the whole complement of planners and doers has to get involved. It's beyond *Arcturus*, now. You know, it's funny, Paul. You randomly scrounge up some little piece of intel from some far-flung corner of the world. You send a couple of guys, Jack and Gordon in this case, in to check it out. Jack snoops around and comes up with something that shakes your world. What Jack pulled out of that jungle house on stilts—well, he hit pay dirt. The Brazilian source dropped just a hint that her boss might have been tied in some way to the truck-bombings. What she led Jack to, in turn led to something, which led to something, which directly ties her boss and Guevara to the bombings! How's that for a day's work? Big enough for you?" the president said. "I have a head of state in *our* hemisphere setting up base camp for a Muslim terrorist operation inside the United States!"

The president became animated again, and Ortega waited before answering coolly.

"Yeah, it's big enough, I'd say so. You said two things. That one seems like an act of war to me. So, what's the second point?" Ortega asked, eager to get the full impact of the developed intelligence.

"Well, if that's not big enough for you, just wait. That's not all. Get this. We think Guevara's cooperating in a second, ongoing operation—right now! CIA scanned back through reconnaissance photography before the 2007 bombings. The analyst on this found the boat the bombers all came in on! It traced right back to Guevara." Before General Ortega could react, the president continued.

"Then, our man at CIA traced it *forward* after it left Mobile Bay where it dropped off the suicide platoon. That was trickier. You know that despite 9/11, we still just can't tell everything going on in every corner of the world at every second. We can't watch every square mile of ocean. Well, this analyst is a good, reliable man. He traced this boat—a now-modified Venezuelan oil tanker named the *Mi Fortuna*—back to Iran where it actually originated, and then he traced it from Iran right back into our own neighborhood. The Islamic Republic of Iran Maritime Cargo Line is a smokescreen. They use this so-called commercial carrier to hide shipments of nuclear and missile-program material. We've been onto them for years. This time, they used one of their several, and equally guilty, affiliates, I guess thinking that we wouldn't notice. NSA watches every move they make and stores the imagery.

'A pattern emerged: these Iranian ships often make quick stops at a remote port on their southern coast, beyond the Straits of Hormuz. Once we knew to look closer, we pulled the photography. The analysts have sifted it all. You won't believe what cargo we spotted it taking on at that port to bring back this way," the president said, pausing for breath. He resumed, getting angry, again.

"Without going into all of the sources and methods CIA used to determine just what it was, the KH-11 photos caught them loading surface-to-surface, cruise missiles, Paul! Six of them. That maniac Ahmadinejad wasn't completely bluffing. These missiles are right now loaded onto this modified tanker. Hidden from view, but they're there. We caught them red-handed putting them on. Had an agent on the ground personally verify it. We don't contact him often—you can imagine how risky that is for him, but this was important enough. He's on the inside at the port. Bottom line, Paul: they are headed this way with six of these missiles. Now!" the president emphasized, clenching both fists.

General Paul Ortega, veteran of many close calls and tense moments, looked back at the Secret Service teams. The perimeter teams all faced out like they were supposed to do; the president's immediate bodyguards, however, looked back at Paul and the president. President Bullington's loud exclamations and body language put them on edge.

"What kind of missiles, sir? To what purpose?" Ortega asked, already planning operations.

"Those are two questions. I'll let the CIA analyst fill you in on the purpose, but our agent saw markings being painted over. Our agent is one of the painters. He sketched a picture and sent it on. Nuclear! Nuclear, Paul!

'Now, as to purpose, I'm going to put you in touch with this analyst at CIA, Nick Ricollo, and I'll let him explain the details. He's a little crazy, but I want you to understand he's operations-oriented, he's on your side. Listen to this later and play it for Gordon and Jack, too," President Bullington said, handing General Ortega an SD card. "I just want you to know the quality of the intel and analysis work you are getting on this one." Then, the president stared hard at General Ortega with narrowed eyes. When the President of the United States spoke again, Paul heard the steel in his voice, cold steel, not the fiery anger of moments ago.

"You asked about the purpose. Trouble is, Nick still doesn't know whether this is Guevara's version of the Cuban missile crisis or if the Iranians plan to deliver the warheads—to shoot them at us, I mean. Are these missiles just for sit-and-show, or does someone plan to sneak them in and fire them at us? Guevara's inviting the Russians down for naval exercises in 2008 didn't exactly signal his goodwill toward us. First, he hosts their navy; next, he buys some commie planes and ships; next, he installs some of their atomic fireworks. Or at least, I suppose he installs them for show. On the other hand, we do not know the final destination for these missiles. Someone may be trying to get close enough to shoot them at us!"

Ortega challenged that speculation.

"Shoot them at us? Cruise missiles? How could they? We can't see every whale surfacing to spout somewhere in the ocean, but we watch our coasts real closely. I don't see how they'd shoot cruise missiles at us," General Ortega said. "Their surface-to-surface cruise missiles just don't have the range."

"Yeah, well, Varus didn't see getting three Roman legions

wiped out in Germany's Teuteberger Forest 2,000 years ago, and we didn't see 9/11 coming, even with Tom Clancy writing about airliners piloted like guided missiles. Remember that video off the Los Angeles coast in 2010? They still don't know what it was. It's what we "don't see" that worries me. Either way, we have a problem, Paul. Any questions, Ranger?" President Bullington asked.

"Any questions? Yes, plenty. If this is too big for *Arcturus* now, why are you telling me all of this? What is my mission? Anything?" General Ortega asked.

"Of course! If they plan to shoot them at us, we are going to be acting fast. We have a foreign head of state to deal with, too. I don't know yet how much of this war is going to take place right here in the U.S. I don't know how much will be out in the open and how much will be covert. As Deputy Commander of SOCOM, you'll see the official warning order through the usual channels. Try to act surprised. As the head of my *Arcturus* team, I want your guys with weapons and equipment drawn, loose straps and buckles taped down, fresh batteries in the radios, canteens filled to the brim, ammo pouches full, and in position to move and fight with rotor blades turning. Particularly, I want Team *Arcturus* ready to operate within the continental United States. That's your mission. That's your Warning Order. I want you, and then Jack and Gordon, to get the briefing from this Italian intel whiz, personally. He's also been told to talk to "No One" when "No One" calls. That's all I can tell you for now until we know more about the missiles and where they are headed. More questions?"

"No, sir. I know my duty—my duties. How do I get in touch with this CIA analyst?" Major General Paul Ortega asked.

"Call this number."

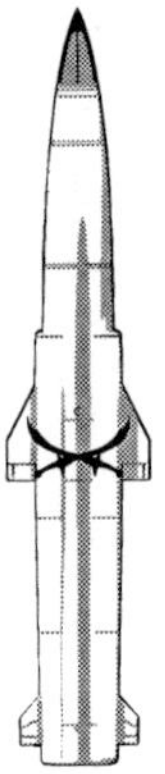

# 42

*Wednesday morning*
*Georgetown, Guyana*
*Aboard the Arcturus*

"We have about 15 minutes, Jack. Here's the MP3 file General Ortega emailed me. He told me the president gave it to him personally and said that we are to listen to it before we talk with the CIA analyst. I don't know why. He just did. Said it would explain something about why we should listen to this particular guy. Ready?" Gordon asked Jack.

Jack sat in the lounge aboard the *Arcturus* with Gordon.

"Sure. I'll take the president at his word. If he says we should listen to this guy deliver a lecture to a class of CIA officer trainees, I'll listen. Odd request, though."

Gordon inserted the SD card and started the playback. He could not know, but he heard Nick Ricollo perform his virtuoso, designed to motivate new case officers. Gordon and Jack heard Nick draw strength from the wounds of his grandfather in Italy. They heard Nick draw from the bittersweet, proud—so proud—legacy left by his own father.

> Kings and generals have sent men to death when they lacked intelligence. The sentence is laughably

and absurdly true, isn't it. Intelligence! Information! Facts! Without it, you are just stupid!

Poor, brave soldiers—the ghosts of poor, dead soldiers—share a common, bitter bond. Many, over thousands of years from Ur to the USA, marched bravely to death because someone made a stupid decision. No, not stupid. Ignorant! *Ignorant* means lacking in knowledge. No information.

Being smart is nice; being smart but lacking in the truth makes you ignorant. Ignorance puts you squarely on the path to make stupid decisions, no matter how smart you are. Men tend to place great faith in their own ability, their own intelligence. That's like expecting to win a cross-country race with the biggest supercharged motor, but not knowing the route. Without information, human intelligence simply isn't. With the wrong information, human intelligence is foolishness. In our business, that's deadly foolishness.

So, here, understand that "intelligence" does not refer to how collectively smart all of you think you are. Get over that. It refers to *information. Facts.* The most brilliant analysis of misinformation still produces garbage. So, as you start your career here, sitting in this hall, understand this.

CIA does information. CIA does this without appreciation. Without recognition. Most often,

> without resources commensurate with the grave duty its people—you—shoulder. People out there die to get you this information. They die in torture chambers. They die in hot, dirty, filthy prison cells. They die suddenly in the middle of the night, their door kicked down. When you open a file, someone may have opened his veins to get it to you.

Nick. Jack and Gordon didn't realize it, but Nick was fulfilling his destiny and gratifying his grandfather's ghost. While he was at it, he trained the next generation to heed the warnings of his own ancestors, who, in this strange way, lived on.

Nick checked his watch, micro-waved his Redskins coffee mug for 10 seconds, shuffled back to his office and sat down. *God, I am tired!* The phone rang exactly on time.

"Ricollo."

"No One. No One is on the line."

"Well, I'll just hang up then." Lack of sleep had worn Nick's patience thin; he simply couldn't resist it. Nevertheless, the not unpleasant caller got right to it.

"Please tell me what you know about the Iranian missiles loaded onto the *Mi Fortuna* and heading this way," Gordon said, rolling his eyes at Jack. "You're on speakerphone." Gordon and Jack sat in the lounge of the *Arcturus*; Paul Ortega had returned to his office at Fort Bragg and turned on his speakerphone, too, muted. Nick began.

"Iran bought SS-N-22 Sunburn cruise missiles from Russia. The Sunburn is an anti-ship missile—surface to surface. It's frightening to our navy; it flies a mere 20 feet above the surface at three times the speed of sound. Basically, once an enemy vessel fires one at a ship, that target ship has under half a minute to react. Let that sink in. You remember the French Exocet the Argentines used in the Falklands War? It's like the Exocet, but enhanced. It's range is under 100 miles, which works if your target is a ship. You pop up, fire, and the Sunburn's on you almost immediately!

'However, one of our agents inside Iran sent us word that the Russians have increased its range to 200 miles. Iran bought them, and now six are headed this way," Nick said. "Damned Russians!" he muttered, more to himself.

Jack agreed with that: *Damned Russians.* "To what purpose? For what mission," Jack asked.

"We do not know that," Nick said.

Gordon and Jack looked at each other. Jack spoke first.

"Well, we appreciate all the information, but anti-ship cruise missiles—even on steroids—are for the Navy to worry about, and you know those guys. They have all this *stuff.* Even if an Iranian ship slipped one under their AWACS and Aegis surveillance and counter-measures, it would not go unnoticed. That ship would be blown out of the water, and we would know that Iran had sent its navy over here to attack ours. That's stupidly suicidal, even for people salivating to usher in the next Caliphate. They must have better ways than that of starting World War III. I just can't see it," Jack said, always a bit short of patience for guys behind desks, and rubbing his still-sore jaw.

"Ah, there you go!" Nick chastised, now fully awakened by Jack's impertinent challenge. "Assumptions! All you *know* is that they are shipping six of them this way. And, you *know* the capabilities that I just told you about. You do not *know* that they plan to launch one from that ship, against one of our ships. Ha! I caught you! Just because it's a ship-to-ship missile, you assumed it would be fired from a ship, at a ship!" Nick retorted.

Jack thought. Now Jack knew why General Ortega had sent the SD card lecture to them. The guy was a little off—*Too much bureaucracy and coffee,* Jack figured. Probably lack of sleep, too. Lack of sleep will make you temporarily neurotic. Jack knew that from personal experience.

But the guy was right. Jack had let what they all knew about the missiles—standard stuff you could Google—dictate what he thought the enemy would do with his toys. The guy charging you with a flintlock might shoot you, but he might just get in close and club you to death with it, too. Or blast it into a hidden powder keg. Or use the flintlock to signal an ambush to start. And, there was always the chance he had up-engineered to something more deadly.

"All right, genius. What do you think they plan to do with it?" Jack asked.

"I don't *think*. Not yet. I don't have enough information to *think* about, to *think* with," Nick said.

"But you never do. Come on. No idea?" Jack asked.

Nick had so enjoyed the exchange. Now it was time to close in for the kill.

"You gave the reasons why attacking our Navy makes no sense. If the Iranians shoot at us, we catch them. We catch them? They are toast. Maybe we even finally invade their country and wipe their government out. Their people will be relieved to see them go. Most Iranians won't shed tears when they see their leaders on the TV news crawling out of a spider hole like a haggard Saddam Hussein and then swinging. So, Ahmadinejad doesn't want us to ID who fired the shot. You are right! So, we reason that they have a different plan. Right? Maybe they plan to sell the missiles to Cuba, or even to Venezuela," Nick said. "Look, I need to know where they take them. More to the point, we want to know who has his hands out ready to accept them," Nick said.

"Well, it's always nice to know what's at stake. Two hundred miles, huh? That's beginning to approach village-to-village ballistic missile range," Jack considered.

Nick said nothing.

"You there?" Jack asked, after the odd pause.

"Yes."

Another odd pause. A long one.

Jack looked at Gordon. Gordon raised his upturned palms in the "Hey, I don't know" gesture.

"Well, it's been charming. Please call anytime. We must do lunch," Jack said.

Ortega checked to make sure his phone really was muted and laughed out loud. Even the usually somber Burnell chuckled.

Gordon gave Jack one of *those* looks and made like he was going to kick Jack in the shin.

Nick re-joined the conversation, completely undeterred by Jack's put-down.

"We discern the threat from the *capability*, not from perceived intent. We can never know what any enemy intends. That's a classic mistake made by history's defeated commanders. So, we focus on what they have the *capacity* to do. I'll have to think about what that additional 100 miles adds to their war fighting *capacity.* You see, I left out a detail. These missiles are nuclear-armed. These are 200-mile range, nuclear-tipped missiles. Thank you, my sarcastic friend, for expanding my thinking. Yes, I'd love to do lunch sometime," Nick ended, cheerfully, hanging up.

"Well, I'll be damned," Jack said to Gordon.

"We'll all be damned along with you if your communications security is no better than that, McDonald. I'm on this call, too," President Bullington said.

*Uh oh!*

"Stay on this, men. Now you see why I want you *Arcturus* boys lurking around down there in the region, staying on this, still unofficially," the president ordered.

"Gordon, Jack, you still on?" General Ortega asked.

"Yes, sir. Until you say otherwise. Any additions to the mission?" Gordon asked.

"CIA is taking over the surveillance op. I want you to stand down," General Ortega instructed.

"Too late. We went on strike," Jack said.

"Gordon, are you sure McDonald didn't lose it there in the Amazon? I had my doubts about him, you know. Some colonel from the 101st wrote him up for being a loose cannon going off half-cocked. You still willing to vouch for him?" General Ortega jibed.

"No way, sir. I'd fire him in a heartbeat, but no one else is crazy enough to take his place. We're stuck with him for the time being," Gordon replied. "Seriously, we broke contact and notified Ricollo at CIA like you told us. The barge pulled a surveillance counter-measure and took a right around the block. For us to follow, it would have looked unnatural. So, we kept going. CIA's watching it now from overhead. It's at open sea and we're in Georgetown, taking on fuel and water and waiting for orders," Gordon explained.

"Good! Keep going north. Make toward Venezuela. One of those Caribbean islands in the Lesser Antilles—Trinidad and Tobago, or Grenada. Yeah, that will work. Grenada. Friendly country. They like us. Ronald Reagan set them free. They won't be surprised at a few Americans showing up. Try to look like tourists. They'll hardly look at your passports."

"Any idea where we might be making our way to after Grenada?" Gordon asked.

"No, really, I don't. I just want you closer to where this is all going down, closer to Venezuela in case something pops, but I think the op's over for you boys. This got big. I had to turn it over to others, and CIA's running it now. Having said that, I'm still in on the ops end—officially this time—because this is gonna go special forces before it's over. We'll need SEALs for the waterborne portions, maybe Delta on land. Don't think the Rangers will be invading any country over this, just yet anyway, but depending on what we find, maybe them, too, later. I'm acting as the Deputy SOCOM Commander, working this through the usual channels instead of through Team *Arcturus*. I like it," General Ortega finished.

"Why?" Gordon asked, who didn't particularly like it.

"It's all offshore from the U.S. at this point, so I have all manner of lawful, legal, usual-suspect conventional and unconventional forces and resources to call on. But, if I need to operate fast, and maybe even spill this action over to within the U.S., well—. You know. I have you maniacs. Looks like now, though, I'll use the Navy or Coast Guard like hungry watchdogs instead of attack dogs: on alert, patrolling, ready. CIA and NSA are like hawks, circling high overhead, missing no sign of movement below, and I have SEALS and MEUSOC Marines bursting to board belligerent barges on the bounding main.

'The Deputy Commander of SOCOM has lots of legal options. I mean, we have identified a threat heading west, loaded with Iranian, nuclear-armed cruise missiles. We increase the flow of intel from CIA and NSA, and stage special ops troops supported by Air Force and Navy to be ready to do the dirty work. And, I smell more game: it's just a question of when we catch Guevara with his hands in this. Hey! I just thought of something!" General Ortega exclaimed.

"What?"

"I own this piece of land. Hills, valleys, woods, kind of like where your lodge is, Gordon. It has this valley that I keep mowed. I've noticed that, when I drive my truck into it, in a few minutes a hawk will appear, circling low. I figured him out. He's expecting the human traffic to scare up the rabbits, squirrels, and other assorted small critters. He's using me to drive his prey out of hiding and into movement that he can see with his hawk eyes," General Ortega explained.

"So, you might use *Arcturus* to beat the bushes to see what flushes out. Is that it, sir?" Jack said.

"You got it. You boys always stir up trouble, or it follows you. Either way, I figure your motoring around down there just makes us that much more ready when it all breaks loose. So, lurk. That's it. Lurk down there in the Caribbean, just like you're doing. Lurk in case that barge does something sinister. Be ready. See the sights in Grenada. You have to admit, I've got you standing down in a nice place. But, be ready: I have a feeling this is not just a delivery service coming our way.

'And, if you catch Guevara accepting Iranian missiles smuggled into one of his ports, he's finally caught red-handed on the wrong side of the Bush Doctrine. Get ready for anything from invasion to assassination," said Paul Ortega, officially the

Deputy Commander of SOCOM, and unofficially the chief of the not-so-legal Team *Arcturus.*

"Any theories on what they actually expect to do with this barge loaded with Sunburns?" Gordon asked.

"No. It sort of doesn't make sense, does it? Cruise missiles, nuclear or conventional, just aren't exactly ICBMs, even if they have somehow kicked the range up to 200 miles. They'd have to get in real close if we are the target. And Guevara, as crazy as he is, knows we could take him out any time. Do they think we are blind? So, no, we don't know what they have planned. We're letting it play out a bit to see. CIA's working on that, too. You fellows got any theories?" General Ortega asked his old friend.

"Yes. What else is there? Blackmail or surprise attack," Gordon observed, soberly. Then, "Maybe, Guevara is just the broker, and he plans to sell them to someone else," Gordon added.

"Request permission to interdict and kill, sir," Jack said. He was serious.

"Geez, McDonald! For now, just stalk. Kill later," General Ortega added. "Out."

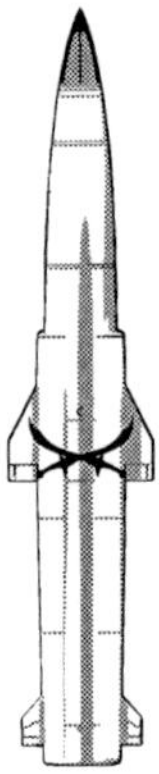

# 43

*Wednesday morning*
*Building storms*

Six hundred miles north of Caracas, Venezuela, the *Mi Fortuna* continued southwest. Captain Kiani found his break between tropical storms Fay and Gustav. The captain left the Atlantic Ocean behind, threaded the Mona Passage between the Dominican Republic and Puerto Rico, and entered the Caribbean Sea. From there, he steered the *Mi Fortuna* due south, straight across the Caribbean toward Maiquetia Port, away from the building storms, and just outside of, and down the mountain from Caracas.

Saya-dar sat in his room at the Hotel Tropical, waiting for the hour of his New York City flight out to approach. He swirled his glass and looked idly at the green mint leaves turning in the strong, sweet drink.

*Like me,* he thought, *just swirling around aimlessly.*

Saya-dar was restless. The hotel bored him.

Why fret? Well-laid plans did not—should not—must not—require his personal leadership constantly. Set the right plans and people in motion and watch the magic. Watch from anywhere. Anywhere in the world. Hotel Tropical was as nice a place as any from where to monitor Allah's apocalypse. Allah's revenge. Saya-dar's revenge.

He could visualize it all. Saya-dar arose from his chair and looked out over the river. A downpour pelted his window, drenching the lush lawn and palm trees. The rain out on the Rio Negro mesmerized Saya-dar; he saw, instead, Allah's rain of fire falling on the American landscape.

The garbage barge should be nearing the coast of Caracas. It would chug on by without stopping. The missiles had been loaded and were now hidden inside the *Khazir*, ready to depart the port at Maiquetia behind the garbage barge. The guilty *Mi Fortuna* had dropped the missiles, had moved around the corner to pick up oil, and was now quietly steaming home—just another oil tanker with a load of oil on board for delivery to Europe—then on to Iran.

Regular commo checks came in. All on time. All correctly authenticated. Saya-dar monitored them all from his notebook computer.

And here he sat.

The targets. He could envision them, too, going up in brilliant flashes of light and searing heat.

Oh, the Americans would detect the launches and trajectories. He wanted to be there when they panicked, but that would be impossible. Ha! Impossible for two reasons. First, obviously, he could not be present in the reconnaissance surveillance room when their equipment detected the launches. He assumed they would. Maybe not, considering what the news reported about that mystery launch off Los Angeles. Regardless, they would not have the time to panic outside of the room where the launches might be detected. Oh, no, all would happen at blistering speed. After the destruction, when they could begin collecting themselves, he thought their data would survive. They'd triangulate back to the launch location.

The Americans would discover only placid, open ocean.

Nothing would trace the launch back to Iran.

Nothing.

Saya-dar laughed aloud at their perplexed faces, these Americans!

Again, he returned to the question he'd already worked out many times: *Was there any way they could trace the launch back to Iran?*

No, they could not. So long as the launch barge, the *Khazir*—named so appropriately—sank where he planned for it to sink. So long as the *jihadist* suicide engineer, did his job. *But that always was the risk.* Saya-dar knew this martyr. He was confident in his engineer cousin's ardor for Allah. He'd launch the missiles and blow the barge.

Besides, while the martyr-to-be did not know it, his missile launch triggered a timer to count down and blow the barge-sinking charges, anyway. Then, the *Khazir* would be scuttled in 6,000 feet of water. Never, never, would it be found. The *Khazir*, its embers within burned out, would drift downward, but not straight down. It would plane and glide, coming to rest on the ocean floor eventually, probably miles from the launch site.

The launch site. What a brilliant plan! CIA might eventually narrow the kind of missile America had been hit with to a few, based on the range, and they might even identify the six as Sunburns. They would be shocked at the extended range. But, oh! The mobile, disposable, launch pad comprised one of his best plans.

They would never figure out the ghostly origin of The Six Fires.

The bungalow worried him. Something had gone terribly wrong there and Saya-dar did not know what. Still, nothing seemed to come of it.

Saya-dar finished the cold drink and read the weather report. All those storms! Make for the North anyway? The preparations had moved from Manaus to Venezuela now, and then the action would move beyond. Saya-dar looked up at the pouring rain, filling the river, in turn, ever filling the Amazon downstream.

The Amazon. Oh, yes, that one detail. *Arcturus* should have been attacked and sunk by now. Saya-dar wondered why he'd not received confirmation from his "brother," Mr. Guevara.

Eight hundred miles around and down the South American coast from Caracas, *Arcturus* got underway from Georgetown. Jack and Gordon conferred and decided to leave the South American coast, pass north of Trinidad and Tobago and strike directly northwest across the Caribbean for Grenada. Bent over the charts, Jack spotted a name that immediately cloaked him with a sense of foreboding.

"Gordon, take a look. In about 10 minutes, we'll pass Devil's Island."

"Want to go sightseeing?" Gordon asked.

"Absolutely not. I've seen my share of hellholes. It just gives you the creeps even to be near the place. You can't help but want to put Devil's Island behind you. The sooner the better." Jack replied, feeling the skin on the back of his neck tighten.

North of *Arcturus,* off Waini Point, Guyana, what appeared to be two fishing charter boats lolled off the coast. The rods with lines in the Atlantic were for show. The boats were over-powered and armed, Somalia style.

Their captains waited only for word to go into action. They'd reported passage of the odd-looking humped-back barge, tugboats chugging away, heading north toward Venezuelan waters hours ago. However, radar still showed nothing tailing the *Khazir* for within the 40-mile radar range to the south of the barge.

"Phone Card," by Crazy blared from below. Appropriate. This seagoing Blackbeard stuff was a sideline. The real treasure-hunting was back in Trinidad selling pirated music and video games. The senior captain should know: he pirated his bootleg CDs and games through the Sea of Commerce and had almost wiped out legitimate profits for artists on the islands. *When the cat's away....* The Captain placed a satellite telephone call to Port of Spain to check up on the latest smuggled shipment of CDs and to ask about progress on his own pride-and-joy project: black market manufacturing. He had turned out hundreds of Crazy's "Phone Card" hit CDs. He had driven the competition off the streets—and had killed one stubborn street vendor to make a point.

This playing around at sea was good business and good PR in case the lunatic from Venezuela ever exercised his ambitions toward Trinidad and Tobago. Hell, he could virtually take one big step from Venezuela and be on Trinidad! Oh well, let him come. The senior captain would do these favors—this business—and be remembered when the time came. He would make his move to become the Principal Intellectual Property Pirate for the whole of Venezuela and from there, who knows? He had doodled a skull and crossbones parody flag logo, with two musical notes replacing the "X" made by the leg bones and a CD replacing the skull.

The senior of the two captains made a call. His Venezuelan contact had no idea why they'd been ordered to pirate the *Arcturus* as it passed, but, now, for some reason, the job was off. The captain didn't care. He assumed someone was willing to pay to dispatch the pirates to collect cash, or drugs, or for vendetta. It didn't matter. The entire cutthroat crew knew that, from time to time, they'd be called on by "someone" in the Venezuelan government to do a job or two. They'd always made out well. The "Buccaneer Coast Guard," they called themselves, would soon be back in Port of Spain, celebrating.

But not today. For whatever reason, their "victims" had slipped away. Or, had simply not shown up for their destruction.

The Captain shrugged. No pirated prize for capture today. Time to get back and guard the true treasure in ill-gotten gains taken by the real, modern, pirates of the Caribbean. The Captain laughed. His haul made Morgan and Blackbeard look like street beggars! Thank the Devil for the order sending him back to look after his landlubberly privateer enterprises!

Maybe the Devil does look after his own—for a time—letting them grow rich until time for the Luciferian harvest of souls.

Waiting on the quay at Maiquetia Port, Venezuela, stood a group of men watching Emilio Vasquez approach.

*Who are they and what could they possibly want?*

Emilio figured he'd find out soon enough, he supposed. With the storms building to the north and stubbornly refusing to move on, he'd probably be stuck here in port for a while. Normally, a few days "down time" in port was a party. This time, Emilio Vasquez absolutely dreaded it.

Emilio ferried out, met the tug's nervous little captain and took over to pilot the—whatever—into the harbor at Maiquetia. *What an unusual-looking barge!* Barge? What was it? Emilio Vasquez had never seen anything quite like it before, with its raised, shaped, steel lid. While he waited for the signal to bring her in, and marveled at the barge's inexplicable features, two men climbed atop the barge and worked their way with paint buckets and scaffolding to her bow—if that were, indeed, her bow.

*K-h-a-z-i-r,* they painted in red—not the usual white lettering. Didn't sound Portuguese to Captain Vasquez. More like—Middle Eastern. Maybe from one of those countries in the steppes?

Certainly, this *Khazir* was the strangest barge he had ever towed into port but he towed it in and secured it to the quay without difficulty, trying not to look too interested. Now docked at the end of the wharf sat a squat, completely covered, rectangular, dull gray-painted barge. Men hustled about readying cranes. Other men stood further out and around the crew, forming a perimeter—men with stubby-looking carbines supplied by the President-for-Life's new Russian friends, Emilio surmised—silently. Barricades cordoned off the whole area from the rest of the piers.

*What are those guys carrying? Who are they?*

Captain Vasquez pulled out his pocket telescope (which he carried as a badge of seagoing authority). The men on the perimeter cordon were definitely armed with some AK type carbine. Evidence of the 100,000 just bought by President

Guevara from the Russians.

*Are these guys Russians? No, those uniforms are Venezuelan Army.*

"What are you looking at, my friend?" a voice asked from behind Captain Vasquez.

Emilio Vasquez startled and shivered. Why was the strange passenger who arrived on the even stranger barge speaking to him now?

"I suggest, Captain Vasquez, you put your spyglass away and forget what you have seen," the stranger said, quietly. "Spies get hung."

Emilio Vasquez collapsed his telescope.

Soon, Captain Vazquez would be sequestered within the cordon. Then, he'd pilot the strange barge out of the port. He'd familiarize another man with both of his big ocean-going tugs' controls. As soon as they reached open sea, Captain Vazquez would be relieved of his duties. His throat would be cut, his body dumped overboard. Somehow, as he pocketed his scope, he knew all of this but saw no way to resist his fate. The crane crews working hard to position their machines between the six containers and the strange barge would meet a similar fate.

Out in the Atlantic, the storms gathered.

"Feed me weather updates—ongoing. Watch those three storms. I have to know where they are going, where they'll hit—everything," Nick said to Colin.

As Colin left, Nick called Burnell about the storms. He didn't know what all Burnell and Ortega had going on down there, but they needed to know. The storms: wild cards. They slowed everyone down, including the surveillance targets. They might also scramble our own assets, holding them on the ground, packing them off to safe ports, masking the action on the ocean from the eyes in the sky.

Nick's mind spun. He could not quite work it all out. For now, he had only to watch to see how it would all play out.

He'd briefed Operations that morning. Nick knew what that meant: someone prepared for action. He'd know who when the time came. For now, his job was to keep eyes on that tanker from Iran, already now in the Caribbean, running from the storms toward Venezuela, and on the two barges off the South American coast heading north—eyes on Carlos Guevara. *Or am I watching the Russians? Or the Iranians? Or all three? Is anyone else attending this diabolical party? Maybe No One.*

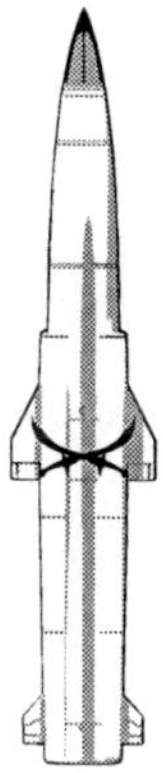

# 44

*Thursday, early morning hours*
*Port of Maiquetia, Venezuela*

The approaching multiple storms blew urgency into their work, even though the hurricanes were forming far to the north and east. The men on the docks at Maiquetia felt more than the quickening breezes. They were not stupid. Never before had they handled such a cargo. This cargo frightened them.

The crane operators set up to offload the Iranian tanker. That oddity, alone, said a great deal. The petroleum facility down the coast should be handling this cargo—if the *Mi Fortuna* carried oil. They muttered among themselves and wondered why they were moving cranes to this remote end of the docks, to pick up cargo from an oil tanker. Containers, but they could not use the gantry cranes. Had to use the modified movable cranes with cables. OK, but why containers on an oil tanker? Are there not enough container ships plying the seas?

The stevedores had a good job. Made good money, for Venezuela, with good benefits. They liked Maiquetia, and Caracas was just over the mountain. Most of the men had migrated from Venezuela's interior towns. Most of the time they worked steadily, worked hard. Running the big cranes and equipment took skill, took training. You didn't put just anybody who showed up on the docks behind the controls and start swinging shippers' precious cargoes around. But, lately, with the market slow-down, the stevedores saw fewer and fewer of the world's flags flapping in the breeze, pulling into port from the Atlantic. Crews talked of dozens of huge container ships, idled, tied up in ports all along the Mediterranean. So, yes, no shortage of container ships drafted this oil tanker into service carrying dry mystery cargo.

Yet, before them floated the tanker, hiding these uniquely shaped, welded steel containers, stowed below deck in what was obviously a specially-created cargo compartment. Although the stevedores high atop the cranes had no idea what these odd containers might hold, they admired the efficiency engineered into the system. Once in place, the tops of the containers and the welded steel plates looked, from a short distance, just like a deck.

More than the nature of this secreted, obviously smuggled cargo, what scared them was that they knew about it. What they knew made no sense. Neither did it make any sense that they had spent the last three days confined to their dockside quarters. A man can play cards only for so long!

Now, though, all made perfectly good sense—in an insane sort of way. The Greek tanker, they all suspected, was not Greek at all. Why would the Greeks build such a ship? Did the Greeks build it? And where were the Greeks who always came on the Greek ships?

In the middle of the night, the crane operators removed the unbolted hatches and plates. Back in the control cabs of the cranes, they swiveled and dipped and drew out the steel containers. From these, the crane operators withdrew long, slender, pointed, finned missiles with no markings. One by one, the missiles were offloaded until they sat like devils on the quay.

When the crane operators finished, they followed their orders and bolted the deck plates back down over them, making the tanker look just like any other.

They had every right to grumble—doing dock-hand work when they were skilled crane-operators—but, this time, they did not complain. In fact, the crane operators tried to appear oblivious. Then, the ostensibly-Greek tanker steamed away to God Knows Where and the strange barge was next. The crane operators crossed themselves in thanks to see the *Mi Fortuna* embark.

Now, though, tugs nudged the ugly *Khazir* into place. The crane operators stood by, wondering what they were to do with this monstrosity. What they saw next frightened them even more than offloading the containers from the *Mi Fortuna* onto the quay.

A different crew emerged from the building at the extreme end of the quay—the building cordoned off and guarded. This crew unbolted heavy plates atop the *Khazir* and then called on the crane operators to move the plates back.

Such a barge, the crane operators had never seen before. It's humped deck rose to a peaked ridge in the center. It's solid deck surface had looked ordinary from a distance, but now, as they lifted the heavy steel plates, they saw that these only mimicked deck plates; instead, the heavy plates they hooked, lifted, and swung to the side were removable hatches. Beneath the hatches, they saw brackets and machinery—hydraulics. By now, they had surmised the purpose for all of this, and it sickened them.

One by one, they lifted the missiles, swung them over "the beast" (as they had come to refer to the barge in hushed tones) and lowered the missiles carefully into place—within the belly of the barge. Six missiles they lowered this way—lowered onto the tailored brackets that would house the missiles on their next journey.

No, these men were not stupid. You did not survive Venezuela's docks, operating the cranes, handling millions of dollars' worth of cargo, and watching the world come and go, without learning anything. They'd seen their share of unusual "custom" cargoes loaded. Never before anything like this, though.

First, plainly some of the men supervising the loading weren't Greek. So many of the world's ships and sailors were Greek; they'd heard Greek spoken on the docks at Maiquetia before. These men looked Middle Eastern and spoke to one another in another language they'd heard before. Ever since their president had become friendly with Iran, their oil tankers would come and go. Oil from Iran, embargoed by much of the world, became laundered Venezuelan oil. Farsi, that's what the mysterious supervisors spoke. Farsi.

The cranes didn't just lower the missiles into stowage either. The crane operators lowered the six onto strong brackets attached to the hydraulics. Crane operators have and develop spatial perception skill or they are off the job fast. If you cannot visualize how your own motions translate into greatly exaggerated lifting, swiveling, extending, lowering motions, you have no place in the cab of the high machines on the docks. Crane operators have been around hydraulic lifts and mechanisms forever. After a time, and with the right innate ability and experience, you can look at how a hydraulic cylinder is attached to a mechanism and you can *see* it performing its work. You can see into its future—its purpose, all without it moving.

These brackets would raise the missiles—horizontal to the deck, as if ready to be offloaded again. The hydraulics would then pivot the missiles vertically until the bases sat on top of the concrete pads the operators now saw poured into the bottoms of the compartments. The brackets would hold the missiles erect at any angle up to 90 degrees. Other hydraulics would—on signal—detach the lifting brackets and fall away from the missiles.

No, the crane operators were not stupid. They could see they were installing the telephone pole-sized missiles onto a concealable launcher disguised as a barge. An odd barge, a harmless looking, decked, dry-bulk barge.

And this is what truly frightened them. They now were certain who the Middle Eastern superintendents were.

And they knew where these missiles would land. They knew it. Where else? And they knew what would follow. Oh, not specifically. They simply knew the United States would retaliate. Massively. Maybe before asking too many questions. They knew all of this just could not go un-noticed and that the U.S. would trace the missiles back to the madman in charge of their country. They foresaw hard, hard times ahead for Venezuela, all because of that one man's foolishness. They knew he would be killed, or humiliated in captivity, dragged away, hands chained together, looking unkempt and haggard, all bluster finally gone.

They knew that would be a good thing. And they knew they had seen too much here, tonight, to live to see any of it. In seeing the barge's future, they also foresaw their own.

# 45

*Thursday*
*CIA Headquarters*

Nick Riccolo watched it all. The storms worried him—for a couple of reasons. One was the advancing, increasing cloudiness. They'd tried to get a man onto the quay. No way. One of the agents in Caracas rented a squalid house on the ridge top above the docks, but he was just too far away and the angle wasn't right.

Their agent tending the bar by the docks had served a lot of beer and gotten to know the crews, but, then, the crews were taken away and never returned. Not even their hard-drinking first mate.

They'd considered SEALs—combat divers. The docks were heavily guarded with spotlights shining all across the water; the harbor was busy; tugboats at the harbor entrance trawled wire mesh screens back and forth at unknown depths. Whomever was behind this was thinking about underwater infiltration and taking counter-measures.

In the end, though, those same spotlights had done-in Carlos Guevara. Reflections illuminated the missiles sufficiently, albeit briefly, for the KH-11 satellite miles above to acquire sharp video. Breathtaking video. Even a shot at a steep enough angle to read the newly-painted name on the side: *Khazir*, whatever that meant.

Nick had rushed it to the DD who'd—again—brought him before the president. Incredible! The video, that is. President Bullington had sworn. The DD had watched, completely calm, his mind already looking ahead toward operations. The DD worried about operations; the president worried about the political ramifications; so, Nick worried about the storms. He worried about maintaining the unobstructed flow of intelligence that those guys doing the operations were going to need. Regardless of what plan Washington might now hatch, weather could foul it up. He'd seen it before.

Nick kept up constant surveillance. Photographs showed the barge completely covered over now, its removed deck plates and hatches back in place, and the six missiles invisible again, but this time, loaded on the strange *Khazir*.

Just before dawn on Thursday, the guilty *Mi Fortuna* steamed away to the east. Ocean-going tugs pulled the *Khazir* out to sea and she struck northward.

"Oh, aren't you quite clever? You slip in and out, disguising your true purpose. You avoid dirtying your hands with the blood and guts of others, but you enable. You are—you are like—you are like Saya-dar!" Nick said out loud but to no one as he watched the tanker, now lighter by six modified, SS-N-22 Sunburn cruise missiles, head east toward Europe to deliver her load of laundered Iranian-now-Venezuelan oil to France.

*Perhaps you will meet with an accident.*

Now what? Here sat Iranian nuclear missiles on a squat ugly barge, this *Khazir*.

So?

What did the Islamic *jihadist* mastermind plan now for his *Khazir*?

Nick thought of something and called SOCOM. He found Sergeant Burnell on duty, as always.

"Burnell, you're good with Farsi. Got one for you. They painted a name on the designer barge, finally. Let me run it past you. Might mean something. *K-h-a-z-i-r.* Yeah, that's right: *Khazir.* How about letting me know if it means something?"

Sergeant Burnell's Farsi was very good. Beyond fluency, Burnell knew the language's history, its many nuances, its richness. This one baffled him, though. He went to the Web.

*Oh. Oh, my!*

Sergeant Burnell called Nick as he had promised. Next, he rang General Ortega.

"Sir, CIA made the name on the designer barge built from Jack's blueprints. Yes sir, the one from that bungalow in the jungle. Very appropriate. Thought you should know."

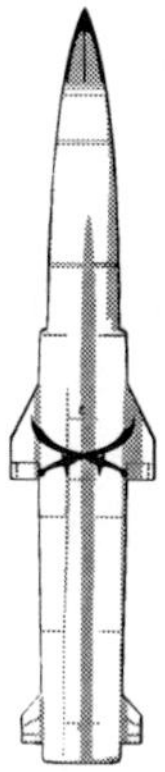

# 46

*Thursday morning*
*Washington, D.C. and*
*Fort Bragg, North Carolina*
*The White House and Special*
*Operations Command HQ*

"Mr. President?" Paul Ortega answered.

"I want to wait," President Bullington simply said.

"For what?" Paul wondered and asked.

"For more rope to play out. Can we? Can we wait?" the president asked.

General Paul Ortega, now Deputy Commander, Special Operations Command, lifelong infantry officer, indulged in something he rarely did: he hesitated.

Yes, the United States could wait, building the evidence against Carlos Guevara. We could watch, mount active surveillance, and build a body of informant and photographic proof that Guevara was complicit in an attempt to launch nuclear-tipped cruise missiles against the United States. The clamorers within the country—the president's political enemies—seemed to always demand that, to howl for "beyond a reasonable doubt." That standard worked great as the burden of proof in a criminal trial, keeping the government in check and off the innocent private citizen's back. But this is war, and if you wait for your enemy to attack in war, then you are frozen in place while your enemy circles and chooses his time to close in for the kill.

For General Paul Ortega—soldier of 35 years, Army Ranger, Airborne, Special Forces, charter member of Delta Force's first selection group—the intel they had right now sufficed for war. From an infantryman's point of view, Guevara represented an enemy soldier with a rifle in his hands, raising it to align the sights on you and press the trigger.

For General Paul Ortega, the proof more than sufficed. However, once the killing was done, the press would take over. The pacifists would howl against this "unilateral" action. The European press would drag out the old "cowboy" invective used to deride President Reagan, and they would smack President Bullington with it. The opposition in Congress would wonder out loud—in press conferences and leaks—whether President Bullington had exercised "restraint." The loonies would call for impeachment. A paper from the State Department would surface, extolling the virtues of diplomacy, without out-and-out slamming the president of course: the political winds would not yet have established their prevailing direction.

The South American press would throw a fit. Secretly, the leaders of Brazil and Columbia, in particular, would applaud. Columbia might applaud loudly and openly. Brazil's old leadership might have made supportive sounds; the new leadership remained unknown, but Brazil's leftist professors and street organizers were sure to foam at the mouth. The Russians would hypocritically issue statements warning about American imperialist designs. The Venezuelans? They would probably breathe a collective sigh of relief that Guevara was finally gone and get on with working out a replacement government, hoping for better this time.

Congress would want to hold hearings about the take-down of another nation's leader. Someone would trot out our constitutional criminal protections designed to keep an intrusive government off the backs of our own citizens, and want to apply the "beyond a reasonable doubt" burden of proof to the president's decision to kill Carlos Guevara. If they tipped their hand about the accuracy of the photo-intelligence, and risked the life of their agents on the ground, they could prove exactly what was on the *Khazir*, but they couldn't prove who, exactly, was behind the plot and what he intended for the six Sunburns.

But, if the president waited too long—.

"Sir, while we do not know just exactly what Guevara, or Saya-dar, or some other committee of America-haters plans to do with the missiles, we know the capability of the missiles and simply cannot allow this threat to build to the point they actually achieve that capability of striking our country. Cruise missiles have a limited range, so they lack that capability right now. We think. We absolutely cannot allow them to get within that range. You cannot wait so long that some Murphy's Law situation messes up your last-minute kill.

'So, sir, you ask me if we can wait.

'I understand the ramifications of stopping all of this right now. Were it simply the political costs to you and to your party, I would say, "Hell, no! Hit now and take no chance at all that they slip anything through!" But, I suppose like you, I'm thinking about the broader potential cost to our will, our moral courage to fight our sworn enemies. Some in this country have less of that than others. Some in this country get nervous when courageous Americans take up arms to defend their country. Once they got over peeing in their pants over what holocaust you had stopped, instead of thanking you for saving their sorry asses, they would start the second-guessing and political sniping. The next president would look back on all of that and be sorely tempted to hold his fire—maybe too long.

'So, Mr. President, I hate to say it, but, yes, we can wait. The 200-mile missile-range allows you to wait—if we're sure they are not enhanced beyond 200 miles. We should give ourselves some margin for error, set a permissible range, and take them out just before that. And we should allow for Mr. Murphy's mischief," General Ortega concluded.

The president said nothing.

"Mr. President? Bull?"

"Agreed. I'll want to know the strike options ASAP. An hour for the first plans. Realistic?"

*Realistic? What was realistic about any of this? An hour?*

"Under other circumstances, sir, probably not, but you'll have them within the hour anyway. We will concurrently continue planning and changing the plans as the situation develops. In case the situation develops more rapidly than expected, I request permission to shoot—to take out the *Khazir* or any other vessel carrying those missiles getting what I deem to be too close. I realize sinking an ostensibly privately-owned vessel has ramifications, too. You know how combat goes; you can never know how combat will go. We do, however, *know* that the *Khazir* carries nuclear cruise missiles, hidden beneath its barge-looking deck. I'm asking for discretion to shoot."

The president simply said, "Granted. I'll have permission typed up and to you ASAP."

"Mr. President, one more thing?"

"Yes?"

"That will take care of the weapons. What about their

sender?"

"Yes, what about Mr. Guevara?" the president asked, his eyes narrowing. "I'll tell you what, Ranger. You just keep an eye on him and make plans. Keep Jack down there. I'll think about whether this will be a kill or a capture—or something else."

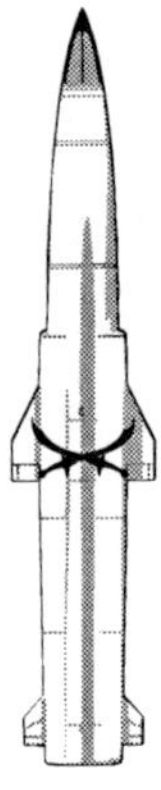

# 47

*Thursday noon*
*Aboard Arcturus, Atlantic Ocean*

"*Arcturus*?" General Ortega asked.

"Jack here, sir."

"Jack, are you keeping your eye on the weather? Those storms are kicking up into hurricanes. Four of them are lining up. Four! Right in a line! This looks like it's going to be some hurricane season. It appears they will hit one after the other. The first one is entering the Caribbean now. You better hole up there in Grenada."

"I'll send you our position, sir," Jack said. "Thank you for caring."

"By the way, I'm putting Burnell on. CIA—that Italian guy—ID'd the name on that designer barge you tracked down the Amazon. Burnell knows what it means. This Saya-dar, man, he is a piece of work. Loves these meaningful names, I guess. Stand by for Master Sergeant Professor Herr Doktor Burnell," General Ortega announced and was gone.

"Jack, this is Burnell. How are you guys?"

"Fine, Bernie, fine. Enjoying the vacation. Actually, our trigger-fingers are itching. Got anything actionable?" Jack asked.

"Funny you should put it that way. The missile-launching

barge is now named the *Khazir.* You'll love this. Very poetic. Very appropriate. *Khazir.* Please take a seat and take out your notebooks and pens. The lecture is about to begin.

"This is ancient Persian, not the more modern Farsi, not a word frequently used, but it is written from time to time, mostly in literature. Rarely. Sort of like we might draw from history to resurrect an antique term. Take like an Old English word we would recognize, but would never use. Try "tarry," or "prithee" or "betwixt". Recognize those words, Jack?"

"Yea, verily, professor."

"You yachtsman playboy types are so, so funny. Well, that's sort of how this word is. No Iranian would use this word in ordinary conversation; it hearkens—Say, I did it, didn't I?—"hearkens"—well, it hearkens back to an earlier time. *Khazir* means the following: "ashes beneath the coals which lie like latent sparks: the fire beneath; the coals beneath the surface."

"'The fire beneath'," repeated Jack. "Thanks, Bernie, I'll tell No One. Out."

Jack briefed Gordon, and they got the *Arcturus* underway. At least they were moving. Into what, they were not sure. So far, it looked like they were bystanders.

"Take 'er around the bend, Chief, then east. Skirt Port of Spain. We're bound for Grenada. We'll be weathering the storms there," Gordon said, addressing the grizzled, tanned 50-something at the wheel in the pilothouse.

"Aye, aye, sir. Coming about," said Chief Harbison, long retired from the U.S. Navy, but never "out" of the Navy.

"And, call the crew together for a briefing here in the

pilothouse in 30 minutes," Gordon added. "Jack, let's plan this next movement and issue a Warning Order," Gordon said, referring to the infantry's, universally used, short-form "Get Ready to Operate" order.

"The crew. That would be Sullivan, sir. Aye, aye, sir," said the Chief again. Chief Harbison was a man of few words.

"Roger," said Jack, who began planning immediately.

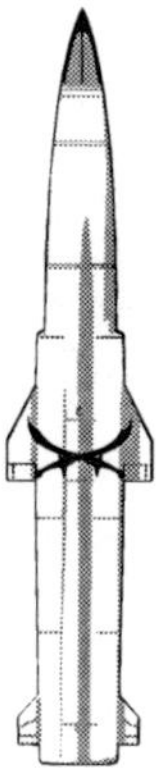

# 48

*Thursday early afternoon*
*Atlantic Ocean, approximately*
*100 miles off coast of*
*Venezuela*
*Arcturus, the pilothouse*

"Our current mission is simple: move, take up position in Grenada, and await further orders. We are not expecting any combat," Gordon added, knowing what was next.

Chief Harbison spoke up. "Sir, last time you didn't expect any combat, *Arcturus* got rocketed out of the water by pirates bearing RPG-7s instead of cutlasses and cannons. Remember? They chased us up a hill. We ended up at The Alamo—only we overturned history and killed them all. When you say 'We are not expecting any action,' it sends chills up my spine! What makes you think we're out of the action this time?"

All grinned, including Gordon. *Arcturus'* first sailing mission had nothing to do with General Ortega's plans and plots. Nonetheless, the team, including Jack and his friend, Bobby, just invited aboard, had blundered across scheming between the Cubans and Saya-dar. It had been "life or death on a lee shore" as Long John Silver might have said.

Gordon answered: "For one, we have no mission. No raid, no ambush, no reconnaissance. Nothing. Just move to a new base. Seriously, this has gotten big. There is a credible threat against the continental U.S. involving nuclear-tipped cruise missiles launched against—presumably—one of our ships at sea. It's developing, not imminent. Since it got big, it went to the Army and the CIA. Still, since we're here in the region and already read in on the problem, General Ortega is having us stage here, moving closer to the expected battlefield, awaiting further orders."

"By Army, sir, do you meant the Big Army is involved?" Chief Harbison asked.

"No, chief, no one's alerted any infantry task forces yet. No invasions are planned, yet, anyway. It's gone to Special Operations Command, and General Ortega is involved—officially," Gordon replied, clarifying.

"Thinking ahead, I can foresee our status going from standby to activate real fast. Let's talk about what other assets are available to us just in case. What about air?" Jack asked.

"None, probably," said Gordon.

"None?"

"None."

"No air support?"

"No, no air support."

Silence.

"Air is all elsewhere, looking after the bigger mission, and, besides, we have to assume that the storms preclude air support—either firepower or transport—until they pass. Bottom line, somehow, mobile cruise missiles on a platform inching toward America take priority over us. Can you imagine?" Gordon said.

"More detail please?"

"Can't," said Gordon.

"Why not?"

"Don't know more. Jack, would you give the Warning Order? That will fill in some of the rest of the plan—but not much," Gordon said.

Jack quickly delivered the Warning Order. The "enemy situation" portion drew the most discussion.

"OK, here's what we know," Jack elaborated. "We got a tip from an agent in Manaus. The tip indicated two things. One is historical, but by no means off our radar. You know we've chased our tails trying to find out who planned that multiple truck-bomb attack back in '07. The trail led nowhere concrete, but the name "Saya-dar" surfaced as the probable mastermind. The bombers all died. The logistics support was very well compartmentalized. A few came forward but possessed only a mere plan fragment. Drop a shipment of diesel fuel here. Pick up a trailer there. The intel from these infiltrated sleeper agents did lead to some specific staging areas. These were all rural areas with sheds built there. These sites were bought and prepared long, long ago, and just sat, maintained, for years. Apparently, this was where the fuel and fertilizer were mixed, and the truck bombs readied.

'Sophisticated but simple. We found fragments of vinyl among the blast debris. These we learned were from commercially available waterbeds. The bomb assemblers used these as tamping, on the sides and top. These waterbed tamping jackets directed the force forward—into the stores. You know the rest. Twenty bombs in 20 department stores throughout the country—mostly the south and Midwest. That's the background. Here's where it starts to connect up to today.

'We believe the bombers infiltrated through the Port of Alabama at Mobile, smuggled in on a modified Venezuelan oil tanker. Our agent in Manaus identified the shipyard where the terrorist mastermind had the tanker modified to smuggle in the infiltrators. Here's why we're running around out here now. Middle-Eastern men coordinated with Carlos Guevara personally and arrived at this Manaus shipyard to take delivery of another vessel: a modified, very odd, barge. The agent, a woman working for the shipyard's owner, ID'd Guevara as a personal friend and sometimes visitor at the shipyard owner's bungalow in the Amazon jungle, south of Manaus.

'We set up surveillance. Before they finished their business, something unusual occurred and the whole surveillance op blew up. The visiting Middle-Easterners were killed. So was the shipyard owner. However, our agent got photos of the barge plans out to us. CIA looked them over and declared them to be a mobile missile platform capable of launching six cruise missiles," Jack said, pausing to let the crew absorb all of this.

Gordon looked at Jack. *Well, he certainly gave a sterilized, nuts and bolts description of a bloody and dramatic business—and neatly left out his own role.*

Whistles. Looking around at each other. Stone faces. The different way men react to hearing such things always intrigued Jack.

"Target?" asked the never long-winded Chief Harbison.

"Unknown. We know that the Sunburn's range is 65 miles. However, during the mid '90s, the Navy actually helped the Russians figure out how to extend the missile's range. Seems they wanted to buy some of them to use to test the Aegis system. The better the enemy's weapon, the better the test. Yes, I know. Unbelievable, but CIA tells us it's true. We're concerned now that the range might be as much as 200 miles."

Eyes got big. Jack continued.

"That's a long, long range for an anti-ship cruise missile. The Sunburn travels at more than twice the speed of sound so having the Russians shoot one at you from up close is sort of like the Karate Kid's "crane technique" against which there is no defense. 'These Sunburns, though, are air-breathers. They have air intakes. This tells us they are meant to launch from above the water.

'So, we just can't put all of this divergent data together. The Navy thinking has been that they don't have to worry about it because any ship the Russians have—and could sell to the Iranians—to launch the Sunburns would have to get within range, and we can detect much further out than that. Here's a sobering thought, though.

'If they do slip inside our defenses, we truly don't have a defense. The Sunburn flies far too fast and just off the water, so we can't detect it coming in. We would have to detect the launching platform—whatever kind of boat that might be—first.

'Finally, the Russians demonstrated these enhanced Sunburns to the Iranian Defense Minister, who placed an immediate order. The Iranians have missiles. They must have found something special about these. We just don't know if they have the enhanced-range model, and we don't know how much the range might have successfully been enhanced even beyond that," Jack ended, deciding to catch his breath, sip some coffee, and let that sink in.

"Jack, that just doesn't make sense then. There is no way we are going to let an Iranian or Russian warship close enough to one of our vessels, even if the range is enhanced," Chief Harbison observed.

"Yes, Chief, you are so right, but these missiles aren't on a warship. To speak of. They are on what appears to be an otherwise common bulk cargo-hauling barge. They are hidden. Disguised. Drum roll please. *Khazir*: 'the underlying embers—

the fire within.' They're not just smuggling missiles somewhere in our region; they have these things on hidden, seagoing launchers, moving our direction.

'The question becomes: 'Where do they plan to aim them and how the hell do they think they are going to get them close enough to any of our ships to launch?' Nuclear or not, if they launch from way out, our ships have the detection equipment to spot them and shoot them down. But, no fleet is going to let another ship get in close enough to fire cruise missiles because, from close enough in, we literally have no defense. No defense. We just can't figure out how they think they're going to get close enough to fire missiles at us and get away with it."

A younger man spoke up, Sullivan, a crewman doubling as Gordon's intelligence specialist. "Sir, I've been watching the weather, just as you said, and we are sailing toward the projected path of multiple tropical storms growing into a chain of 'canes," he said. "Why don't we just go ahead now and take this *Khazir* out, and this Saya-dar along with it?" Sullivan asked in a very logical way.

Gordon spoke up.

"There are good reasons. There is another villain mixed up in this, and we hope to flush him out. A mistake. A call. A desperate move. Maybe a document found after we take out the missiles—whatever that is going to look like. Bottom line: we're letting this play out a bit since the Khazir is so far from being within range and since it is right there in plain sight. That is not our call; it comes from higher-higher."

Gordon motioned for Jack. "Think about this for a few minutes, fellows. Take a short break. I'll be back in 10 and we'll cover any more questions you have. Sullivan, maybe you can get us another weather update," Gordon said. No one asked a question or added anything. They just thought. No wonder they sat silent. What a tale to hear!

Jack and Gordon walked outside the pilothouse and plopped down in the aft lounge's overstuffed chairs and sofas.

"Those are good men, Gordon. How'd you pick them?" he asked.

"The Chief. From Long Island. Joined the Navy right out of high school at the tail end of the Vietnam War. Then, it ended. He got out after his four years and drifted. Fought for prize money. Drove trucks. Stayed in the Navy Reserve the whole time, though. Gravitated back to the docks and was supervising stevedores there when the Iranians took over our embassy in 1979. He saw this as a personal declaration of war and went active duty again. Saw the need for special ops, as well as huge, crushing, naval power, and went SEALs. Retired after 24 years and I picked him up. Not only did I get an expert at piloting all manner of small boats, I got a warrior, too.

'My intel guy, Sullivan. Smart cookie. Master's in English literature from Stanford. Speaks—I don't even know how many languages. Every time I ask, he's picked up one more! Could not stay out of the fight his country found herself in though, so he joined the Army. Buck Sergeant in the $82^{nd}$ Airborne Division where Ortega spotted him. He wanted Delta, but Ortega got him first. He's invaluable. He's like having a CIA Analyst Section on board. There's no way I want that Ricollo guy at CIA even to know Sullivan exists or he'll try to steal Sullivan away from us.

'Both of these men came from families where someone served before them. Common thread—kind of like your own, Jack," Gordon said. He referred to Jack's grandfather, a flyer. Army Air Corps during WWII and U.S. Air Force when the pilots got their own service.

"Say, Jack, here's something I never asked you. Why did you pick infantry ground-pounder? I'd have thought you'd follow in your ancestors' footsteps and climb into airplanes. Not even a chopper pilot. How come?" Gordon asked.

"Ha. Simple, really. As a kid, I spent time in the woods, hours and hours, just exploring. I got real comfortable with the woods. Just couldn't see going up there where there are no trees for protection," Jack explained.

"Now look at you! Where are the trees?"

"Good point. Your *Arcturus* is pretty nice for a PT boat, though. Let's go back in and see what they have processed and come up with," Jack said. "I can't wait to hear what they surmise from all of this."

Sullivan—as predicted—asked first.

"These other vessels, what about them? The tanker and the barge ordered by NYC?"

"The tanker—the *Mi Fortuna*—headed back the way it came. Due north. Right now, it's on course to pass between The Dominican Republic and Puerto Rico. About half way there. We think it's behaving for now, carrying oil to a European friend."

Here, Jack started pointing at a map of the Caribbean tacked up.

"*Mi Fortuna* came that same way, through the Mona Passage, and steamed straight south into port at Maiquetia, just outside of Caracas. We shot pix of the secreted missiles being off-loaded late Wednesday night from the *Mi Fortuna* onto the *Khazir*. CIA is watching, but it appears the *Mi Fortuna* is eventually bound now for home—Teheran. It's really Iranian," Jack explained.

"Where is it now?" Sullivan pressed, looking for a potential target.

"Not far east. CIA will track it. Relax, Sully. We can't do

anything to it yet because that would tip off whomever is behind the missile transfer. We may let it get home and see what they do with it next. We may not wait that long. It's there and not getting away. So, disposition of that target: unknown for now and irrelevant," Jack said. Then, he added: "Like you, I'd like to see that ship disappear somewhere across the vast Atlantic. Who knows? Maybe it will. Looks like we're not going to be in on that, though."

Sullivan continued: "OK, then, what about the humble, no-name garbage barge?"

Gordon frowned. "Good question, Sully. We just don't know even whether it fits into to anything. The shipyard at Manaus where the *Mi Fortuna* was modified first to carry terrorist infiltrators, and now to deliver these missiles, is an operating, otherwise legitimate, money-making business. The NYC Port Authority order appears to have been just a coincidence, although we're looking at the procurement process there and identifying specifically who made the decision to buy from Fats. Anyway, besides taking custom orders from Tangos, Fats operated a regular business. That's why it was such good cover. That, and the fact that—city of a million or not—Manaus is far out of the way, even for its own government. The NYC order could have nothing whatsoever to do with the plan. We can't figure out yet how it might fit in. A ruse, maybe? How? Nevertheless, the garbage barge is north and west of us right now.

'Check this out. The garbage barge worked its way along the Venezuelan coast while the *Khazir* was taking on its missile cargo. Nothing surprising about that route, either. It's the ordinary except that the garbage barge passed by the port at Maiquetia right about the time the *Khazir* headed out. Coincidence? Now they are traveling almost together. Like the rest of us, both the

*Khazir* and the garbage barge may button up during what looks like is going to be Hurricane Ike," Gordon finished.

"So," Sullivan played it back, seeming to be talking to himself, "We have a tale of three ships. The Iranian oil tanker that delivered nuclear-tipped missiles to Venezuela is headed back east and being watched; we have discovered a cleverly designed, sea-going launch pad disguised as a barge—actually it is a barge. Finally, we have a stray garbage barge, built by the same rogue—but now deceased—shipwright, finished and dispatched just ahead of the missile barge, quietly chugging northward to be handed over to its buyer in New York City. All of this sailing-around action, and here we are in the middle of it, but on hold."

"Yes, that's about it." Jack summarized. "Fishing. We're supposed to be fishing."

"Weird," Sullivan said.

"Huh?" said Gordon. "Might you elaborate?"

"Behind all of this is a planner, a brain, this mastermind, lurking undetected—as of yet. Maybe we can focus there as we fish from the *Arcturus.* We're too far away from everything else happening, Gordon. What if we abandon our safe harbor in Grenada idea, and move further north?" Sullivan asked.

"You've been watching the weather closer than anyone else. You know what's building. We've already had tropical storms Fay and Gustav, and now Hannah and Ike are working up speed. Grenada is too far south of the usual hurricane path. Moving north puts us right in the potential hurricane path. Is that what you're suggesting?" Jack challenged.

"I'm proposing we move to the sound of the guns: even if they are not yet going off. Looks like the action is going to explode much further north. We should set up our patrol base further north and be ready," Sullivan concluded.

"Where?" Gordon asked. "Got any place in mind?"

"As a matter of fact, I just happen to have map-reconned a spot. I found a sheltered harbor, tucked away into the south side of the Dominican Republic. I say we skip Grenada, make for the Dominican Republic's south coast, beat the hurricane, batten down the hatches, ride it out there, and be ready to move when the shooting starts," Sullivan said.

"Show us, please," Jack said, indicating the map.

Sullivan stood, approached with a rolled up chart under his arm, and tacked it over the Caribbean map.

"Here," he said, pointing to a spot within a bay on the south side of the Dominican Republic coast. Sullivan turned to gauge the reactions. The men stood and thought. Then, Jack spoke up.

"I bet you were one of those guys who always seemed to know where the soccer ball was going to be kicked to next. I like it. Let's do it," said Jack.

Gordon looked at them both: *The impulsiveness of youth!* Still, combat developed fast, and rarely did the enemy strike exactly on our planned schedule. Gordon hated unmade decisions.

"When we get the call, it's going to happen fast," Gordon said slowly. "We are too far away. We will run back out to sea if a hurricane heads our way. We will move toward where we think the ball will next get kicked. Good thinking, Sully.

'Forget Grenada. Set course for the Dominican Republic, Chief. Here, take on fuel at Barahona Port and then head here, 45 miles west of Santo Domingo. We'll put in there and wait out the storms. In the meantime, check weapons and do your maintenance. I don't like it a bit. Something is up, and we're going to be in striking distance when they hit," Gordon said and adjourned the briefing.

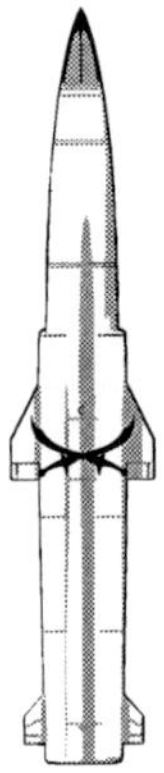

# 49

*Friday*
*CIA Headquarters,*
*monitoring Tropical Storm Ike*

Tropical storm Ike gathered power. It had stalled and sat. Now, it gathered, picked up, and moved west-northwest. Meteorologists watched and grew more anxious over its potential power.

Nick Riccolo also watched the reports come in. He, too, grew more concerned. Where was all of this going? How severely would the storms affect surveillance?

Ike picked this time to build toward hurricane velocity and alter its course northward. Suddenly, it shifted into the much more the usual Hurricane Alley course, sweeping toward the Leeward Islands of Antigua and Barbuda, on its way toward maybe Puerto Rico. Westward still lay Hispaniola, the island home of two countries: already-devastated Haiti, and the Dominican Republic.

Nick buzzed the DD. "Boss, they've picked a bad time, but they're on the move. The missile-barge left Maiquetia and is heading north. Without the hurricane, it could be in U.S. waters in three days."

"And with the hurricane?" the DD wanted to know.

"Who knows? That's not all."

"OK?"

Nick explained the developing situation. "The barge bound for NYC is staying roughly together with the missile barge. Together. They're going the same direction and are at roughly the same speed, 40 miles apart. Radar range of each other. Figure that."

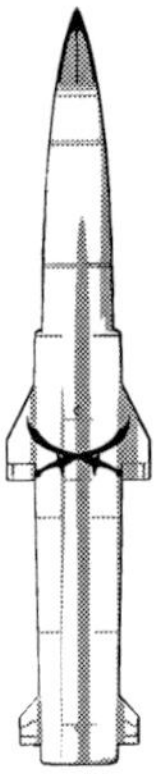

# 50

*Friday*
*Port au Prince, Haiti*

The hot sun burned hotter than usual as Jacques Moreaux dismounted his motorcycle and steadied himself on the gravel. The heat rose from the rocks to envelope him. Sweat trickled down his arms, making his palms slick. The riding-breeze was gone, gone, gone, and the Haitian heat beset him again with punishing vengeance—punishing Jacques who tried to escape by riding.

Head throbbing. Feeling a little queasy. Prestige. Needed a cool bottle of Haiti's surprisingly good, ice-cold beer—Prestige—or two—or three, maybe.

The Unknown Slave stood before him. Jacques kicked down the stand, locked his bike, and took purposeful, careful steps toward the opened front of the bar. Inside, no one looked up, at least yet. The bartender spotted his regular customer, Jacques, heading for a table and waved to him. Oh, yes, Francois would be glad to see Jacques. He knew Jacques would spend money and probably buy for everyone else in the place, too.

Jacques' eyes focused on a white, round, plastic table with four plastic-molded, forest-green chairs scattered about. The two-color mix served as "designer" decor here. He picked one out and eased in. *Yes, better already.* Francois appeared, smiled and set the ice-cold Prestige before Jacques. *Oh, yes, much better already.*

Jacques gripped the cold bottle with both hands. He lifted it to his face and cooled his cheeks. The first sip gave peace to Jacques—no easy accomplishment, considering Jacques' bent—his line of work.

Jacques Moreaux, Port-au-Prince entrepreneur, man of means and contacts: Jacques Moreaux, pirate.

It's not that Jacques set out to be a pirate. At first, Jacques merely smuggled. People. They were the easiest. Paid good, got on board, afraid to complain or he might keep their money and refuse them passage. He swaggered, blustered, glared, barked orders and told them to shut up or he'd feed them to the sharks. For the most part, he dropped them off where they wanted. Had to make an example a time or two, but it would have been bad for business if they reported back to the home folks with some horror story. The Dominican Republic. Puerto Rico. Maybe even the states. Now *that* trip made Jacques really good money.

Then, the South American drug-runners got in on it. A man called on Jacques at The Unknown Slave and began to talk business. At first, Jacques thought him like any other: no visa, no future, and looking for passage to a better place. Probably a small-time criminal back in his home country and, thus, unable to get a visa, maybe even unable to get a passport.

But, the conversation evolved. Soon, Jacques realized that the money he was playing for was beyond smuggling a few hapless Haitians. Easy enough: no smuggled people on board, though. That was one of the conditions. Cargo only, no piggy-backing income by taking on a few passengers. They might see something; might attract attention. Just cruise up to this cove or that inlet, help unload and leave.

It made Jacques rich. But, then, the DEA and the U.S. Coast Guard got involved down here. The risks got bigger. Jacques watched his competitors go out of business one by one. That would have been good news but for the way they went out: captured, arrested, convicted and thrown under a jail somewhere.

So, what now?

Retire? Buy some property? Become legit?

Jacques could do that. He had enough money. Not all the money in the world, but he was flush. He'd not live in luxury, but he'd live well and never have to work again. He could take the boat out and fish for real, not as cover for some smuggling operation.

But, men who needed his services knew where to reach Jacques, and the need was still out there. The market drew Jacques back in. The market and the mobile phone. Truly a marvelous device. Perhaps a devilish device.

The mobile phone made it all so easy. It expanded Jacques' contacts far beyond word-of-mouth.

And so, René had called him again, left a message, pressing for a crew. Several crews. René wanted *all* of Jacques' crews! This would cost some money. And all they had to do—at first—was watch. After they found this *Arcturus*—well Jacques would deal with the *Arcturus* once they captured her.

Seemed harmless enough. Just another American or European pleasure yacht.

Jacques remembered the first one. He really hadn't intended to kill everyone on board, but, he reflected later, he had known that was how it would end. His client needed a boat—a legitimate boat, not some drug-running cigarette boat. Something with a yachtish name on it, something registered, something that could get back into Miami attracting no particular interest. All Jacques had to do was spot one, board her, and take the boat.

Thinking back, Jacques recognized that his customer had left the fate of the owner and crew a bit vague. Undefined. Unspoken. Best that way. But, once aboard, what was Jacques supposed to do? Where could he put them ashore? These days, they could be picked up in minutes and be on the phone. In less than an hour, he'd be in trouble. No, the piracy had to go undetected for three days—time for the drug-runners, he assumed, to load the yacht with their own crew and cargo and make the run across the Caribbean into Miami.

So, there was Jacques. There was the man and his woman. There was all of that open, isolated sea out there, and the isolated, sandy beach in the tucked away cove, with no one else around. There was that pistol in Jacques' hand. The woman looked so good, in her solid white shorts and tight top, tanned skin, and so, so slender and graceful body.

So, after thinking about it just a little, Jacques just shot the man. Jacques was not exactly an accomplished pistol shooter. Hit him in the shoulder first, and the man started cursing and the woman started begging. So, Jacques shot him again. And again. Finally, five shots did the job. It taught Jacques a lesson. He'd better upgrade to a higher caliber and do some target practice, and get better. Blood everywhere! Quite a cleanup for later.

After Jacques killed the man, the woman, terrified, screamed too, then looked at Jacques' ice-cold eyes and got quiet. Real quiet. Saw her own fate and death, but held out just that tiny little hope that she'd survive this. Not to be, but he let her have the hope. Told her he'd let her live so long as she cooperated. She cooperated. Real quiet like. Afterward, he shot her, too. Both bodies dumped about a mile out, past the drop-off.

Jacques had stood back after mopping up, and taken stock.

Easy. And even fun. Not particularly fun killing the man—and having to clean up—but fun with the woman and there just didn't seem to be a down side. Witnesses gone. Money left lying around in his pocket. A few other valuables, the more unique of which Jacques had the sense to dump overboard. He wanted to sell those, but just didn't need the extra pocket change considering what he was being paid to pirate the yacht and deliver her to the drug-runners. No sense being greedy. No guns with serial numbers that might be traced, if he kept them or sold them. They should have had guns, but, nope, they didn't. Not Jacques' fault. It was a lick on them.

Jacques took the boat—which he knew the drug-runners would scuttle later—dumped anything traceable, and forgot about it. Next time, maybe he'd just dump them over alive and let the ocean take its course. Or dump them in and then shoot them. Cleaner that way. Eventually, he'd settled on the neater technique of tying captives up and throwing them overboard while still alive. Getting tied up implied that you were going to live. *We are tying you so you'll be still and not try anything. That way no one will get hurt.* That hope. The hope dangled out there. It made people passive. Jacques came to laugh at the shocked, horrified look in their eyes when his men began to drag them by the feet to the gunwale to throw them overboard. Too late! All trussed up, gagged, a few pistol whips about the head, and they got the message. Splash. Gone. Sharks and other little friends below the surface would take care of the rest.

That's how Jacques survived as the others got grabbed from their homes and bars. Fifteen years, he'd survived. And thrived. Now what? What had it all come to? What was he all about?

Jacques lifted the cold, dripping Prestige and drank deeply. He'd quit thinking long ago about the people he'd killed. He just didn't worry about it anymore. It had bothered him some at first, but it was just so—well, so necessary. They shouldn't have been running around out there unguarded, unarmed, anyway. Foolish. Might get pirated! Besides, he'd had his fun at it, too. After the first, killing people on board the pirated yachts grew easier.

So, what did he have to show for it? Well, he had that 200 hectares around the island, high on a bluff above the south side of the Dominican Republic. Someday, someone would want to build a resort there and he'd make a fortune. He had his influence. The Haitian police left him alone. They left his family alone. That was worth something. And, he had his boats and crews. He had people depending on him for their livelihood. He was a man of responsibility.

Ample money waited for him in bank accounts—and more hidden away.

Was that it? Was that what all of this was about? Drinking cold beer at The Unknown Slave, keeping the police off the backs of his family members, and making payroll? Would he do this differently if starting over?

Would he live here? After all, why live in Haiti? The DR, PR, or the U.S., maybe. Maybe even the Bahamas. Why Haiti? Yet, here he sat, wobbling in the plastic chair, looking out onto the street where Haiti's noisy drivers and motorcyclists honked their horns and raced by like madmen. A rooster crowed behind the building. He turned and Francois eyed him, ready to sell him another Prestige. *Why not?* Jacques thought, nodding his assent.

Jacques looked around. Chipped, peeling, brilliant green paint. Worn tiles. The bar wood wore away under the patrons' elbows. Trash blew by in the quickening sea breezes that played out in the street. Urchins peeked in, waiting for the rare visitor or tourist to emerge so they could beg some money. Fat chance here!

The plastic chair shifted with a little springiness, but held. Jacques rested his arms on the chair's armrests and leaned back. The Prestige vanished just as Francois arrived with a fresh one—always so cold!

The beer worked on Jacques. Some became the life of the party. Some became morose. Some became mean, belligerent. Some got horny.

Jacques' emotions hardened. He became keen, focused, cruel—even more cruel.

No, he'd stay. He was only 45. He still had time to make, perhaps, another fortune. The bribe prices grew, the terrorism-related security precautions threw up some roadblocks, but, basically, his trade went on.

He tried to pirate yachts out far enough into the Caribbean so that no newspaper could report that so-and-so disappeared while sailing anywhere near Haiti, the waters his crews usually plied. He strictly stayed away from waters eastward where the Dominican Republic's Navy and the U.S. Coast Guard coordinated to keep close watch. He left the Westward Passage between Haiti and Cuba carefully alone. He had executed one of his captains for piracy there and reinforced the lesson: the U.S. Coast Guard, the U.S. Navy and God knows who else watched the passage for drug-runners and Cuban mischief, particularly with Guantanamo just across the passage from Haiti. So long as the crime fell away from and between the boundaries, no country picked up much interest in it.

*That Holloway girl!* If she'd disappeared at sea, en route, poor Aruba could have escaped all of the international attention. Jacques didn't need that kind of attention. Make Haiti dangerous enough and The Unknown Slave would become The Known Slave. The Army left the place alone for now, but throw Haiti back up on the international news screens and soldiers would kick the white tables and green chairs aside and begin billy-clubbing the patrons. Someone would break and talk. They'd point to Jacques.

No, Jacques remained careful. No matter the money, he stayed away from murder on the island and from killing the few tourists who dared set foot into Haiti. He left the DR's tourists alone, too. Just too close, and the first thing the Dominicans would do would be to begin wailing about Haiti and pointing fingers west across the border. The wary Dominicans kept their eyes on their restless, impoverished neighbor, and their M-16s pointed in that direction.

So, he hunted further out. Liked to get yachters making their little forays out of the Bahamas, before they made landfall anywhere on his island. That way, they were in "international waters." Worked like a charm. Oh, that international piracy outfit reported the disappearances, but they didn't do any investigation or prosecution. Just reported. Let them.

Jacques liked checking their piracy map at http://www.icc-ccs.org. It was like keeping score. He got a charge out of seeing them "pin" his crew's attacks.

Jacques laughed.

Francois looked up, puzzled, since Jacques sat alone, but for Prestige. Francois wiped the bar absently and refilled the paper napkin holders. Francois liked Jacques as a customer, but he feared the man who made The Unknown Slave his court. Francois carefully eyed Jacques and considered his customer.

There sat Jacques, black, black in the Haitian way, short hair graying, face taught, limbs long and thin, but wiry. Cheekbones sticking out, but not from lack of eating. Jacques was putting on a bit of weight, Francois thought. That was OK; he could stand a few pounds. *Business must be good,* Francois surmised. Seeing no one, and seeing Jacques return to quiet solitude; Francois returned to wiping down the bar, seeing Jacques open his netbook computer and fire it up on the Wi-Fi internet connection Jacques had insisted Francois install.

Jacques had the Google Live Piracy Map maintained by International Commercial Crime Services set as his Home Page. He congratulated himself on his law-enforcement effectiveness; he achieved visible results. Just look at that map! Africa and southeast Asia loomed fraught with piratical dangers. "Pins" all over the place! Not in Jacques' immediate area of the Caribbean, though! Jacques had taken care of that. With all of the U.S. patrolling at sea, pirates around here really were land-based fishing boaters, more like burglars darting out to board some cargo ship in the harbor. Those ridiculous teenage thieves had boarded that Ro-Ro at anchor, waiting to deliver used cars. They had broken into the ship's stores and grabbed what they could before the crew sounded the alarm and chased them off.

Jacques had them rounded up and cut out their tongues. Word got out and Port-au-Prince harbor became as secure as Boston or Cherbourg. Every once in a while, some little gang who hadn't gotten the word would hit on some commercial vessel, usually trying to slip aboard and burgle the ship while anchored. Pilfering, not piracy! More like a home burglary, but it counted in the ICC's eyes and would make the map sticking a warning pin right there in Jacques' home port. So, Jacques did the government's job for them: he took care of the blundering boat burglars of Port au Prince. *Voila*! Check the map and compare with the rest of the world. Relative peace reigned in Haiti's ports. (Of course, his agreement with the Venezuelan dictator required that he not molest the Venezuela-Guyana coast, and he'd had to do a few muscle-operations on the dictator's behalf there, too.)

To hell with it! He was at home here in Haiti's corner of the world. He had respect. He'd keep it that way. The road for Jacques led from the south Caribbean's high seas to right here instead of afar!

"Francois, *mon ami*! Bring me another and join me, my friend!" he shouted.

Jacques' phone lit up blaring Crazy's "Phone card" intro as Jacques' favorite, current ringtone.

"Hello, this is Jacques."

René always came straight to the point. "Captain Jacques, I have a new job for you."

"A job? Now? With these storms coming in?"

"Yes, a good job."

"Should be. How good?"

"We should meet. Can you meet me at The Unknown Slave in 45 minutes? I'll buy you a glass of cold Prestige and fill you in."

"Certainly. Indeed, I am there now."

"I'm sure you are," René said, unable to contain both his sarcasm and excitement over the money he expected to make, subcontracting this job out to Jacques and his Port-au-Prince pirates.

Promptly, in 45 minutes, René strode into The Unknown Slave. The back of the room was dim. René spied Jacques slumped in a corner, obviously drinking the popular Prestige beer heavily, already.

"Jacques, get up!

"Huh? OK."

René ushered Jacques through the doorway's hanging-bead strand covering and over to a table. René nodded at Francois, who diplomatically cleared the room for René.

The Unknown Slave bar held its own special place of dishonor, even in Haiti. Granted, its open front bustled with customers as Francois served up his notable, savory, roasted chicken, but its cluster of small, back rooms played host to far more sinister rendezvous.

René pulled up a chair, leaning in close to Jacques.

"How many men can you get together?" he demanded of Jacques.

"For what?" Jacques wanted to know.

"A fishing trip! What else?" René responded.

"No, really, I mean for what? Burglary? Murder? Piracy? Women? What? What skills do you need of my able-bodied seamen? Have you been watching the weather? Besides, we would have to get organized and outfitted, you know. I need to know for what," Jacques said, pretty coherently for a man who had been enjoying Prestige all afternoon.

That's why René used Jacques. Competent even when cockeyed drunk.

René sat back, pondering how much information to share.

"Prestige!" René ordered from Francois, bustling about through the bead strings. "Make that one, not two," he added, looking at Jacques. "Yes, I suppose you do need to know," he said, more calmly. "Here is the proposition.

'Gather your crew. Patrol along the Dominican southern coast as far east as Santo Domingo, and south along the Haitian coast as far as the end of the island." He held up his hand to stay Jacques' protest. "Hear me! Pay special attention to the border area at Pedernales. If a yacht called *Arcturus* shows up, take it!"

René said, forcefully, pounding his fist on the plastic table for emphasis. He enjoyed the bravado, too.

Jacques was not impressed, but he was curious, and emerged somewhat more from his fog.

"Take it. Take it where?" he said.

"Fool! Take it! It is your prize! I am told it is a very nice boat. You are to kill all on board. Rape the women first, if you like. Rape the men, too, I don't care."

Jacques laughed. "Who is hiring us?" he asked.

René frowned. "The call came from someone I do not know. However, I know an important person whom he knows. I have a—a friend in—a friend who sends me mariner's work from time to time. When he refers me to someone, and if they use the right words, I am to ask no questions. But, I do have a picture of my employer: here!" René said.

René shoved an envelope full of $100 bills across the table to Jacques, pulled out the top one, and snapped the crisp bill in Jacques' face.

"Benjamin Franklin continues working his diplomatic voodoo, *mon ami*," René said.

"Huh?"

"That's his picture on these $100 bills. Benjamin Franklin, the great American—ah! You are so stupid! You are lucky I am your—your broker for lining up these little privateer adventures," René reminded Jacques. "I am your rainmaker!" René boasted.

"What is my cut?" Jacques asked, side-stepping the insult and focusing on the pertinent details.

"Perhaps you are not so stupid after all. I meant no harm—just using the term—affectionately!" René looked around, raising his finger to his lips in the universal warning for silence. "Tell no one or our lives will be in danger. Our homes would not be safe,"

René said.

"No one would dare invade our homes! They would fear the retribution I would exact!" Jacques protested.

"Yes, men here who know of you would fear your revenge, but the amount of money this job pays would embolden them," René explained.

Jacques sobered up completely and pulled his chair closer. Until now, he had played along only for information, and just to play along and break the boredom. What René proposed lay right around the corner of the island, required him to patrol way too close to the Dominican Republic, and thus, lay outside of the precautions Jacques' had set for himself as the safeguards of his success.

But, something about René's furtive behavior and the hint of great wealth convinced him to at least hear the proposition. He started to lift his hand to order another Prestige, but stopped. Instead, he looked René in the eye and whispered, "You have my full attention."

"We will be rich men after this job," René said, and then began to explain the details.

The details frightened Jacques. The money over-rode the fright.

"What about these storms?"

"Passing to the north," Jacques replied, dismissing his concerns.

"You hope."

"Yes, I hope. They may shift, but for now, all of the news is that they will hit north. The mountains will protect us on the south side of the island from those northern storms, as always," Jacques asserted.

"You hope," Jacques repeated, but looking at the money.

"Almost always. So, what are we to do?" he asked.

"We will be paid well, my friend, but listen to me! There is more! If we bring back the captain's log book from the *Arcturus*, here is your bonus," René said, leaning close enough to whisper.

Jacques's eyes grew big. "Impossible!"

"Believe it, *mon capitan*! Believe it and prosper. Some rich man wants these rich Yankees dead," René said.

"What about the storms?" Jacques replied, all precaution gone, just angling for a better price out of habit.

"Storms! Far away! Think of the money! Besides, for this kind of money, you can hire help. You do not have to stay at sea, personally, running from Dominicans or storms up and down the coast. All you have to do is show up and—seize the *Arcturus*!" René said. "Hire more help!"

"Help?" Jacques asked. Playing dumb, he had learned, induced the other man to talk.

"Help! Yes! Do you think I am an idiot? I know you hire coast watchers all around the island. *Enriquillo! Los Blancos! Los Patos! Barahona! Monte Sorpresa*! Do you not have cousins in all of those little Dominican towns? Your job is to be ready, to watch, and to move in for the kill. I do not care how you do it. Simple!"

"Yes, I have coast watchers—men in the ports around the island I can call on. But, that's a lot of coastline to cover. That costs much money."

"Really? I know what it costs! Shocking how little they charge you. You just get your men sobered up and have them watching from the Windward Passage in the west, and almost to Santo Domingo in the east. I want you to pick a port in the center of the DR coast and wait there. No drinking! You must be ready to move fast," René said.

"Barahona has both good bars and good shelter" Jacques said, again exhibiting surprisingly lucid logic considering the number of cold bottles of Prestige he had downed. "We will remain ready."

"I will need verification. Report to me the instant your watchers spy the *Arcturus*," René ordered.

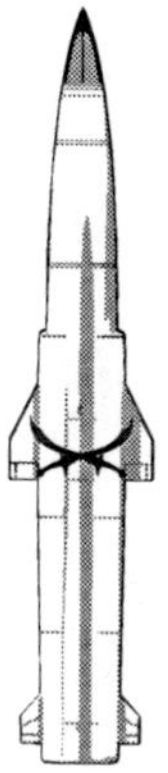

# 51

*Friday*
*Aboard Arcturus*
*Barahona Port, south*
*Dominican Republic coast*

"Paul, we're going to have to button up, now," Gordon reported by satellite phone. These storms are on the move. We're between Hannah and Ike. Looks like the next one will pass by Santo Domingo on the south side of the island and make landfall westward. Poor Haiti! About to get hit again."

"Understand, Gordon. The latest from CIA is that the barges are also heading north. You'd think they were convoying. I suspect they will hold while the storm passes. Where will you hole up?" General Ortega asked.

"A place called *Monte Sorpresa* Bay. 'Mount of Surprise.' 'Surprise Mountain Bay,' I guess is the literal translation. Hope that's not prophetic. It's a little Dominican Republic town, tucked deeply into a nice little bay. Surprise Mountain rises up steeply just to its east and should shelter us from the winds. The town lies at the foot of the mountain. Way out of the way place. Remote. Most of the tourism's on the north side of the country. It's quieter on the south side. Only one road in. That road leaves the coastal highway that serves this whole area, drops down the mountain toward the bay, and then goes from asphalt to gravel into town."

"Very well. Let me know when you are in position. We're all depending on CIA's surveillance now," General Ortega said.

"What about us next?" Gordon asked. "Mission?"

"When to take out the barge is the question of the hour. I don't see a role for you and yours. The Navy and Air Force will be the shooters on this one. I'll let you know when they take out the barge," General Ortega said. "Say, you be discreet down there. I don't want you boys stirring up any attention," he cautioned.

"It's going to look a little odd to the few locals, and we'll stay at sea as long as possible, but I don't see much choice. They'll probably figure we are just American or European yachters wanting to get out of the way of the hurricanes. We're told it's a quiet place. They'll sell us fruit and bottled water and pay no attention to us otherwise. No surprises at Surprise Mountain Bay," Gordon promised.

# Part V: Mountain of Surprise

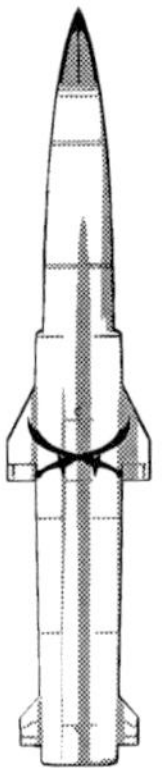

# 52

*Friday afternoon*
*Port of Barahona,*
*Dominican Republic*

"*El Jefe'*, this is—well you know who this is. I have been keeping an eye out for you! Is that not funny, *mi amigo*! Get it?" the one-eyed watcher said.

"Yes, yes, yes. Hilarious. Why are you calling me?" Jacques answered.

"Patience my friend and often benefactor, patience. First, let's talk business. Let us confirm our terms."

"Our terms? I told you the terms already. Yes, go on, then," Jacques commanded.

"You said you would pay $500 to the man who spotted this yacht, *Arcturus*—to the man who could tell you where it is, right?" the caller angled.

"Yes. I did say that and I will. Can you verify that by texting me a photo?"

"*Si*, I can."

"Then, do so at once!" Jacques ordered.

"Not so fast, *El Jefe'* my Creole captain; *oui*, I should call you *mon capitan*, no? How am I to be paid?"

"Send me the picture. If it's the *Arcturus* and she is where you say she is, you'll get paid. Send it—or else! You know of my men."

Jacques snapped his phone shut. *Fools! Little-minded fools! Trying to re-negotiate with a master negotiator!*

No more than a minute later, his phone beeped. Jacques thumbed the keys to bring up the picture. Tiny. Grainy on the phone's screen. He could not be sure. He'd need it printed.

From an Internet-call and copy-machine shop down the street, a color photograph emerged. A yacht's transom. The name: *Arcturus.* Jacques rented time on one of the shop's PCs and corrected the picture's color and lighting. Then, he sent the improved picture by email message back to his own phone.

Jacques called his watcher.

"I have it. You earned your money. Where is the yacht now?"

"Moving out to sea, as we speak."

"What? Not docked? You were to—! Never mind! Where? Which way?"

"Ah, let's see. I am not so stupid either my Creole friend and generous employer. Following the *Arcturus* must be very important—and dangerous. You paid for spotting her and verifying her identity. Following her will cost you extra. This is—this is *surveillance*! This is very dangerous work."

"Damn you! I said…! Never mind. Never mind. How much do you want?" Jacques asked, seeing René's envelope full of money and impressed with his spy's craftiness and greed. Besides, the deal had been *find* the *Arcturus.* He'd found it.

"Five hundred more."

Jacques swore for effect, but would have paid $1,000 without hesitation.

"Very well, you thief," he said into the phone, the rank hypocrisy of his words utterly lost on him. "Go to this address in Barahona and report to Senior Alvarez. Greet him with "*Cuba*

*Libre*!" and he will pay you," Jacques directed.

"You are wise, *mon capitan*," the man replied to Jacques. "The *Arcturus* cleared the jetty at Barahona and headed east and north, along the coast, my cousin watching from there reported," the caller said, tired of the game and the banter, and wanting his money.

"You have done well, *mon ami*," Jacques said, pulling his map from his pocket. "Perhaps we may do business again sometime," he added as praise, genuinely impressed.

"Anytime, *mon capitan*. I am honored to help you," crooned the caller, very pleased with himself.

Next, from Barahona, Jacques sent the picture by text message to give René' the good news. Jacques called back to René in Port-au-Prince, and then settled back onto the bar stool waiting for his next watcher to call. Jacques had relatives all up and down the coast from Barahona. It was only a matter of time.

Smoke wafted thickly over René and throughout the back rooms of The Unknown Slave, which he had occupied as his own temporary headquarters. For some reason, the place's stench awakened his ambitions. He smelled how its stew of odors and street-dust permeated the crude wood rafters, the palm-leaf roof, and the stained stucco walls. *I am made for better than this! I will escape this city and the Arcturus will be my ticket out! My ship is coming in!*

René ordered an ice-cold beer upgrade—a bottled Bohemian, imported from Brazil—and sat back. Smooth, cold lager. René took a long, cool drink and exhaled his frustrations. Jacques pirated and ran illegal immigrants but René's shipping business was different, more like filling custom orders or auctioning rare pieces. The sex-slave trade had taken a hit since all of the TV coverage in Aruba. Sure, it was picking up again, but one could never tell when it would all come to light and he would go to jail. Getting out now seemed just so right. He could make a small change and simply start smuggling poor Haitians into Venezuela to work the cooperative farms there. Was that legal? Must be. They were government farms.

René looked to the *Arcturus* picture on his phone again, seeing both his lucky star and his ship coming in.

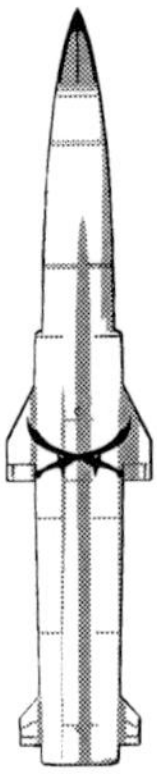

# 53

*Friday, late afternoon*
*Aboard Arcturus*
*Monte Sorpresa,*
*Dominican Republic*

The Atlantic quieted as soon as *Arcturus* cleared Salinas Point and entered Salinas Bay. To the right lay the old colonial-era salt works. Five miles across the bay and further to the east, lay the naval barracks and piers of the *Marina Guerra* units—a Dominican Republic naval and helicopter base. Only half a mile ahead, though, just where the chart said it would be, Jack spied the narrow entrance to a secluded, shallower bay: *Monte Sorpresa. Arcturus* motored smoothly to the mouth of *Monte Sorpresa*, stopped, and anchored.

The men conferred here, "re-conning the patrol base" as Jack put it in landlubber-ese. Good land tactics worked at sea, too.

Jack stood leaning on the rail, at the bow, sizing up their port-in-a-storm through his binoculars. To his left, the port consisted of a single boardwalk dock about 12 feet wide and 100 yards long. The heavy plank walk separated *Monte Sorpresa* Bay from *Monte Sorpresa* town's main street—its only street. Vertical support pilings, hung with nailed-on, blue and white-painted old tires, marked where yachts and fishing boats would tie up to the cleats fastened there. A blue and white-painted, tin-roofed Harbor Master's shanty of no more than six feet by six feet jutted out from the center of the dock boardwalk, as if to assert command over the bay and town. A ladder led from the shack, down to a white and yellow skiff, surprisingly, the only boat tied up at the long dock.

Behind the shanty and dock, and lined up in a row along the 20-foot wide, dirt street, stood the town's buildings. The few *Colmados*, small stores mixed in with other shacks and houses, stood in random order, none painted the same color. Jack spotted one café and a bar at the end. Nothing was open, though. Heavy wooden shutters stood straight, closed and fastened, giving the whole town a very tight, deserted appearance. Not even one of the *Colmados* was open for business.

Across the 100-yard wide bay, to Jack's right, spread along a narrow beach, stood scattered a half dozen, colorful, palm leaf-roofed shelters. Jack reasoned the beach comprised the playground of *Monte Sorpresa's* residents. Food vendors there packed up their plastic tables, checkered tablecloths, and chairs to wait out the storm. Jack watched the few of them left ferry their furniture across the bay to the town.

Most of the normally open-fronted businesses stood with wood-framed corrugated tin covers latched in place against the expected storm. A few people not yet quite battened down were finishing getting their covers in place. Only a few people hustled up and down the plank walks that ran in front of each of the 20 or so shop and house fronts.

Jack surveyed in widening arcs, checking behind and above the town and bay. Indeed, *Monte Sorpresa* was well-situated to wait out the storm. From right behind the town's row of buildings, brushy mountain foothills took off, rising steeply. The brush quickly gave way to trees, and *Monte Sorpresa's* steep, green slope pressed in close to the town on its way up to the mountain peaks that form the spine of the Dominican Republic. Jack knew from the map that he was looking at the tail end of that spine. Looking further up, Jack spied the 4,000-foot heights of Surprise Mountain—*Monte Sorpresa*—that gave the town and bay their names.

The men conferred below. Pleasantly surprising, they all had to admit. For once, a mere map recon worked out. Ideal place to shelter, really—and *Monte Sorpresa's* people were clearing out. Probably getting to higher ground. Maintaining a low profile here would be easy. All looked fine. For an extra security measure, they kept the *Arcturus* anchored outside the harbor, as if undecided about where she would weather the storm. They cooked supper, ate, and waited for dark to enter *Monte Sorpresa* Bay. An hour passed. A single, bright, light bulb on a metal arm screwed to a tall piling came on at the dockside shack, as if to beckon them.

As *Arcturus* slid toward the town's dock, a couple of dogs and a bent, skinny, older man emerged from the Harbor Master's shanty. The dogs barked and sniffed and peed on the pilings while the man limped toward the arriving *Arcturus.* He announced himself as the Harbor Master as Sullivan and Jack tied up at the cleats nearest the shanty. The *Arcturus* needed most of the dock on that side of the shanty. The Harbor Master's skiff and the fishing boats now tied up at the dock were all on the other side of the shanty, as if the Harbor Master had ordered all of the remaining berths left for the *Arcturus.*

Jack greeted the man, but scanned past him. Except for the old fellow and his dogs, the darkened town now appeared utterly deserted to Jack. No lights on in the buildings, but maybe the shutters and covers kept him from seeing any sign of people holed up inside. Gone? Where would they go, and why? By land to the Navy base across the bay? Why there? It, too, was securely sheltered on the larger Salinas Bay, but not like this place.

"Where is everyone?" Jack asked, keeping his tone natural and easy.

"Gone," the man said, waving his hand generally behind, toward the buildings, confirming the merely obvious. Then, not wanting his answer to be taken as evasion, he added brusquely in the Dominican way: "Storms! Gone! Storms!"

Jack looked hard at the man. Hardly looked like a trained-up enemy. Hundred and fifteen pounds. About 70 Jack guessed. Probably lived here all his life. If not, the dogs constantly jumping for his attention were certainly good props for the disguise. The man's clipped "Storms! Gone!" explanation still didn't shed much light on why the town was deserted. Anyway, these people from the different little towns mostly knew each other and the townspeople of *Monte Sorpresa* would have relatives living away from the about-to-be-lashed shoreline. It was probably their standard hurricane routine to button up and go play dominos with the cousins, aunts and uncles. *Monte Sorpresa* would definitely do.

Gordon paid the harbor-master's outrageous 3,000 Dominican pesos fee, ignoring the demand and handing him a $100 bill without arguing as the crew tied up. The Harbor Master grunted a perfunctory sound instead of "Gracias," turned on his heel, kicked the dogs back into the shack, and disappeared. With his disappearance, the entire town looked utterly deserted.

"All in all, a most unusual greeting, Gordon," said Jack.

Later, during the debriefing, Jack would self-assess that he should have paid more attention to the cognitive disconnect between the old man's "Storms! Gone!" excuse and the sheltering qualities of *Monte Sorpresa's* harbor. If *Arcturus* chose *Monte Sorpresa* for shelter, why had the town's inhabitants abandoned their nice, tight little cove? Good question.

"*Mon capitan*! *Mi amigo*!" the watcher pleasantly greeted Jacques, piling compliments on him as both chief and friend, switching between French and Spanish.

"You again? I am surprised," Jacques responded, checking his watch. He was surprised. He expected no more help from this man. Certainly, not at midnight.

"You paid me well, monsieur. I want you to call on me again. So, I am going beyond my duty to report this news to you," the caller said, marketing his services.

Jacques dialed down his attitude. No need to be rude. The man had done his job.

"Your *Arcturus* has moved, but it has now taken shelter. She is docked." The caller let it hang.

"Thank you for your diligence, *mi amigo*. How do you know this, and do you have a new location?" Jacques asked.

"*Si*. The fishing village of *Monte Sorpresa*. It lies about halfway between Barahona and Santo Domingo. Not much there, but..." he paused for effect.

Silence. So, the caller continued.

"I have an uncle there. He called. The town's best feature is its small bay. It lies right at the base of the mountains. Plenty of depth to handle storm surges without bouncing boats off the bottom. Mountains on three sides block the winds. Even during the worst, the town's buildings have always survived. Very sheltered. Your *Arcturus* anchored outside *Monte Sorpresa* Bay last night and just sat there. My uncle spotted her and called me. We were not sure if she would stay at *Monte Sorpresa* or move on, but I instructed my uncle to get the good people out of town —until the storms blow over. No witnesses that way. They have all gone to stay with relatives inland. My uncle stayed to watch to see what the *Arcturus* would do. When night fell, the *Arcturus* weighed anchor, entered the bay, tied up there, and paid my uncle very well for the privilege," he announced.

Again, Jacques was impressed.

"You've done well. Very well. I'll ask for more money and share it with you if I get it," he lied.

*Liar*, thought the watcher. *I will play my best card now.*

"There's more," he led. "You will find that I am worth the extra money you are going to secure from our employer. My uncle found lodging for them. They will be found—here, I will send you a sketch map. I know this place and can guide you in. See, *mon capitan*, your crew will not have to go looking for them. You will find them all bundled up, waiting out the storm, all in one place. Keep me in mind. My network (meaning his group of relatives) here is extensive," the caller said.

"I will," Jacques said, not lying. "Thank you. Good-bye."

Jacques marked *Monte Sorpresa* on his map. Next, he arranged the map with the best lighting he could achieve and carefully took a close-up digital picture. He messaged it to René. Jacques then called René and wheedled René for a greater share. He got it.

René pushed his chair back and called his brother-in-law to

ready the boat. This was too important to leave to subordinates, even to the surprisingly competent Captain Jacques. He would join Jacques and his cutthroats on their boat at *Monte Sorpresa.* Besides, this would be fun.

*All of my misfortunes are about to end,* he thought, congratulating himself.

He was right about his misfortunes ending.

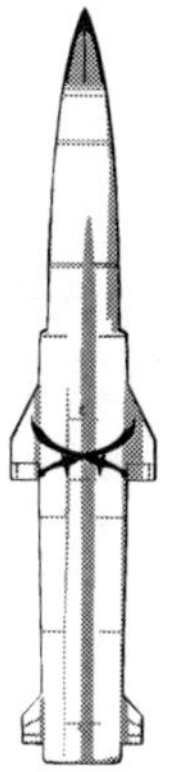

# 54

*Saturday*
*Storms over the Caribbean*

The islanders knew the hurricane drill well. They'd lived through so many, the storms almost became routine. A longer power interruption, but routine. At least expected. Fresh water supply messed up for a while. A few hapless souls somehow got caught in the surge. Usually villagers without TV and lacking someone texting them to keep them up to date, or teenagers horsing around. The cities battened down and rode the storms out.

The U.S. coast lay more exposed. More financially vulnerable, really. All of that expensive beachfront property! And then there was New Orleans, a city mostly lower than sea level, an invitation to disaster.

Between June and September, storms form far to the east between the Caribbean and Africa, heading northwest. Some merely dissipate. Others build steam and draw the attention of the National Weather Service and the news networks. Interested watchers track each storm online as they march northwest. The trick is, they may fan out and make landfall anywhere from below the Dominican Republic to Maine. They may curve up from the Yucatan to strike the U.S. Gulf Coast and then continue across the American south as flash-floods causing rain. Or, they may skip Cuba and the Bahamas and spill out fury in South Carolina.

That much was ordinary about the three storms following hurricane Fay, east of the Caribbean. What was not ordinary was the proximity and force of these three storms. Gustav, Hannah and Ike lined up in a nice, neat straight line, but astoundingly right behind each other. Storm upon surge. Surge upon storm.

The U.S. presidential election coverage had overshadowed The Weather Channel, but the wind-whipped correspondents stayed on duty. Fewer watched though. It appeared that New Orleans would avert Katrina II and the rest—well, everyone else just seemed to cope.

Once again, with a lineup of storms piling onto each other and feeding each other's frenzy, the American public's news media looked elsewhere. So, when the roiling mass of these storms broke north over the island of Hispaniola, much of America wasn't watching. Some, though, watched very closely.

Nick Riccolo fretted. His last picture of the barges came in showing them 1,500 miles east of Cuba, still chugging north. Then, the swirling, turbid skies got in the way, and he lost sight. He dispatched P-3 Orions. He'd held off on overflights until now, concerned that the barges might detect lower-flying reconnaissance. Now, though, he had to take that gamble. Besides, the storm-trackers would be aloft, too, and the P-3s could masquerade as storm trackers. Trouble was, the P-3s had a hard time re-acquiring the barges. The winds built. The column of storms advanced. Then, one veered north across Hispaniola but another crashed into the island's south coast.

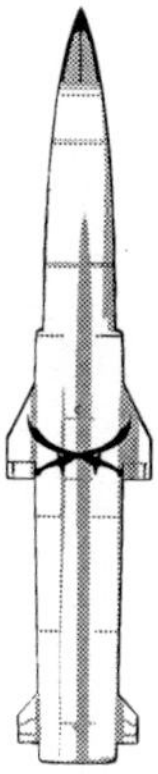

# 55

*Saturday*
*Monte Sorpresa Bay*

At dawn, Jack watched the red skies fester into an angry, boiling, red and black mix from the deck of the *Arcturus.* For what must have been the hundredth time, he glanced at the surrounding mountains like they were walls. He caught himself hoping the walls would hold. *Monte Sorpresa* stood above the others, as if either to reassure, or to warn.

After the sun rose fully, Jack went looking for the Harbor Master. He didn't expect to find him, but decided to shop for shelter and transportation before just confiscating it. Instead, though, he found the Harbor Master in his dockside shed.

*Why?* thought Jack. *Expecting somebody? It's not like this place is the shipping hub of the world.*

Nonetheless, there the man sat. And, while saying little, he was helpful. In no time, Jack had arranged for (paid the man for) shelter above the town on the mountain, and for a truck for getting up there. Jack had no idea whether the man owned either the concrete block house or the noisy truck he used to get up there to recon their new base, but the man eagerly implied the right to receive the rent payments.

Jack reported back to Gordon, Sullivan, and Chief Harbison,

busy selecting what to bring from the *Arcturus* that they might require over the next three days.

"I found us a solid little hut up there," Jack said, pointing vaguely up the street where the narrow valley and road rose to the hills behind the town. The old, but colorful, GMC truck waited for them on the dock, parked ready for loading and evacuation.

"Our rented transport," Jack said, pointing to the truck. "Our hut is about 15 minutes up that road. It's going to be quite solid—built of concrete blocks and with a poured concrete roof of all things to find—but it's quite basic. Got its own water cistern. Outdoor toilet. All rented from the skinny old Harbor Master, who at least acts like he owns this whole town," Jack said.

The men began unloading the *Arcturus*, transferring equipment and food to the truck. At mid-afternoon Jack and Gordon watched with interest, but without alarm, when the old converted shrimp boat chugged in and docked at the far end of town nearest the harbor entrance. No outriggers for nets. Painted white with red on the gunwale, paint peeling in places. Crew looked a bit rough, but, hey, that was no surprise either. Went with the watery turf.

No outriggers? No name.

No name?

No old Harbor Master around to collect his fee, either.

The other captains must have decided to go to open sea and ride this out, Jack guessed, surprised other boats had not arrived to tie up, too.

"Sullivan, would you check before we head out and see what the latest weather reports say?" he asked.

"It's time to head for the hills," Sullivan reported after ducking into the pilot house to check the weather. "Latest reports have it about to strike the island, just west of here—Haiti and the southwest Dominican Republic. Mostly, it will hit Haiti, but the DR down here where we are is going to get blasted with severe winds and rain. We're not in the eye, but we're on the edge of the hurricane. Hey, here's what's got the U.S. really worried: another one is stacked up right behind them. Looks like she'll head up the U.S. coast," he added. "I would like to stay with *Arcturus* for now. I think one of us should monitor the radio until the last minute," Sullivan said. "I can walk up when it's time."

"OK, Sully, don't you wait too long. Give me a radio check every half hour, roger?" Jack said.

"Wilco," Sullivan agreed. "Every half hour. If I get to the point where the storm messes up our radio commo for some reason, I'll abandon ship and work my way up this dry river bed excuse for a road and join you boys in the mountain chalet," Sullivan promised. "Give me 30 minutes after missing a radio check."

Jack, Gordon, and the Chief climbed into the truck cab while Sullivan waved from *Arcturus*, ear to the radios until the absolute last minute.

The multi-colored, off-road truck bounced and groaned up the hillside, jerking as the erratic ruts shook the passengers like roundhouses to the jaw. Still, the old, U.S. Army surplus, deuce-and-a-half truck, in its heavily modified and colorful form, ground on. Jack fought with the steering wheel as the ruts became mixed with large rocks that really should have been broken up into gravel. Jack supposed the road became a fast-running stream bed during storms and the soccer-ball sized rocks served more as riprap to break up the erosion than as paving. He estimated they'd climbed about 1,000 feet above sea level when the track rounded a bend.

There, situated in the bend of the near-elbow turn, sat a square concrete hut. Jack parked behind, blocking the road above, re-considered, and moved the truck slightly downhill to block the approach, orienting the truck downhill to speed up any getaway.

"Let's get unloaded and settle in. Still time to call room service and to catch the game, huh?" Gordon said.

The wind now whipped in a frenzy, even on this, the lee side of the mountains. Palms lashed at each other. Fronds broke and lashed at the hut's window's crude, wooden shutter slats.

The men had work to do. Weapons, water, food, some furniture to unload, all taken from the *Arcturus*. They'd had no idea how long they might be off *Arcturus*. They had to take into account the possibility of losing *Arcturus* to the storm and being stranded on the island. The wind drove their preparations hard.

By the time they finished, afternoon had given way, the shift to night hardly discernable from the darkening day. At eight, the first raindrops fell.

"Wonder why we've not heard from Sullivan?" said Chief Harbison, who looked on Sullivan almost as a son and felt responsible for the much younger man. "He's overdue on his latest commo check."

"See if you can raise him," said Jack.

"Already tried," Chief Harbison said. "Radios! You know how they are. Piss near one and it quits working. Always work fine back at the company area when everybody is drawing and testing equipment. Hit the field and they quit working," growled the Chief.

Legendarily true, according to soldiers, but the newer radios were pretty reliable. This shouldn't be.

Sullivan's thirty minutes passed.

The men looked at each other, then at Gordon.

"I'll go" said Jack.

"What do you want to take with you?" Gordon asked, pointing to the weapons laid out for maintenance on a blanket on the hut's floor.

"I'll take that AA-12 and my own sidearm," said Jack. "I don't like the fact that we can't raise him on either radio. I can see one radio going down, not two," Jack said, voicing the worry shared by all three men.

"Expecting trouble, Jack?" Gordon asked, eyebrows raised at Jack's selection of the devastating AA-12, selective fire, 12-gauge shotgun.

"Always," Jack responded. "You know how it is. I don't want to get fined for not bringing enough gun to the gunfight. I'll leave the truck and take the motorbike," Jack said.

"Sure? You know we just rented the bike for good measure because the old guy threw it in for $10. We don't even know if it works," Gordon said.

"Yes, I'll give it a try. I want to get down there fast and see what's going on. I'll take this handheld radio, too. I'll radio you when I get down there, but, if I'm not back in an hour, something's going on," Jack said.

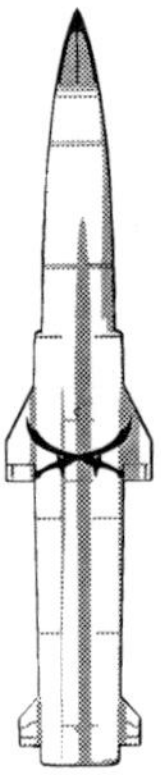

# 56

*Saturday Night*
*Monte Sorpresa*

Jack flipped the gas tank lever, turned the key, and hit the kick starter. The bike required a few tries, but it sparked to life on the fifth kick. Jack shifted into gear and worked the clutch, finding it loose and in need of adjustment, but it engaged and held.

Jack looked back. Good men. Good weapons. The .308 rifle and a couple of M-4 carbines. Jack tightened the AA-12's sling and prepared for takeoff.

Jack let the clutch out and took off—carefully—down the treacherous track.

After five minutes of working his way around rocks, he stopped.

"Radio check, over."

"Loud and clear," the Chief answered.

"Next check in five minutes," Jack decided and said.

"Roger. Five minutes, over."

"Out," said Jack.

Jack's ride for five more minutes brought him to the edge of *Monte Sorpresa.* He stopped before entering the streets and radioed again.

"Radio check, over."

"Roger. Lickin' chicken," said the Chief reverting to radio slang for "L" and "C" meaning "loud and clear." "Are we there yet?" the Chief drawled.

"No, kids, not yet. At the edge of town. I see *Arcturus* in the distance. Since we have commo, I'll make the next commo checks on the 15-minute mark. Cancel my 'back in an hour' order. Now, instead, if I miss a commo check, come for me, come for me by the moonlight, Roger that?" Jack asked.

"Roger. Out."

Jack cut the motor and the headlight, letting his eyes adapt to the dark, and surveyed the scene before him. Dusk had faded by now, and the village looked entirely closed up. Shutters were bolted. He saw no sign of their supplier contact, the old man. No light on in the Harbor Master's shanty; the single electric light was off. He saw no sign of anyone. Anyone. The same boats tied there yesterday when they arrived strained at their moorings up and down the town's single wharf, but no fishermen worked at the pier. Not even the men crewing that old shrimper. *Now, where did they go?* he wondered. *Must be already holed up and headed for the hills to their own place,* Jack surmised.

Jack listened. He opened his mouth slightly to take any pressure off his eardrums, and to enhance his sense of smell with taste. He couldn't hear anything other than the wind whipping around, and the sound of the increasing raindrops reverberating off multiple and differently-tuned, tin roofs. Jack waited, listened, sniffed, and watched, letting his night vision adapt. He absorbed *Monte Sorpresa's* creaks, groans and other background sounds the mind tried to filter out.

This was Jack's "security halt." The ears and eyes and nose and skin all receive so much information. The brain must filter some of it out to avoid overwhelming the perception. If you were not careful, you carried this ambient filter with you into a new setting, perhaps a dangerous setting. Into combat. The security halt was a simple device taught to soldiers to acclimate to the sounds—even the feel—of a different setting. Jack's senses sharpened as he perceived more of what his receptors had already been taking in, but had gone unnoticed.

The town of *Monte Sorpresa* lay all lined up, stretching away down the street on Jack's right, looking very innocent, facing the bay, in a single row. A narrow, rough alley ran behind that row. The hills rose so steeply behind the alley that they denied the town any additional streets. A few storage shanties snuggled into ripples in the mountainside. Other than those, the entire village of *Monte Sorpresa* faced the bay on line, street to the storefronts and house entrances, alley behind. *Monte Sorpresa* was very confined, Jack observed.

He didn't like it.

Where were the people? Even with hurricane driven gales approaching, he expected to see someone hustling about. Chasing a chicken. Checking the shutters. Making fast the lines, checking them one more time. No one.

In fact, he saw and heard a few loose shutters flapping against the houses, as if neglected, abandoned hastily.

*Why is no one securing those? Maybe it's standing operating procedure for all of these people to make the short run over to the Navy base during hurricanes.* The locals in more exposed towns went to visit relatives on higher ground during the hurricanes, but it struck Jack that *this* should be the place where the relatives come to, not leave from. The sailors should leave their more-exposed base and rent quarters here.

Jack pushed the bike into the alley to the right, behind the first building. He crept further into the alley, cut left into the shadows between the first two buildings and crouched in the shadows. For now, he kept his hands free and the AA-12 slung across his back. Jack's right hand moved to his side—to the Glock 17's fat grip. With his index finger alongside the frame, he touched the raised square on the extractor, sticking up from the pistol's slide. This confirmed—again—that he'd chambered a round. Now, Jack moved forward two steps, got down on hands and knees, got so low his cheek brushed the cold mud, and peered low around the corner, down the dirt street.

To Jack's right—the line of wood-framed shops and houses now shook noisily, tin amplifying the twisting and groaning noises as the wind tried to pull planks off their nails. No tile on these roofs. Then, the street. Empty. Dust kicked up by the wind earlier that day was now patted down by the increasing raindrops. *Monte Sorpresa* looked like a scene from a western. He half wanted to step out in the middle and slowly swagger down the street. "Bad Day at *Monte Sorpresa*"; "The Lost Treasure of *Monte Sorpresa*"; "Death and Surprise on a Dirt Street." Something like that.

Then, the docks. Pilings sticking up incongruously high, low, medium, none the same height. Normally, gulls topped these—maybe a pelican—but the wind beat them away tonight. That single, unlit, metal-shrouded light fixture blew back and forth by the vacant shanty.

Only three boats rocked at the pilings and the pier. The Harbor Master's skiff stood ready, tied up tight by the shanty's ladder. *Arcturus* bobbed close by Jack. The new boat—the shrimper—floated by itself, in the dark, at the end. No sign of the crew. *Where are they?*

The wind quickened and fattened raindrops began to slam

against the sides of the buildings and into the boats. Few reached Jack just yet, sheltered from the horizontally driven rain by the ramshackle buildings.

No lights. No people. No shouts. No dogs. Even the ever-present chickens weren't.

Jack eyed *Arcturus*, where Sullivan ought to be at the radio. Waves whipped up. He'd have preferred to slip into the bay and quietly work his way along in the water, but the storm made that impossible.

Now, the intensifying rain smothered all other sound. Good. Visibility decreased to only a few feet as dusk washed away into turbulent night.

Jack backed away into the alley. He sheltered on a back porch enough to get the radio out of the rain and tried Sullivan again. Even before being met—again—by the silence, Jack expected no return call or answer. He made his radio check with Gordon on schedule and then slipped the radio into a waterproof bag. This, he tucked away into a cargo pocket and checked his watch.

Jack ran to the back of the next building, jumping the rain barrel's overflowing pipe at the last second. He slid into the two-foot space between the buildings and crawled in the mud up to the front. Here, he was closer to *Arcturus*, but still a good 30 yards away.

The wind now howled. The three boats jammed against the rubber tire pieces. Tin banged and clattered and threatened to tear away and fly off, but it held. No other sound but the frenzied, watery cacophony could permeate this night.

Jack started to dart to the *Arcturus*, but formed another plan. *Speed is a form of security*, Sergeant Alvarez instructed Jack's weary patrol of remaining Rangers. Jack chose speed.

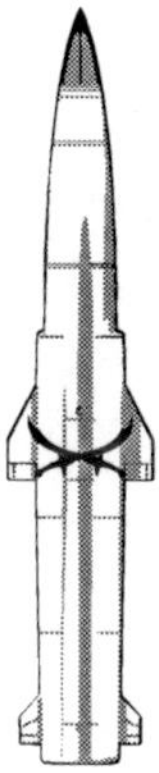

# 57

*Saturday night*
*Behind Monte Sorpresa*

Jack crouched, rain stinging his face, and ran down the alley away from *Arcturus*, behind the line of other buildings, and toward the far end of the wharf and the shrimper. Reaching the end, without pausing, Jack took a deep breath, darted left into the space between the last building and the hillside and stopped. In retrospect, his sudden appearance probably saved his life and the mission.

As Jack stood straining to see into and beyond the narrow space, a quick series of lightning flashes far out in the bay backlit two men crouched over another man lying face down in the mud. In freeze-frame, strobe-light, snapshot scenes, Jack discerned the two taking turns kicking the downed man and rifling through his clothing.

While one man cut away the victim's shirt, the other reared his right leg back, aimed his toes toward the downed man's ribs, and let loose with a vicious, bone-breaking kick—hard enough to crack ribs and pierce the lungs. Only the dark uncertainty about whose side Jack should choose—if any—held him in check. The next lightning bolt burned into Jack's brain a flash-image matching the shirt, pants, and equipment belt Sullivan had worn when the rest of the team left him on *Arcturus.*

The kicker recovered his balance, staggered into a solid stance, and drew back to kick Sullivan's head. Simultaneously, the second man, still crouching and searching pockets, turned to get out of the way and caught Jack's darker-than-the-alley form. He began to rise from pilfering the man's pockets and to reach for what Jack perceived to be a weapon. Too late.

Jack sprang forward in the dark, drawing his long Randall Number 1 fighting knife at the same time. He landed both feet first on the crouching man's surprised face and neck, then sprang away to begin slashing back and forth at the standing assailant. The razored man screamed—his screams drowned out by the insane rain pummeling them all.

Jack slashed again, hard down and then back up, using the Randall's sharpened, back-half of the blade. He felt more than saw what he wanted. He felt the resistance of the man's neck muscles and tendons give way, and then felt the Randall's strong blade grate, cutting across the spine. No way he'd missed the jugular.

The crouching thief struggled to his feet, but too late. Jack's double-booted smash to the head stunned him. Trying to rise, he stumbled back and fell into the mud, face up.

The man screamed in Creole: "No, no, no, no, don't!"

Lightning flashed.

In the brief flash, Jack saw Sullivan's attacker, his face and eyes alit. Terror in them. Jack saw terror.

Rain mixed with blood ran off Jack's steel blade and down his arms. The man raised his own arms in futile defensive gestures to ward off blows. Jack's blood was up. He sprang forward again and fell onto the man, blade first. On his knees in the mud, gripping the knife's black Micarta handle now with both hands,

Jack plunged the blade past the man's upraised hands. The knife point caught squarely on a rib and stopped.

The man howled.

The wind howled.

The killer within Jack howled back, and he plunged the blade again, this time more controlled, a bit lower, and found the man's belly and diaphragm. Jack wrenched the knife in a twist and opened up the man's guts on the draw stroke.

As Jack got up from the mess he'd made, the man lay in his intestines, screaming and screaming for his momma, but his screams quieted, and he died with Jack's boot planted in his mouth to suppress the last pleas.

*Breathe! Breathe!* Jack's lungs sucked air hard. The warm rainwater slaked the thirst Jack didn't realize he'd developed.

*Sullivan!*

Jack stumbled over the bled-out body of the kicker, lying in the dark alley, and fell across Sullivan. Sullivan groaned and cursed.

*Alive!*

Jack struggled to his feet. He crouched. He listened. He looked. More enemy could be just around the corner. That's why he'd avoided using the Glock. At a crouch, he sheathed the Randall and swiveled the slung AA-12 to the front. Now, Jack stalked carefully to the street front—still at a crouch, the Randall back in its sheath, the AA-12's muzzle up, at high-ready tracking everywhere Jack's eyes went. Peering out around the corner, keeping low, on his hands and knees, Jack checked left and right. Nothing. Satisfied, he crawled backward to Sullivan.

"Sully, Sully, can you hear me?" Jack whispered.

The rain fell, dripping off Jack onto Sullivan, who lay soaked, in a puddle.

The tin rooftops rattled in maniacal staccato.

Sullivan heard him. Sullivan had been here before. Battered, close to death, that is. If you survive it, you realize you can survive it. Even being shot doesn't mean you can quit because it's over. It ain't over. Not something you wanted to get used to, but....

Today was not Sullivan's day to die. Not in this place. Not with these wounds. Some other day, perhaps. His side hurt like hell! Sullivan was not in shock, though. After a few times of being wounded, the body didn't go as quickly and deeply into shock. Sullivan struggled to breathe. Knives pierced his chest, or at least it felt like it. He could tell he had a broken rib and a punctured lung. He assessed his condition. Thinking helped him. Jack's voice urging him to answer helped him.

The intended kick to the skull would have killed him. The kicker had killed men before with his strong legs, powering his toes into their vitals. He had perfected his technique on the soccer fields. Team mates thought him so focused. Yes, he was: focused on committing murder and training for it even as he made the shots. Now, the kicker lay still—never to kick or kill again—adding his offal to the muck Sullivan and Jack lay in.

"McDonald? McDonald? Is that you?" Sullivan rasped.

"Yes! McDonald. Lie still while I check your vitals, you scruffy bastard." *Scruffy? Seems to fit the occasion, but surely I can muster up a better alley-side manner than that.*

Jack checked pulse. He checked for bleeding wounds not yet detected in the dark. Sullivan took desperate gasps when Jack had to roll him over to check for wounds in the back. Had to do it.

Wouldn't be the first time a guy looked OK from the front but was bleeding to death from the back. None.

"Sully! Suck it up! You're not hurt! You'll live. No bullets. No knives. What's the damned problem? I'll radio and reach the rest of the guys. Then, they can bring the truck down for you. That truck ride back will hurt more than this!" Jack said, trying to keep Sully distracted.

Sullivan was not amused. He knew Jack was trying to bluster him out of shock. He had tried the same little motivational speeches while he had his bloody hands stuffed into other guys' guts. He didn't need it.

"On *Arcturus*! They. On *Arcturus*! Watch out! Attacked. Took over *Arcturus*!" Sullivan said in broken phrases between rib-twisting gasps.

"How many? Sorry, Sully. I have to ask," Jack said.

"Eight, I think. Huh! Six now. Six. Good boy! Get me some help, Jackie, please! Get those bastards first, though!"

Jack searched for his radio. During the scuffle, it was knocked out of his pants pocket and he had not attached the "dummy cord." *That's why they call them dummy cords. Where is it?*

Jack groped through the mud and the kicker's remains and found the hard case of the radio: lying in two inches of water, out of its waterproof bag. He knew it would not work, but tried it anyway. Nothing. Again. Nothing.

"Sullivan, I can't raise them. I'll be back. I'll get to the radio on the *Arcturus*. Look, I've got to take care of these pirates before our team comes looking for us and stumbles into them. I have to find out what has happened on the *Arcturus* and get who else might be out there trying to ambush us. Agreed? Sully?" Jack asked.

"Agreed, dammit! Just do it. Do it, you hear? I'll be all right," Sullivan said through clenched teeth.

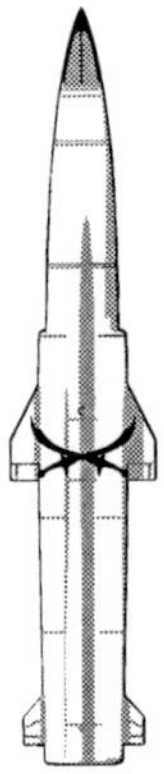

# 58

*Saturday night*
*Above Monte Sorpresa*

"Murphy! Inevitable! Always at the worst time!" Gordon fretted over what he should do about Comrade Murphy's leering appearance in his operation.

Jack was gone an hour. No radio check on the last quarter-hour.

Gordon checked his watch again. Harbison looked at Gordon, expecting a decision—the decision he wanted.

"Leave it all here but weapons, ammo and radio. We'll have to do this on foot. We'll probably slide right back down into *Monte Sorpresa* on our backsides. Here's the plan," Gordon said.

"First, movement to *Monte Sorpresa* straight down the road. No choice. I don't like it either, but there it is. Get fast to *Monte Sorpresa.* We will halt at the edge of town and radio again. If no answer, then second, we recon *Monte Sorpresa.* We'll go in behind the buildings, all the way to the end of the street, then along the docks. We'll clear the street and only then return to the *Arcturus.* First rally point is the first building we come to after getting down this excuse for a road.

'Actions on contact? Go combat patrol immediately," Gordon

said.

"I'm with you. Let's move out," the Chief said.

And they did. These men were used to putting one foot in front of the other and driving on. They might have jumped in from 30,000 feet. They might have washed ashore in pounding surf. They might have leapt from helicopters, ferrying them deep into enemy territory. They'd done desert landscape more like Mars than Earth; jungle hell; snow-covered mountains.

They'd never before encountered quite anything like this. The triple whammy of lined-up hurricanes bounced off the mountains sheltering *Monte Sorpresa* and sent ripping winds wildly about. And the rain!

The road they negotiated on the way up ran with flooded mini-canyons, rivulets crashing into each other, tearing roadway away in chunks.

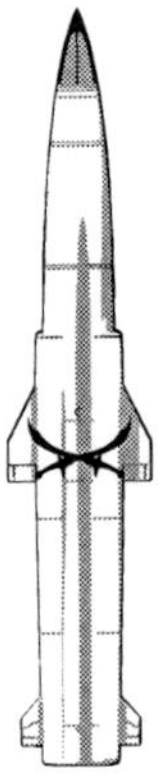

# 59

*Saturday night*
*Monte Sorpresa docks*

Jack recovered his breath, crouching at the corner by the street. He watched *Arcturus* at the other end, and scanned the street back and forth. He looked at the converted shrimper across from him. He looked back at Sullivan. Sullivan propped himself up on his elbows and gave Jack a thumbs up.

One Jack. Two boats. Six more men. At least. Jack retrieved the Glock from its molded holster and checked chamber—again—to absolutely know he'd chambered a round. Of course, he had, but he'd probably check chamber again just to make sure his first shot didn't merely go "snap!" He felt and confirmed the presence of his two spare magazines. Muddy, but the Glock never seemed to care about mud.

Six men. Time for the AA-12. He'd need the AA-12 to make up for the disparate numbers.

Twenty, 12-gauge, 3" magnum, buckshot-loaded rounds waited their turn in the fat drum magazine. The AA-12 CQB (Close Quarters Combat) built by Jerry Baber inspired awe in everyone who shot it. Jack couldn't imagine a more devastating close-range gun. Perfect for shock and neutralizing multiple bad guys fast. He could fire single shots, or he could let loose with full automatic fire, made workable despite the 12-gauge booming because of Baber's ingenious low recoil design. Couple the AA-12 with the straight-from-science-fiction FRAG-12, fin-stabilized high-explosive round, and the AA-12 was one wild weapon, indeed. This was not the shoulder-kicking, single-shot, single-barrel gun your great-grandma cleaned the snakes out of the chicken-house with. Jerry said you didn't even have to clean it, and Jack figured he was about to find out, having dragged it through the mud.

Sullivan groaned.

Jack needed to move fast and get Sullivan help. Briefly, he considered heading back up the road to the hut to stop Gordon and Harbison from coming. That just wasn't realistic. He'd barely made it down. He'd not make it back up on the motorcycle at all. Besides, the remaining pirates might come looking for their missing mates at any time—and find Sullivan. He could not leave the pirates in town with Sullivan.

No, he had to act now. Which boat to clear first? Decision: the pirate shrimper. Closer to Sullivan and—there it was. Might as well clear it first.

Approach: fast and straight in. No one could see more than a few feet in the rain anyway. Any watcher should think one of his mates had gone out and was running back—running to get out of the wind and rain.

Jack pushed himself up and forward into the mire of the street. Glances down the street revealed no one—nothing, at least that anyone could see. He ran in short, squarely-placed steps to avoid falling.

Sixty feet of this found him at the wharf. No movement or sound. He scraped mud from his boots to re-gain their gripping power, walked to the edge of the quay, waited for the shrimper's deck to sway down and over his way, and leapt aboard.

Jack moved quickly to the pilothouse. In through the hatch. Butt stock tight into the shoulder. Muzzle up. Scan for enemy. No one there. The galley and quarters next.

Jack pulled back the hatch leading below, felt for the gangway, and lowered himself. Dark, but quiet. The Surefire flashlight hung underneath the AA-12 illuminated the cabin. No one was aboard here either.

Very well. They didn't disappear into thin air. They were aboard his *Arcturus*!

Up the middle. Jack crouched and began stepping down the wharf toward *Arcturus*. He searched the Harbor Master shanty before he passed, but it showed no sign of life.

The rain stung and washed over his face constantly. The sound—on the wharf—on the tin rooftops—on the water—was a roar. No one would hear his approach, no matter how careless he was. That much was for sure.

Forty feet from *Arcturus*, Jack paused. He looked at the end of the street where the road—what was left of it—climbed into the hills, toward the center mountains. He hoped he'd see Gordon and the Chief emerging, but saw only the frenzied rain obliterating the dark, mountain-shadowed end of town. Lightning flashes illuminated the frothing rivulets pouring from the base of the road. No reinforcements. It was time.

Jack stepped from the wharf onto the rocking *Arcturus* as the deck pitched upward to him. The *Arcturus* thudded against the dock. No one would feel his footfalls. He crept toward the door of the main cabin. Reaching the glassed door hatches and the first window, he crouched to peer in. Surely, that's where they'd be. The only other larger room was toward the bow—the pilothouse and lounge.

Jack heard the cursing from behind him and swiveled to face a surprised and drunken man. Beard. White T-shirt. Hair disheveled—whose wasn't in this mess?

Jack pressed the AA-12's trigger and touched off two 12-gauge blasts. Although flashes from the muzzle lit the tumultuous night briefly, the storm suppressed the sound. This meant time. Jack used it and went to work.

Jack took two long steps, the second carrying him over T-shirt's buckshot-filled body, thrown backward against and hanging from the lower rungs of a ladder. A second, stunned, much shorter and fatter man stood frozen coming through the passageway behind the body. Bad response.

Trigger press. Two muffled explosions and flashes and the man flew backward, slammed in the chest by all 12 of the two shells' 000-sized pellets. Loaded with "triple-ought" buck shot, it blasts out pellets the size of ball bearings. Work the high school physics: lots of 12-gauge energy. The practical, lethal reality is that catching all of those at six feet shreds your chest with the force of a sledge hammer—only pinpointed into each pellet.

What does all of that do for the shooter? Simple. Jack McDonald knew the man was dead. It just wasn't necessary to verify and follow up.

Jack had held the AA-12's stock firmly into his right shoulder, below the collarbone, barrel pivoted up, scanning for more targets. The quick blasts had caught the man at sternum level. The force threw him rearward, but also turned him and his body toppled over *Arcturus'* side. Splash.

Jack made a fast decision. Rather than standing on the exposed deck waiting to see who showed up next, he charged forward to *Arcturus'* pilothouse. Jack gathered his strength in his left leg, prepared to kick the door and assault; instead, he didn't have to.

Muffled or not, the two men in the pilothouse had heard the sharp "whumps" the AA-12 had spoken, and they came to investigate. Jack almost ran into the third of the six exiting the hatch. Unfortunately for this man, Jack already held the AA-12 elevated to "high ready," which meant face level for this particularly short-stature pirate. Jack lunged and jabbed with the shotgun's crenellated, face-ripping muzzle—a "muzzle strike"—into the man's face and felt it solidly connect. The man screamed and grabbed his face as he crumpled. Jack jabbed again and again with the shotgun's barrel, slamming like a tire iron with repeated muzzle strikes. The man's facial bones gave way, his right eye mashed, his lower front teeth broken out, his jaw cracked. Three of the six down.

Jack charged past him, kicking and kneeing him out of the way, lining up the barrel for a shot. The fourth man stood, open-eyed, looking Jack full in the face as if Jack were a customer entering his store. Puzzled. Maybe more; unbelieving. This man lacked experience. This deficiency in his training delayed his response and cost him his life.

Killing and being killed is just not part of most people's ordinary experience, thank God. In gentle, now supposedly more civilized, western cultures, we fantasize that we have isolated violence to career criminals, to the deranged, and to unstable, overseas hell-holes. We subcontract our personal defense out to the military and police, fantasizing that violence is just something we will never be called on to do. The fact that terrorists hit major urban hotels, train stations, and commercial centers somehow fails to shake us from this comfortable illusion. Even the close-to-home headlines announcing rape, murder, and armed robbery down the street fail to shatter our ineffective psychological defense-mechanism of denial. It's just too scary for us to deal with. We expect to rise to coffee, hear the morning news about some *other* person's misfortunes, compare sports scores, eat breakfast, and go to work.

We expect to arrive there, greet, joke, work, and come home. If we stop for gas or to run errands on the way, and must exchange words with someone, we expect a courteous give-and-take with other working people doing the same chores, and then we count on a routine ride home, listening to the radio.

At home we expect to relax and enjoy the evening.

Completely alien to our experience is evil, personified.

We abhor "violence," unwilling to consider that violent combat, with or without weapons, may save our life. We resonate to some politician proclaiming that "Violence is never the answer."

Thus, the first response when accosted by some street thug, home invasion robber, or bully is denial. We may look down or around and back away to maintain the illusion that this is just not happening. We may make feeble protesting attempts at reason. Our hands rise in feeble defensive gestures, but not to strike or strangle.

In stark contrast, the hardened killer already knows his own intent and capability. Our displays of weakness unfetter his rage. "I own you!" he hears through the pounding blood vessels in his own head. Our attempted negotiations play as mere mewling to him. Pacifist noises and tones tell him he controls the victim. Weakness emboldens him.

Men and women who choose to coldly consider that some such monster may pounce on them arrive at a different conclusion and prepare for a different reaction. Experience and training prepare the intended victim to *become* the monster—just for this occasion—and, therefore, to survive. *Become the occasional monster!*

Training cuts through the passive tendency and gets right to the business of survival tactics. When face-to-face with violent death, only ferocious, immediate, focused, carnivorous rage turns the tide in your favor. You have the bonus of surprise, for the demonic beast before you thought he would slaughter a sheep.

Of course, the right gun helps.

The fourth man faced Jack, frozen, exhibiting no sign of any trained response, and Jack lingered on the trigger long enough to automatically fire two rounds.

Without slowing down, Jack cut left, then circled the pilothouse to his right, until at the opposite side hatch. No need to stand in one place waiting for someone else to arrive at the sound of the last action.

Jack searched for the remaining two targets, peering over the AA-12's sight, still at high-ready. Satisfied that the pilot house was cleared, Jack exited the hatch and checked for more targets.

Nothing. No one.

Jack pivoted quickly, checking behind him, then moved forward, shotgun still held at high-ready, the AA-12's butt firmly in his shoulder, barrel extended and up, but below his own line of sight so as not to obscure what lay before him. Elbows tucked in tight to the sides and chest. Jack lifted each foot high to avoid tripping. His shotgun barrel moved and searched in tandem with his eyes.

Later, he'd regret his next move and resolve to keep his excitement more in check.

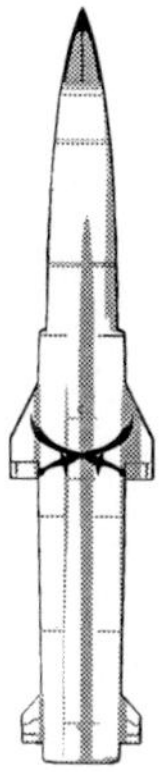

# 60

*Saturday night*
*Aboard Arcturus*

Instead of using the AA-12 to breach the door, Jack kicked the door to the aft deck cabin and used his forward momentum to lunge—only to hit the strong hatch's determined resistance, and bounce off!

*Real, real bad! Doesn't happen this way in the movies!*

Bullets shattered windows to his front and right, the shooter reacting to Jack's noisy but ineffective kick. Jack ran. No sense standing still right where they expect him to be. Jack collected his thoughts, his tactics, his breath.

*Well, I found 'em. "Successful recon-in-force" is the way I'll write that up,* he thought absurdly, panting.

Now, the door burst open. An AK boomed on full auto. Jack's AA-12 was already up. He pressed the trigger and held this time—for how many rounds, he was not sure. He did not wait to see the effect either. Before the "smoke could clear" he ran back to the pilothouse, through the door he'd only stepped out of a minute ago, and through the pilothouse. He forgot the bodies.

Jack's feet thudded against the literally deadweight of "Mr. Untrained" and down he went, painfully. His left elbow slammed the deck and his face bounced off the steel receiver of the AA-

12. His finger was outside the trigger guard, as it was supposed to be, so at least the fall did not cause him to commit the heinous "negligent discharge."

*Up! Up! Fast!*

Jack was on his feet.

*Flex left arm! It works! Ouch!*

Out the door.

This time, Jack's luck had run out. This corpse had its revenge: when it tripped Jack, the sixth and last man bought time.

All Jacques knew was this: He'd been promised really good money! He expected to massacre vacationing gringos. No one had briefed him he might step into a nest of gunmen. The most action he expected was the begging, crying and pleading he'd hear as they raped the women they found, and as the women watched them cut the men's throats. He still didn't know what had happened to destroy this idyllic plan, but he knew one thing. His second cousin—young Felipe'—was dead. As was his employer, René!

He'd seen death before, this pirate captain had. He'd raided before. He'd pirated yachts before, too, all up and down the Caribbean south of Hispaniola, as far down as the Amazon's confusing and vast estuary. He'd kidnapped. He'd sold little girls found aboard the yachts to the Arabian sex-slave merchants. Rape, kill, scuttle. Rape, kill, scuttle. Who was even to know that this or that sloop wasn't lost at sea?

He'd fought a few times, too. Not all of the victim crews went passively to their fate. He'd shot and been shot—and survived three 9 mm slugs removed from his torso.

It was not so bad! Later, in bars, drinking with his crew, he'd joked, pulling them from his pockets and rattling the bullets in a Cuban cigar tin for laughs. Eyes always got big.

Jacques had wrestled the one man on the nice sailboat. He was surprisingly strong, too, for his age. That man had punched hard and broken bones. However, Jacques had won that match and enjoyed killing the man and raping the woman, before throwing them both to the sharks.

So, what seemed like an onslaught by multiple armed men all over the boat was not an entirely foreign experience to the pirate, Jacques. It's just that Jacques had been in the company of five other men, expecting no trouble, and Jack McDonald was more than Jacques had signed on for. Seeing Jack appear as if in an instant—seeing this weird weapon in his hands, and seeing the fury on Jack's face, he dropped immediately to his face as Jack's buckshot—intended to hit at high chest level—blasted by his head. The man froze prostrate—not a bad response, all things considered. He was had, dead to rights. No resistance would save his life.

Jack glared at him over the AA-12's barrel, eyes burning a hole at the man's vitals and just bursting to let loose more buckshot. Jack's fingertip pressured the trigger, the "slack" taken up, the trigger's mechanism ready for the slight move required to send the open bolt forward to stick its firing pin into the primer.

Jack actually admired the man's composure. No whimpering. No futile flailing at the air with his hands, which might be taken as an attack. Just the repeated words in Spanish and Creole, clearly meaning, "I surrender. Do not shoot." Over and over, singing the song of the vanquished.

*A prisoner! Not a bad idea*, Jack realized. Then, *Who the hell are these guys?*

"Down, down, down! Stay down and do not move!" Jack bellowed at his prisoner in Spanish, using the power in his voice and expressed rage to dominate the prisoner.

*Secure the area, Jack!*

Jack scanned about left and right quickly.

Six men total. If Sullivan was right, all the enemy were "present or accounted for." Before Jack could decide on his next move, the ship-to-shore radio belatedly squawked. Holding the angry AA-12 in check, still targeting the pirate's mid-section, Jack lifted the handset by rote reaction and answered—in the clear, without the usual radio "pro-words" and call signs. He was too fired-up for call signs.

"McDonald's. May I take your order?"

A pause.

"Jack?"

"Yes. Who other McDonald did you expect? May I help you?"

A pause. Laughter in the background as he heard Gordon's familiar voice come back on.

"If that's you on the *Arcturus*, we're to your front and coming in, Jack. Two of us. Verify you are on the *Arcturus*," Gordon directed. "Don't shoot."

"Shoot? Would I do that?" Jack asked. "Roger. I verify I have *Arcturus*. I say again: I have *Arcturus*. Two men, pass through friendly lines, you signal four flashlight flashes, I say again, pass only on your signal, four flashlight flashes."

"Wilco. Four flashlight flashes."

"Roger." Seeing the light flash four times, Jack came back onto the radio: "I have four flashlight flashes. Pass," Jack said, panting, now exhausted.

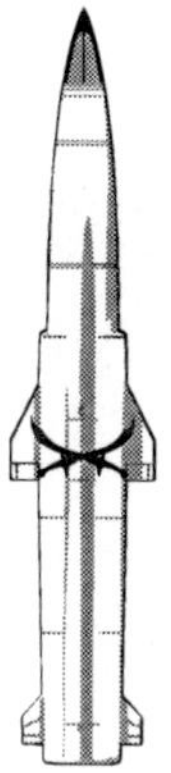

# 61

*Sunday morning*
*Monte Sorpresa Town*

"Who were those guys?" Sullivan groaned from the chaise lounge, paraphrasing "The Sundance Kid." Then, "Jack, someone—gunning for us," said Sullivan, straining for breath through cracked ribs.

"Shut up, Sully. Rest. Someone local," added Chief Harbison, guiding *Arcturus* back out to sea.

"Why do you say that," asked Gordon.

Sully was all ears, eager to hear the Chief.

"The locals knew to clear out. Someone warned his nephew who warned his cousin…," the Chief said, trailing off, thinking.

Gordon's Iridium satellite phone warbled.

"Excuse me, fellows. Maybe you can start the cleanup now that we're out of Port Nightmare," Gordon said, stepping out, into the pilothouse.

"Gordon here."

"Gordon, couple of things. First, where are you?" asked General Ortega.

"Under way, just 20 miles east of the harbor at *Monte Sorpresa*. You won't believe what happened here in our shelter-from-the-storms port." Gordon briefly recounted the night and ended, "We really were just trying to take a break. Honest."

"You just can't take Jack out anywhere, can you? Seems everywhere you take that boy, he breaks things," General Ortega said. "Gordon, I need to know your status. How'd you weather the storm—other than Jack's rampage?"

"Sullivan is hurt, has some internal injuries and will need surgery for his jaw and arm. He'll be down for weeks while he heals, but he's OK for now. The rest of us are all right. Thank God for Jack. These guys were setting up to ambush us," Gordon said.

"Why? Sent by who?" the general asked.

"Don't know yet. Heavily armed, Creole and Spanish-speaking indicates Haiti and Dominican Republic. I now suspect that Saya-dar set this up somehow. Just like we spotted him on the Amazon, he probably spotted us. We now know he has dubious friends down here in Latin America capable of making these—these arrangements," Gordon said, referring to President Guevara. "Hey, we captured a prisoner," Gordon added.

"Huh? McDonald didn't kill 'em all?" General Ortega jibed.

"No, Jack always tries to spare one of them, you know. We just haven't had time to fully question him yet," Gordon said, too tired to joke further.

"Well, well. We'll have to see where and who he leads you to. I have a feeling he might point back to a certain South American dictator. Get your prisoner to Santo Domingo. Let me know where you've holed up, and I'll send a team to take him off your hands. Too bad you can't just drop him off at Guantanamo anymore. It's close by."

Chief Harbison heard it all and, before Gordon could issue new orders, he was already turning the wheel.

"Aye, aye, Santo Domingo, sir," the Chief confirmed to

Gordon. He added, "Sir, they knew we were coming. Set us up. I tell you, sir, these are deep waters. There is a whole lot more to all of this than we are seeing. I wonder where all of this is leading."

"Yes, and I wonder who is behind this all," said Gordon. "This is no accident."

# Part VI:
# Whispers to a Child

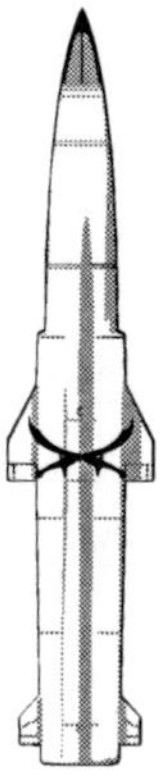

# 62

*1979*
*Columbia University,*
*New York City*

Sex was easy, little thought given to the ramifications—until the young nursing student missed a period, threw up, and felt—odd. She'd told Hassan at their table in Columns and Colonnades where they whiled away the hours over Styrofoam cups of bad coffee.

He'd listened like stone, his face hard, his countenance unreadable.

She'd cried.

Later, she begged him to let her have the baby. He'd hurt her—slapped her. He'd pulled out this roll of money from his pocket and thrown it down in front of her. She'd "take care of it! Soon! Real soon!" he'd ordered. He'd pay for it. "There! Take the money! Do it! Speak of this no more! Take care of it!"

"It."

Her baby.

Hassan was so darkly handsome. So full of fire. He held the other students enrapt with his impassioned oratory, eyes locking with theirs, intense face commanding their attention, making sure they learned of all of the indignities suffered by the Palestinian people at the hands of the Jews—and the Americans.

Other girls at the table became regulars, too. She could tell that they also wanted him. She couldn't blame them. Tanned, slender, exotic, hair curly and unkempt reflecting his wild emotions. Hassan.

But, she'd had him. Again and again. He'd taken her body and her heart. Never did she consider his actions out of line with the teachings of the Allah he was always professing before them.

Superior. Always superior to the West. The "degenerate West!" "Allah's perfect way." Somehow, enjoying making love to the young American college student from Niagara Falls squared with Allah's great plan. She couldn't figure that out, and didn't try very hard.

But, somehow, her baby did not square with Allah's plan.

She'd lain in her dorm room bed after he'd had her again and left, crying in deep, unstoppable sobs. She'd told him, expecting him to be so proud for them both. Proud she would bear him a child. Instead, he turned into someone she didn't know.

She really *didn't* know Hassan Najibullah. Hassan would soon return to his native Palestine to "work" for his uncle in Hamas. His sole mission in the United States was to learn English, to establish credentials and knowledge—knowledge of the Americans' ways, roads, of conversation topics, styles, customs. He was to become an American.

And, always, he was to smile. Smile before their older adults anyway. He could preach all the fiery anti-Israel diatribes he wanted in the student union's cafeteria corner where he held court. So, his Mullah had instructed.

Hassan burned hot with shame when he confessed to his

Mullah what he'd done. He expected retribution or even expulsion from the mosque—from the brotherhood!

Instead, Mullah Obaidullah had taken his hands and praised Allah for the "bastard half-breed infidel growing in the belly of his American whore!"

"Return, my son. Make peace with the girl. Quickly! Before the maiden acts on your command. Withdraw your cash offer. She will have this child. The child will be yours, always. Allah's, always. You will disappear from her life and from the child's, but Allah will never disappear from the child's soul. Allah will whisper to the child someday and the child will answer—if it is the will of Allah. And, from afar, without ever seeing the child again, you, too, will whisper to the child in a way that only a father can."

Then, the Mullah turned and struck Hassan full in the face!

"You have committed a great sin and penitence is required of you!" Mullah Obaidullah hissed. Hassan was shocked. Not at the stinging rebuke but at the unpredictable turn of the Mullah's attitude.

Then, just as quickly: "It matters not. She is but an infidel whore. She was not your sister in Allah. For that crime, you would die!" Mullah Obaidullah warned, pointing an indicting finger at Hassan like a knife. "Come, walk with me."

Hassan recovered and obliged.

As they walked through the park outside the mosque, Mullah Obaidullah instructed Hassan. As they passed Americans hurrying back to work from lunch, strolling their toddlers, walking their dogs, Mullah Obaidullah told Hassan exactly what he wanted Hassan to do before disappearing to Palestine.

"Learn about this woman, the mother of your child. Her full name. Her parents' names. Her home. Copy her papers, her driver's license. Her checkbook register. Anything identifying her. Soon, you will disappear from her life, but we must locate the boy someday. You must document the links that will lead us back to him. Someday—" and Mullah Obaidullah stared off into the sky.

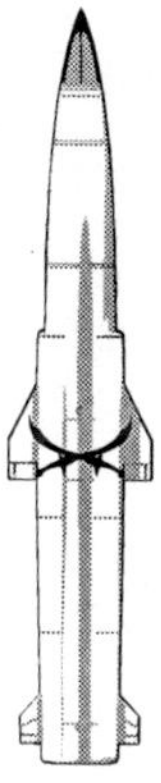

# 63

*1989*
*Niagara Falls, New York*

The heartbroken young nursing student got over her lost love and moved on to other lovers, but the child's grandparents adopted him, giving him their name. No putative father stepped forward to assert parental rights. Their daughter now vowed her hatred for the child's father and asserted (falsely) that he could have been one of several.

James and Linda Lewis talked it over and finally considered it a blessing that the baby's father had disappeared. Their adoption petition took some time, given the constitutional difficulty of terminating parental rights, but Hassan's lawyer permitted a default judgment after service of process, and so the legal end of things was final. Hassan Najibullah was no more in the child's life, and the boy would henceforth be "James Lewis, Jr." James Senior and Linda vowed to show him all the love they had. They did.

The fourth-grader, James, heard his teacher's voice coming from somewhere, but the blue-bound books on the shelf to his right beckoned and held his complete attention. All in two neat rows. Worn, hardbound covers bent, covers scuffed, but colorful.

How he yearned to read one right now! He'd finished half of them already. What would he do once he had met all of his friends?

George Washington.

Paul Revere.

Sam Houston.

Davy Crockett.

Jim Bridger.

The Mayo brothers.

Thomas Edison.

Captain John Smith.

Ethan Allen.

Jeb Stuart.

U.S. Grant.

Books to stir a young boy's mind. Men to stir his heart. Books to awaken the man within, to summon him, and to shape the man he would someday become—was becoming, even now.

Miss Alberta saw James looking at the books and left him alone. Miss Alberta saw all. Had he been a slacker, a disrupter, or behind, she'd have gently commanded his attention. Jamaal—"James"—was bored, and she knew it. Couldn't be helped right now, though. The multiplication tables stood as a milestone before all of them and others needed some help—not James.

Miss Alberta smiled inwardly, even as she addressed the rest of the class. While he might not be paying attention to her right now, it was not about James paying attention to her. It was about James *learning*. Learning life; character; learning to be a man.

She'd happened across the books at an old, second-hand market, lying in a wooden box next to other boxes filled with "LP" records from the '70s. Old. Last print date in the set was 1953. Certainly, they were highly politically incorrect. Someday, some student would comment at home. Some parent would take offense. The principal would sigh, walk down the hall, and come to her room to see for himself. She'd ask Alberta to sit down. She'd regret having to order her to remove the books. She'd be surprised that Alberta would acquire such "controversial" material on her own and introduce it to her classroom. The "contraband" rule violation would earn her a write-up.

For now, though, the books sat quietly, but not silently, anachronistically out of place, and revolutionary in their messages.

The blue-bound books stood strong. The books spoke of rebellions, of conquest, of danger, of character, and of heroic deeds. Of killing, even, although 90 percent of the stories covered the historical hero's childhood. Yes, the blue-bound biographies stood counter-cultural among the other, much more upbeat, modern covers and collages of mostly meaningless stories and pap propaganda.

Boys came into her class hungry for stories that inspired courage, chivalry, character—all the things writers these days wanted to inspire, but just couldn't. Too many constraints, imposed not so much by law as by implication, by understanding. ISI: "Inherent societal insipidity." Modern stories struggled against so many "specifications." This whole era was suspect. This figure too uni-dimensional. This one, too—yecch—violent! This one might offend this group. *Andrew Jackson, Boy General.* You get the point. Something could be found in each of the men's lives to disqualify all of them from study during this much more advanced and—civilized—century.

The writers were hampered; the editors and publishers were hampered; the school boards were hampered; and the books were hampered.

So, the boys came and went from her fourth-grade class. While there, though, Miss Alberta worked hard to capture their attention. She did, for the most part. Always, she was quick with the next question for them to answer: the one requiring their logic, their moral compass-work, their bringing to bear the hard work of their own *reasoning* to answer their own inquiries.

Some rose to the occasion—sometimes. Some never did. Those broke her heart.

The blue-bound biographies: she thought of the men in them—and some women too—as her "covert, culture, spirit-warriors." *Francis Marion: The Swamp Fox.*

So, young James (really "Jamaal" she knew from his records) Lewis incurred no teacher-wrath that day. In the final period at the tired end of the day, he'd have his desk-work turned in early. She'd watch him quickly get a drink of water and return to his desk, perusing the shelf after the workaday work was done.

No, *the little rascal!* (She chuckled inwardly.) He was perusing the shelf now. That way, when the school day wound down, and he had free time, he would already know which story he would delve into and would waste no precious reading time considering.

Alberta Jones wondered how the lives of men long dead would change young James—as she started on "the sevens tables." Inwardly, she smiled again.

Miss Alberta had earned the right to smile. She brought her gift to the classroom. She somehow knew what each boy and girl needed. She knew how to challenge and grow the girls. It was the boys she looked on with such sadness. Somehow, school short-changed them the most. The blue-bound books appeared as if by magic to fill the void left by their world. Even in the richness of her quiet wisdom, she could have no specific idea what the living ghosts of those men would forge in young James's soul and mind.

James grew. James went on to many other teachers and classes, but always the quiet inspiration of Miss Alberta spoke to his spirit. As did the voices of the men and women in the blue biographies.

When James Jr. drove his used Impala out of the driveway, left Niagara Falls for Washington, D.C., and grinned as he waved his good-byes, his adopted parents burst with both grief and pride. As they turned to walk back through the storm door into their now quieter kitchen, James reassured Linda. He'd be back, and besides, this was the moment they'd so carefully prepared him for. Now was the time for James to go and face the world. They'd raised him to love his home, his country, and his God. He'd face Satan and the world's wicked, tricky forces, but he'd stand. He'd stand. He'd persevere. He knew The Truth, and The Truth made him free. If it were possible, they'd be even more proud of him someday.

They really didn't think it was possible to be more proud of Jamaal. It was possible. They would be. For now, though, Linda wiped her tears as they prayed for their son's safety and future.

James not only arrived safely at college that day. He thrived. He plucked flowers of truth from fields of weeds. He took verbal strolls through the foolish fantasies of some of his teachers and laughed with them as he decimated their arguments, so arrogantly urged.

James inspired tired professors who wondered how much longer they could strive against the cultural onslaught. Would western civilization survive? Some days, it appeared not. "Would the farce movie prophecy, *Idiocracy*, be our legacy?" they asked select others from their colleagues. Then, James—and a few others—entered the classroom at each new term—and these professors were renewed! They rose to their duties, their calling. They taught, inspired, and guided. They drew from and gave, and were refreshed.

Then, James acquired a Master's degree in political science at The American University in Washington, D.C. His incisive logic and fire for learning turned some of his instructors against him. He stood impervious to anti-American rants, and laughed at Marxist mantra. Keen professors respected the courteous, ready-to-laugh, but rapier-minded James. They stepped to the classroom more eagerly than usual, drawing inspiration from their student. The synergy between student and teacher girded the entire classroom, and all learned. Whether they agreed with him, or wished him on some other lecturer, professors noticed something special about James Lewis, the tanned, angular, brown-haired, brown-eyed, slim young man on scholarship from Niagara Falls. For that is where Jamaal (James Lewis) Najibullah grew up.

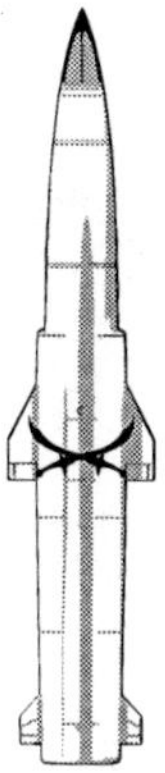

# 64

*Spring, 2001*
*Washington, D.C.*

Like others, James was caught off guard when it all ended. Graduation? What next?

One early afternoon in May, 2001, James Lewis sat on a brick patio at an outdoor café, umbrella overhead keeping off the already bright Washington sunshine. The cherry blossoms peeked out, students walked by, and James sat bewildered and sad that he'd soon leave this behind. Oh, he was optimistic about his future but he lacked the specific direction that eludes so many of us. James pondered whether to celebrate graduation with a second Sangria when an unfamiliar voice broke in.

"James Lewis?" the man asked, cheerfully, not waiting for an invitation to sit—just pulling up one of the French-styled, round-seat, iron-framed chairs so popular at sidewalk cafes the world over. The man placed both hands on the small, circular, steel mesh table surface and smiled benignly, signaling for the waiter.

"Sir, I do not know you. Who are you and why have you presumed to sit down at my table?" James asked, not unkindly but pointedly, appropriately defensively.

"Fair question and well-asked," the man answered without answering. "I will answer them both, but first I *must* ask you a question." Before James could interrupt and shoo the odd man away, the visitor continued.

"James, James. Jamaal. Do you know who you are?"

James shifted. The man stared. Not maliciously. Not insanely. Intently. James would have dismissed him, but the question revealed something.

For in truth, while James was very firm in who he was *now*, he didn't know who he had been.

The Lewises had told him he was abandoned by their daughter and adopted. They had all cried. They all affirmed their love. He loved them now in a way even somehow deeper.

But, the truth did what it so often does: the truth opened further questions, a bigger, deeper, more mysterious and marvelous world to explore.

James didn't worry about it: he was James Lewis. He had good upbringing and a sharply-trained mind. He did, indeed, know who he was.

But he didn't know who his father had been.

James sighed—audibly—and involuntarily.

His mother had left Niagara Falls years ago and had abandoned her own parents and him. New Mexico they'd last heard. He'd not worried about it—until right now.

This man's knowledge of his secrets angered James.

"Who are you and why are you asking?" James challenged the nosy stranger.

The answer shocked James.

"Because I know who you are, who you *were*, and who you could become. That is why I am sitting here talking with you. I have sought you out.

'Please, James, hear me out. I mean you no harm. Hear me out and, afterward, I will offer you something. You are, of course, free to walk away from what I have to offer you. I have a business proposition for you, but much, much more than a business proposition. I believe you will accept what I offer you. I believe you cannot resist. I believe I will offer you something you were made for—something that will fulfill you. So, I ask, just hear me out," the man said.

The well-dressed, 42-year old recruiter pulled his chair closer, waived for the server, ordered wine, and began to earnestly lay out his plan for Jamaal Najibullah, a/k/a James Lewis.

Five months later, on September 11, 2001, at 10:30 a.m., Jamaal stood affixed before the television set suspended above the bar. With others. A few murmurs but silence for the most part. Some cried. Others sat stunned. One man cursed.

Jamaal left a 10-dollar bill on the counter and walked back to his New York City office. He wiped a tear. He sat at his desk. He pulled open a drawer and fished out the old card from a stack of a few others he had tossed into the drawer. No name. No company. Just the two numbers. A phone number and another. Random, like a computer password was supposed to be.

A woman answered. Jamaal gave the second number. On hold. The call was forwarded. A man answered. Jamaal recognized the voice.

"I'm ready," Jamaal had said.

"I know you are. I knew you would call," the Central Intelligence Agency case officer said to his recruited agent. "Who knows but that you have been placed here for just such a time as this?"

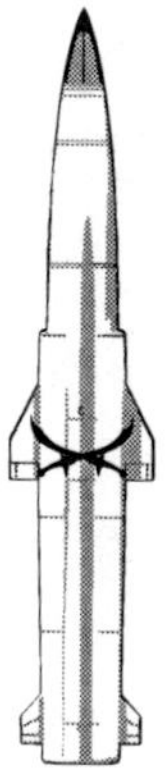

# 65

*April, 2002*
*Warwick Square, London*

The Shade—Saya-dar—remained a mere shade to sharp western eyes by exercising caution. Security. Have security rules. Never violate them. Protect your identity at all costs. He did not intend—at least yet—to join the martyrs he helped create.

So much work lay before him! Take Jamaal, the young aide to the junior Senator from Illinois. Saya-dar had put Jamaal into motion over 20 years ago. He had watched so closely, planning his growth as an American power-player. Yet, he'd never met Jamaal before, until now.

Ah, meeting with Jamaal defines the dilemma. Security versus action. Every action poses its set of risks. Risks sparked counter-measures. The counter-measures themselves were actions which sparked risks. The not-so-apparent risks caused even Saya-dar to lose sleep. Lately, despite heavy doses of Scotch, he had risen from his cabin on the *Babylon* in the middle of the night. Always at 3:00 a.m. Always. Always to the same frightening vision: black-clad infidels armed with M-4 carbines, boarding his *Babylon* from the stern. Securing each room "as seen on TV," methodically streaming into each successive cabin in their "stack" formations, fanning out, angry spears of tactical light stabbing the night, securing all directions, searching, and working their way confidently toward his own berth. They were poised outside his cabin door even now! One of those battering rams in hand sometimes—and sometimes one of those water-tamped, door-blowing devices. Flash-bang grenades ready.

Saya-dar had no death wish, but neither did he fear death. Death ended his operational life—a life spiced by the luxuries available only through fabulous wealth—and that is what made Saya-dar so careful. Both the sensual pleasures and secretly working his operations against the West thrilled The Protector of the Faithful. And there was that, too: guarding Islam. Serving in the courts of Allah, as Allah's necessary, covert operator. Let others grovel, blow themselves apart, and wonder if they had done enough to achieve escape from hell, much less merit the virgins! Saya-dar calculated that, if there were an afterlife, and if Allah were its King, then his brilliant service to Allah put him in the court of Allah's close confidants—and more than over-rode his vices.

But on those nights of the black-clad men, the Saya-dar arose and mixed yet another drink with trembling hands. The conscious vision next visited upon him was more deeply disturbing than the subconscious nightmare.

Saya-dar saw himself as one of their prisoners! Orange coveralls. Hair long, unkempt, matted. Arms and legs in chains. Downcast, utterly exhausted look. Deprivation from Scotch, the fine foods Saya-dar always enjoyed, and the women. Total and ugly contrast to the finery gracing Saya-dar's life now. Filthy infidel hands directing his every move. Their eyes watching him. Lack of his freedom to roam the world in his war against the West. Shaming him before the entire world!

Fear: a gift from Allah. Fear was Allah's voice teaching him security and humility. Yet, like so much else of life, fear given rein paralyzed and destroyed. Fear could destroy physically, but that *other* fear-effect worried Saya-dar even more.

Fear caused the coward to simply "stay home." That, Saya-dar had vowed, he would never do. He simply enjoyed his exercises in lust for power too much. He could never retire from his career as Islamic terrorist financier and mastermind. Saya-dar, The Shade, The Protector of the Faithful, simply *must* operate.

Ah, again, there arose the dilemma. Cause and effect. All action created some tangible change in the material universe. All. Some traces left were so miniscule as to be virtually undetectable, but the West's technical ability to sniff out even those microscopic shifts in the universe's equilibrium grew chillingly—and impressively.

So did the West's skill at laying out the massive quantities of data netted in its searching, and then sifting it, sifting for patterns. Seeming anomalies, changes that pointed to other changes which pointed to—him?

Saya-dar arose from his couch and drifted toward the bar. He glanced at the clock on the wall behind the bar. The glass and brass timepiece seemed to scold him for sloth: 11:00 a.m. in London. Saya-dar began calculating the time zone difference between London and Spain where he'd just left—shuffling about mentally for a rationalization to take his first Scotch whiskey of the day so early. Something important was forming in his mind, and he needed the clarity.

The amber bottle with its sophisticated label called to him and he answered the call. *Only one*, he answered back.

We should thank the distiller. The Scotch whiskey bewitched Saya-dar a little—emboldened him a little—induced him a little toward the inevitable compromise between security and action. The burning, comforting, earthy liquid also made it just a bit easier for this most cautious man to swallow what he knew were slips in security.

The time was when no one on earth matched Saya-dar's phantom-like mastery over so much misery. But, as his successes mounted, his ambitions accelerated with them. Grander action required him to recruit others, and to supervise them. Eventually, Saya-dar had revealed himself to a few others. Four, to be exact. The Ayatollah, his nephew, and the two young men Saya-dar had personally selected and groomed to live and grow within the United States and Britain.

Saya-dar and Jamaal met first in London where Jamaal kept an apartment for a month. The United States taxpayers generously, but unwittingly, provided the cover. The four-week International Banking Regulation Conference Jamaal attended took a long weekend break, planned far ahead for sightseeing.

Now, Jamaal knocked at Saya-dar's door. Saya-dar greeted Jamaal warmly. Someday, his Jamaal would rise far in America. He already had. If Saya-dar must sacrifice some increment of anonymity and security, then preparing Jamaal—his prize student—his highest placed sleeper agent—his prospective "Manchurian Candidate" justified the risk.

"Sheik, I am honored. I have much to tell you about the work I am doing with the Americans!" Jamaal said, greeting Saya-dar with a kiss.

"All in time, my son, all in time."

That time arrived.

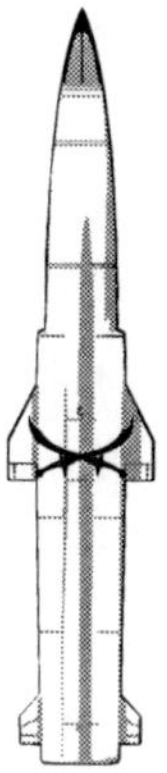

# 66

*New York City*
*Present day, Thursday,*
*after the attack at*
*Monte Sorpresa*

"Hello, Jamaal. *Salam*!" Saya-dar spoke into the phone.

"Peace to you, also, my father. To what do I owe the honor of this call. I am surprised to hear from you. Are you in the city?" Jamaal asked.

Saya-dar laughed.

"No, my son, I am not in New York at this time," Saya-dar lied. "Far to the south. That is why I am calling you. Would your affairs be arranged such that you could leave New York City for a time?" Saya-dar asked.

"Leave? Perhaps. Yes, if I must. When? Why?" asked Jamaal.

"Soon, all shall be revealed to you. Soon. Would you be able to leave New York no later than a week from now? You would need to leave and go inland. Chicago, perhaps."

"Chicago?

"Yes, Jamaal. Do you have friends there?" Saya-dar knew he did.

"Why, yes, I do have friends in Chicago," Jamaal replied.

"Splendid! Then, arrange to visit them. Visit them soon.

Seriously, Jamaal, I know I am being mysterious, but hear me. Are you familiar with the fate of the twin cities of Sodom and Gomorrah?" Saya-dar asked ominously.

"Indeed. I am. Wicked cities not unlike the one in which I live. Vile places inhabited by unbelievers who threw God's laws back into his face but who foolishly expected, nonetheless, to live. Vile cities destroyed by the very hand of God. All consumed by fire—and brimstone—whatever that was. All except for those few God agreed to save in promise to our father Ibrahim," Jamaal added.

"Correct. You are correct in every respect! Our father Ibrahim pled with God for mercy, and God, in His great mercy, spared Ibrahim's nephew Lot and his family. This is why I am calling you, Jamaal," Saya-dar hissed urgently. "I will come to you and explain all. I will meet you in New York, and we will leave together. Stay there now, but you must prepare to get out! You must get inland. Prepare, pack, arrange your affairs but be discreet. You will be gone for a time, but you will prepare as if for a short trip only, to visit your friends in Chicago. Do you understand?" Saya-dar pressed.

"I believe I do, O Saya-dar, but I should be sure. My leaving suddenly could arouse suspicion. Can you tell me what I am running from?" Jamaal asked.

"Fire and brimstone, O my son, fire and brimstone. Run, and do not look back or you will suffer the fate of Lot's wife," Saya-dar warned, looking down and across Manhattan's 5$^{th}$ Avenue, only 20 blocks north of where Jamaal sat at work.

Jamaal Lewis lowered his phone, stunned. Dazed, he

studied the LG flip phone's face. Still lit, it's blue and green tropical island "wallpaper" reassured him of time and date and of who he was: "Jamaal's phone." He could almost make out the waves crashing on the glistening, white, sandy shore in the picture. Staring dumbstruck at the beach picture, he saw a curtain of red fire fall from the sky over the picture. He saw schools of dead fish rise. He saw grotesque bodies of horribly disfigured human beings float by. They bobbed and washed ashore and piled up. Birds circled, lowered, and began pecking at them.

Pecking at their corpses. Corpses of his countrymen. His friends. The people he worked with. The people he worked for. The vision sharpened and he saw his parents' bodies lying among the corpses.

Yes, plainly the time had come.

Jamaal thanked God for his Verizon-inspired vision and shook it off. He lunched today at the City View Cafe, only blocks away from his senator's office. One of Jamaal's favorite spots. Jamaal got up, told the server not to clear his table—he would be back—and stepped out onto 5th Avenue.

Jamaal Lewis, 30 years old. Handsome. Suave. Educated. Educated in the classics, too. Educated in the writings of Montesquieu. Locke. Adam Smith. De Tocqueville. The Jewish prophets and the Christian Bible.

Jamaal Lewis. Saved from death by a Mullah, sent out from Arabia long ago to grow from within. To strike when the time came. To occupy. To change. To do conquest from within the Great Satan—unknown to the Great Satan until too late. Selected to govern in the new land once the apostate government had been overthrown.

Jamaal Lewis. Jamaal considered the words he had read in

America: "You shall know the Truth and the Truth shall make you free." By the mercy of God, Jamaal knew the Truth. The inescapable truth. The awful truth. The objective truth. No matter how many pilgrimages, murders, recitations, or *jihadist* beheadings of Westerners, no man could escape the awful, indicting, damning Truth: "All, like sheep, have gone astray, each of us has turned to his own way; But the LORD has caused the iniquity of us all to fall on Him."

All. The *jihadist* could never "earn" God, no matter how many infidels whose necks he sliced. No matter how many infidel children he exploded along with himself. No matter how well he kept all of the many religious laws and their arcane interpretations. The *jihadist's* martyrdom was a fool's act of impotent self-destruction only, not a glorious salvation to anyone.

Jamaal Lewis. Holder, by now, of a Ph.D. in political science from the American University. Sophisticated, urbane—convicted of the Truth. Truth verified by his own observations: The more men try to achieve perfection through their zeal for deeds, and the greater their faith in their own righteousness, the more monstrous they become. Always, it seems, our zeal to force our own will on people means killing people. Always. How else could it be? The stain of sin is stamped on our souls.

Jamaal Lewis: horrified at the carnage in his vision.

Jamaal Lewis. Agent. Sleeper agent for Saya-dar's Islamic *jihad*, turned double-agent working for the CIA. No, for America. For his new home. For his parents. For his birth mother, even though she had abandoned him. For the land that accepted him. Hardly a perfect land, but a land at least trying to hold fast to the dream of freedom for all.

Jamaal Lewis: agent for the Truth. And this is the truth Jamaal knew that condemns the worldwide *jihad*: No holy warrior can ever, ever do enough violence or good to somehow overcome his own sin and merit acceptance to God. That's for God to do, and He does so joyfully.

Jamaal Lewis. Placed in the United States of America by God for just such a moment as this, just as was Mordecai in Persia. Jamaal laughed at the connection he felt with Mordecai, reaching across time, trading lands, the Jew placed in Iran—the modern Persia—and the son of the Muslim placed in secular New York.

Jamaal knew not where his call would lead. He knew only that his time had come. He stepped to the phone booth in the 23rd Street station, fiddled for change, directed his coin into the slot, and left a message at his case officer's number. Jamaal said the matter "is urgent." He stared at the phone, then returned to the café and his lunch table.

Now, Jamaal stared at his cold cup of chicken-rice soup and the remainder of his half chicken-salad sandwich. City View served good food. The crowd from the Flatiron Building made it a regular stop. Jamaal ate there at least twice a week.

He was no longer hungry, though. Not for a second did he believe he'd stayed the hand of God. If God designed to destroy New York City, nothing could stay His hand and the city's fate. He had, however, stayed the Saya-dar—the Shade of Death—from rolling over his city. No, he had not yet stayed Saya-dar; he had merely taken the first step.

Laughter from the side stirred Jamaal from contemplating his city and his lunch. He glanced around, yearning to see ordinary people, in ordinary conversation. Yearning to *be* ordinary—something he knew he could never be again. Never had been.

A man and a woman, having coffee now after lunch was cleared. Lovers?

From their conversation, Jamaal caught bits and snatches. A publishing company editor and a literary agent debating the merits of the book the agent hawked. Here they were, next to Jamaal, lunching next door to the Flatiron Building, these days at the City View Café instead of some more expensive restaurant, saving some money.

"Unique terrorism thriller...," the agent pressed.

"People have moved on from terrorism," Jamaal heard the editor reply, catching his bored, dismissive gesture.

Jamaal marveled at the casual irony and wished the terrorists had moved on from their bloodlust.

Jamaal arose, left his lunch, left the editor who had moved on from Islamic terrorism, paid, and stepped out the City View Café's door. He breathed deeply, trying to recover his composure and ability to think clearly. Across the angular block, New Yorkers hustled back toward work, the lunch hour quickly expiring. The Flatiron Building jutted out oddly. Madison Square began to empty of lunch-going New Yorkers like himself. Jamaal walked toward the park, found a bench, and sat.

New Yorkers like himself.

Like himself. Sinners, more in need of mercy than destruction. Yearning in a way they could not recognize from an oppression they could only sense.

Like himself: going about ordinary life, all while wolves howled all around, waiting and watching for a sign of weakness, swirling around, circling for an opening through which to close and kill.

To kill people like himself.

Like himself.

Americans.

The inanimate herald of destruction—the paradoxically, serenely-wallpapered mobile phone—buzzed in his suit pants pocket. Jamaal retrieved it and checked caller ID.

"Gabriel" the phone announced.

*Hardly the Archangel,* thought Jamaal, but, together, he and the CIA would stop the Angel of Death from casting his shadow—his Shade—over the city Jamaal had been given as his home.

# Part VII:
# The Fire Within

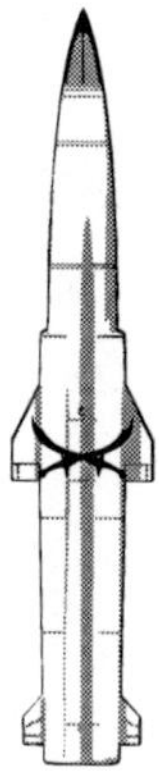

# 67

*Thursday morning*
*CIA Headquarters*

Nick sipped coffee. Before him lay the *Khazir's* blueprints. He lifted his phone and called Colin Ferguson.

"Can you clean your desk for an hour and come in here?" Nick asked.

"Yes, sir. Give me 10 minutes."

Right on time, Colin whisked in and sat down. Nick began.

"Good. We're going to reason through this. The key to what we don't know lies right in front of us, right here," Nick said, jabbing his finger at the blueprints. "Get comfortable and settle in for a while."

Nick opened his media player and started Chopin's concertos, turning the volume down. He relaxed. Colin watched his mentor, mentally rearranged what schedule he had, disposed of those tasks for now, and cleared his mind. A moment passed. Quietly, Nick began.

"Tell me what *they* tell me," he directed, pointing to the silent blueprints.

"Oceangoing. We know that from the size. Too big for rivers other than the Amazon and large enough to make blue water voyages. No propulsion on board, no engines of its own;

therefore, tugs. Oceangoing tugs."

"No, no," interrupted Nick.

*Already! What did I say?*

"Stick with what we *know.* No inferences yet," corrected Nick.

"What did I *say*?" Colin asked.

"You said 'tugs.' You've concluded that it requires oceangoing tugs for its propulsion. You don't know that. You know 'no propulsion.' You know how it is moving right now. You don't know how else it might move, or what other use might be made of it."

Colin thought the objection silly, but kept that to himself. Instead, he said, "Well, we know the barge lacks its own engines. Therefore..."

"Stop! No 'therefores'—not yet, anyway!"

"Size—big," Colin continued, nonplussed. He was used to Nick's style.

"Propulsion—none," Nick led by example.

"OK, I get it. Hull reinforced with this odd concrete slab, but only in this one area," Colin pointed out. Pointedly, he added: "I see here heavy couplings like those that are for fastening hawsers to a tug."

"Framework that we now know carries missiles. Removable hatch over section of the barge where we now *know* missiles are stored. Rest of the deck permanently fastened down," Nick said.

"Hydraulics?" asked Colin.

"Yes, hydraulic lifts underneath the missiles," Nick conceded. "What do we know about the reinforced concrete pads?" he asked.

"They look like they are about a foot thick, strong enough

to sustain and support a missile launch. And, there's all this interior plumbing for moving ballast around. Very unusual," Colin said.

They continued this way until neither man could make any more fact observations, looked at each other and began.

"Now, let's start to surmise a few things. Now let's infer. Now that we have inventoried the facts, let's theorize. They have to know we'd spot this long before it could threaten us. I mean, a football field-sized pad is visible, to say the least. At open sea? Why do they dream we'd *not* spot them?" Nick asked.

"Answer: they don't dream that at all. They don't *expect* us to spot them," Colin reasoned.

"Yet, right there on the surface, how could we not spot them launching unless—?" Nick stopped. He looked at the blueprints again and back at Colin.

Nick reached for the phone, but it rang before he could call the DD.

The DD wasted no time; he did not even wait for Nick to answer.

"We now know at least one target. There may be more," the DD rushed to tell Nick.

"Let me guess: New York City—again," Nick ventured.

"How'd you know?" the DD asked.

"Really, chief, it's not hard to guess. Very symbolic for them. We know this already. They seem fixated on NYC. Also, they've hit New York at least twice before already, and we've foiled three other NYC plots. Then, the FBI busts those

Afghans in Queens starting up a bomb factory. So—*duh*—NYC is a high-probability target as opposed to, say, Topeka, Winnetka or Kokomo."

Nick's reasoning was always ironclad even if he was, sometimes, a smartass.

Nick added: "Besides, they did hometown America two years ago so they're behind on New York."

"Yeah. OK, smart guy, an agent just verified your theory. Your theory is no longer theoretical. I don't know how you came up with it, but—well, I'll explain. Meet me in the conference room, with the DD—Operations and the liaison from SOCOM. Ten minutes. We'll stay on intel and analysis, and I want you on this until the end, but it's shifting to ops now. We'll need to act."

"You can say that again," Nick agreed.

Paul Ortega did not blink while receiving his own briefing. Not surprised at all. Just pleased that the CIA had done good work.

Pretty amazing work, actually. They'd ID'd the target even though the missiles were still far, far away. Wondered how they did it. Who did they have placed so inside that they ID'd the target—at least one target—so quickly? Well, good work, anyway. Thank God for the spooks. If there were any job more thankless than soldiering, that had to be it.

SOCOM already had teams standing by, tasked to take on the threat. These teams could be deleted from, added to, or re-configured once the threat materialized and they knew more. Maps and charts covered the tables. Liaison officers between the different special forces units coordinated. SEALs and Marine MEUSOC teams met each other and studied the charts together. New York City's head of security for the Port Authority (PATH) sent a liaison, and it seemed like old home week. PATH's security head was a retired Marine with a double career: 20 years in the Corps and then a new career on NYPD's SWAT team. This former Warrant Officer 4 (WO4), former cop, just couldn't hang up his gun. The new PATH security chief and part-time tactical pistol trainer fit right in. After briefing his official operations group, General Paul Ortega called Gordon.

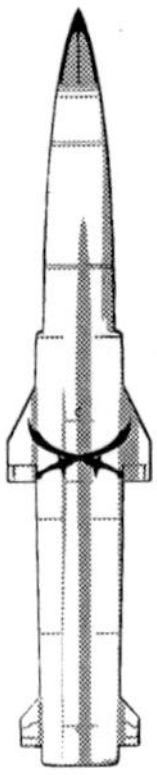

# 68

*Thursday night*
*CIA Headquarters*

Nick Ricollo did something he'd never done before. He panicked.

First, he rubbed his shadowed, stubbled face and blinked. Then, he compared photography and double-checked. Then, he panicked.

The missile barge—the *Khazir*—The Fire Underneath—The Smoldering Embers—had disappeared. He'd lost it!

His blood pressure spiked. He sweated. He would have loosened his tie, but he'd done that hours ago.

*Gone! How could that be?*

Not the storms. Those had passed mostly south. They just spread enough thick cloud cover and wind around to blind the surveillance for a while. For 12 hours. Before, the *Khazir* was tracking right there with the NYC garbage scow.

Now the *Khazir* had vanished!

Bermuda Triangle?

Nick felt like *he'd* disappeared into the Bermuda Triangle. No way around it. He quadruple-checked the before-photography and compared with now: there was the NYC barge, 1,000 miles due east of Jacksonville, chugging along, and its shadow—the missile barge was—gone!

Nick cleared his throat, sipped coffee, and buzzed the DD.

"I need to see you, Boss. Now," Nick said.

"OK. What's up?"

"No, please come down to the video display room as fast as you can. I have to show you something," Nick said.

Nick was this way only when it mattered.

"I'll be right there, Nick." And he was.

The DD stared too.

"Analysis?"

"Hell, if I know!" Nick admitted.

"That's no analysis," said the DD calmly. *He's been up too long on this. Needs some sleep.* The DD was about to say so, but Nick cut him off.

"I'll get some sleep later, Boss. Now's not the time for me to go home and go to bed. We'd been banking on the limited range, even of the enhanced missile, giving us plenty of time. It was still far out of range when it disappeared, but it could have been gone for 12 hours and—."

"Well, before Charon ferries us all across the Styx on his cursed barge, find it!" the DD said, unusually tense.

Nick stood in his office door, stared ahead and rubbed his burning, blurry eyes. Twelve feet away, mistily somehow behind the two photos on his wall, Nick saw thousands of corpses, all in the uniform of the United States, dead soldiers and sailors washed ashore, bodies piling on top of each other. Nick squinted at the sepia photograph of the young officer and tried to focus. His grandfather, World War II vintage campaign hat slightly cocked, smiled back. His eyes shifted to the black-and-white newer photograph of the young man in the black suit: his father. He looked back sadly now, not with the strength Nick always drew from. Back to Gramps. His grandfather's photo seemed to chide him. Now, it was like a specter chanting the same thing over and over: *Bad intelligence! T-h-i-i-i-s is what happens when soldiers get bad intelligence! You've got to do something!* the specter hissed, ending with a dramatic, swooping hand gesture indicating the lifeless corpses of comrades, floating somewhere, somehow in the wall there behind the pictures.

*Thanks, Gramps!*

Nick was dazed. He shook his head and got coffee and drank half the cup immediately. He returned to his office, plopped into his chair and buzzed for Colin. A few minutes later the young analyst appeared. Nick just looked at him. Colin looked worried.

"Boss, you look like death-warmed-over," Colin said.

"Thank you for the accurate assessment. Sit and think with me. No, first, let's get coffee."

Colin noted that Nick already had coffee, but he went along with him to the nearest break room anyway.

Back in Nick's office, more fresh caffeine in hand, they began.

"Here's the situation. After that chain of storms cleared the sky north of Cuba and the Bahamas, and after the clouds thinned, we re-acquired the NYC barge," Nick began.

"I know. Only one barge, though. The *Khazir*—the missile barge—disappeared," Colin answered.

"Yes. How—? Never mind. You know. Objects do not disappear. This is the time-space continuum. At the sub-atomic level, quarks are said to disappear, but matter does not simply cease to exist—cease to reflect light—."

"Mr. Riccolo?"

Colin never called Nick "Mr. Ricollo."

"What? What? I was onto something," Nick snapped.

"Sir, you sound like you're onto LSD. You absolutely must sleep. Your powers of reasoning are fading—even—(Colin coughed here)—twisting," Colin said.

"Twisting?"

"Yes, sir, twisting—out of control. Get some sleep. I just came back from the lounge where I got four hours. I'll pull out the blueprints once again and the charts for the western Atlantic and Caribbean, too, and go over them all. Once you've rested, let's get our heads together. I'll tell you any new observations I make and you will—no doubt—astonish me with your fresh analysis!"

"Astonish?" asked Nick.

"Astonish!"

Nick sagged and gave up. Colin was, of course, right.

"I'll be in #231," Nick said, referring to one of the dorm-like rooms where a single bed and clean sheets awaited exhausted officers and analysts who did not have the time or peace of mind to just go home.

Nick passed the coffee machine and this time left it alone. He slid his card through the lock sensor, pulled off his shoes, pants and tie and lay down.

*Ahh! My God, it feels good!* He began consciously forcing relaxation and deep breathing.

*Nick.*

*Grandpa?*

*Yes. Hello grandson, how are you doing?*

*Well. No, not well, Gramps. I've lost six nuclear missiles bound for NYC and don't know where to find them.* In Nick's exhausted half-sleep, the last of the sentence came out absurdly in the same cadence as "Little Bo Peep."

*Well, they're out there.*

*How do you know, Grandpa?*

*They have to be, don't they?*

*Yes,* Nick conceded.

*Nick, you solved it yourself a little while ago.*

This dream drama grew more strange. He'd *loved* to have solved *it* but, instead, he'd *lost* it.

*Right, Grandpa. Let me sleep. Please, sir,* Nick added.

*Yes. Sleep. Sleep. Sink into that other reality where your mind takes you all manner of places, but your body lies stock still.*

*Right, grandpa.*

*Seriously! Like right now. You're here in this room at Langley, but you're talking to your dead Grandpa! See what I mean.*

Getting more strange by the minute.

*Once you wake up, Nick, you'll see reality and you'll know I was never here. You'll see past the neural-chemical and spiritual illusion and see the reality. After all, Nick, I'm dead, right?*

*Can't argue with you there, Grandpa.*

*But you think you see me.*

Nick stirred and drifted toward deeper sleep.

*Nick!*

*What, Gramps? What?*

*Listen to me!*

*Why? You said yourself, you're dead!*

*I'm helping you see the puzzle you've already solved.*

*How? Huh? How?*

*Matter does not just disappear. Even in the best magic tricks, the magician employs the environment to manipulate perception. It's human perception that flashes the picture the magician wants everyone to see. The material reality is different. It's beneath and behind all of those prop manipulations. Hell, boy! Do I have to out and out tell you?*

*Tell me what?*

*How this Saya-dar has pulled down the Shade to cast a shadow so you can't find his hidden fire beneath.*

"This dream is getting pretty real," thought Nick, or did he speak it?

*Nick?* The Gramps of Nick's vision spoke more gently now. *Think of Saya-dar as a master magician. A master of deception. He has no stage, no assistant, no hat, no magic table or box. What does he have?*

*Only the open ocean and this weird barge, Gramps. We know that already.*

Gramps groaned. Either impatiently or because that's what haunts do. Nick couldn't tell.

*What else?* Gramps challenged, growing a little louder, Nick thought. Too loud for a dream.

*Nothing,* Nick thought. *Nothing else is out there. No props, no magic hat. Come on! Nothing,* Nick concluded.

*False statement! Nick, you remember the story of Agassiz and the Fish?*

Nick jerked. Yes, he remembered the story both his father and grandfather had delighted to tell him. This was getting really, really weird.

*Nick, what did Agassiz the Professor have his student do?*

Nick somehow gave the answer almost reflexively. He'd spoken it to his father and grandfather so many times when they challenged him as a boy. So, he just spoke the answer: "Observe! Make observations!"

Later, Nick would not be able to tell whether he had actually spoken the answer, or dreamed answering his grandfather.

*Right! Now, observe, boy! Make observations, and make more observations. Make observations and you will find this Saya-dar's magician's props. You will observe reality and blast past the illusion created by your own manipulated perceptions. Observe, observe, obs....*

Nick slept deeply, and dreamed. He dreamed of a young student seated in a lab, gazing at a single fish specimen laid out on the laboratory table in a specimen tray, just as his Professor, the great biologist Louis Agassiz, had told him to do. For a solid hour, the student sat, gazed, and made notes.

Nick saw him get up and report that he'd noted observations and was done. Nick saw the great teacher laugh and say, "No, no! Return and make more! This is your sole assignment for the next months!" The dismayed student obeyed and slowly, once he tuned his mind to *perceive* what he *saw* before him, he began to make many more observations.

The specimen tray blurred and a miniature barge appeared before the student in its place. Barge—singular—for one of the two barges was now gone. Only the innocuous garbage barge remained. The student's face and body changed and he became Nick. *Now, there is an observation,* the now student-Nick thought, and he began to make a note. Yes, more than just open ocean had appeared when the clouds cleared. It seemed meaningless and unattached to anything going on, but there it was. So, make the observation: the NYC-bound, plain, old, garbage barge, plied the waters ever toward New York, now only 50 miles from where they'd projected the missile launch barge should have also been.

*Observation #1: While not the barge they were looking for—.*

Nick sat up in the squeaky bed, fully awake in an instant.

The barge they were *looking* for!

The audience before the magician! Sleight of hand: Make

them—us—see something other than what is reality. Limit our perception of reality to what we are *looking for*. When we do not *see* what we are looking for, *it* seems to have disappeared. But a solid, steel barge, half the size of a football field, could not simply disappear.

The stage: the sea. The props: the sea. No, not just the sea. Our eyes. Our photographs from *above!* Just like the audience, we see, but only within *limits*—from one point-of-view only. *As if through a glass, darkly,* Nick mused over the Biblical simile bubbling up in his thoughts.

The P-3 Orions and satellites: those were the audience-observers. Recognizing the limitations on their distant, single line-of-sight was another *observation*! What *other* observations had he overlooked?

Observation: The NYC barge they'd so casually dismissed. *It* remained.

Nick jumped out of bed and stumbled over his own shoes, thrown haphazardly about. He pulled his pants on, jammed his feet into his shoes, and stuffed his tie—which wasn't much to look at anyway—into his pocket. He startled his boss in the hall but ran past him, back into the room where the photography was projected onto the wall.

This time, Nick went straight to the more recent, post-storm photos and pinpointed the NYC garbage barge. There they were: four tugs. Four, large, sturdy, ocean-going tugs, two per side.

Nick looked for the earlier pictures. Where were they? Already filed in Archive to make room for the most recent photos looking for the missile barge? Nick laughed aloud, and dug through the tub of printed photographs instead.

There: black-and-whites of the pre-storm garbage barge—towed by two sturdy tugs. Two, not four. He hit the buzzer for Colin just as the young man walked in, grinning, but surprised to see Nick.

"Boss?" *Supposed to be sleeping!* "What? Never mind. I've figured it out! Look!" Colin said.

Colin held copies out for Nick to see. Three, printed, black-and-white photos dated earlier showed two barges, each with two tugboats. Four in all. The third picture—the most recent—showed only a single barge but the same number of tugs—four.

"Tell me, Colin, how did you arrive at your conclusion?" Nick asked, gripping the young assistant's shoulders.

"But, I haven't told you my conclusion yet!" he said.

"How, how, how, Colin, did you know to make the observations that brought you to your conclusion?" Nick pressed.

"Huh? Oh. Well, that," Colin said, surprised, still wanting to tell Nick what Saya-dar's complete plan entailed, sort of like your cat bringing up a dead mouse and dropping it on your doormat. Colin wanted to brag a little bit. Here Nick was asking strange questions, seemingly uninterested in how this fiendish terrorist mastermind planned to incinerate and poison New York.

Colin Ferguson, 27-year old CIA analyst, graduate of the Bush School of Government and Public Service at Texas A&M University, student of Nick Ricollo—student of a young American infantry officer wounded decades ago at Anzio—student of a CIA officer remembered anonymously on the Wall of Honor—pointed to the old, odd, framed picture Nick kept on the wall of a fish lab-specimen.

"That's how," he said. "Observations."

Nick did something he'd never done before. He hugged Colin. Then, he buzzed the Boss.

"Boss. We know where the missiles are. Exactly. *Khazir*! The name says it all! It's time for operations," Nick announced. "Fast."

# 69

*Thursday night*
*Hotel Conde, Santo Domingo,*
*Dominican Republic*

Jack gave up and lay in his bed, recuperating. He'd been here before, sore muscles, bruised knees. Just took time.

His muscles ached from the violent exertion of the fights in Monte Sorpresa. He kept himself in top condition but nothing taxed the body like combat.

He'd pulled a hamstring darting forward. A groin ligament yielded from slipping in the mud, probably.

Besides, the job was over. It seemed anyway. He smiled. Their mission had seemed over at Gordon's lodge two years ago and all hell broke loose. And, their mission seemed over at *Monte Sorpresa.* Surprise!

Priority now: get the body ready for the next mission. Next, clean the AA-12? "No maintenance, no cleaning required," they said of the AA-12. For right now, he'd test that claim. Later, he'd lube it anyway. Put some Slick 2000 on it. *Where did I put that bottle?* Jack's mind wandered, poised just before sleep.

Consuela. Her warm hands. Her liquid chocolate eyes. He wondered how the Brazilian jungle queen fared in her new job. His gut told him she'd fare well, indeed. He wondered—he wondered.

She'd been so brave, this *Rainha da Selva* he'd named her, nicknaming her the Portuguese title for *Queen of the Forest.* She'd laughed, but plainly enjoyed her newly elevated station in life.

Jack wondered if he'd ever see her again.

She'd endured things he would not let himself imagine. He'd remember her at her bravest: barefooted, guiding him silently in the dark to the blueprints that set all of this into motion.

The blueprints.

The barge—the *Khazir*—now missing.

Missing. How?

The thoughts just kept coming, so Jack gave up on sleep and let them dart back and forth.

Missing barge loaded with its cargo of six nuclear-tipped, SS-N-22 Sunburn missiles.

Acquired by Iran from the Russians, and enhanced in Iran. Those missiles. Range unknown. Thanks to some source in New York, they now knew the "to where" end of that range. But, range *from* where?

The blueprints.

No one believed the missile-launcher barge had sunk. If so, why had the NYC barge not also sunk? The seas that far off the Carolinas and Virginia coast had not been churned by the storms to the south that much—that far out to sea: just clouded in with lots of rain.

It was possible she'd sunk, but they could not afford to assume that. What other possibilities emerged?

Jack shifted to try to quell the pain in his left knee. No use. *Hope it's not the ACL, again.* He sat up.

The blueprints.

He pulled on his jeans and shirt and stepped barefoot outside his room into the kitchenette. Jack stretched. The Chief passed by, walking toward the adjoining room, grinned at him and said nothing.

Jack pulled up a cushioned stool and fired up Gordon's laptop. He wiped his fingertip across the biometric security sensor and was accepted. He opened the folder for this op. He scrolled through the numerous images and found those by date that he'd made at the bungalow. There. The blueprints. Jack sat back. He looked at the Chief returning to the room. The Chief looked back, but said nothing. Chief Harbison was just letting him recover, whatever that looked like for Jack McDonald.

*Why am I doing this?* Hard to see on this screen anyway. Besides, CIA or NSA or DIA or some other __IA was pouring over this with the best and brightest minds around.

The blueprints. Pick out each anomalous feature. Infer from it anything it has to tell. Jack started an Excel worksheet and began listing the features he'd not have expected to find on a barge design. OK. There they all are.

Next, Jack checked the latest message traffic between General Ortega and Gordon and found the key that turned the lock to the secret: "Missile barge disappeared! Repeat, disappeared! Trying to re-acquire. Visibility now good, but target is gone."

The Excel sheet. The features. The anomalies.

*No! Not anomalies!*

Anomalies are things that are not supposed to be there, like a paper clip on an X-ray of your guts. Oops! Anomaly! Guts don't sprout paper clips.

Someone engineered these so-called anomalies into the barge, making them chosen design features, planned in and paid for, each with a specific purpose, not quirks or oddities or out-of-place mistakes. They would be out of place only on some *other* barge designed simply to haul corn, or soybeans, or gravel, or coal. *I must stop thinking of these unexpected features as anomalies. What do they tell us? What do they do? What could this barge do? What are its capabilities? From its capabilities, infer its purpose.*

Plainly, the barge could launch the missiles. It exhibited that capability unquestionably. Switches would start hydraulic pumps; pumps would move pistons; pistons would operate the hydraulic, steel, rail launchers which would raise the missiles. The missile engines would fire against their hardened, poured-concrete pads and lift off. Saya-dar had built a scary, mobile, sea-going, missile-launching platform and magazine for hiding and firing six, nuclear-armed, cruise missiles.

Fine, but, the U.S. constantly patrolled its coasts at multiple levels. Saya-dar must think he could not get these missiles close enough to the U.S. to launch and escape detection. In our age of missile defense shields, detection meant counter-launch, and our technology had gotten pretty good at that, despite all of the vociferous opposition to such missile shields. Saya-dar must know….

Conclusion: Saya-dar did not *believe* the launch barge would be detected and deterred.

Why? Why would he not believe that we would catch him as he closed to within cruise-missile range on our coast, and that then we would stop him cold?

*Maskirovka*! The Cuban intelligence head, Colonel Casteńeda, had told Jack that Saya-dar loved to exclaim the Russian word for the Soviets' "masking tricks": *maskirovka*! Deception. Feints. Disguises. Deception was part of great war plans from the beginning of history—if the commander had the time. A good commander continued to look constantly for the ability to feint, or trick the enemy.

*How could Saya-dar deceive us? They are at open sea. They. They are at open sea. They. Plural.*

Visions of "No Man" Ulysses and his men slipping silently out of a hollow wooden horse flashed. Later, Jack and Gordon would toast the delicious irony: that the key to figuring out Sayadar's trick lay in Greek mythology—ironic because the Greeks had been such bitter enemies of the Persians. Ironic, too, since Gordon's own *nom de guerre* drew from Ulysses' assumed, trick name, recorded in *The Odyssey!* How marvelous is the human brain that it makes all of these connections and produces such astounding conclusions!

Jack arose stiffly from the stool, stretched his sore joints, and left to find Gordon. He found Gordon conferring with Sullivan by the radio. He signaled Gordon the urgent need to talk.

"Gordon, I think I know where the missing missile-launch barge is. It is truly the *Khazir*. 'The Latent Fire Underneath.' Where is the visible garbage barge now, in relation to NYC?" he asked urgently.

Gordon startled at his voice, pointed to the chart lying open on the table.

"Here, off the coast of Virginia by 500 miles. Still headed northward," Gordon said.

"Gordon, it is imperative that we talk—you talk—with General Ortega now. The NYC barge is towing the missile barge. It's—."

"No, Jack, you don't understand," Gordon interrupted. "I got a message telling me the missile barge had vanished—or sunk—or something, but it's gone." *Must be the pain killers.*

"No, sir, the *Khazir* is gone from *sight* but the embers that burn underneath are not gone at all. The garbage barge is towing the *Khazir* underwater, piloted remotely to keep it beneath the waves and beneath NYC's barge, but close enough that the humble garbage barge masks the missile barge's sonar and even its visual profiles. It's traveling in the *shadow* of the NYC barge. It's traveling in its *Shade.* NYC's barge is a Trojan Horse. The Shade strikes again. *Khazir* is the Fire Underneath—literally."

Gordon looked at Jack. Then, after a moment, he said: "I'll get General Ortega on the phone right now."

But, the phone sounded as Jack reached for it.

"McDonald here."

"Jack, Paul Ortega. Put us on speakerphone and get Gordon. You're not going to believe this. Are you ready to move?"

"Ready? Yes, sir!"

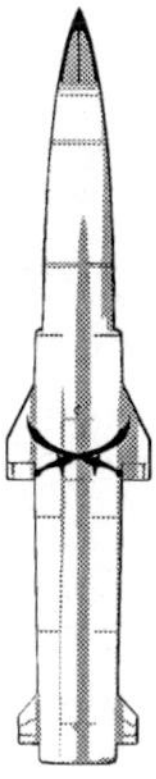

# 70

*Thursday night*
*The Khazir,*
*beneath New York City's barge*
*North Atlantic Ocean*

The hydraulic depth controls had challenged Saya-dar the most. In the end, low-power sonar constantly gauged the distance between the hull of the garbage barge above and the deck of the *Khazir* below and behind. Software caught and erased ambient sounds and engine noise, and produced the necessary pure, bounce-back, sonar, distance readings. These signals fed to the servo-motor controls which, in turn, operated the *Khazir's* stubby planes. These—in conjunction with ballast pumps—controlled the smaller missile barge's depth and distance from the hull of the NYC barge perfectly. It had all worked so well, having his covert launch pad tethered to a non-threatening, nondescript barge, ordered up by the enemy and eagerly anticipated for delivery. Indeed, Fats' sales VP was already passing on to Saya-dar heated complaint calls from the Port Authority of New York.

"PATH is not accepting either your owner's funeral or hurricanes as excuses for late delivery."

"No, the delivery is not yet late, and it had better not be, either."

The unwitting sales VP assured PATH that the delivery

would be on time.

All that stood between New York City and a hail of six-missile destruction now was 200 more miles of sea-travel. New York's life was virtually chugging away at 10 knot speed. Saya-dar had been considering using the sophisticated guidance systems to spread the missiles out to hit Baltimore, Philadelphia, Boston and, of course, Washington, D.C., too, but, in the end, Saya-dar chose to reduce the plan's complexity and go for drama instead. Multiple warheads landing all over Manhattan would make Saya-dar look—invincible. Allah would return, to the city already wounded, showing them He could strike wherever and whenever He pleased.

Three thousand miles separate Belem in the Amazon estuary from the port at New York City. A northern course from the mouth of the Amazon, staying just off the South American coast, brings a ship to the Trinidad and Tobago islands. From there, a captain may either hug the South American coast and enter the Caribbean Sea, or he may choose to skirt the Caribbean Sea and the Bahamas taking to the rough, open North Atlantic.

After the first 2,000 miles of the North Atlantic voyage, a captain nears Bermuda, oddly jutting out of the Atlantic far from the chain of pleasant Bahamas islands separating the Atlantic from the Caribbean. Off Bermuda, the ocean depth sharply plunges again. Bermuda lies 1,000 miles from New York City and due east of Charleston, South Carolina.

Once in range, Saya-dar's engineer aboard one of the ocean-going tugs—posing as a tugboat able seaman—would issue the remote command. The great towing hawsers would fall away from New York's new garbage hauler. The big, strapped-on, electrical connection between the garbage barge and the *Khazir* would disappear beneath the waves with the hawsers, leaving the garbage barge disconnected and appearing innocent.

The pumps below on the *Khazir* would answer to the remote signal, purging the *Khazir's* ballast tanks. The planes which had been constantly fine-adjusting the sub-surface *Khazir's* depth to hold 100' below the NYC barge would level and cease their work. Slowly, the *Khazir* would break the surface behind NYC's barge which had so thoroughly screened the *Khazir's* approach to the American coast. The NYC barge would continue placidly onward toward its purchaser and new owners—people who were never to know its first mission.

All else would proceed automatically. At the surface, and freed of water pressure, a pressure-sensitive switch would feel the relief from the water-weight which had been pressing down on the deck and the switch would trigger the missile hatch to blow free. The hydraulic lifts would raise the missiles. Once raised, and the inertial guidance system on, only then would the firing sequence start.

The entire operation would require less than 15 minutes once the engineer armed and pressed the single remote "Start" button he kept in his pocket.

Freed of the missile weight and detecting that the firing sequence was complete, the system would—with no further command required—detonate charges placed at the *Khazir's* hull and tamped by the poured concrete launching pads (designed to perform this double-duty) to direct the explosion downward. Simultaneously, the ballast tanks would blow to open them to the Atlantic's cold embrace. The *Khazir* would simply fill and sink. If any searchers were to happen upon the exact location of the launch, they would find nothing. No oil slick from fuel. No floating parts: these should all still be in place on the barge—sunk intact by being filled with sea water.

Above, the six, modified, Sunburn missiles would stabilize in the direction of New York City. Inertial guidance would keep them low to the water, unseen by any radar. Skimming closer to New York, the pack would rise high enough for the radar-seeking head to lock onto the Empire State Building. This soaring landmark radar target permitted the missiles to approach hugging low to the water, sometimes less than 10 feet off the surface, depending on sea conditions.

As the hidden fires beneath rose, flew, and prepared to ignite the city, the sinking *Khazir* would, effectively disappear underneath nearly a mile of sea, just off the continental shelf.

The Americans might somehow track the launches back to their point of origin. Saya-dar *figured* that. However, they would see only the humble, harmless garbage barge. The only clues that could link New York's barge to the *Khazir* were the electric switch that disconnected the electrical control cables, and those heavy steel towing cable brackets. The Captain had orders to remove the radio controls and throw them overboard.

*Who knows?* Considered Saya-dar. *Perhaps I may use such a plan again and again. Probably, they will never know where the missiles came from.*

For now, though, the *Khazir*, The Fire Beneath, the submersible launching platform, glided 100 feet beneath the waves, hidden below. The latent coals beneath the ashes waited to spark to life and burn in furious vengeance.

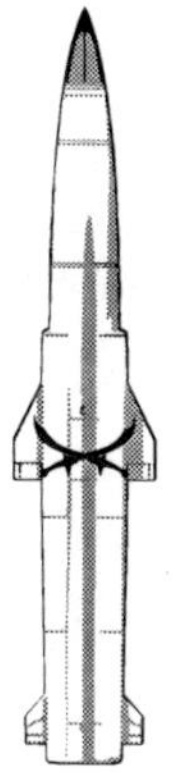

# 71

*Friday morning*
*Hotel Conde*
*Santo Domingo, Dominican Republic*

"I don't like it, Gordon. I don't like it at all. She's been through hell. She's not trained-up. If that's not enough to nix the idea of her going on this mission, you saw what kind of surprises she's capable of. Use someone else. Use CIA," Jack said to Gordon.

"Can't. She is the only one who can ID the Iranian man who ordered the missile barge—this *Khazir.* He is that very same man who met with her boss, right there in her bungalow. She had eyes on. She can ID him. No one else knows what that guy looks like. You killed everybody else who could have identified him! I can't ID the guy. You can't either. He may or may not be this Saya-dar.

'Casteńeda can ID the man he knows as Saya-dar. But, if this Iranian master-terrorist in the Amazon is the same man as this Saya-dar, then Saya-dar would recognize Casteńeda immediately and blow the whole operation. It has to be someone on our side who has laid eyes on Saya-dar, but someone he is not likely to recognize. She said it was fleeting, from a different room, and he didn't see her—she thinks. You know this. *Right?*" Gordon asked—said, really.

*Yes. I know this. I know it. I just hate it. For Consuela.*

"Then, let her ID him by video," Jack said.

"Come on, Jack. Video will be great—if everything gets set up just right—if it all works just right. If, if, if…! You're trying my patience with your protective instincts," Gordon said. All of this was wearing, and Gordon was tired.

"Are you mad at me for trying to protect her? Is that what you think is going on? Maybe I am. But, I tell you, Gordon, I'm right about this. She's not trained for this, and this is a complicated operation. You know what my favorite trainer, Roger Patrick, says."

"Not again! You're always quoting that Marine," Gordon complained.

"'If you're not trained, you're a *liability*,'" Jack quoted from the legendary gun-fighting trainer's endless repertoire of tactical truths. "She's just started. She's a 'noob,' Gordon. She's tough, but she does not know operations. She has been through all manner of trauma, not all kinds of training. SOCOM's psychologist hasn't interviewed her yet. No one expected her to take off on a murderous binge—but she did. Did you see that video of her? Like a banshee! She butchered Fats! Unpredictable!" Jack said.

*Pretty impressive, though,* Jack thought, but kept to himself. *Justifiable homicide if ever there were one, maybe a bit lacking in the immediate risk of great bodily harm, but, hey, just a little detail. She gave old Fats some jungle bungalow justice!* Jack tried to look grave, but it was hard, thinking about Consuela's revenge. Secretly, he was pleased.

Gordon sighed.

"I know, Jack. You are right on all points. It really isn't fair to her either. I feel—sorry for her. Fact is though, she joined up. That's our number one job requirement: Show up for the fight. She has showed up. There are no super-spies: just good people who come to the fight. Don't know why they do, but they do. Some are better than others, and some have no aptitude at all. But, they show up.

'Then we train them. Yes, they show up first, and get trained up second—usually. But, you have to admit: she's hardly the usual. I'd like to have seen her complete The Farm. I've got trainers lined up for her. I have her registered for your Roger Patrick's tactical pistol course. I'm getting her into one of Mad Dog's knife-fighting courses, too, only I have to wonder if that's necessary after watching her in action. Mad Dog might hire her to teach.

'Look. Here's the hard reality. You're a hard reality kind of guy, right? Well, here it is, McDonald. She's the only available resource who can connect Saya-dar to Fats and his bloody barges, and we're out of time. You saved her, but you can't protect her forever. That's not all," Gordon added and paused, frowning.

"What?" Jack asked.

"She insists on you. She trusts you. She insists that you are there to shoot on her behalf, if necessary. She knows she's not ready for this herself—although if you ask me, she fares pretty well in a fight—and she insists on your being there to protect her if it all blows up. I don't like it, but I can understand that; she's new to all of this and can't be sure we are all who we say we are. But, you, Jack, you, she is sure she can count on because you didn't leave her out there to be raped and fed to the piranha and crocodiles. So, it's got to be Consuela and it's got to be you. I need to know you are on board with me on this; so, are you, Ranger? What are you gonna do now, Ranger?" Gordon asked.

Jack knew Gordon was right. The deep-inside, loyal, double-agent had handed them what might be the only chance to get the monster when he surfaced in New York. If this terrorist they almost caught in the Amazon were really also this Saya-dar, then they could not afford to miss the chance to get him—perhaps the same monster who dispatched the 20 truck bombers. If they missed, how many more hundreds of thousands would he go on to kill?

The bloody facts led to a bloodless conclusion: as much as Jack ached for Consuela's peace and healing, she had to go back in. A New York "bungalow" this time. It was true: only she could ID the Iranian in the jungle as this same Saya-dar. They needed to raise the positive probability of killing him every way they could. She raised the odds of mission success. Period.

Besides, he had to admit, she'd signed on anyway. She was Richard's willing recruit. She'd "taken the King's shilling," as Richard put it, just like Jack had done. "I laid the shilling on the head of the drum, Richard old boy, and she took it up on her own, took up the recruiting sergeant's enlistment bonus, she did. She volunteered," Richard had told him.

Once you volunteer, your "career" never went like you thought it would. Jack could vouch for that. She was supposed to have trained for a year and gone back undercover in Brazil, and worked Guevara in Venezuela from there. Instead, Gordon planned to infiltrate her as Jamaal's housekeeper in New York City. She'd be right back there again—in the presence of yet one more evil, evil man.

Of course, Jack had to admit: Consuela had her ways of handling evil men.

Gordon's phone buzzed.

"Cyclops? This is Hank. I have two coming up. Man, woman, appear to be Connie and Clyde. Cannot—I say again—cannot verify yet. No surveillance spotted. No security spotted, over," Chief Harbison said to Gordon.

Gordon stepped to the window of his second-floor room at Hotel Conde Penalbe in Santo Domingo, pulled the curtain back, and looked out over Independence Park. Chief Harbison remained in his place in the square below, on the iron park-bench, feeding the pigeons immediately to his front. Gordon smiled and motioned Jack over.

From the center of the plaza in front of the oldest church in the New World, strode a man dressed in a khaki suit and white shirt, no tie, looking very European-colonial on this 90-degree day. On his arm stepped a woman of medium height and build, dressed in business casual, as if she might work for one of the western companies in Santo Domingo, or for one of the foreign embassies. The woman gracing Richard's arm glided gracefully along with him toward the hotel entrance.

"Look at that, will you? Mr. Dapper 'I'm not a spy' Pye and his "My Fair Lady," looking quite Her Majesty's Diplomatic Corps administrative assistant," Gordon said to Jack, pointing.

Jack had to smile. Somehow, no matter where he was, Richard Pye seemed in place, relaxed, and utterly delighted to be there. And Consuela! Jack shook his head in amazement. From backwater Amazon housekeeper to quite the urban, *latina*, professional woman-about-town. Apparently, they'd decided her social polishing was a higher priority than her tactical training. Well, that would have to be a missed ordering of priorities. They shot right past the combat vitals and sent her to charm school. *She doesn't need charm training much*, thought Jack, who kept it to himself.

A knock on the door. The challenge. The password. Gordon opened the door while Jack stood at low ready to the side just in case.

"Gentlemen, and I use the word generously! We meet again. May I introduce the Lady *Señora* Consuela—currently Her Majesty's Special Envoy to the Dominican Republic for Fair Trade, assisting with the certification of their excellent organically-grown coffee!" Richard beamed and announced.

Consuela smiled happily from ear to ear, white teeth shining, long black hair professionally trimmed somewhat shorter. Her loose white blouse worn out over her own khaki pants complemented Richard's linen suit. At 5' 6" tall and 125 pounds, she cut a striking figure, no doubt garnering all manner of hissing from the local *tigres*-would-be-Don Juans who chose that odd means of trying to impress the passing girls.

Gordon handed each a chilled bottle of water and directed them to chairs. Before moving to hers, Consuela silently moved straight to Jack, wrapped her arms around him, and pressed him close, kissing his cheek. Speaking no word at all, she then took the offered water, found a chair, sat, turned to the group, straightened and prepared to hear her own part in the new mission. Jack blushed as the two other men smiled.

Gordon began.

"Downtime is cancelled. Sorry about that. You knew that was too good to be true, anyway. Every time General Ortega tells us we are out of the action—well, you know that means load your magazines, draw your equipment, check your batteries, oil your entrenching tool, write your will and get ready for action!"

Gordon ended, while the men laughed and Consuela looked puzzled. Gordon continued.

"Jack, why don't you take a walk? Take Consuela with you. Richard and I have some planning to do. No, no, I insist. This is an order. Work on getting back to 100 percent. Besides, you didn't get to say good-bye to Consuela at the bungalow. The two of you take some time and be back here say, in two hours," Gordon said, and, with that, he ignored Jack's protests and pulled his chair up to the round table at the window, where he and Richard conferred.

Jack escorted Consuela out the door, past the desk where the sharp young man clerking this shift tried not to be too curious at the collection of English-speaking people meeting at the old hotel. Jack and Consuela stepped down the curving stone staircase, through the bar and out the hotel's arched entrance into the street-level cacophony.

Motorcycles buzzed by like tight swarms of angry bees. "Taxi?" yelled the passing drivers, in English, slowing down only imperceptibly, if at all, but getting eye contact. Tourists lounged at the ground floor's sidewalk café tables. All manner of people strode up and down the Conde's pedestrian walk, free for this short stretch from the incessant traffic normally whizzing up and down Santo Domingo's streets.

At first, the two walked quietly through the park by the old church, but foot merchants and tour guides pestered them, unwilling to leave the couple alone. Jack turned northward and led Consuela toward the river. The streets away from the colonial district's heart quieted a bit. To the left, through an arched opening in a low wall, Jack spotted a serene, bricked walkway between two buildings, with a few benches shaded by palms. He led Consuela through the arch, to the far corner of the small park, and invited her to sit in the shade.

"I thought I would never see you again," Jack said.

"I knew I would see you. I was determined to see you. That is one reason I have agreed to work for the British. Did you read my note? The note I left in your pocket?"

"Yes, Consuela, I read your note and kept your lawyer's name and address. I thought it would be my only way of finding you again," Jack said. "Instead, you are working for the British and apparently, you've joined our team."

Then, Jack posed the question that had demanded an answer since the two were separated at the bungalow.

"Consuela, you knifed Fats. You didn't just knife him, you butchered him. Why?" he asked, coming straight to the point.

Consuela looked back, looking perplexed at first, then defiant.

"He was a monster, Jack! I learned something I'd never have believed," Consuela replied.

In the soothing shade of a palm, sheltered from the city by a wall built 400 years ago, Consuela told Jack her full story. At the end, through her tears, she saw his shocked face, and stammered.

"I have no one else to tell, Jack! I wanted you to know why I did what I did. I could not stand that you left without knowing what I had learned."

Jack sat stunned. He strained to try, but could not grasp the enormity of what Fats had inflicted. Truly, this bungalow was a stifling house of evil. His own recon shack must have been the very place where Fats murdered her parents! That explained why Fats never went there.

Unable to get his mind around the beast she had killed, and

afraid of what he felt for this remarkable woman, Jack put his arm around Consuela and sat quietly by her side. He felt so awkward when words failed him. His embrace communicated all Consuela wanted to know: that Jack did not shun her for what he had seen her do—nor for what she had been made to do. Finally, in the best way Jack McDonald could, in the way that Jack McDonald could best identify with her, he dispelled any worry she still held that he judged her.

"Consuela, you and I both sent evil men to hell back there. You sent more than evil men to the Devil. You killed your own demons. You freed yourself from the clutches of the Evil One himself. You are very brave! I am honored that God put me into your life at this critical moment. I am honored to have been able to join with you to kill your would-be slave-masters. My only regret is that one got away."

"That is not my only regret, Jack," Consuela said next.

"What do you mean?"

"You have a life that is most out of the ordinary. Where in such a life is there room for *normal*? Would you give up your life as a soldier for your country to make a home for—a wife?" Before Jack could answer, she stopped him.

"I do not think you would, and I would not want you to. You are called to be a soldier, but that calling has its price. Perhaps, someday, you will grow weary and withdraw from your line of work, but I do not think so. And, I would not want you to. I am so proud of you, Jack. You are my rescuer. I, too, feel called. I wanted the life I saw other women have, but now, I do not think I could ever live so *normally*. I have seen too much, and I have too much to be grateful for. Your people have offered me the opportunity to pay back that debt, and I am ready," she said.

Jack understood. Part of him ached to redeem both of their

lives—to stop the killing, running, and hiding, and to just settle down. Jack thought of Boatman's seclusion and his family and he envied the man. But, he knew Consuela was right. Jack McDonald out of the Army had been lost—a man without a mission. Gordon's offer to join the *Arcturus* team redeemed Jack from being lost back into fulfilling his calling—his mission. Consuela, somehow, saw all of that so clearly for them both, and she was right. As much as his heart ached for peace, peace for both of them would not be defined by escaping from combat. Besides, as Jack looked at Consuela, he knew another truth. This wild woman had endured so much and only now had found release from her bondage. Yet, her release became fulfilled through her answering her own call to duty—to protect people far away she'd never met. That call must be powerful indeed to break through her bonds, to draw her out, and then back into danger. Neither she, nor he were ready to quit the field and leave behind the duty that called them both. For now, anyway, it was really unthinkable, Jack decided, and marveled that Consuela knew that already.

Jack stood and took Consuela's hand. The two rose, hand in hand, and found a small sidewalk café. Jack held the chair for Consuela and ordered wine. Consuela and Jack spent the rest of their two-hour respite there, at a tiny round table in the shadow of Christopher Columbus's presence in the new world, treasuring their brief time to explore their own new discoveries.

Gordon started the Operations Order for the next phase of Operation Piranha.

"Mission: Capture the Iranian terrorist who, we suspect, is the same man as this Saya-dar. This is the bad guy who planned and executed the truck-bombings two years ago. We will make the capture no later than midnight, Eastern Standard Time, on the 18th, immediately ceasing his ability to communicate orders. Only if you determine that capture is impossible, then kill him. However, you *must* stop him no later than the deadline. That is imperative. I say again, *imperative.*

'Enemy situation: unknown. Great, huh? We do not know what security or weapons accompany the man. We do not know how he will arrive in New York City, or who he may bring with him to his link-up with our double agent. I'll cover the terrain in more detail later, but think Upper West Side.

'Friendly Situation: Our agent—a double agent posing as a deep sleeper agent working in the U.S. for Saya-dar—resides in New York City at this address."

Here, Gordon pointed to a map of Manhattan projected onto the wall, indicating 88th Street between Amsterdam and Columbus Avenues.

"Here," he added, passing out aerial photographs of the AO (Area of Operations) to each, showing roughly five blocks on Manhattan's Upper West Side, between Central Park and the Hudson River. "The target is not a safe house; this is the agent's ordinary residence. He's an aide to the senior senator from New York and holds down the NYC office for the senator."

That drew raised eyebrows and a whistle. Gordon continued.

"This Saya-dar requested an urgent meeting with our agent on the 18th. The agent whom we will call "Jay" expects Saya-dar to arrive at his rented apartment—here's a picture of it—for this meeting."

Gordon showed a picture of a well-maintained, sandstone-colored, three-story townhouse sandwiched between two similar connected structures. The two on the side were constructed of red brick, all with the characteristic stone stairs leading up to the first floor above ground, complete with a gated passage down to the "walk-down" apartment underneath. Classic for Manhattan's Upper West Side.

"The walk-down is vacant. The walk-up is Jamaal's, including the second floor. The top floor is occupied by a literary agent, and his wife and daughter. Right now, they are registered for a conference in Orlando, with tickets and reservations at Disney World through the next seven days. They checked in and made reservations at the Bistro de Paris on the Disney World grounds for three nights from now—he must have sold a blockbuster this year. They are expected to have a good time in the Magic Kingdom. We do not expect them to return early. We may decide to use their apartment in their absence. Big Brother is watching their charge cards and, if they check out early, we'll know.

'Jay is a 30-year old American of part-Arab descent. The rabidly Palestinian-supporting Senator is a traitor. The Senator is waiting for his own *jihadist* orders and believes his aide to be loyal to Saya-dar. That's how Jay got the job in the first place—through Saya-dar. In fact, Jay "turned" on his own long before after being raised by an American family and living here for years. No one doubts his loyalty to America."

This confusing use of Gordon's double-entendre name, "No One," drew looks.

Gordon saw the confusion he had created and continued, explaining: "I mean, seriously, *nobody* doubts him. No One does not doubt him. Arrgh! I do not doubt him. Neither does anyone else on our side doubt him. Consider him a loyal American. He reported to us on his own volition, but was recruited by CIA years ago.

'The rest of the Friendly Forces section of this gets tricky. A

CIA surveillance team is on standby in case this maybe-Saya-dar moves the meet or in case you have to let him leave. If you for some reason have to let him leave, they are prepared to become a snatch team and capture him. We do not want that. Doesn't look good if the CIA is running around America grabbing people. But, they will, rather than take the chance that Saya-dar escapes. They change from surveillance only on my orders, and I order that only if you—Jack—tell me I must. They do not know about you, who you are, or what you will be doing—only that they must stand by.

'The command center—that would be me—will be here," Gordon said, pointing out a high apartment building on the west end of the block of residences between 88th and 89th Streets. This gives me good surveillance. Also, I have ordered up two sniper teams from the Army. Not sure yet if they will be SF, Delta, or Rangers, but Ortega has promised me the best tactical marksmen in the Army who are not already in the Middle East. They will occupy rooms in both of these two high apartment buildings anchoring down the west end of these two blocks, the one I'm in, and the other. Together, they cover the blocks formed by 89th Street on the north, and 87th Street on the south—pretty much our whole operational area, at least that is visible from their vantage point. You do see the elementary school on the east end of the block? We certainly hope we will not need the snipers but, if we do, they're there to stop Saya-dar from getting away. If not needed, they go home separately and we will never see them—nor they us. Questions?" Gordon asked, pausing.

"We ought to set this up like an area ambush, Gordon. If he—say that he—gets past me somehow, we need a plan for taking him out. How about a couple of sniper teams covering his possible escape and evasion routes?" Jack suggested.

Gordon considered a moment.

"We'll do that. I'll take care of laying on that support. More questions?" Gordon asked.

"OK, here's the Concept of the Operation. We all re-deploy to NYC by military transport tonight. I've arranged for ground transportation from here to this airfield just outside Santo Domingo. Richard drops off there. You fly to the military airfield here north of New York City, on the West Point Military Academy reservation. Very isolated. There, we will find a man waiting for us with the keys. You will know him.

'Once we occupy the safe house across the street from Jay's apartment, Consuela will report to Jay in the guise of his housekeeper. She will deliver three video and audio transmitters which she will place about the apartment—I'll show you where, later, Consuela.

'Additionally, she will carry an RFID tag: a radio-frequency tag embedded in her clothing. That's in case Saya-dar decides to move the meet and take her along.

'This is simple in concept: Saya-dar will arrive. The surveillance equipment will show him at Jay's apartment. You, Jack, will get that report from me. You will next hear directly from me that Saya-dar is entering the apartment—infecting the apartment as they say. That's your cue to move in. Consuela will have the back door opened—left unlocked. Jack will enter and take Saya-dar prisoner. Kill him only if you must. We badly need to interrogate him and know for sure whether he planned the 2007 truck bombings. More to the point, we need to know more about what else he has in store for us. So, Jack, be nice to him. You know what I mean by that: don't put one into his head if you don't absolutely have to. Finally, we want to make sure we wrap up this Fire Beneath attack and all who participated in it. Oh, I forgot. Friendly forces again: the CIA has an interrogation team standing by in a safe house close by to question him. He's going straight there once you're done with him. There is no telling what else he might have planned for us so every second counts.

'When you have him, report to me. Wait at Jay's and secure the site until the CIA's interrogation team arrives to pick him up. I will ID them for you before they come in. You and Consuela then leave by the back door and make your way to this address—Gordon pointed again to a location on 34th Street—for your debriefing. That will end your mission. From there—if we are all still alive—we go to dinner and celebrate.

'So, just to summarize, redeploy to NYC by military transport. Van into the city. Report to the stakeout house here NLT 2000 on the 17th. On my order, Consuela, in disguise, reports to Jay, plants the cameras and mikes, tests, verifies. Consuela will assure that Jay's back door is left open. On my order, Jack, you move in and do the POW snatch on Saya-dar.

'Here are some coordinating instructions. Front of Jay's apartment is 'red'. Back is 'white.' Roof is 'blue.' Jamaal is Jay. Consuela is Connie. Jack is Mack. Harbison is 'Hank.' I am Cylcops as usual.

'Alternate Plan Annex. Here goes. This is the Murphy's Law Annex to the Op Order. Saya-dar will probably contact Jay and arrange to meet him elsewhere. I would. You would. We think he trusts Jay completely but he really should arrange another meeting site at the last minute. It's just good OPSEC. If so, we'll hear about it on our mikes and Jay will IM us. He may give Jay an address or he may set up a chain of destinations and phone calls. If they do that, a CIA surveillance and snatch team takes the whole operation from there. We'll have to get him in front of Consuela for identification later, after the snatch. Questions?"

"Bodyguards?" Jack asked.

"We just don't know," Gordon admitted. "I warn you. Sayadar is at least a 'hard' target skilled at detecting surveillance. He may be an 'overt' target with his own counter-surveillance out there right now. Back to the 'Enemy Situation—Enemy Forces' section for a minute, he's avoided western detection for how many years we don't even know, possibly decades. He may be better at this than we are! Do not expect him to come waltzing up 88th and ring the doorbell below.

'However, we think he's coming to New York for one urgent reason: to evacuate his trusted agent. Why he thinks he has to do this personally, we don't know. I don't see it, myself. We suspect he's motivated by an element of personally wanting in on the kill here in his target city, but he has got to get Jamaal and get out to a place from which he can watch. This may make him abandon some of the counter-surveillance he might otherwise have mounted. But, don't count on it. So, back to your question, Jack. I understand why you're asking. You're the one going in for the kill—the snatch. But, we don't know what muscle he might bring along."

"Let's catch a plane," Jack said.

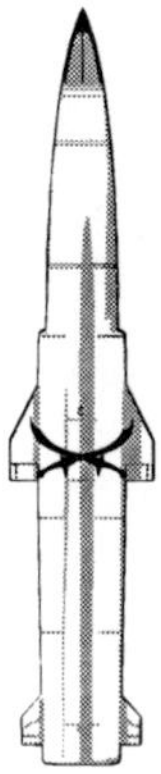

# 72

*Present day, Friday*
*Manhattan, New York City*

Saya-dar relaxed high above $5^{th}$ Avenue in the building owners' private lounge on the $34^{th}$ floor. Below him and above him, the offices and stores—the building's tenants—went about their business, completely unaware of their building's covert purpose. The "Safe House Lounge" in room 3432 stayed well-stocked. The owner made sure of that, for he never knew when his special guests might arrive.

Saya-dar swirled the whiskey sour and stared absently out the floor-to-ceiling window. The iced drink cooled his hand. He laughed at the irony. Immediately across $5^{th}$ Avenue, facing him, was the Burgundy Building, its mirrored glass surfaces reflecting back to Saya-dar his own building's light-brown granite, horizontally striped with contrasting darker brown granite, just as the Shah of Iran himself had ordered when he built his own New York headquarters 30 years ago. In only a year, the Shah toppled. New money and power arose in Iran. That power seized the state bank that loaned the money to build the Shah's New York offices. That power, too, found use for a presence in New York. The Americans were so busy going about their commerce. Why, if a terrorist organization were to need a "branch office" in the midst of the enemy, why would it buy some rusting warehouse in a rusting corner of a rusting city? That's what TV versions of terrorists' operations facilities looked like. Steel shelves full of machinery or tarnished, leaking chemical drums. Dark, abandoned storage rooms and dismal offices with a few pieces of fraying furniture. Vacant loading docks long left behind for other, better buildings. Sure, these made ideal movie sets for action scenes. However, they lacked class.

Saya-dar had considered such quarters. Indeed, he owned several across the United States for just such occasions when "some assembly was required." But, not for his flagship. Not for his headquarters. Oh, no. Hide among them! *Maskirovka*!

And so, while the deposed Shah's stock was down, dragging the building's price along with it, Saya-dar acquired it—or at least the controlling interest. A Channel Islands corporation hid his ownership. Teenagers swarming into the hot retail chain store below hid the true purpose. Doctors, dentists, insurance companies and corporate headquarters camouflaged the building's other and sinister designs. The flagship tenant bank might as well have been named the "First Bank of the Jihad"! Where better to operate—and successfully too—than in New York? When the Saya-dar required a place to stop over, he rented no motel room.

And so, on this day, he had simply strolled up to the recessed keypad panel around the corner from the anchor-tenant bank's main doors and wiped his finger across a biometric keypad. One of two doors had opened. Saya-dar had taken this rarely-used private elevator to the $34^{th}$ floor. Minutes later, shiny brass elevator doors had drawn back, his banker had rushed over, seized his hands, and ushered him back into another private elevator and upward to Saya-dar's lounge high into one of New York's signature skyscrapers. Now, Saya-dar rested, collecting himself for the time when he would also collect his prize agent and get him out of this doomed, damned city before fire fell from the sky.

When Saya-dar brushed his index fingertip across the sensor, the sensor triggered another switch. This switch closed a circuit controlling power to a transmitter. This transmitter alerted an office across from Saya-dar's lounge in the Burgundy Building. The FBI surveillance team's monitor lit up and beeped, catching the team members inside by surprise. It was not often that the keypad alerted. They'd chased down the idle curious bank customer. Some people just cannot keep their hands off of electric controls, dials, buttons and gadgets. Each one had to be followed and checked out. So far, their six-month long surveillance operation had failed to net them anyone. They'd spotted the money trail and the phony off-shore corporation as hallmarks of a terrorist money-laundering and financing scheme, but had been shocked to learn it led to one of New York's prestigious signature skyscrapers. They had set up to see who might be enjoying New York's hospitality and, so far, had compiled quite a list; but, they knew they lacked the head of the empire.

The three cameras flashed pictures of the special guest. The images uploaded automatically into image comparison software and started the process. Ten minutes later, the assistant team leader conferred with the team leader, printed identification of the guest in hand. The surveillance team prepared to pick up the "target" and see just where this Iranian financier playboy might next go. Was he just a privileged dupe, enjoying the lounge as a courtesy? Maybe he was a hanger-on. Perhaps, though, he was up to his ears in *jihad.* Only way to find out was the good old-fashioned way: tail him.

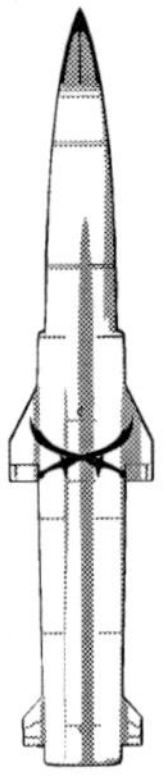

# 73

*Present day, Saturday*
*New York City*
*88th Street between Amsterdam and Columbus Avenues*

"I'm impressed. A nice walk-up two blocks from Central Park. We could do worse. Actually, we *have* done worse, Consuela," Jack had said to Consuela as Gordon showed them the stakeout immediately across from Jamaal's "target" rented walk-up. "There's good Chinese take-out food around the corner, too, an essential element for stakeout crews who are too undisciplined to stay put."

They assumed Saya-dar watched the area around Jamaal's apartment even now. The team had hung a thin, black, cloth screen from the ceiling. From the outside, it would appear that the window was unobstructed, but that the room was dark. The occupants would be able to see out. Around the walls, folding tables stood with the surveillance electronics set up. U-Haul boxes sat, now empty and collapsed in a corner, having disguised the equipment dropped off from the classic orange and white van. Tiny undetectable lenses peered out from the windows, covering the approaches, as well as the park-like common area behind all of the connected townhouses. The bank of monitors on one of the folding tables showed people bustling by on the street below.

Consuela stepped from the back bedroom wearing a white,

uniform-style dress.

"Are you ready for this?" Jack asked.

"*Si.* Let's do it," she replied.

Fifteen minutes later, Consuela left out the back door, worked her way toward Central Park where she might have gotten off a bus, turned down 88$^{th}$ and met Jamaal at his door. Jack now lay just around a corner in one of the few openings between the houses connecting 88$^{th}$ Street with the area behind the houses, hoping no good citizen would report him as a drunk.

Gordon radioed each for a commo check.

"Jay here," Jamaal spoke.

"Connie here."

"Mack here."

"Ghostbusters 1 here. Lima Charlie," the Delta Force sniper team leader replied from up the block, giving the radio word slang for "loud and clear." Ghostbusters 2 repeated the same, from the other apartment building.

"Connie, are you ready?" Gordon asked.

"*Si.* Yes. Roger," Connie corrected.

Jack shuffled to his feet and toward the back common area to circle closer.

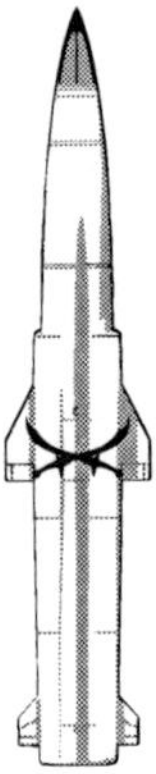

# 74

*Saturday*
*5th Avenue*

Saya-dar checked his watch. He'd rested almost an hour. Almost time. He grew excited. He raised his whiskey sour and finished the cold, soothing liquid. Saya-dar drew a deep breath and forced his nerves back under control. Time to go.

First, though, Saya-dar logged onto the computer terminal provided and placed orders shorting several of his stocks, and buying gold and oil. What delicious timing!

He descended by the private elevator. As he stepped out onto 5th Avenue and walked north passing St. Patrick's Cathedral, the FBI's stakeout team leader ordered the surveillance "box" into action. The young couple picked Saya-dar up easily. Indeed, they had all expected a challenge but, today, they found their target seeming to be out for a casual stroll, deploying no active counter-surveillance measures. The other surveillance operators stationed on different streets moved with the rest of the "box" toward Central Park.

Saya-dar considered his time and decided to head into the park. If he had any regrets at all, the loss of the park would be one. He might as well enjoy it's dipping, curving paths once more. Twenty minutes later, he emerged from Strawberry Fields imagining the fiery, poisonous carnage. At the 72nd Street Metro station he caught the A Train the 14 short-blocks north to 86th Street, swaying as the train slowed and stopped. Containing his building sense of urgency, Saya-dar flowed with the others rising and shuffling out the door. He joined the crowd working its way upward to the city street. At the top of the escalator, he fought the urge to turn west and make straight for Jamaal's. Instead, Saya-dar crossed Central Park West and ducked down along the Transverse Road dipping down into Central Park.

Four healthy-looking thirty-somethings—runners with big, black numbers pinned to their shirts, rounded a bend, appearing before him suddenly, and passed him by, frighteningly close. They had emerged from nowhere and seemed to be coming straight at him. One, pony tail bouncing, hands clenched, looked at him and reached up, tugging something on her shoulder. Water, she was only sipping water from one of those plastic tube devices.

The young woman did sip water, but, after passing Saya-dar, she spoke into her modified Camelbak microphone: "Beta 1 is off the spider and has infected the Charlie Papa farm at Transverse Road Number 3. No smoke detected. Possibly intending the 86thLizard. No. Wait. Beta 1 is still free. Now dead at the farm bench. Cunningham no longer zero-zero."

What strange language to use to tell control that Saya-dar had re-entered Central Park, might have been heading toward the nearest bridge where 86th Street crossed underneath West Drive, but had stopped instead at a park bench, and that the runners had to pass him by and stop surveillance! The runners no longer had "command" of their target and had passed Saya-dar to the next team.

Saya-dar now sweated, too. He knew he was on the verge of out-of-control. *This is when you make mistakes! This is when you abandon the principles that have kept you alive! I wish I had kept up my operational training. I have grown too complacent!*

Saya-dar took a seat on the nearest bench and peered around him. All appeared so *ordinary.* He fought back the pressure to check his watch again. Instead he appeared to react to a vibrating mobile phone. He retrieved the phone from his front pocket, checked the time on the display as he raised it to his ear and pretended to answer the call. He relaxed, stretched back and appeared to absently begin looking around as he talked. He saw no one familiar. No same garment. No same face. No one stopped, appearing to wait for him to move again. None of his fellow train passengers still lurked about. Still, it had been long since Saya-dar had run counter-surveillance exercises, and he knew his skills were rusty.

Plenty of time? No! The clock had run out. Even now, he could see the *Khazir's* decks falling away, the missiles rising to cause their "sunburns" on the denizens of this city. He *must* get up and get to Jamaal and get them both out of New York. Why so nervous?

Saya-dar knew why he was so nervous. In his mind's eye, he foresaw the *Khazir* rising to break the cold grey surface of the North Atlantic. The agitated Atlantic churned as if angry at the leftover storms and squalls. His mind's eye watched in fascination as the Sunburn missiles—his missiles—arose steadily to the vertical, no longer the fire contained *within.* With a roar, the stage I motors ignited, shooting the missiles away from their reinforced concrete pads poured into the *Khazir*. The stage II motors ignited and the flaming embers—no longer beneath—arced steeply westward, hugging the choppy gray surface. At 1,500 miles per hour, the modified cruise missiles would cover the 150 miles from the continental shelf to New York City in a mere six minutes. Once launched, nothing could recall them. Nothing the Americans had could stop them either, he was sure. He could not imagine how the Americans could even detect them in time to strike them down, if they detected them at all. Launched from close enough, the former anti-ship cruise missiles became a phalanx of surprise attack, surface-to-surface missiles, like tactical field artillery. Saya-dar liked to think of them as Iran's intercontinental missiles, only making most of the trans-continental journey plodding slowly, hidden in the belly of the most mundane of vessels. Then, emerging from beneath, the fire within would come alive at twice the speed of sound and complete the journey, consuming the city in nuclear holocaust in under six seconds from launch.

*Why, oh why, have I come here personally? Why would I do this?*

Saya-dar knew this was a tactical mistake. Saya-dar leaned back and rested his arms along the top of the bench, stretching his feet to his front again as if carefree and off work for the evening. He actually felt himself relaxing.

He knew why he'd come. Saya-dar wanted to celebrate the fire and brimstone he was about to rain down on this city. How to do that other than to be here—one more time—to observe New York all about its self-absorbed urban hustle. He would link up with Jamaal, explain all to the young man, and savor the shocked—then joyous—look on his prize sleeper agent's countenance. Jamaal would realize that he was about to witness a great victory, the culmination of years' worth of preparation. He and Jamaal would, together, witness great revenge against the Americans.

Witness from afar, that is. Saya-dar breathed deeply and arose steadily to his feet. *Time!* He was out of spare time. Meeting Jamaal here to evacuate the city was exciting, but cutting it so close bore its costs. He was sure his attack was undetected: look at all of these New Yorkers going about their business as usual. Yes, Saya-dar was confident in his secrecy. How could the Americans know what fire lay beneath the ship *they* had ordered?

Saya-dar rose, renewed—alive—secure. Besides, he had his fearsome bodyguard already at work. He breathed deeply, again, as if enjoying Central Park—which he was—and made straight for Jamaal's less than two short-blocks and two Upper West Side long-blocks away. Standing at Central Park West, waiting for the light to change, Saya-dar phoned Atash, his bodyguard.

"I am ready. Go to prepare the way, Atash" Saya-dar commanded.

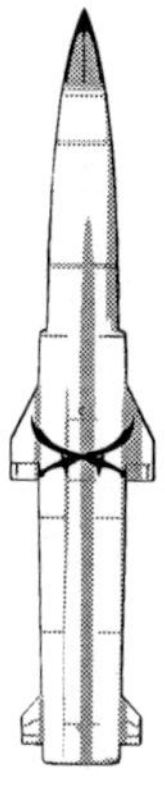

# 75

*Saturday*
*88th Street and*
*Amsterdam Avenue*

Atash's unblinking eyes never left the woman who turned from the sycamore-shaded sidewalks and took the steps up to Jamaal's rooms. He hated her. No, he did not know her, or her purpose, but that was not necessary for Atash to hate her. She represented an unknown: unknowns represented threats. She *carried* things in her hands and those represented threats.

*Weapons?* questioned Atash. Perhaps, although the tote slung from her shoulder by a single strap looked ordinary enough. He shrugged.

Cleaning crews come alive at night in the city. Nothing unusual about that except that this was a bit early. Of course, nothing about this mission was usual. Jamaal was no usual person. Saya-dar's agent lived and worked in NYC. So, it was natural enough, Atash reasoned, that Jamaal hired a housekeeper like so many other affluent Americans.

She looked Latin-American. Looked like a housekeeper. Atash kept his binoculars on her, hands propped on his knees, peering out of his 5th floor apartment on the west end of the block, chosen for its perfect view straight down 88th street, covering Jamaal's door. Atash sat in the dark, about five feet back from the window, chair elevated on a wooden box he'd hammered together to better his view. Gauzy gray curtains fluttered in the windows to keep him further hidden as he stood counter-surveillance, one floor above Gordon and one floor below Ghostbusters 1.

For Saya-dar had, indeed, developed his own counter-surveillance measures. The standard involved various tricks designed to flush out the team members following you. That is how the great game is played, but Saya-dar was anything but standard. Saya-dar had long ago assessed the skills of the western intelligence agencies and found them superb at foot surveillance, in particular. Therefore, the usual counter-surveillance measures—he had reasoned—stood so little probability of success that he might as well use "the book" against them. Indeed, deploying counter-surveillance would simply confirm that he was, indeed, a target. Instead, he liked to lull them into a sense of complacency, if possible, by mounting no counter-surveillance following him about at all. He abandoned the known tactics that "targets" employed which marked them as targets. Saya-dar liked to deploy what he thought of as "deep, target-critical" counter-surveillance: he deployed his bodyguard—Atash—The Fire—to watch his destination and guard his immediate approach, for this was the zone of greatest danger.

Saya-dar thought of the huge man from the mountains of Iran just south of the Armenian border. Atash's job was to eliminate danger before Saya-dar arrived. Saya-dar thought of Atash as "The Flame," burning all who dared to stick their hands into his flames. Saya-dar shuddered, remembering Atash's specialty: torture. He had not believed the stories, and, so, he watched Atash one night, at his work. Then, Saya-dar believed and made Atash his bodyguard. Any man who could be that cold was capable of filtering out all of the emotion, the chaff, the distraction of life in general. *If Atash ever learned what I did to his brother...*

Atash watched Consuela enter the front door. In only minutes, his master would arrive, and it was Atash's job to clear the way of all risks. Maybe Jamaal kept the housekeeper on appointment on his calendar, anticipating she'd be done in the hour before the scheduled meeting with Saya-dar. Jamaal could not know what Atash knew: that Saya-dar would arrive an hour earlier as a security measure.

Nonetheless, Atash reasoned: there the woman was, inside the apartment where his master would shortly arrive. She would have to die if she did not leave quickly on her own. Time to move. Atash had already selected his path from his own stakeout to Jamaal's. The dumpster behind the tall building nearby would serve to deposit her body. In Atash's line of work, you always had thick, plastic disposal bags, and you always looked for places to hide the bodies.

Atash's phone vibrated.

# 76

*Saturday*
*$87^{th}$ Street and*
*Amsterdam Avenue*

Jack exited the back of the stakeout on $88^{th}$ and turned west toward Amsterdam to circle around the back of Jamaal's apartment. He worked his way through the maze of patios and common areas, turning left again at the tall apartment building housing Cyclops' observation post.

Jack crossed $88^{th}$ against the pedestrian light at Amsterdam, crossing with the mass of pedestrians so he did not stick out from the crowd. He dragged along just a little, as you might expect a drunk, unemployed, homeless man to shuffle. Then, he continued ambling down Amsterdam, but cut left at $87^{th}$, and then left again immediately into the parking lot behind the tall apartment building there. He tried to look disoriented and aimless.

The back corner of this 20-space parking lot connected to the common area behind Jamaal's townhouse. Jack dragged himself to the back corner of the parking lot where he could see down the common area through the low trees. Here, Jack fell into the stacked, black plastic bags of refuse piled there, awaiting pickup. Just enough clumsiness to look real, not enough to make a big racket. Just before rolling to get eyes on the back of Jamaal's apartment, patio garden area, back entrance, and fire escape, Jack glimpsed Atash rounding the corner behind the tall apartment building and stepping into the parking lot just like Jack had done.

*What is that monster lumbering down the alley? Pretty big extraneous variable running around in my equation. Following me? Who is that guy? Murphy himself? Murphy's sure grown! How did he spot me so fast?*

Jack moaned loudly and rotated over onto his back, losing his watch over Jamaal's back entrance, but now able to watch the man-mountain approach through relaxed eyelids. Jack watched in disbelief as a monster of a man walked straight up to him, looking quickly 360 degrees around in a most non-civilian, switched-on way, and then returning to focus on the sprawled-out "Mack."

*Didn't take long for this plan to fall apart! I think this is gonna hurt!*

Jack considered and lay still to see what developed next. He keyed his mike to hold on "transmit." Cyclops was about to get his ears full.

Big! Maybe 275 pounds, but the mass was carried in a frame 6' 5" tall, shoulders wide, wide, wide. About mid-thirties: no gray hair. Eyes dark brown, almost black and set wide apart above a huge nose, and—*Weird!*—the eyes showed no emotion. Very calm. Very—professional, was Jack's immediate impression from his bleary-looking, squint-eyed peering as Atash approached and squared off over him.

Jack moaned drunkenly, swayed his head back and forth, blinked like he was trying to regain his consciousness, and appraised Atash the entire few seconds. Face dark and also wide, black beard trimmed close, black pleated pants (more room for weapons storage and concealment), black sport coat loosely worn (great for hiding guns), dark maroon, button up, button-down collar shirt. No tie. All clothing discreetly in style for New York or Europe, but perfect curtains for a black, double-stack magazine, large caliber, semi-automatic pistol—with extra magazines. Nondescript as you can be and still be a man-mountain. This time it looked to Jack like Murphy had sent his chief enforcer out to bend Operation Piranha to his will.

*Security,* Jack reasoned correctly. *If I get him, I blow taking down the target. If I don't, he may kick me into next week! Dilemma!*

"Huhhhh?" Jack belched, stirring in the shadow Atash cast. Through bleary-looking but quick eyes, Jack spied the fixed-blade knife and the pistol beneath the sport coat. Those shoes! Must be size 14, thick-soled with leather, not rubber—black smooth leather, probably steel-toed, work-style shoes—good for kicking.

"Huh? Guh mahnin' deh buddy" Jack said, faking a wrong-time-of-the-day greeting as he shuffled amidst the rubbish to sit up. He flashed a woozy, boozy-looking smile.

"Say, yous not a cop, ah ya buddy?" Jack asked Atash, coming to a bit, as if now a little worried, maybe a little more sober.

"Go! Now!" Atash hissed in return, through his clenched teeth, partly from controlled, fire-like rage, and partly as a tactic—controlling the situation and the threat by frightening the bum with his manner, tone and voice—and his size.

"Huh? Yeah. Go. Right. Sure. Yeah, guh buddy, no problem. No problem wi' me, man. I am *movin'* on," Jack said, shuffling but not vacating.

"Shakin' it here, boss," Jack said, trying to delay and joking with Atash, who probably hadn't seen *Cool Hand Luke,* Jack then figured. This got more fiery-eyed, clenched-teeth hissing. With some growling, now Jack heard.

"Must *go*! Police coming! I called police! They take you away. Go, go, go!" Atash urged, frowning and leaning forward menacingly: pretty effectively, too, Jack thought.

*He can't risk killing me right here. Someone might see. Decision time. Got it.*

"Yeah, OK, OK big man, no problem, no problem," Jack agreed smiling stupidly, trying to be as harmless and charming as a street-drunk could be. He clamored over a smelly, broken bag, strewing eggshells and coffee grounds. Jack struggled to his knees, then feet, and wobbled slowly back through the alley where the garbage trucks would approach. The bug-bot camera Jack had palmed out of his pocket and left by the pile of bags began transmitting.

*Uh, oh!* Gordon spied the blinking #4 light labeled "Mack Bug 1" and turned to monitor Jack's bug camera's observations. *So soon? What could have made Jack deploy his bug-cam so soon? Oh. That! Him. That's some serious muscle! Yeah, that would do it all right.*

Gordon fiddled with the joystick and the bug-looking device crawled backward, lifting its "eyes" to stare up at Atash.

*Security has arrived. It was too good to be true.*

"Mack, this is Cyclops. Tango is Frankenstein," Gordon said, naming the new arrival into the tactical situation. "That's Frankenstein staring, watching you, not reaching for weapon. I say again, *not* reaching for weapon. Range now 20 yards," Gordon said, flicking the bug-cam's eyes back and forth. "Copy?"

"Mack. Roger. Over."

"That's Frankenstein still not moving. Still not moving. No weapon, I say again, *no* weapon. What is your plan?" Gordon asked.

As if to answer, Jack slowed 30 yards from Atash, just short of the 87$^{th}$ Street sidewalk and "tripped," lying face down in the mulch by a shrub, and next to the silver-gray Prius parked there.

"See Mack?" Jack asked.

"Roger, that's Mack at corner of 87$^{th}$ and Parking Lot. To all Ghostbusters: one Tango—Frankenstein—in common area AO behind target, west end. Armed with at least large-caliber pistol and fixed-blade knife. Six feet, five inches, 285 pounds, wearing black, open, sports jacket on black pants, maroon shirt, black hair and beard. You'll recognize him, believe me! I ID this Beta as 'Frankenstein'," Gordon said, congratulating himself on how appropriately he named the enemy security monster.

Frankenstein watched the filthy bum leave, watched him trip, watched him fall, watched him *not* vacate the area. Atash glared at Jack in disgust as Jack's insubordination stoked Atash's flames. The stinking vagrant had stumbled and fallen again, this time just short of the sidewalk lining 87th street. Atash raged at his own hesitation. He felt the fire of his name glow, becoming a white-hot consuming inferno. His eyes lasered into the prostrate, unmoving lump of human detritus and Atash stepped forward to kill the man.

Atash's phone vibrated.

Atash hesitated, answering the call and hearing his master, clearly angry.

"Atash!" hissed Saya-dar. "Where are you?" Saya-dar demanded.

Atash halted. White heat built, rose, flushed his face. He felt it rise inside his head, threatening to blow the top of his head off. Atash was afire. His very name meant *fire.* How could he *delay*?

This man—his master—caused him such frustration! Allah did not mean for Atash to be under such tight control. Allah meant for Atash to consume! Yet, this service, this master, always curbing his rage, holding back his violence. Atash jerked at his harness, kicking to tear the reins from Saya-dar's hands. Atash burned!

Yet, Atash halted. Still glaring at the unmoving Jack, he spoke in response.

"Behind Jamaal's, at the west end of the block," Atash gave as the controlled answer, trembling but reporting evenly. "I am in the little park behind the buildings."

"I am almost outside Jamaal's! You get here, too! Immediately!" Saya-dar ordered.

So, Saya-dar made Atash's decision for him. Atash obeyed. His eyes flicked from Jack back to the common area and Jack was forgotten. Saya-dar had so ordered it. The flame evaporated, as if fuel had been cut off. In a way, Saya-dar had made it easy. Atash burned to kill any threat in the area, but Saya-dar himself had pulled him away. Therefore, it was decided. The homeless man would live another day to infect his city.

All the better, Atash rationalized. The smelly, greasy bum would leach sustenance from New York for a few more days, and then perish along with the millions of his betters.

"I am only 100 meters out. Situation?" Saya-dar demanded.

Tense. Curt. Abnormal for him. Atash didn't like it; his boss was coming apart, losing it.

Frankenstein stood over the alley. He looked left, through the low shade trees, toward the back of Jamaal's apartment. He still had the rest of Jamaal's fire escape and back entrance common area to secure: about 100 yards of winding walks, patios, fences, flowers, trees, a few benches, perhaps. Lots of adjacent windows and porches, though. Granted, he needed to check the whole common area between the houses facing 87th and the houses facing 88th, plus that break between the buildings on the east end opening out onto 88th street, but Atash was out of time.

Atash felt a rare pang of remorse and grief. He wished his brother, Kadir, had been along to help. They had always worked as a pair—brothers—Atash and Kadir, in Saya-dar's service. *Fire* and *Power*: Atash and Kadir. Together, they had fought and guarded Saya-dar as The Mighty Fire, The Consuming Fire.

Unfortunately, Kadir had died protecting Saya-dar on his last raid into the United States. Had Atash been there.... The wash of guilt shook Atash. He had not been there to see his brother die. He really still did not know quite how his mighty brother, Kadir, The Powerful, had perished—while Saya-dar had escaped.

"That's Frankenstein scanning back to Mack, now scanning back to the common area. Not moving. I say again, that's Frankenstein snagged at point Orange," Gordon reported.

Atash tried to visualize the rest of the perimeter he wanted to check. Glancing back at Jack, he considered: perhaps he should have just killed the man. Perhaps someone would have seen and called the police. Only 100 meters out. Time. Atash needed time.

"Wait," Atash the Frankenstein said.

"Wait? For *what*? I am ready *now!*" Saya-dar hissed through clenched teeth.

This time, Frankenstein ignored his master. He would obey, but he would secure the common area. His tactical dilemma solved, his grief over his brother, Kadir, dissolved, Atash threaded his huge bulk surprisingly quickly through the patios, fences and trees behind Jamaal's, noting the raised fire escape ladder behind Jamaal's apartment. He continued more swiftly than he would have liked behind the other apartments to the east end of the common area and cut sharply left through the opening between the buildings. Now facing 88th, Frankenstein turned left, doubling back down 88th Street and startling a woman walking her dog.

"Gone. Frankenstein has left the AO. No. Wait. Wait. That's Frankenstein at range 150 yards, moving this way—west—on 88th street in front of target. That's Frankenstein climbing steps at target side Red. Connie, that's Frankenstein at Red intending to infect target. Lower the White-side ladder now, now, now!" Gordon said, urging her to lower the ladder behind Jamaal's quickly. All of a sudden, this was happening fast.

"Cyclops, this is Connie. Roger lower the ladder now. Wilco," Consuela replied. This was all happening much faster than she'd anticipated. They were supposed to have at least another hour!

Jamaal and Consuela ran to the back porch. Together they lowered Jamaal's fire escape ladder as Jamaal's doorbell sounded the first measure of Beethoven's 5th Symphony. Jamaal turned and ran back inside.

"Mack, this is Cyclops. Execute entry. Execute entry," Gordon ordered, seeing the ladder lowered through the eyes of the bug-bot and, simultaneously, watching Frankenstein ring Jamaal's apartment entrance doorbell. *Oh, this is close!*

Jack startled an older woman who recoiled as he arose and turned back toward the parking lot. As the woman hurried away, he made straight for the common area behind the row of stone and brick fronted townhouses.

"Leave your bug-bot in place," Gordon instructed, deciding that camera eyes in the common area were a good thing.

The bug—no more than the size of a modest roach—watched

Jack run past and stop, waiting for the ladder. Jack looked up, arms outstretched. His eyes met Consuela's as she lowered the ladder. Then, apparently distracted by some noise behind, she turned quickly away and was gone.

"Situation? Cyclops, situation?" Jack asked.

"That's Frankenstein at Jay's apartment. On the walk-up steps. Intending Red door."

Jack pulled himself hand-over-hand up the ladder onto the stamped-steel landing above.

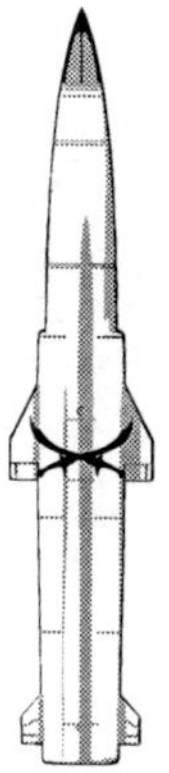

# 77

*88th Street*
*At the door to Jamaal's*
*Upper West Side townhouse*

The lazy always got off, it seemed; the diligent get screwed.

A sick relative. Jamaal's forgetting to call and cancel. Perhaps Jamaal did call, but his housekeeper had permitted her pre-paid cell phone minutes to lapse, missing the call and the voicemail message that would have saved her life. *Inch'Allah*!

Atash could not accept the housekeeper seeing his master. To see Saya-dar was death except for the few he permitted to know his face. Only a handful knew him as Saya-dar. Atash, the bodyguard secretly named Frankenstein, decided as he stood at Jamaal's 100-year old, solid wooden door, that it was to be the housekeeper's misfortune to have shown for work. Atash stood slightly to the side, turned at an angle, weight mostly on his back foot, knees bent.

The door lock's metal-on-metal noise clacked. The door began to swing open. Atash shoved and lunged, his Tarik 7.62mm, semi-automatic pistol coming up, front sight flicking back and forth, following everywhere Frankenstein's eyes darted, ready.

Atash darted quickly to his left, stood, turned, and took up a position in a corner from which to check the apartment's main room and other doorways. The young man regained his balance, then merely stood and gawked at him in surprise.

"Close the door, Jamaal. Close the door!" Atash ordered.

Atash was in, scanning from a vantage point with his backside covered, wall to his rear. Atash had simply left his mobile phone on, in his pocket. He transmitted, speaking as if to no one.

"I am in. Entry cleared, I say again, cleared. Wait one minute. Wait one minute," Frankenstein said as the woman in white emerged from somewhere in the back of the apartment and gaped at him, broom in hand.

Atash would need only one minute to check the rest of the apartment and then he would kill the housekeeper. First, secure the apartment against people with weapons. Then, kill her—strangle her without leaving a bloody mess.

*Too bad,* Atash thought, glancing more carefully at her as he swept by. *She is very beautiful and looks so innocent. Too bad.*

Saya-dar fumed! What took the oaf so long? *Not his brother, that is for sure!* Saya-dar disposed of the brief flash of guilt and regret, still seeing Kadir's shock at Saya-dar's abandoning him to death.

Inwardly, Saya-dar fretted. He knew—he felt—his own carefully-cultivated sense of caution evaporating. Exigent! Urgent! Not enough time! All of these things spelled "haste" and he knew what haste did to operational security. Haste is the very antithesis to security.

Saya-dar held himself to the bench in the West Side Community Garden on 89th, a mere 100 yards away. Cold, calculating operational skill warred with his lust for American blood. Warning bells pierced his eagerness to see his prize agent and whisk him to safety, out of the city before the *Khazir* became "The Fire all Around" instead of "The Fire Beneath."

Why? Why was he now taking chances at this very time when all was about to come together?

Because all was about to come together. That's why. Thrilling! Irresistibly exciting! Even now, the PATH garbage barge must be approaching the coordinates where it would cut free from The Fire Beneath and sail on, as if innocent. He could save his pre-planned, diversionary *maskirovka* bombing for another day. He did not want to have to launch that operation; its dramatic and bloody success would detract from the Six Angels of Death he would soon dispatch over New York. It would take only a touch of the Send button to send hundreds to their watery grave on the other side of the world just to create a diversion, but, it appeared, Allah in His great mercy would spare them this night. Still, if anything at all went wrong at this point, he'd make the single mobile phone text message "send" to launch the *maskirovka* bombing held in reserve. Such devastation would do more than create a distraction. Such devastation would, itself, work Allah's revenge. If he did not use the bombing as *maskirovka* today, he would terrorize the entire West by consuming their children on his next operation.

"Hurry up!" Saya-dar said through gritted teeth. He would wait no more. Saya-dar arose and walked south, crossing 89th and working his way past the row of classic, renovated townhouses there toward 88th and Jamaal's front door.

"Secure, Master. Secure," Gordon heard Frankenstein report over the microphones Consuela had placed inside Jamaal's home. Over the video, Gordon saw Frankenstein turn to look at Consuela like a tiger looks when it identifies prey. *Uh oh.*

"About time!" Saya-dar snapped, now walking down 88th Street toward Jamaal's front door steps. Then: "Good. Very good, of course. You've done well. Meet me at the door right now. I will ring. Let me in and meet me at the door. Once I'm in, you take up your position at the door. Now. Out."

Saya-dar closed his phone. Saya-dar really should have left his bodyguard "on the line," his phone on. He should really have given Atash more time to do his job.

"Mack, this is Cyclops. That's Frankenstein in the kitchen, intending the living room. Intending door Red. Frankenstein at door Red. Hold. Hold."

*Hold?* Jack coiled on the ladder just below the landing, and held almost impossibly. This Frankenstein moved about on Jamaal's main floor only feet away, just over the wrought-iron back porch and rail, just through the kitchen, and with Consuela right there. Jack knew what he'd do if he were Saya-dar: He'd order her killed!

"Roger that, Mack?" Gordon broke in. "Hold? Roger the 'Hold' order? No! Wait. That's Frankenstein at the Red door, facing away from you. Oh. That's Beta 2—The Ghost—approaching Red door. That's Ghost ringing the doorbell. That's Frankenstein telling Jay to let Ghost in. Go, Mack, go! You've got two targets, though. Take Frankenstein out. Try to take Ghost alive. May God be with you," Gordon said.

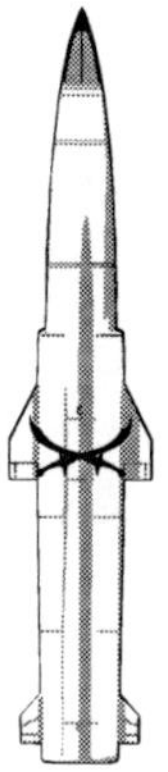

# 78

*Jamaal's back porch*

Jack locked his eyes onto the half-glass, back porch landing door—the White side door—as he hauled hard up and swung his legs low over the porch floor, keeping low. Rolling onto the metal floor, with his right hand he pulled the pistol-to-carbine conversion he had kept from Brazil from underneath his ragged coat disguise. Thinking about Frankenstein's bulk, Jack wished for a caliber beginning with "4." He slithered to the window by the back door and popped his head up for a last-second look-see. No time for his second bug-bot to help out.

Jack peered through the kitchen, into the living room, where he saw Consuela's back. Consuela's right hand held a broom, but Jack could not see her face. She, like Frankenstein, faced Jamaal's front door. Orders: capture Ghost—maybe this Saya-dar—finally.

Maybe not. In seconds, he'd have whoever the man was in Jamaal's living room.

The back door. Had Consuela left it unlocked? Her life depended on his going through that door unimpeded by even a second's delay.

Frankenstein with hand on door knob. Door opening. Get

down and ready to rush.

"Mack, this is Cyclops. That's Ghost at Red door. Red door opening. Ghost infecting target. That's Frankenstein and Ghost both infecting living room. Red door closed. Execute, execute, execute," Gordon said.

Saya-dar passed beneath the shading sycamores and hurried up the massive stone steps. He punched the doorbell. The door opened. Instantly, he took in the situation before him. Frankenstein stepped back to clear the way for him to enter. Jamaal stood, surprise on his face, then extending his hand.

*Who? Oh, the housekeeper.* An extraneous detail. A woman, Latin-looking, about 40, standing, resting on her yellow-handled broom. Too bad. She would have to be disposed of now. He cursed Atash for not already strangling her.

"Welcome, my father!" said Jamaal, approaching with open arms.

"Jamaal! My son! Come to me!" Saya-dar said, delighted to see his recruit again.

Jamaal smiled and looked Saya-dar full in the face as he stepped toward Saya-dar. Saya-dar raised his arms to embrace the young man, as Atash closed the door behind him.

Saya-dar's eyes darted around as Jamaal approached, and then returned to look at Jamaal.

*The eyes. The eyes. What do I see there?* Saya-dar wondered, alarms beginning to sound.

The door behind Jamaal, behind the housekeeper, swung open. *The housek—?*

Low, from behind the door frame, appeared the stubbled, dirty face of a man behind an odd black device gripped in his hands—

pointing into the room. Saya-dar saw nothing but heard clicking sounds, like blocks of wood being clacked together quickly. He saw his Atash's eyes go wide, his face splayed with blood. As Atash's knees buckled and the big man crumpled, Saya-dar instantly understood. Instead of embracing Jamaal, he gripped Jamaal low around the waist, crouched and lunged at the gunman, shoving the off-balance Jamaal backward in front of him like a shield.

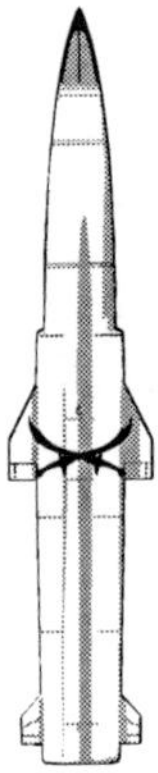

# 79

*Jamaal's living room*

Consuela looked as innocent and non-threatening as possible. *What now?*

The huge man ignored her. *Good!* She watched him move to the front door and open it. Consuela stood in fascination, watching all unfold before her. There now stood the man she had seen in the Amazon. She was sure.

She'd seen him only once, but the lamp by Fats' couches had lit the room with a soft amber glow. She'd watched silently from the veranda. The way Fats deferred to the man, he must have been important. They spread the papers before them. The strange man said nothing as he studied them. Then, he rolled up the papers, raised his head high, his noble profile backlit to Consuela, paid Fats and left.

Consuela had ducked down and padded on her bare feet around the corner of the veranda where she came face-to-face with one of the other Middle Eastern visitors.

"What are you doing here?" the intense man had challenged,

grabbing her shoulders and shaking her. He handed her off to the big man, who Consuela now knew as Frankenstein.

She'd stammered an explanation to both, but she could tell no one believed her. The suave man, plainly the boss, had stood back with arms crossed. The big, big man had gripped her arms hard. Fats had arrived and looked at her like he never had before. Like he knew something about her that she did not know. Like he knew something about her *future.* Fats had looked—resigned—as his Middle Eastern guest glared at her. Fats had made no move to interfere with the big man's assault, the big man's face only inches in front of hers, his breath hot and oddly spicy, like cinnamon. She had felt his spit spray as he raised his voice, demanding again to know why she was "skulking around out here." His huge hands had squeezed her biceps, hurting.

Again, her voice quavering as she had tried to explain even while the stranger shook her: "Just trying—to make sure—porch cleaned up—for you." "Getting—your—drinks!" (There were no drinks and this fact was not lost on the men.)

Then, the shorter, cleaner man had come. He had peered into her frightened face and then had looked at Fats. He had gently touched the huge man's arm. That had caused the huge man to loosen his vise grip and he had removed his hands from Consuela's arms.

"There, there," he had spoken soothingly to the huge man as if he were an upset child. "I'm sure all of this will be OK. All will be OK. You meant no harm, did you, my dear?" he had asked Consuela.

Fats had remained silent. He had not moved to help her, just looked at her, his face set like stone.

The Middle Eastern leader she'd seen in the living room was gone, out of sight. He did not join the other men outside as they debated Consuela's fate.

"No, *señor*, no. I meant no harm. Just—cleaning up. Doing my job."

"Yes, and you do it so well," Mr. A had replied, looking around, noting the now-glaringly obvious fact that all saucers, ashtrays, glasses, and trays were removed from the veranda. Turning back to her, he had addressed her again, smiling.

"Yes, my dear, you do your job so well! Did you by any chance *see* the man who was just here?" he had asked suddenly, holding her gaze and gripping her wrists tightly.

She had broken his gaze as she lied to him. At that moment, Consuela had known these men who wanted to use her would also kill her—or worse. And her benefactor, her guardian—he would let them. He would let them do whatever they pleased and would not save her from whatever fate they planned for her.

Consuela had run for her room. The two foreigners had laughed.

It was at that moment that Consuela had known what she would do. She knew to whom she could go. The man she was not supposed to have seen held some secret. He was important. He, and Mr. Guevara, and now Fats, all intertwined in some great evil with these men.

She had burned the man's image into her mind and slept. She would see the British Consul in Manaus. She could give them the faces of the Middle Eastern men. Somehow, she had just known those evil faces would be important to them.

Now, however, in Jamaal's living room, Consuela stood frozen. Frankenstein crashed forward, toppling onto the floor, unmoving.

But, not the newly-arrived Middle Eastern man Gordon had labeled "Ghost"—the man she'd spied in the bungalow at Manaus. Yes, he was the same man. Of that, she was sure.

He moved surprisingly fast.

"Jack!" she cried.

Jack did not shoot. Consuela saw why; Jack could not shoot without risking hitting Jamaal.

As Saya-dar drove Jamaal into Jack—now getting to his feet from his crouch behind the door frame, she saw Saya-dar's hand move.

As Saya-dar propelled Jamaal forward Saya-dar's right hand released Jamaal, and went to his side. Up came the hand. A black blade flicked.

Consuela leaped forward, gripping her broom handle. She swung the handle in a sideways arc and caught Saya-dar squarely on the right side of his cheek. Blood spurted from the vessels lying close to the skull's surface. Saya-dar jerked and eyed Consuela with shock.

Consuela swung again, and again, this time cracking Saya-dar's upraised right hand, knocking the knife to the floor, then swinging past Saya-dar's defensive hands, catching him full in the face, just above the nose. Consuela improved her grip and drew back preparing to strike again, this time, downward, hard.

"Consuela!"

She checked her swing and looked at Jack. Jack grinned, but kept his eyes on the dazed Saya-dar, now collapsed to his knees, face covered in flowing blood. Jack had questions to ask Saya-dar. He had seen Consuela attack before, and did not trust her to quit.

Jamaal stood to the side. Consuela and Jack flanked Saya-dar, now recovering, wiping his face with his sleeve, furtive eyes flicking around desperately. Jack peered at him over the barrel extension of the Roni; on his other side, Consuela paced cat-like with her broom drawn back, ready to strike.

"Get down! On the floor!" Jack boomed in Farsi. This was one of those soldier-phrases Jack knew well.

The man gawked at Jack, then at Consuela, then at Jamaal in disbelief, then back at Consuela, eyeing him like a fiend and still gripping her raised broom like a shillelagh. Saya-dar plunged his hand into his pocket grasping for his phone. He would press "Send," and at least have the revenge of his *maskirovka.* He fumbled the flat device out of his pocket, and groped with his injured hand to unlock it and press the "Send" button.

As he fumbled for it, phone flew from Saya-dar's hand and clattered to the floor. Saya-dar looked at his numbed hand, now bullet-bloodied. He looked up. The maniacal-looking man with the odd silenced carbine sneered at him and said in English: "Give me an excuse."

Saya-dar declined the invitation and, instead, turned—slowly, painfully—toward Jamaal.

"I must know why. Why?" he rasped, trying hard to regain his composure.

Jamaal spoke.

"Simple. You are evil. These people, yes, Saya-dar, they are fallen, as am I, but you are evil. My parents taught me to do good, *resist* evil, and savor the adventure along the way. Tonight, I have honored my parents and my country, and followed all three parts of their wise counsel by delivering you to this man—and to this woman.

"Enough! Get *down*!" the man with the ugly, silenced pistol screamed at Saya-dar. "Now!"

Saya-dar saw his death in the man's eyes, but looked at the phone, blood-smeared, but undamaged.

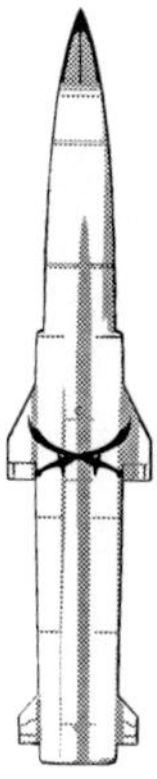

# 80

*Present day, same Saturday*
*Aboard the Genoa*
*to Barcelona Ferry*
*The Ligurian Sea, off the coast*
*of Barcelona, Spain*

Laughing, cutting up every step of the way, the high school seniors had spilled from Genoa's narrow, cobble-stoned alleys. They connected by TXT and collected by cliques on their way to the harbor. Jokes and flirting lent a carnival atmosphere. They hardly saw the architecture of the port from where Columbus hailed, inspired more by each other and their complex young relationships. Only the bright orange and blue-flashed backpacks each slung in common marked them as a group tour. The handy daypacks signaled a class of American kids—almost adults—on a fling.

They'd flown from Detroit, touching down briefly in Amsterdam where enough English signs held back the feeling they'd alighted in the Old World. They "oohed" and "ahhed" flying over the Alps, glorious in the reflected, clear daybreak. At the crack of dawn, they landed in Rome. On the bus and out into the frenzied get-to-work traffic, they worked their way into marvelous adventure.

Too few days later, once again by bus, they sang, joked and flirted on their way to the next stop: Barcelona, this time by sea!

Their tour guide had enjoyed the group and hated to see them go, though he'd now have a few days off. After the bus did some more winding through Lazio's coastal highways, the highway dropped, and they entered the old, old port of Genoa.

Genoa—*Genova,* to the Italians. Genoa's lore and charm and history and mystery were just too much to take in, particularly when in competition with modern day, coming-of-age romances.

As day turned to afternoon, their Barcelona-bound ferry departure time beckoned. All aboard! All made it.

Up the gangplank, onto the ferry, up her stairways, following their teacher-chaperone. Cabins assigned. Bags dropped. Time to explore.

Garish, bright 1970s-looking decor yelled "Vegas, baby!" more than it exuded the atmosphere befitting a 10-hour, seagoing voyage through the Ligurian Sea, the route arcing from Genoa westward toward the next dawn and Barcelona. Brass and glass. Kids from all manner of nations roved in clumps, checking each other out, chatting in the restaurants, visiting the theater, and—oh yes—slipping into the bars when chaperones weren't looking.

Despite the party-boat colors and noises, most, nonetheless, settled down by 2:00 a.m. A few stayed topside until the cutting wind grew intolerable and they, too, gave it up and turned in.

Likewise for most of the truck drivers. Truck drivers the world over look and act a lot alike. Quiet men, attending to their business, comfortably wearing work clothes, looking for a few minutes rest and some good food. Their rigs, driven on at Genoa, stood all lined up deep in the hold, waiting for their drivers on the lowest decks; the next deck up held the cars. The higher decks held sleeping passengers rocking gently with the waves, and the highest contained the entertainment decks, where a few truckers lounged, unwilling to just yet give up the bar.

The Bosnian truck driver propped his nondescript body against the stand-up bar, and rested one foot along the bottom rail. He slowly nursed one last espresso. Not as good as the strong Arab coffee he had when in training. Of course, all coffee is better outdoors, in the wild, in the morning chill. But still, it was good. He savored this one especially.

He quietly rebuffed the irritating efforts of the other drivers to start up the usual chit-chat. Not tonight. He just couldn't fake any interest.

Not tonight.

The truck driver checked the clock on the wall, slowly—ever so slowly—marking the passing minutes. He stuck his left hand into his jeans pocket and confirmed that his cellphone was still there. Checked the display. Still charged up. Plenty of bars of signal. Plenty of battery.

The bartender thought he must be waiting for an important call. Worried he'd not heard from his wife or girlfriend by the sober look on his face. *Women*! thought the bartender. Why else would the portly, swarthy man still be clinging to the bar at this hour, nervously checking his phone every 10 minutes as if willing a love-message to arrive? He should be getting his head down—getting some sleep so he could competently swing that big rig off the boat in the morning. That drive out of the port and through Barcelona would not be easy. Propping your body on the bar all night would not help. Oh well, closing time at three o'clock anyway.

*Hmm. Odd,* should have thought the inspectors back in Genoa when they checked the Bosnian driver's truck. *Why are these bags of concrete on this trailer not on pallets? Someone will have to unload each bag by hand. Glad I'm an inspector, and it won't be me.* That's what they should have thought, but they did not, and let the commonplace load pass.

Indeed, at that moment, Cristobal, one the port inspectors in Genoa who had opened the fabric sides of the truck to verify the load, fitfully pondered that question, unasked earlier. He slept restlessly. Got up. Used the bathroom. Got a drink of water. Looked for a place on the pile of dirty glasses and dishes and finally worked his water glass into a space that looked like it wouldn't topple the stack. The act of working the water glass onto the overloaded, randomly stacked, dish drainer triggered it: now he knew what bothered him.

No pallets! That was no way to organize a heavy load. Made no sense. He reached his decision.

Cristobal stumbled in the dark, swore, but retrieved his mobile phone to call the port duty officer. He would advise the duty officer to have the captain give the order to open the truck again and to question the driver.

He remembered the driver. Could have been Italian from his looks, but the accent quickly dispelled that notion. From the Balkans, maybe. Maybe one of those hundreds of Albanians illegally sneaking ashore on Italy's rugged eastern coast to find work. Maybe illegal. All the more reason to make the call. Cristobal stubbed the keys on his mobile phone, a sense of dread rising. *No pallets!* So, what could have been hidden beneath all of those loose bags, bags they did not search beneath because of the weight?

Two batteries and a satellite phone sat in a hard plastic box atop a small crate. Six, one-pound blocks of crystalline, pure white C-4 explosives, stolen in Bosnia, in turn filled the crate and rested directly on the truck floor, the crate surrounded on all other sides by 60-pound bags of neatly stacked cement.

The "load" in the circuit leading from the batteries was two silvery, cigarette-sized blasting caps, stuck into two of the C-4 blocks. The satellite phone's alarm feature saved battery power and avoided blowing up the driver before loading by powering up the phone 5 hours after the hour of scheduled departure. The bomb-maker had set the phone to "Vibrate" so that a call sent battery power down the wires normally connected to the tiny electric motor that buzzes silently. The bomb-maker had removed the electric motor and replaced it with a small relay that would close and complete the circuit once energized by the current from the phone's battery. With a completely closed circuit, the C-4 would detonate. If one blasting cap or battery failed, the other would ignite the blast.

Cement—the wonder material—discovered by the Romans and perfect for their massive construction projects. Perfect for this destruction job. A whole truck full of bags all stacked, one on top of the other. No pallets. Bags so inconveniently loaded and heavy that they discouraged any port inspector from probing beneath the stacks of cement bags lining the soft-side truck.

The weighty cement bags perfectly tamped the explosive, surrounding it on all sides but one. They would turn and focus the blast force downward, straight toward the steel hull. The blast force would have only one un-resisted direction to go and it would seek that direction. In minutes, the cold Mediterranean Sea would fill the lower deck under pressure, water gushing through the large hole. The *Glory of Barcelona* night ferry would turn on its side, fill even more, and sink before the sleeping passengers could stumble out of their cabins and up elevators or stairs to the lifeboats on the top deck. Along with the *Glory of Barcelona* would sink young dreams, romances, laughter, and lives. Saya-dar would break parents' hearts across Europe and the United States—if he chose to trigger the mass murder that he had thought of as a mere diversion.

Saya-dar could have set the charges to detonate automatically, on a timer, or at a particular GPS location. However, that would have launched his *maskirovka*—his masking, deceiving plan to draw attention from his real attack against the United States—regardless of whether he needed it. Sending American and other Western teenagers to Davy Jones' Locker was too delicious a plan to waste, if not needed. Of course, if a random wrong-number caller exploded the charges, Saya-dar did not care much. So, instead, Saya-dar chose to ignite the detonation personally, on his command, only if and when he saw the dramatic feint tactically useful.

Saya-dar also chose a man. A duped man, explicitly willing to blow himself up along with his victims. The man was, indeed, necessary for driving the explosives aboard the ferry. Unfortunately, for him, it was also necessary for him to stay with his truck; security would certainly notice a driver walking down the gangplank, abandoning his rig to arrive in Barcelona without him. So, the driver had to die. However, a dedicated *jihadist* might not be thrilled at martyrdom just to maintain his trucker ruse. He would want to *be* the bombing. He would want to press the trigger, to take the final act that forfeited his own life, but also killed the hundreds of infidels across whose corpses he would lightly trip into Allah's Paradise.

And, so, Saya-dar left him placebo instructions. At Saya-dar's call, the bomb driver would press the Send button on his own mobile phone, in firm belief that he actuated the bomb's detonator switch. Of course, he would either be dead by then, or, Saya-dar would have sent the short, harmless-sounding cancellation message to save this destruction for another day.

Three a.m. The bartender watched the truck driver check his mobile phone one more time. (Hopefully, he's checking the time, the bartender thought.)

The driver knew the bartender was watching him, wondering why this particular truck driver was the only one who had not turned in long ago. They'd all make Barcelona in only hours now, and this driver would supposedly be in control of a big rig, hauling a load, wending his way overland, perhaps south for a load of Valencia oranges, or perhaps for a load of ceramic bathroom fixtures from the Roca plant south of Barcelona.

The driver set his coffee cup on the granite bar, placed both hands before him, and arose. He looked at the bartender, nodded his head, and then left two Euro coins on the bar. He breathed deeply and bade the bartender "Good night," in Spanish.

He started to turn to leave, halted, looked at the bartender, and emptied his pockets of the rest of the coins. Came to about 7 Euros. The bartender gaped and finally stammered out "Gracias."

"Think nothing of it. Enjoy," the trucker said.

The truck driver-terrorist ambled slowly toward the central bank of elevators. Instead of pressing the button, he paused, reversed and stepped out of the nearby hatch onto the deck. The cold blasted his uncovered face. Felt good! Felt alive! He propped against the rail and gazed down, down, down into the black abyss of the Mediterranean Sea. Sharp, moving, living wind above—cold, cold life-stifling sea below.

The driver checked his watch. Fourteen minutes until the time.

All Saya-dar had to do was press the "Send" button and the number he'd pre-entered would direct his signal across the world to flash on the bomb's phone, ordering and heralding death. The *Glory of Barcelona* would become the *Glory of Allah,* and take the infidel children to the bottom.

The truck driver had not planned on driving off the *Glory of Barcelona* in the morning. He'd thought his eternal body would have been driven, instead, by chariot into Allah's presence, preferably immediately to the 70 virgins featuring highly in his fantasies about Paradise. He expected his broken earthly body to be swallowed by the Mediterranean like all of the other people on board. All of those laughing teenagers, heedless of Allah, mocking his greatness, sinking lifelessly into the salty sea. He and they; all sharing the same swirling fate, except that he expected to rise to Paradise while Satan dragged them to hell. In Paradise, Allah would praise him before all others there and reward him in ways he could only imagine.

But—not tonight. He expected Saya-dar's command or cancellation, but the 14 minutes passed without incident. Lacking Saya-dar's commanding call, the default was "cancel." For some reason, not tonight. *Inch'Allah.*

*But, what could have gone wrong?*

Saya-dar gaped at his hand, then at the phone. The phone seemed to mock him. Would his shattered, bullet-broken hand press the Send key, or even pick up the satellite-phone trigger device lying on the floor. Saya-dar lunged for the phone again, realizing the man had shot his hand, but still unwilling to give up.

But, instead of gaining the cell phone bomb trigger, rough hands slammed him face-down onto the floor. Saya-dar screamed in pain as Jack landed on him, jabbing his knee into the small of Saya-dar's back. Then, Jack kicked Saya-dar's legs apart and jammed the barrel extension muzzle behind his ear. Strangely, even though dazed, Saya-dar thought he recognized the American voice threatening to kill him.

Below the would-be martyr-trucker-bomber at the rail of the *Glory of Barcelona*, deep in the hold, but above the truck deck, slept the young Americans, along with French, Japanese, Spanish,

Italians, Germans, and a few Russians, with their teachers and chaperones. They had traveled from their various schools, toured Pompey's ruins and Rome's grandeur, and now they all slept and dreamed of Spain in the morning.

Jack McDonald would never know what his single, well-placed shot to Saya-dar's hand had stopped. No one would know, but Saya-dar.

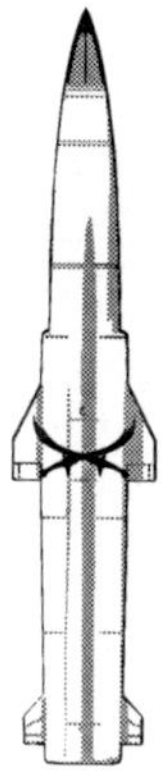

# 81

*Sunday morning*
*SUBASE*
*New London, Connecticut*

Captain Irving Gavinger read his orders again. Yes, they said exactly what he'd thought.

"Mr. Condrey," he called, "Come here and tell me if I'm reading these right," Captain Gavinger said to his Ship's Duty Officer.

Lieutenant Baron Condrey, the SDO, strode over with a puzzled look and read. He was matter-of-fact, that Condrey.

"You are ordered to sail immediately, with urgent priority, due south, to locate and destroy all vessels expected to be found at a point …" he read, including the written latitude and longitude. Remaining details helped identify the vessels and their course and speed, but offered no explanation whatsoever as to why, other than the chilling order: "It is *imperative* to the security of the United States that you accomplish this mission as quickly as possible, and regardless of which vessels you find at this location. You will be furnished additional target identification information. Confirm their destruction when you have accomplished this mission."

"What's to interpret, sir? Training's over. We are to take the *Seawolf* out and sink some ships," Condrey answered.

"Yes, I can see that," Captain Gavinger replied. "You see the same thing, then, Bear?"

"Aye, aye, sir."

The men looked at each other.

"Then, muster the crew and let's get underway to intersect the target. We will obey our orders," the Captain ordered.

Bear complied.

On the dock, before boarding, Captain Gavinger waved Bear over again.

"Look, here, Bear, at the other side of the mountain. This came in while you were scrambling the crew. Check out these additional coordinating instructions and the concept of the operation. This is wild."

> You are supported by the *USS Connecticut*, already patrolling, but now ordered to the same location as are you. *Connecticut* will not arrive before you. Surprise is critical. You are not to warn, hail, attempt to stop, or attempt to board the target vessels. You are to destroy any target vessels found, without the *Seawolf's* being detected.
>
> A combat swimmer team will be flown to you. Rally point where you will surface to receive team is to be determined. Otherwise, you are to make full dive speed directly toward the target. After target is destroyed, you will deploy combat swimmer team to verify destruction, if feasible.
>
> No enemy forces are anticipated. None. Targets are not expected to be accompanied by patrols of any nature, including sea or air. Targets are not expected to carry defensive weapons.

> Targets are civilian cargo-hauling barges with accompanying tug boats, one barge equipped with modified SSN Sunburn missiles believed to be capable of striking the United States once within 200 miles of the coast. The missile-equipped barge is believed to be submarine. This is not an error. The missile-equipped barge is believed to be a towed submarine, beneath a surface barge, in turn towed by four ocean-going tug boats. You may find the missile-equipped barge either sub-surface, or on the surface. If on the surface, expect that it is preparing to immediately launch nuclear missiles at New York City. That is right: nuclear.

"Let's get on the boat, sir, and get the *Seawolf* underway," Bear said. "Right now. We can be there in three hours, minus the time it takes to rendezvous with and load the combat swimmers."

Someone thought better about slowing down for any reason and messaged the *Seawolf* that the combat swimmers were cancelled—to rendezvous with the *Seawolf* only after the submariners torpedoed the target vessels. Mission: verify target destruction. Repeated updates honed the *Seawolf* in on the *Khazir's* location and course.

Captain Gavinger ordered two, Mark 48, Advanced Capability (ADCAP), heavy torpedoes readied for firing. His orders: just destroy, striking the bow. Usually, he shot for an explosion under the keel, but not this time. Whatever. Orders were real precise about that. He detected no active or passive counter-measures.

No escort. This was like shooting fish in a barrel. No challenge.

Captain Gavinger stood off at 1,000 meters and ordered one torpedo fired. All of that high explosive, plus the unused propulsion fuel, could destroy far larger ships. The high definition, low light, digital images sent down from the photonics mast made it plain: utterly, totally destroyed. A barge of all things. More like target practice.

Once the combat swimmers arrived, Captain Gavinger ordered the *Seawolf* surfaced where she rendezvoused with the swimmers who returned and seconded his confirmation. Captain Irving Gavinger, a Navy submariner for 20 years, had done his share of the unusual. He could only trust that he and his crew had saved lives.

They had.

Miles to the east and south, the United States used the *Mi Fortuna* to test its C-130 mounted laser cannon. General Ortega watched the real-time video from SOCOM HQ and knew they had a winner weapon.

In Caracas, stewards prepared champagne for the president. After the ice melted in the bucket and the bottle remained corked, they then brought coffee. The coffee grew cold. Eventually, they brought meals, all while President Carlos Guevara stayed in his room, glued in fear to the American news stations. The food remained untouched as President Guevara contemplated the unknown hour and means of his death.

New York went about its business. The city was over the terrorism thing, anyway.

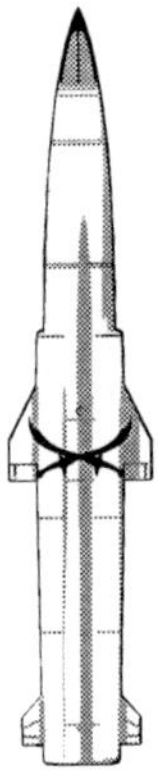

# 82

*One year later,*
*late Sunday afternoon*
*Downtown Manhattan Heliport*

The Blackhawk helicopter touched down at New York's Downtown Manhattan Heliport, attracting a few stares. However, only a group of men in blue jeans and light jackets got off.

"Sir, this is really too much," Grant Gammon protested.

"Yeah, I know. I'll give it to you this time. Granted, it truly is," said President Bullington, sympathetically. "Get it? 'Granted?' Well, look Grant, while we're going this far, we might as well walk over there and pay our respects at the Vietnam War Veterans' Memorial. Your men got the park secured yet?"

"Yes, sir. Secured."

"Besides, crossing South Street is the most dangerous part of this little outing," the president offered, lamely.

Gammon coordinated with the team already securing the park, all undercover. The men crossed. President Bullington halted at the memorial and sat for a few minutes, praying, while the area teams finished checking the streets and reporting. Then, as the streetlights came on and a light rain began, the group walked the block to the restaurant President Bullington had insisted on, entered by the back door and walked upstairs, avoiding the Pearl

Street entrance to Fraunce's Tavern altogether.

General Paul Ortega, Gordon Noone, Jamaal Lewis, and Richard Pye, seated at a table by the fireplace where a painting of General Washington hung, rose as President Bullington stepped through the double doors. Later, they would compare notes and swear that both presidents—the first and the current—showed a twinkle in their eyes.

President Bullington shook hands all around and waved everyone else back into their chairs. Taking the cold glass of beer proffered, President Bullington looked around and said quietly, "I slip away and come here when I can. Funny, isn't it? The President of the United States has to slip in through the back door like he's delivering steaks from a truck out back. Yet, at this same tavern, 200 years ago, the man who was to become the first President of the United States probably tied up his own horse right out there at the front door."

Turning to Richard, the president barely contained his laughter.

"You must be Sir John's prize spy! Of course, you are not a spy, you are not here, you never were here, and we never met you. How deliciously outrageous, don't you think, Richard, that you return here, to New York, and to Fraunce's Tavern to beat it all, in collusion with General Washington and with us, helping us save the very city from which your bloody redcoats set sail for home!"

Richard Pye politely agreed. It was pretty outrageous, but it all seemed right.

After dinner, the men relaxed with port and cigars. While the others chatted, the president motioned Gordon aside to stand with him at the fireplace.

"I wanted to congratulate the entire *Arcturus* Team but I know you are trying your best to keep them secret. I've got something I want you to give to Jack," the president told Gordon, handing him a manila envelope.

"Might I ask what you are handing my operator?" Gordon asked.

"Pardons, notes of thanks, and signed waivers of Executive Order 12333," said the president.

"Not all killings are illegal assassinations under 12333," Gordon said.

"With these, Jack won't have to worry about the nuances. We can let the lawyers and scholars of a future, and more gentle time, debate all they want," the president said. "Know this. I've got their six. I want Jack to know that. Besides, no doubt, you and I have more work for him."

"You said 'pardons, notes and waivers.' Plural?" asked Gordon.

"I suspect you didn't send young McDonald out alone on this one," the president explained. "I'd like to meet that remarkable young woman Richard recruited. We owe her. Without her—well, I don't even want to think about it. Where are she and Jack, anyway?" the president asked. "I'd hoped they could make our celebration."

"Who? What young woman? Jack who?" Gordon "No One" Noone said, adding, "You might say they are hosting their own quiet little dinner party. They have their own little gift for you. You can read about it in tomorrow's paper, sir. In the words of my hometown's newspaper, pray that 'A good time will be had by all.' Well, by almost all."

The President of the United States eyed him quizzically, over the rim of his glass of port. Gordon Noone just laughed.

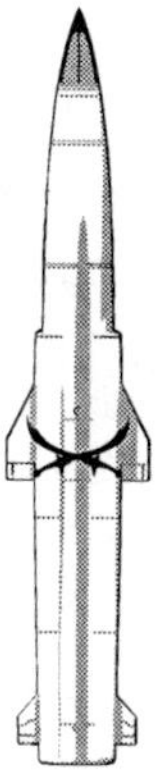

# 83

*Same time*
*Villa Rio,*
*South of Manaus, Brazil*

Consuela poured white wine for Carlos Guevara and smiled at him.

"I'd much rather do business with you. How good of your uncle to provide for you! He could not have left his shipyard in more—lovely—hands," Guevara said, sipping the wine, licking his lips, and peering over the glass's rim at Consuela.

"Yes, my uncle was always so thoughtful, was he not? So kind? So—attentive to the needs of others, wouldn't you say?" Consuela said, pouring herself a glass and raising it to her lips, moistening them only, not drinking any. She held the glass there, eyes twinkling at Guevara over its shimmering surface, forcing her eyes to smile.

"Kind? Yes, I suppose." Guevara shifted, thinking Fats to have been anything but kind to this woman, though she was now freed of that monster. Her remark nudged him off script, but his lust seized an opportunity suggested by her odd words and drew him back onto the amorous stage.

"Are you also thoughtful and *attentive* to the needs of others?" he asked leaning in with hands folded.

"Consuela sat calmly across from Guevara at a small but sturdy, antique, wooden, linen-covered table, set elegantly but simply with chilled Riesling in an earthenware cooler, loaves of the French-style bread so loved in Brazil, and a board of imported cheese. They sat in an intimate tiled courtyard, atmosphere hushed even more by water cascading placidly from a fountain landscaped into the corner. Palms and lush philodendra not only shaded the two from the tropical sun's rays, now about to disappear over the low stucco wall separating the courtyard from the villa's grounds—but also the plants screened the courtyard from curious eyes beyond the wall. Beyond the wall, grass carpeted the gentle rise to the jungle at the top of the bluff overlooking the Amazon River below.

"Am I attentive to the needs of others?" Consuela mused, expression still obscured by the wineglass, but voice melodic, eyes still smiling at Guevara. "Yes, something about me desires to come to certain men, and to do what they desire me to do," she teased, opening her eyes wider, now broadening her smile and leaning slightly toward the man. Consuela let both the hint and the mystery hang for a moment, then relaxed, sat back some, and added: "My uncle helped his friends and filled their—orders, you might say. I intend to continue the business he left me. I will do the same," she said. "I will fill the orders that meet the needs of others. I will satisfy my most cherished customers beyond their expectations. That is why I invited you to join me at my new house. 'Customer relations,' as the Americans might say," she said, teasing with her smile again.

Guevara coughed, wiped his mouth with the corner of his napkin, and rose from his chair.

"Is that the only reason you invited me here, Consuela? Customer relations?" he asked, more hoarsely.

Carlos Guevara had lusted after Consuela, the housekeeper, during his visits to Fats' bungalow. He thought Fats might offer her. Now, with Fats out of the way and Consuela inheriting as his only heir, he'd thrilled to her invitation. He foresaw continuing his business ventures, only now with the added bonus of spending time with Consuela instead of the crude, but useful Fats.

"No, no, no, *El Presidente*," Consuela said, laughing, tossing her hair and shaking her finger, teasing him. "I plan much, much more than you and I collaborating on new barge sales," she said, eyes locked onto his, now genuinely smiling, face alight and merry, rising to meet him.

The sun dipped lower, urging her on, gilding the white villa on the cleared hilltop overlooking Manaus and the Amazon River below. The low, stucco courtyard wall, capped with terracotta and crisscrossed with vines, would soon block the setting sun—but not the line-of-sight from the higher rise 100 yards across the grounds.

As a suitor lovingly crafts mood from sensual elements of setting, Consuela painted her scene with the brush of perfect timing. Perfect, that is, from the standpoint of tactics.

For nothing else obscures like the shadows of the night. Well-practiced combat, choreographed to perfection in the daylight, degenerates into clumsy chaos once the sun is down. Consuela counted on just that twilight shift to chaos to cloak her escape. The sun burnished the tops of the giant philodendron leaves, flashing her the signal that the time was right—now.

Consuela rounded the table and came to Carlos Guevara, letting him take her in his arms. She raised her head and exposed her neck, which he hungrily kissed. Consuela's hands drew him in, firmly but gently at first so as not to alarm him. She felt his biceps, which he made taut to boast to her of his strength. She moaned softly, as if aroused. Encouraged, he indulged himself with more kisses, lower this time as his hands began to caress and explore.

Consuela sighed, backed away, raised her skirt just above her knees, lifted a leg and rested her thigh on top of the sturdy table. She reclined and held her arms outstretched, inviting *El Presidente* with her hands, her eyes, and her body. As he came to her, she locked her legs firmly, but still not alarmingly around Guevara, and, as he pressed harder against her, she reached one hand aside for the slender, silvery, dagger-designed steak knife wrapped inside her own rolled-up table napkin.

Again, except this time concealed only feet away, Jack McDonald watched the video surveillance monitor show Consuela lock her victim in a death embrace. As she lay back on the table, clearing the way for Jack's shot at Guevara, Jack nudged the button that closed the deadbolts in the double-doors separating the patio from the villa, and arose.

In one motion, Jack threw open the lid over his hide-hole in the landscaped corner. From this soil, mulch and tangle of vines sprouted first a stubby sound-suppressed carbine, then the camouflage-darkened face behind it.

Jack whistled. He watched with both eyes open, through the Aimpoint T-1 Micro, unmagnified, optical sight. Since Jack kept the dot lingering atop Guevara's scalp—to allow for the offset between point-of-aim and point-of-impact at this close range—nothing obscured Jack's vision as he saw Guevara's last living response. Completely without the characteristic bravado, the former paratrooper screamed just before Jack's single shot—followed closely by Consuela's knife—ended his tenure as self-appointed president for life and perpetual enemy of the United States of America.

The sniper team on overwatch on the hilltop moved no muscles other than those responsible for aiming the eyes. Invisible from their hide just inside the jungle tree line, both sniper and spotter saw it all and waited. The calculations had been made and put on the scope. The attack unfolded just as they had planned—as they all had not only planned, but also shaped by Jack's locking those doors, and by taking advantage of the low wall around the patio.

First, from around the corner of the villa, the perimeter bodyguard team sprinted along the stuccoed wall, bound for the courtyard gate. The spotter whispered their every move, and, as the faster bodyguard stopped to touch the gate handle—which he found stuck—the sniper's trigger finger pressed. Addled by seeing his partner's head disappear in a fountain of red, the man's leftover body not yet collapsing, and then further startled by the boom from up the hill, the second bodyguard stalled and reacted poorly by turning around toward the sound to look for the threat. Almost as if courteously, he presented a rifle-range perfect, immobile, facing target for the rifleman who had already cycled the short Desert Tactical Stealth Recon Scout .338 Lapua Magnum's massive bolt handle, chambering the next 300-grain open-tip round. The sniper sent this shot to the heart, anticipating the bodyguard's delayed, but panicked reactions kicking in. The big bullet blew out the man's heart, expanding, transferring its energy from flying lead missile to flesh, bone, wet human mass, redundantly slamming the guard backward into the wall so violently that the impact snapped his spine and caved in the back of his skull as if the first death were not sufficient.

Jack understood that the sniper's two booms secured the rear. Keeping the carbine up, he held his support hand out for Consuela and helped her into the hide hole. Though holding both the carbine's muzzle and his eyes locked on the doorway, Jack could not resist matching Consuela's broad smile as she passed and then disappeared down the steps behind him.

Now, the two front and inside bodyguard teams battered at the dead-bolted doors. With a bump of the hip, Jack hit the oversized button releasing the deadbolts and Guevara's final four bodyguards tumbled into the courtyard's killing zone. The sudden entry threw them off, but their eyes required just moments to take in the scene of their leader's lifeless corpse with the blade handle still protruding upward at a neat angle, chromed steel shining in the sun's last rays. Synapses fired, requiring almost imperceptible time slices to perceive the details of Guevara's death, and their brains immediately screamed multiple, complex instructions back to the four men.

In that less-than-one neurochemical second, Jack shot each one once, one round to the chest, playing by "roadhouse rules" where everybody gets one. Jack worked his way "first come, first served" from the lead man to the last one, killing him even as he tumbled through the doorway. In the next second, Jack swept his carbine back across the four falling men, a bit more deliberately this time, a bit more slowly since the men were already dying, each man meriting a head-shot in case he wore body armor. Certain they were dead, but keeping carbine up, ready, sweeping for targets, checking for that surprise—perhaps that laggard joining the fray at the last second, that wild card, that extra movement, that ambush by Death himself leering at the reckless—in this manner Jack McDonald made certain the job was done.

Satisfied the protection detail men had been alone and were now permanently down, Jack McDonald lowered his carbine, shifted his trigger finger off the trigger, and breathed. Eyes lingering only briefly on the scene before him, Jack turned from the destruction and joined Consuela, waiting at the bottom of the short ladder. Together, the two Amazon avengers nodded to the cleanup team approaching through the tunnel, and slipped away.

# Dedication

It is May 2nd, 2011, and I am making final edits to *Amazon Avenger*. The newsdogs are going nuts over the fatal fact that United States special operators hunted down and killed bin Laden. While I am angry at whichever fool in our government exposed the shooters as Navy SEALs, and while I am angry at whomever ID'd the USS Carl Vinson as the vessel hosting bin Laden's burial at sea, I am, of course, absolutely bursting with pride on behalf of our military forces. I expect this novel, my second Islamic terrorism thriller, to hit the market, appropriately, by this Memorial Day (which I will celebrate by attending a machinegun shoot and taking pistol training).

So, I am dedicating *Amazon Avenger* to two young officers I encountered years ago—one as a first lieutenant, and one as fellow Ranger. Both entered the shadowy world of the special operator, rose to the rank of general officer, and retired after more than 30 years of dangerous service to our country.

I recommend to you *Never Surrender*, the autobiography of General Jerry Boykin, whom I met and served with briefly when he was a much younger first lieutenant in the 101st Airborne Division at Fort Campbell a long time ago. LTG (ret.) William G. (Jerry) Boykin helped start up Delta Force and spent his career in special operations. Jerry successfully dodged both the bullets—well, not quite all of them—and the reporters, but after he entered the swamp of Washington, D.C., he found himself the center of a surprising controversy for speaking the truth, plainly, about the nature of Islamic *jihad*. We need such men badly.

I am pleased to dedicate *Amazon Avenger* also to one of Jerry's comrades, a man who endured Ranger School with me long ago,

# Dedication

who reported to the 82nd Airborne Division as a young lieutenant, and who seized the opportunity to sign on with Delta Force, rising through the ranks to high office at Special Operations Command (SOCOM) as did Jerry Boykin. You have not seen him on television; since he managed to fly mostly under the radar despite being named in one movie, I will respect his anonymity here. His humble answer, when I asked him why he stayed in, was that he got to serve with some fine men, and felt that, perhaps, he was able to help them out and do them some good. I'd say that is an understatement the size of his linebacker stature.

The character in *Arcturus* and *Amazon Avenger*, General Paul Ortega, is, in part, a fictionalized composite of these two men. I am dedicating this novel to them both, at this special time of celebration of a great victory. This is my way of expressing humble gratitude to all of the men—and women—who, year after year, fly to hot, filthy places, who catch .50 cal. rounds and mortar fragments, and who peer over the barrel of an M-4 ready to press the trigger on behalf of fellow-Americans.

Do good, resist evil, and savor the adventure along the way,
M.J. Mollenhour, 2 May 2011

CPSIA information can be obtained at www.ICGtesting.com
228698LV00001B/1/P

9 780979 967245